HOME IN CHENGDU

Where the Heart Nestles
There the Home Settles

此心安处是吾乡 　上

成都市人民政府外事侨务办公室 编

中国文联出版社
http://www.clapnet.cn

图书在版编目（ＣＩＰ）数据

家在成都 / 成都市人民政府外事侨务办公室编. --

北京 : 中国文联出版社，2018.6

ISBN 978-7-5190-3569-3

Ⅰ．①家… Ⅱ．①成… Ⅲ．①访问记－作品集－中国

－当代 Ⅳ．①I253

中国版本图书馆 CIP 数据核字(2018)第 087571 号

家在成都

作 者：成都市人民政府外事侨务办公室	
出 版 人：朱 庆	
终 审 人：朱彦玲	复 审 人：周劲松
责任编辑：李成伟 张凯默	责任校对：傅泉泽
封面设计：贺 焘	责任印制：陈 晨

出版发行：中国文联出版社

地　　址：北京市朝阳区农展馆南里 10 号，100125

电　　话：010-85923060（咨询）010-85923000（编务）010-85923020（邮购）

传　　真：010-85923000（总编室），010-85923020（发行部）

网　　址：http://www.clapnet.cn　　http://www.claplus.cn

E－mail：clap@clapnet.cn　　panshijing@clapnet.cn

印　　刷：天津画中画印刷有限公司

装　　订：天津画中画印刷有限公司

法律顾问：北京市德鸿律师事务所王振勇律师

本书如有破损、缺页、装订错误，请与本社联系调换

开　　本：710×1000	1/16
字　　数：260 千字	印　张：27.25
版　　次：2018 年 6 月第 1 版	印　次：2018 年 6 月第 1 次印刷
书　　号：ISBN 978-7-5190-3569-3	
定　　价：76.80 元	

前　言

　　在人的一生里，从故乡出发，往往终点却是第二故乡。你会把哪座城市当成自己的第二故乡？也许，一万个人会有一万个答案，而在西南的巴山蜀水里，有这么一座城市，正成为越来越多外籍友人的第二故乡。这座城市就是有着 4500 年文明史和 2300 年建城史的成都。

　　一年成聚，二年成邑，三年成都。今天的成都，延续着曾经的天府之国的包容、豁达，加入了闲适和恬淡，更充满着活力与希望。目前，以投资、就业、留学、考察、旅游、生活、探亲等各种目的在成都停留的境外人员、常年居留的外国人逐年增长。为了让越来越多的外籍人士来到成都、爱上成都，像主人翁一样在成都生活、发展，2016 年初，成都市政府启动外籍人士"家在成都"工程，整合市级 24 家有关部门涉外公共服务功能，从政府公共信息发布、涉外公共服务保障、涉外公共服务提升等方面改进和提升涉外公共服务水平。

　　"家在成都"工程是做什么的？"家在成都"是"信息畅通"，"家在成都"开通了自己的英文网站、微信、手机应用 APP，开播了英语电视栏目和广播双语栏目，开通了英语服务热线、涉外法律服务热线。编印了外籍人士在蓉生活、办事、就医、投资、出行、旅游、参加宗教活动等多种"家在成都"特色指南，保证外国友人即使第一次来成都，或者不会中文，也能随时了解成都的大城小事，做一个"成都通"。

"家在成都"是"服务惠通"，为方便大家在成都创业、就业、就医、就学、出行，推出外国人来蓉工作"一窗式"服务，出台了吸引外籍人才的政策，建立了人才绿卡制度，为外籍人才来蓉创新创业提供全方位服务，提供外籍人士"一站式"就诊服务，还充分保障外籍人士子女在蓉入学权利。

"家在成都"是"人心相通"，外籍友人在社区也有自己的"街道办"——"外籍人士之家"和"外籍人士创新创业之家"。这些挨着家门口的"家"方便外籍友人办理停居留手续，申请中国绿卡，结交中国朋友甚至创业。"家在成都"还邀请大家参加吟诗剪纸、赏灯采茶等丰富多彩的涉外文化民俗活动，参加就学、就医、创业等主题体验活动。"家在成都"希望外籍友人越来越顺畅地融入成都生活，让他们不仅把家安在成都，更把心留在成都。

作为"家在成都"工程的子项目，《家在成都——此心安处是吾乡》文集正是希望用文字走进外籍人士的成都生活，记叙他们多彩的"异乡"故事、他们与成都的"不解之缘"、他们在成都文化感染下的变化和融入、他们对成都的优质服务以及对成都和谐人文环境的认可和欣赏。本书分上下两册，其中上册采写于 2016 年秋冬，下册采写于 2017 年冬至 2018 年春，这 24 位采访对象，或因其所在领域的不同，或因其与成都结缘的因由不同，或因其在成都发展的情感诉求不同，他们的故事也被大致分类在"创·梦在成都""教·学在成都""乐·享在成都"三个主题之下。

第一个主题"创·梦在成都"，着力于关注创新创业领域的外籍友人和为成都城市建设发展做出重要贡献的外籍友人，他们或自己践行着创新创业，或在自己能力范围内创造着各式各样的环境和条件，去助力人们在成都圆自己的梦。如以色列驻成都首任总领事蓝天铭，在以色列驻成都总领事馆设立的四年多时间里，经过蓝天铭的悉心浇灌，以色列与成都在经济、文化、教育、科技等领域的合作取得丰硕成果。如儿童应用"熊猫博士"的设计者、荷兰创业者泰斯，2008 年，泰斯和妻子林燕一同来到成都创业，他们推出的第一款儿童应用"熊猫博士"传达出的便是他们对熊猫、对成都最为真挚的热情。在这一主题下的文章主人公正在用自己的身体力行参与着成都的每一步创新创造。他们愿意在成都这一方充满创新机遇的热土继续创业，继续筑梦。

第二个主题"教·学在成都"，关注一些与教育领域相关的外籍友人，他们或是因为留学与成都结缘，或在成都教育领域就职，或是因为重大科研项目的国际合作而执教成都。如为四川做出杰出贡献的古巴专家、电子科技大学中国——古巴神经科技转化前沿研究联合实验室特约教授裴德乐。2011 年，裴德乐第一次来成都参加一个会议，就被这座城市深深迷住了，他发现这里才是他梦想的生活地。那之后，裴德乐受邀成为电子科技大学的特约教授，为所在行业的科研做出了不可磨灭的贡献。还有来自新加坡的青年指挥家洪毅全，放弃了众多世界著名交响乐团的邀请后，他选择了正在快速发展的四川交响乐团，选择了汲汲渴求人才的成都。他用手里的指挥棒，为四川的交响乐翻开了崭新的一页，也让自己在天府文化中汲取了丰富养分而夺目绽放。

第三个主题"乐·享在成都"，着力于关注一些乐在成都、爱在成都的外国友人。如文艺达人、来自美国的江喃。江喃眼中的成都在飞速地发展、变化着，地铁载满了市民穿梭在城市的下方，街上一辆辆共享单车整齐地摆放着，抬头看，一列高铁正驶向远方。然而，这里不会有如北京、上海般急促的日常工作节奏，成都这个以悠闲著称的城市，如同环绕它千年的流水，不急不躁，却悠久流长。还有来自美国的刘杰森医生一家，刚来时人生地不熟，常常需要朋友邻居的热心帮助，现如今不仅习惯了晒成都的太阳，也不断地用自己的医术和爱心无私地回馈这个城市。他的三个孩子从小和成都的孩子一起上学读书，和成都的孩子一起说唱童谣、嬉戏打闹，成了地地道道的成都娃娃。而今年，他和妻子从成都市长手里接过了中国的"绿卡"，成了真正的成都人。这一主题下文章的主人公，他们在成都奉献着、分享着，他们乐在成都。

三个主题下的24篇文章，初步勾勒出成都之所以能吸引世界的魅力所在，也浓缩了这些来自四面八方的新移民在成都的生活百态。

此心安处是吾乡！2018年6月，成都召开对外开放大会，会后发布《关于加快构建国际门户枢纽全面服务"一带一路"建设的意见》及《建设西部对外交往中心行动计划（2017—2022年）》。《意见》和《行动计划》是成都对外开放的信心和接纳四海宾朋的诚意。我们欣喜地看到成都不仅有姿态更有切实的行动，为身在异乡的外国朋友营造欢乐体验、创业梦想、送去家的温暖，让外籍人士来了不愿走，离开还想来，在心底种下"蓉情万种"。希望若干年后，无论他们有没有离开成都，成都对于这些外籍人士来说，都远不只是中国西部的一座城市这么简单，恰如书中文章里出现最多的关键词，相信成都终将是这些外籍友人的"第二故乡"，或者是他们"永远想念之地"！

FOREWORD

Many people in their lives start their journeys from their hometowns but end up, finally, in a second hometown. Which city is your second hometown? Ten thousand people would perhaps give ten thousand answers. In Southwest China, there is a city which an increasing number of foreign friends regard it as their second hometown. This city was established 2,300 years ago and enjoys a 4,500-year history of civilization. This city is called Chengdu.

It is said that during its first year Chengdu was just a settlement. By the second year it was a town and by the third year it had become a city. The modern Chengdu has inherited tolerance and generosity from the historical "Land of Abundance". Moreover, it features a unique balance of leisure and dynamics. At present, Chengdu is seeing an increase in foreigners, including long-term resident foreigners, year on year. They invest, work, study, investigate, travel, live and visit their families in Chengdu. In order to attract more foreigners to make them not just come and live in Chengdu but also love and assimilate into Chengdu as locals, in early 2016, Chengdu Municipal People's Government launched the "Home in Chengdu" project in a bid to integrate and improve foreign related public services provided by 24 relevant departments at municipal government level. Basically, these public services can be divided into three parts: public information, public services and public activities.

What exactly does the "Home in Chengdu" project do? It is about the free flow of public information. To provide free access to public information, "Home in Chengdu" has opened up its own English-version webpage, WeChat account and App. It has facilitated the broadcast of English language TV shows and bilingual radio programs in local channels. And it has availed foreigners with an English language hotline to solve their problems. To ready foreign newcomers for life in Chengdu, this project has also prepared special manuals concerning daily life, business, medical services, investment, traffic, travel, and religious activities. With these materials, foreigners can become well-informed about Chengdu, even if it is the first time for them to come and they are unable to speak Chinese.

"Home in Chengdu" provides convenient public services. To help foreigners with entrepreneurship, employment, medical care, education and traffic, it offers one-stop services to foreigners who wish to get working permits in the city. It has issued policies on attracting talented professionals. It has created a green card system for foreign talents and gives comprehensive services to foreigners who come to the city for innovation and entrepreneurship purposes. It also offers one-stop medical services to foreigners and ensures their children's access to education.

"Home in Chengdu" endeavors to create a helpful and harmonious community for foreigners. Foreigners living in Chengdu can also have access to "neighborhood offices" in their communities. These offices are called

"Home for Foreigners" or "Home for Foreign Entrepreneurs and Innovators". With these special "homes", foreigners need not travel far to apply for residence permits or green cards, to make Chinese friends, or even to start up a new business. Besides, "Home in Chengdu" organizes folk cultural activities like poetry readings, Sichuanese paper cutting, lantern appreciation and spring tea picking. Also, it stages thematic experiential activities related to attending schools and hospitals or starting business in Chengdu to help foreigners better adapt themselves to the life of Chengdu. It hopes, through its effort, foreigners can not only settle down but also are willing to nestle their hearts in this city.

As a sub-project of "Home in Chengdu", the collection, *"Home in Chengdu—Where the Heart Nestles, There the Home Settles"* describes the colorful life stories of foreigners living in Chengdu, their affection for the city, their transformations and recognition of Chengdu's culture, and their appreciation of the city's quality services, as well as the city's harmonious cultural environment. This collection consists of two volumes. The first volume was written in the autumn and the winter of 2016, while the second volume was written between the winter of 2017 and the spring of 2018. With different professions, different reasons for moving to the city and different expectations from Chengdu, these 24 foreign interviewees have been grouped roughly along three themes, namely "Dreaming in Chengdu""Studying in Chengdu"and"Enjoying Chengdu".

The first theme, "Dreaming in Chengdu", focuses on foreign friends who specialize in innovation and entrepreneurship or who have made important contributions to the development of Chengdu. They have broken new ground or personally started a business, or they have created various conditions within the scope of their ability to help others realize their dreams in Chengdu. Mr. Amir Lati, meanwhile, was the first Consul General of the Consulate General of Israel in Chengdu. In more than four years since the Consulate General of Israel was established in Chengdu, Mr. Amir Lati took the initiative to extensively carry out economic, cultural, educational and technological exchanges. Another story is about the Dutch entrepreneur Thijs who has designed the children's mobile app "Dr. Panda". In 2008, Thijs and his wife Lin Yan started a business in Chengdu. Dr. Panda, the first app for children that they launched, conveys their passion for pandas and Chengdu. The protagonists of this theme devote themselves in and witness the progress of Chengdu's innovation and creation. They would like to continue pursuing their dreams in Chengdu, a city filled with opportunities.

The second theme, "Studying in Chengdu", focuses on a few foreign friends who are involved in the field of education, either because they are connected with Chengdu through their studies in the city, because they work in Chengdu's education sector, or because they teach in Chengdu via international cooperation on major scientific research projects. Pedro Antonio Valdes Sosa is a strong performer from Cuba who has made significant contributions to Sichuan. Now, he is a guest professor of the Advanced Research Union Laboratory of China-Cuba Nerve Transformation for Science and Technology established by the University of Electronic Science and Technology of China and the Cuban Neuroscience Center. In 2011, Mr. Pedro attended a conference in Chengdu for the first time. During that time, he became fascinated with this city and then discovered that Chengdu was the place of his dream. After that, Mr. Pedro was invited to be a guest professor at the University of Electronic Science and Technology of China. And there is youth talented conductor Darrell Ang. After giving up loads of offers from world's renowned orchestras, he chose the fast growing Sichuan Symphony Orchestra and the talent-craving Chengdu. With the baton in his hand, he has unfurled the brand new field for Sichuan Symphony Orchestra, while at the same time, he has absorbed the essence of Tianfu Culture and fulfilled himself.

The third theme, "Enjoying Chengdu", highlights foreigners who enjoy their life in the city. Jonathan Kott is from the US. In his eyes, Chengdu is a city of rapid development and changes. Beneath the city, the metro system shuttles its full loads of passengers. Alongside the streets, public bicycles are placed in an orderly fashion. Along the railways, bullet trains run at high speeds. However, unlike fast-paced and stressful cities like Beijing and Shanghai, Chengdu is famous for its leisure and placidity. Here, rivers have been flowing through the city for a thousand years with neither haste nor hurry. There is also Dr. Jason Logan from the United States, who was unfamiliar and often needed the help of friends and neighbors when first arrived in Chengdu. Now, he is not only used to going out when the sun is rising in Chengdu, but also constantly and selflessly cares the city with his own medical skills and love. His three children have been studying, singing lyrics and playing together with Chengdu kids. This year, he and his wife took China's "green card" from the Mayor of Chengdu and finally, they became real Chengdu locals. The protagonists of this theme enjoy their life in Chengdu and they are committed to giving back to the city and sharing with people of the city.

These three themes and their 24 articles primarily reveal the charm of Chengdu that has attracted the world's attention, and delineate various life stories about these newcomers, having come from all over the world, finally settling down in Chengdu.

Home is where the heart is! In June 2018, Chengdu held Opening Up Conference, after which it issued its Opinions on Accelerating the Building of an International Hub to Fully Serve the Construction of the Belt and Road and Action Plan on Building the International Exchange Center in West China (2017-2022). Both of the documents represent Chengdu's confidence and sincerity in welcoming foreign friends from all over the world. We are glad that Chengdu not only has such a welcoming posture but is also taking practical measures to provide its foreign friends with a joyful experience, their startup dreams and the warmth of home. Now, more and more foreign friends are either reluctant to leave Chengdu, or eager to return after having previously left. In their innermost heart, a seedling named "Chengdu" grows stronger. Years later, whether or not they have actually left Chengdu, hopefully in their minds Chengdu is not merely a city located in West China. Just like the key words mentioned most frequently in these articles, Chengdu is a second hometown for these foreign friends, and it is a place that they will never forget.

目　录

【乐 · 享在成都】

CATALOGUE

Realizing Dreams in Chengdu

Teaching & Learning in Chengdu

Enjoying Living in Chengdu

创·梦在成都

>>> 蓝天铭（以色列）

以色列驻成都首任总领事

Amir Lati, Israel

The First Consul General of the Consulate General of Israel in Chengdu

愿做一座桥　情牵丝路梦

他，是来自迦南之地，那里是《圣经》中流淌着奶和蜂蜜的地方。

那里曾是大漠荒原，也是绿洲天堂。

那里遍布亚述、巴比伦、纳巴太、罗马、拜占庭、十字军、阿拉伯、奥斯曼几千年的文化遗产。

那里也是犹太教、基督教、伊斯兰教三教共同的发源地，两河流域孕育的，是和中国一样的文明古国，直到今天，依然是世界的焦点！

他是蓝天铭，身为以色列驻成都首任总领事，在蓉城很多场合，经常会看到这位高个子、戴眼镜、中文流利帅哥的忙碌身影。忙碌的原因，恰如他的娓娓道来，领馆是丝路上的一座桥，桥的两岸是两个国家，领馆人员会尽心尽力维护好这座桥，为两个国家牵线搭桥。

求学抉择结缘中国

"飘动的羊毛多么纯净，切开的面包多么洁白，我们的城市正在崛起，风景不断展开。"这是亚伯拉罕·施龙斯基的一首诗，少年时代的蓝天铭喜欢朗诵这首诗，只是他读诗的时候未必能想到若干年后，自己会来到如诗歌里描摹的那般、正在崛起的一座城市。1974年，蓝天铭出生在以色列南部最大城市贝尔谢巴，和成都类似，贝尔谢巴是座历史十分悠久的城市。《圣经》中说："那一天以撒的仆人来，将挖井的事告诉他，说我们得了水了。"水源之井所在被命名为"示巴"或"别是巴"，英文名是Beersheba，今天，贝尔谢巴这座城市被称为以色列的硅谷，同样和成都有相似性。

　　和家乡所有小男孩一样，童年的蓝天铭在马路边飞驰踢球，玩泥巴，在沙漠边追逐打闹，在绿洲追逐牛羊和骆驼的踪迹。伴随着眼底世事流转，少年长大了，服完兵役之后，22岁时，他只身来到耶路撒冷，在希伯来大学主修经济与东亚研究。在学校里，他曾在日语与中文中选择不定，大概是冥冥之中自有注定，他选择了中文，开始系统学习中国的历史文化和国际关系。

　　他也曾想过听从家人朋友的建议，学习化学从事科研，或学经济，当白领。毕竟从专业到职业还有很长一段距离。事实上，直到大学三年级的那一年，一切才明晰澄澈。以色列外交部工作人员到学校宣讲，听完介绍后，蓝天铭醍醐灌顶，他终于知道自己想要什么——他第一次了解到外交部工作的丰富多彩，更能直观触摸到文化的交流与脉搏的跳动，"去外交部工作"，他耳边似乎有这样的一个声音响起。因为自己主修中文，所以蓝天铭把他的第一目标锁定在中国。同年，蓝天铭意外得到了中国政府的一笔奖学金，并获得了到北京大学学习的机会。面对这份惊喜，蓝天铭迅速做出决定，收拾好行李，动身前往中国。在中国，蓝天铭听鸽哨、登天坛、看故宫、喝豆汁……生活过得有滋有味。

　　除了和中国的同学以及老师交流，读中国经典书籍也是他去了解这片古老沃土的方式，当时他特别喜欢看鲁迅先生的作品，《狂人日记》等经典文本经常会翻来覆去地读。求学经历还让他明白"读万卷书不如行万里路"，要真正了解一个地方，不能坐在房间里，须走出去看世界。他一路行走大街穿小巷，听着人们对古老而现代中国的叙述，嗅着泥土的芬芳，看着似曾相识怡然自得的生活方式。那段时间也使蓝天铭更加深入了解了中国，以及他所热爱的中国文化。

　　此时，梦想又一次来敲门，他得知以色列开始选拔外交官。客观地讲，以色列外交部对外交官的选拔可谓严格。然而功夫不负有心人，蓝天铭以雄厚的综合实力如愿通过了以色列外交部的考试，从 2000 多名外交部考生中脱颖而出，成为那 1% 的幸运儿。之后，他先后在以色列驻澳大利亚、韩国，以及驻非洲使馆工作，2006 年，他终于再次来到中国，出任以色列驻上海总领事馆副总领事。2014 年，以色列驻成都总领事馆开馆，蓝天铭作为首任总领事赴任成都。

从绿皮车到高铁他看到中国速度

以色列驻成都总领事馆的领区包括四川、重庆、云南、贵州。成渝之间，动车快捷又舒适，是蓝天铭往返成都与重庆主要的交通工具。车窗附近，看着窗外的巴山蜀水，他还是会回想起 17 年前自己初到中国挤火车的场景。

1999 年，当时蓝天铭还在北京留学。恰逢十一长假，他和朋友相约旅游，行程从山东经过河南，到了返程时，在火车站他感受到了车水马龙、人山人海，排到公路上的买票长队让他傻了眼，黄金周一票难求，为了如期赶回学校，他只得买了站票。

于是，在熙攘的人群中，他惊喜地发现另外一种生活或者说另一种旅行的方式，有人提着鸡，有人背着大包，有人挑着扁担……那时候赶绿皮火车是件"热闹"事。年轻的大个子蓝天铭，来不及仔细端详，检完票就往站台冲，终于在角落占到一个位置。虽然满头大汗坐定，但挤火车的经历与情感也瞬间定格，包括车厢里那种充满热度与烟火气的市井人情……

那段经历之对于蓝天铭来说印象深刻，原因还在于中国这些年的发展太快，变化太大，当时人们赖以出行的绿皮火车如今几乎消失殆尽，取而代之的是四通八达的交通线和干净舒适的动车，航空港的建设伴随飞机的普及，正在从中心城市普及到全国各地。到成都之后，他常常会挂在嘴边的，中国的发展并不只是北上广，还有四川这样的西南腹地，四川的发展也不单只是成都，还从成都辐射到绵阳、德阳等。

愿做文化桥梁　穿针引线搭桥

"士不可以不弘毅，任重而道远。"对比同样古老的希伯来文"别为了已经洒掉的牛奶哭泣"，费解而充满韵律美的中国古语似乎更有忧患意识，蓝天铭也始终把中国圣人的教诲深谙于心。2014 年 11 月 17 日，以色列驻成都总领事馆正式开馆，那天，高大帅气的蓝天铭快步走上红地毯，意气风发。以色列驻成都总领事馆是继上海、广州、香港后，以色列在中国设立的第四家领事机构，领馆设立的两年多时间里，经过蓝天铭的细心浇灌，广泛开展文化与教育交流，大力推进与中国西南地区的经贸往来和在"创新创业"领域的交流合作。设在武侯区的成都以色列孵化器，就是他和他的团队与成都市共同推动成立的，这个投资型国际孵化器，目前已经接受过超过 1000 个项目的咨询，先后孵化近 60 个科技创业项目，举办各类双创活动 40 余场，2016 年 9 月 29 日被纳入国家级众创空间。

之所以选择成都，他用凝练的语言表述，"商机，这里有巨大的商机。"以色列曾经在地中海创造了灿烂的文明，直到今天，在海上依然拥有很重要的地位，而其航道正位于"一带一路"战略沿线。在"一带一路"战略沿线覆盖的六十多个国家中，无论是人均 GDP 还是科技实力，以色列都比较领先，并且以色列的创新能力与中国的广阔市场具有极高互补性。

在其位，谋其事，一口流利中文、踏实做事的蓝天铭如此勉励自己。在成都的两年多，700 多个日夜，他因务实精神而博得了太多人的认可，他所在的以色列总领事馆也成为在成都较忙的总领事馆之一。

"四川位于中国腹地，自古以来，巴蜀文化对中国文化的影响不可忽视。如今，四川作为西部大开发大本营，无论是经济还是文化，都与以色列有非常巨大的合作空间。"谈到四川的过去与现在，他的了解程度会出乎你的意料。

热爱成都 热爱中文

蓝天铭的中文非常好，和热情好客的成都朋友见面，他会主动用中文打招呼。在他看来，中文有个成语叫作入乡随俗，他对于中文的热情，一面是不由自主地喜欢，另一方面也是工作使然。他总认为自己有着一份担当，身为总领事，他需要在成都长期生活，需要和成都人沟通和交朋友，需要去学说最地道的中国话甚至成都话。

工作之余，蓝天铭会主动加强中文训练，在成都每周他都会去上中文辅导课。对于语言学习，蓝天铭颇有心得，他认为平时积累最为重要，没有什么捷径可言。一旦工作生活遇到生僻的字或者词，他便会立刻请身边的助理帮他记下来，再抽时间把记下的词融会贯通。他热爱这座城市，热爱那些美好的风景和食物，他需要和当地人交流聊天，需要感受这座城市的脉搏，能够自己独立处理生活上的事情。平日里，他总说自己说的其实是成都话，是"川普"。

中国的圣人孔子说过一句话叫"己所不欲勿施于人"，几乎在同一时期，在以色列也有位圣人说过类似的话，《圣经》中记载为"doing unto others as you would have them do unto you"。圣人之间并不相识，也没有互动和交流，但是思想却有异曲同工之妙，不同地区和国家文化的相通，让他对语言，对中文充满热情。就在最近这段时间，蓝天铭开始练习中文的书写，他要成为一个熟悉成都味道和成都文化生活的"成都通"。

蓉城生活　不会想家

他的家人和他一样，特别热爱这座让人来了便不想走的城市。早在 2008 年，蓝天铭妻子便已经来过成都旅游，回去之后还与他分享在成都的见闻，无论是充满韵味的人文景观还是丰富可口的成都美食。口耳相传，妻子的描述使得蓝天铭对成都这个陌生的城市充满了好奇和向往。所以到后来，蓝天铭调任成都后，家人也欣然同行。

蓝天铭有两个女儿，大女儿四岁半，小女儿快两岁了。过周末时，他会提前向有小孩的职员打听成都近郊哪儿适合小孩子玩，工作之余的时间会尽量放在孩子身上。在成都，工作中的蓝天铭是解决问题的高手，但身为两个女儿的父亲，家庭生活的温情与琐碎，足以让他瞬间卸下所有盔甲，变身一个温柔奶爸。

今年 9 月，蓝天铭一家回到以色列，当孩子奶奶用希伯来语问大女儿是否要吃饭，大女儿竟不自觉地冒出一句中文"不想吃"，着实让奶奶摸不着头脑。面对此情此景，蓝天铭颇有些意外之喜与哭笑不得。语言环境与家庭熏陶，使得他的两个女儿可以同时听得懂英语、希伯来语和中文三门语言，这也是丰富的文化交流造就的天赋。

工作关系，在中国数年的时间里，蓝天铭的足迹踏过了十多个省份，感受了中国大江南北的山川之美和人文风情，蓝天铭始终认为成都最具有生活气息，林林总总的公园是他工作之余常去休闲玩乐的地方，成都的慢节奏让他能够在繁忙的工作外寻得几分舒适与安心。他常常说，即使是没有工作的原因，自己也一定会来成都。

关于未来，蓝天铭将会在四川做更多的项目，他与四川许多企业和机构都在进行良好的交流。他将这种交流解释为"多个朋友多条路"。蓝天铭也希望会有越来越多来自中国西南腹地的政府代表团、企业、商人、学者、科研人员、学生、旅游者前往以色列，同时也将更多的以色列经济技术力量带到西南地区，让成都和以色列一道见证"一带一路"的建设，彼此参与对方的发展。他把中以合作称之为"天作之合"，也始终坚信成都与以色列的交流"正当其时"，特别是科技等高新领域的合作令他充满期望。

2017年，是中以建交25周年，蓝天铭与他的团队也将通过一系列活动，以多种方式为中以友谊提供发展新契机。蓝天铭与成都之间，想必会有更多的精彩故事，让我们拭目以待。

May I Serve As a Bridge along the Silk Road

He comes from the land of Canaan, described in the Bible as a land of milk and honey.

It used to be a complete wilderness, yet its oases always presented the vision of Heaven.

It is home to cultural heritages spanning thousands of years, created by the Assyrians, the Babylonians, the Nabataeans, then the Roman Empire, the Byzantine Empire, the Crusaders, the Arabs, and the Ottoman Empire.

As the shared origin of the three major religions—Judaism, Christianity and Islam, it has witnessed the glory of the Mesopotamian culture, an ancient civilization comparable to ancient China. Today, it still makes headlines in the world.

Our hero in this narrative is Amir Lati, the first Consul General of the Consulate General of Israel in Chengdu, a tall figure frequently seen in Chengdu on different occasions, wearing glasses, fluent in Chinese and always busy. The reason for his full schedule, as he said, lies in the fact that the consulate must serve as a well-maintained bridge connecting China and Israel along the Silk Road.

Study in China, Form Ties with China

"How pure is the floating wool, and how taintless is the sliced bread!

As our city is rising, the vista is unfolding." This poem by Abraham Slonski was especially favored by young Amir Lati. Only that he could never have imagined that, several years later, he would indeed end up in a rising city resonating to the poem. In 1974, Amir Lati was born in Beersheba, the largest city of southern Israel, and also a city steeped in history just like Chengdu. Its name can be traced to Bible: "That day Isaac's servants came and told him about the well they had dug. They said, 'we've found water!'" The location of the well was called Shibah, or Beersheba in English. Today, the city Beersheba is becoming Israel's Silicon Valley, a goal Chengdu is also in pursuit of.

Like all the other boys back in his hometown, Amir Lati spent most of his childhood time playing roadside ball games, making mud pies and chasing after cows, sheep and camels by the oases. Time flew and he soon grew up. At the age of 22, after completing his military service, Amir Lati went alone to Jerusalem, where he was to pursue a degree in economics and East Asia studies at Hebrew University of Jerusalem. Finally, he had to make the difficult choice between Japanese and Chinese. As if fate had called, he finally fixed upon Chinese, kicking off his systematic study of China's history, culture and international relationships.

At first, he thought about following the advice of his loved ones and becoming a scientific researcher majoring in chemistry, or a white-collar worker through economic courses, for, after all, any occupation somehow requires an academic foundation. It was not until the third year in university, however, that things became clear for him. The Ministry of Foreign Affairs of Israel happened to be holding campus recruitment at his university. The recruitment proved enlightening to Amir Lati, who finally got to the depth of his desire: for the first time, he was given a glimpse of the colorful life in the Ministry of Foreign Affairs, where he believed he would feel. The tangible pulses of the cultural exchanges. "Then go there!" A voice seemed to be ringing in his ears. Majoring in Chinese, Amir Lati instantly set China as his top goal. In the same year, he was granted a surprising scholarship by the Chinese government and also a chance to study at Peking University. Amir Lati, in his immediate response, soon packed up his things and set out for China, where he was to listen to whistling pigeons, visit historical places of interest, drink fermented soybean milk, and live a most enjoyable life.

Always talking to his Chinese classmates and teachers about China, Amir Lati also read classical Chinese books to know more about the country. His favorite Chinese author was Lu Xun, an author whose most typical work, A Madman's Diary, was the one that Amir Lati kept reading. As a student, Amir Lati knew that "it is better to travel ten thousand miles than to read ten thousand books". To get a real understanding of the world, one must not be confined in his room, but go out. Travelling through streets and alleys, Amir Lati got to know stories about both modern China and also a country with profound history; indulging in the fresh smell of the soil, he was brought to the presence of an amiable and enjoyable lifestyle, exploring even deeper into China and his favorite Chinese culture.

Then another chance came: Israel began to recruit diplomats. Objectively speaking, the screening examination was rather strict, yet Amir Lati, hardworking and highly competitive across the board, passed it, standing out from more than 2,000 candidates and joined the one percent winners' group. After that, he was sent to work at the Consulate General of Israel in Australia, then Republic of Korea and Africa. In 2006, he went to China again, this time serving as Deputy Consul General of the Consulate General of Israel in Shanghai. In 2014, the Consulate General of Israel in Chengdu was set up, and Amir Lati became its first Consul General.

Seeing China's Growth through its Trains

The consular district of the Consulate General of Israel in Chengdu covers Sichuan, Chongqing, Yunnan, and Guizhou. During his routine trips between Chengdu and Chongqing, Amir Lati mostly takes the bullet trains, which are fast and comfortable. As he sits beside the window and looks outside, the memory would flash in his mind of seventeen years ago when he just came to China and elbowed his way to take a train.

It was during the National Day holidays in 1999 when Amir Lati was a foreign student in Beijing, he and some friends traveled from Shandong to Henan. Then, on their journey back, he was found dumb at the ticket selling hall, where long queues were extending far away onto the roads: the National Day holidays made train tickets even harder to get. Anxious to return to school on time, Amir Lati and his friends had to buy the standing-room-only tickets.

However, amid the crowds, Amir Lati was amazed to find another way of life, or rather, another way of traveling: some people were carrying chickens, some had super-big bags on their backs, some were bearing shoulder poles. Back then the most widely-seen green-colored trains offered much fewer seats than needed and people just scrambled aboard, including Amir Lati. Even before he had time to double check, his young and tall figure had already rushed out like an arrow shooting towards the platform. Finally, he got seated at a little corner. The whole chaotic scene—his battling for a corner to sit down, and the way he sweated—together with the tension and anxiety, was frozen at that moment, and even the heat and smoke of secular taste in the carriage was unforgettable.

It is an impressive memory for Amir Lati, especially in the context of China's rapid growth and ever-changing look. The formerly popular green-colored trains are almost extinct, giving way to interconnected transportation links and clean, comfortable bullet trains. Meanwhile, as air travel becomes more and more popular, airport construction has begun to spread from major cities to other areas. After he came to Chengdu, Amir Lati always said that China's development was not only witnessed in Beijing, Shanghai, and Guangzhou, but also in Sichuan, the southwestern hinterland. And Sichuan's development did not only depend on Chengdu but also must take into account other cities like Mianyang and Deyang.

Committed to Serving as a Bridge between Cultures

As a Chinese saying goes, "An educated gentleman cannot but be resolute and broad-minded, for he has taken up a heavy responsibility and a long course". In Hebrew, there is also a saying: "Don't cry over spilled milk". Comparatively speaking, the more implicit and beautifully rhymed Chinese language seemingly does better in showing a sense of crisis. And the wisdom of China's wise men never ceases to inspire Amir Lati. On November 17, 2014, the day the Consulate General of Israel in Chengdu was officially established, the tall, handsome Amir Lati walked briskly onto the red carpet in all his splendors. The Consulate General of Israel in Chengdu, whose consular district covers Sichuan, Chongqing, Yunnan, and Guizhou, is Israel's fourth consulate in China after those in Shanghai, Guangzhou and Hong Kong. Over two years into office, Amir Lati, having made meticulous preparations, launched wide-ranging cultural and educational exchanges, largely strengthening economic-and-trade ties between Israel and Southwest China and boosting the two parties' communication in "innovation and entrepreneurship". The Chengdu-Israeli Incubator in Wuhou District, Chengdu, came as the fruit of the joint efforts of Amir Lati's team and Chengdu. As an investment-oriented international incubator, the Chengdu-Israeli Incubator has so far consulted on over 1,000 projects, incubated close to 60 sci-tech entrepreneurship projects and held over 40 activities themed on innovation and entrepreneurship. On September 29, 2016, the Chengdu-Israeli Incubator was listed in the national maker space.

As for the reason why Israel chose Chengdu as a consular base, Amir Lati's answer was succinct, "Prospects. Here lie great business prospects." Israel has historically created a most glorious civilization along the Mediterranean Sea. Its maritime edges persist to this day, and its seaways fall rightly on the routes of the "Belt and Road" initiative. Among the 60 countries along the "Belt and Road" routes, Israel is taking the lead both in per capita GDP and sci-tech strength. What's more, Israeli innovation ability and China's broad market could be highly complementary.

The Chinese motto "once you take office, you have to be wholly committed" has always been inspiring to Amir Lati, who speaks good Chinese and is a conscientious doer. For the last two years, over 700 days, his goal-oriented approach has gained wide recognition across Chengdu, and the Consulate General he heads ranks among the busiest. Amir Lati knows

Sichuan's history and the current developments exceedingly well. "Located in the hinterland, Sichuan has played a non-ignorable role in shaping Chinese culture throughout history. Today, it serves as a stronghold of China Western Development, and there is huge space for cooperation between Sichuan and Israel, in both economy and culture." When speaking of the past and present of Sichuan, his knowledge may surprise you.

A Fan of Chinese Aiming to be a Chengduer

Amir Lati speaks Chinese very well. Whenever he meets his hospitable friends in Chengdu, he will call them in Chinese. For him, the Chinese saying "When in Rome, do as the Romans do" makes great sense. Actually, his love of Chinese is as much spontaneous as obligatory for in his eyes his role as the Consul General requires that he has to make a point of living in Chengdu for the long haul, mingling with the Chengduers and speaking the most native Chinese or even the Chengdu dialect.

In order to improve his Chinese, every week after work, Amir Lati will attend Chinese tutoring classes in Chengdu. And he also has his own learning method: there is no better shortcut than the day-to-day accumulation. In life or at work, no new Chinese word will be neglected by the eager-to-learn Amir Lati, who often has the words put down by his assistants and then learns them by heart when he has time. He is in deep love with this city, its scenery and food, and he is anxious to talk to the locals, feel by himself the pulses of the city and rely more upon himself in daily private affairs. He often jokingly says he speaks mandarin with characteristics of Chengdu dialect.

The Chinese wise man Confucius once said, "do as you would be done by", which is also echoed by one of his Israeli peers, who writes on Bible that "doing unto others as you would have them do unto you". It is amazing that the two wise men, though they never met nor talked to each other, could share the same thought. The connection between different cultures mesmerizes Amir Lati and ignites his enthusiasm for language learning and Chinese. Very recently he has begun Chinese handwriting exercises, for his goal is to become a "walking map", and a real "Chengduer."

A Happy Man with His Family in Chengdu

Amir Lati's love of Chengdu is also shared by his family, who view Chengdu as a city that one never wants to leave. As early as 2008, Amir Lati's wife traveled to Chengdu. Upon returning she shared with Amir Lati her experiences in Chengdu, its profound cultural landscapes and delicious food. Her description encouraged Amir Lati's curiosity and longing for the strange city. So when Amir Lati took office in Chengdu, it was quite natural that his family was very pleased to go with him.

Amir Lati has two daughters: a four and a half-year-old and a nearly two-year-old toddler. Ahead of the weekends, he, as dedicated father, always seeks advice from his colleagues, who are also parents, as he tries to figure out whether there is some fun place in the suburbs to which he could take his kids. He spends as much after-work time as possible with his children. At work, he is a powerful problem solver, while at home, this father of two is instantly disarmed by love and happiness, and turns into a tender guard.

This September, Amir Lati brought his family back to Israel. When invited to dinner by their grandma in Hebrew, Amir Lati's eldest daughter spontaneously responded in Chinese, "I don't want to eat", making Amir Lati a bit frustrated yet much amazed. Favorable circumstances and family education have enabled his two daughters to have a good understanding of English, Hebrew, and Chinese. That couldn't have happened if their rich cultural communication was not launched.

During his years of time in China, Amir Lati's work has taken him across more than ten provinces and all kinds of beauty inherent to the Chinese natural and cultural landscapes, all of which fully unfolded before him. Yet for Amir Lati, Chengdu is always the most vivid landscape. Its ever-present parks embrace him during his leisure time, and the slow pace of living here always soothes his weary soul after busy work. As he often says, even if it hadn't been for work, he would still have come to Chengdu.

In the near future, Amir Lati plans to launch more projects in Sichuan, which are already under discussion between his consulate and the local companies and organizations. These discussions, in his eyes, act as an approach to bring more friends and more opportunities. Meanwhile, Amir Lati wishes to see more government delegations, companies, businessmen, scholars, researchers, students and tourists from Southwest China to go to Israel, bringing more Israeli economic and technical strengths to Southwest China, involving both Chengdu and Israel in the "Belt and Road" initiative and boosting their cooperation. He views the China-Israel partnership as a "match made in heaven", and he believes that the communication between Chengdu and Israel falls in the right moment, especially over their cooperation in high-tech areas like sci-tech.

The year 2017 marks the 25th anniversary of the establishment of China-

Israel diplomatic relations. Amir Lati and his team will endeavor to create new opportunities for the development of such friendship by holding a raft of activities in multiple forms. The story between Amir Lati and Chengdu will go on and on. Let's wait and see.

023

>>> 泰斯（荷兰）
软件公司创始人

Thijs Bosma, the Netherlands
Founder of a Software Company

熊猫与博士

2012 年，一款名为"熊猫博士餐厅"的儿童应用一问世，应用中这个戴着博士帽，形象憨态可掬的"熊猫博士"，便迅速赢得了世界各地的孩子和家长们的喜爱。这款知名的应用正是出于成都一家软件公司之手，这家公司的创始人，名为泰斯，来自荷兰。

2008 年，泰斯和妻子林燕一同来到成都创业。作为他们推出的第一款儿童应用，"熊猫博士"中的"熊猫"意喻创意输出地是熊猫的故乡成都，"博士"则代表泰斯"寓教于乐"的儿童教育理念。

大熊猫作为最广为人知的中国国宝，是世界自然基金会的形象大使，是世界生物多样性保护的旗舰物种，也多次代表中国给其他国家送去问候与祝福，如"出使"一般，代表了中华民族较高的礼遇之一。选择从"熊猫"出发，创立公司并开发儿童应用，泰斯夫妇可谓用心用情而为之。

在上海邂逅中国女孩

泰斯出生在荷兰首都阿姆斯特丹附近的一座小镇，如世间千百万个小镇一样，这里朴素简约而又不失单纯。泰斯在这里极其普通地度过他的幼年、少年时光。在周围人的眼里，泰斯没有任何的不同，循规蹈矩、按部就班，然而谁也没有想到，他在鹿特丹商业大学完成大学学业后，毅然选择了飘洋过海到中国，去探究一个更大的世界。

2006 年，泰斯只身一人来到上海，起初他在一家荷兰公司从事市场方面的工作，这份工作虽辛苦，却也应了"一份付出一分回报"的哲理，泰斯在这家公司赚到了他人生的第一桶金，这不仅为后来的创业提供了经济基础，与人交往、业务开展方面的经验更是无价之宝。而最值得赞叹的是，他在上海时，邂逅了他的爱人林燕。而后，林燕不仅成为了他的灵魂寄托、生活伴侣，更是他事业最默契的伙伴。

泰斯和林燕的恋爱之旅好似一部浪漫的爱情电影，他们始于一见钟情，向往携手一生。

当初，林燕以中文教师的身份出现在泰斯的生命里。第一次相约见面，泰斯内心深处那颗爱的种子便不禁悸动，然而终究是初相识，以"不冒犯"为前提，泰斯努力克制着自己的感情。随着接触越来越多，两人顺理成章地熟络起来，渐渐从师生发展到朋友。然而好景不长，半年后，林燕便远赴欧洲求学深造，两人只能通过电邮和电话保持着固定频率的常规联系。

这段异地不得见的时光，于泰斯可谓苦煞人也！他越来越确定自己对林燕的思念，他再也不想刻意控制对林燕的爱，他开始隔着电波疯狂地表达着对林燕的关切，坚如磐石般等着她回来。

终于，爱和时间改变了他们的师生、朋友关系。2008 年，完成了学业的林燕回到中国与泰斯携手创业，一起为美好的未来奋斗拼搏，地点则选择在了成都。

在成都创业打拼

问及为何会选择到成都创业？泰斯浅笑而语：因为成都有中国的国宝熊猫！关于成都，泰斯是完全陌生的。唯有熊猫是他"耳朵边的熟客"而已。然而，即便是如此的不相熟甚至有些不相干，他还是选择到成都来，到有中国国宝的城市来。

当然，这看似是游客心理，泰斯却绝非如此草率，他明确地知道自己是为创业而来。于是他和林燕展开了城市筛查及对成都的深入研究。成都越来越国际化的城市建设理念是新颖的，而其固有的则是人口众多，拥有了不逊于一线城市的劳动力市场，不仅如此，其劳动力成本也远远低于北上广地区，这对于一个初创公司而言具有相当大的吸引力。

再加上成都市政府在推广科技创新方面的优惠政策很多，而且成都拥有 50 多所高等学府，培养了大量专业的软件编程技术人才，能提供的基础人才供给充沛。充分权衡之后，成都成了他的不二之选。2008年泰斯和林燕创立公司，当时的他们对公司的定位是"从小而精做起"，他们的办公室租赁在市中心的一栋写字楼里，全部员工只有五个人，主要业务是游戏外包。

尽管公司小而精，但五脏俱全，无非是个人肩负职位与责任的问题。管理层的泰斯和林燕，分工极其明确：有着丰富的工商管理经验的泰斯负责对外法务，投资者关系等；林燕则主要对内负责产品和人事管理方面。凭借过去在上海公司积累的经验，他们的公司发展得平稳顺利。

公司发展稳定，作为外国人的泰斯，也逐渐适应了在成都的生活，除了让他感觉火辣辣的辣椒以外，两年的上海生活让他对中国整个大环境都比较熟悉。但对比上海这个快节奏的国际大都市，他也明显感觉到了成都节奏的缓慢，"如果说成都的平均步伐如果是 1 的话，上海就是2"。所以，他每次从上海出差回到成都感觉一下子就慢下来，身体和思想也都缓慢了下来。用泰斯的话来说，慢意味着有缓冲的时间，能让自己更加平和淡然。

相比其他城市，成都一直以独特的精神面貌以及丰富的生活内容吸引着来自不同城市的人。成都还是一个极具包容性的城市，在这里你可以体味到不一样的极致生活，感受到来自世界各地的文化特色，以及周到的品质服务。当然，成都也在步向国际化的道路上步步前进着，不断发展着。

初来成都创业期间，泰斯和林燕两人几乎每周无休，生活和工作都在一起。他做了一个计算，两人每天平均在一起的时间 16 个小时，而且这种长时间的在一起已经 6 年了，人们常说七年之痒，但泰斯并不觉得。回想他们的创业生活，两位异乡人，带着共同理想来到一个陌生的城市，在公司草创初期，同甘共苦、同舟共济，反而觉得能一起吃苦就是幸福。有时候一个人想到一些开心的事情，马上就能和对方分享，对方秒懂的莞尔一笑，更让他们彼此觉得很幸福心。也正是这种苦乐与共的紧密，让他们有了更多的时间互相了解和沟通，也变得更密切和默契，工作上配合的更好。

这种状态一直持续到有了孩子之后才开始转变，作为母亲的林燕把更多精力放在了孩子身上，而对于泰斯来说，家庭和工作双重的压力也使他经常忙得不可开交。但他享受身为丈夫和父亲的责任，乐于承担这种压力，也愿意与妻子一起将家庭与事业经营下去。此时，在时代的大背景下，电子行业快速发展，数码产品开始普及，泰斯也迅速抓准时机将公司的发展推向新的领域。

推出"熊猫博士"

2012 年，泰斯推出公司第一款游戏——"熊猫博士餐厅"，在 App Store 刚刚上架，就赢得了良好的口碑。三年的时间里，泰斯的公司累积推出超过 20 款的"熊猫博士"系列游戏。数据显示，直到 2015 年，它的全球下载量超过 4000 万次，成为仅次于 Disney 和 Tocaboca 的全球第三大儿童游戏开发商，同时也是最大的付费儿童游戏独立开发商。

常常有客户问泰斯，为什么选择熊猫作为人物形象呢？泰斯的答案很简单，就如开篇提到内容，泰斯会告诉人们，自己的公司位于大熊猫的故乡中国成都，大熊猫是这座城市的骄傲和象征。作为创业者的泰斯个人和可爱憨厚的大熊猫结下了不解之缘，也希望世界各地的孩子和家长能一起分享他对大熊猫的喜爱之情。

在"熊猫博士"应用中，泰斯通过给孩子们设置一个开放式的场景和一些道具，让孩子们做自己世界的主人，没有规则，没有分数，没有传统思维的限制，孩子们可以自由发挥想象力，按照自己喜欢的方式去探索和发现。"熊猫博士"能够给父母提供所期望的教育价值，游戏中没有错误答案，没有分数的压力，没有过重的负担。

不仅如此，"熊猫博士"还完美融合了角色扮演的元素、兼具开放式的游戏玩法和富有表现力的游戏角色。泰斯希望，"熊猫博士"带给孩子的不是书本上的内容，而是通过玩这个应用，熟悉他们周遭的世界，例如进入机场后的流程，医院是干什么的，园艺工作者的日常工作内容等。这些看似普通的生活常识，让游戏更有趣，同时游戏中布满了各种隐藏的小秘密，孩子们会为自己在玩游戏时获得的角色成长而产生极大满足感。

每一个孩子的学习潜力都是不可限量的，而只有在一个轻松的、寓教于乐的环境里，孩子的学习效果才是最好的。在"熊猫博士"游戏中，孩子们并没有进行刻意的学习，而是沉浸在开放式的角色扮演中，不知不觉学习了知识，在潜移默化中养成了良好的生活习惯。毫无疑问，对于家长来说，最关心的莫过于孩子的成长安全，最放心的就是知道孩子所玩的游戏是安全和值得信任的。泰斯的"熊猫博士"便是让孩子们有机会去尝试因为年纪太小而不能体验的活动，比如做一名厨师、一名巴士司机或一名医生。与"熊猫博士"和他的小动物伙伴们一起，孩子们可谓是在一个安全而又充满乐趣的环境探索这些日常生活中的职业。

在泰斯和林燕的打造下，"熊猫博士"受到了大众的关注和喜爱，原因在于这款应用的游戏内容大多数都是以 3D 形式呈现，以 Q 版动物形象作为主角，配合欢快的音乐和简单的玩法，非常适合小朋友。在儿童游戏中，这一系列在画质和玩法上都属于较高的水准，在画面上也十分精良。

最重要的是，这款应用的游戏在知识性上也经得起考量和推敲，小朋友和家长都能从中获益良多。这一点，在 App Store 的评分和评论中可见一斑。此外，"熊猫博士"系列游戏最大的特点是在游戏中基本没有任何的语言文字，玩家通过引导和交互就能明白游戏的玩法，这种避重就轻的设计使得其产品在多个国家的 App Store 获得了官方推荐。

立足成都走向世界

2015 年，在"熊猫博士"迎来 4000 万下载量的同时，泰斯和他的公司也搬进了位于来福士广场的新家。而公司的人数，也从最初创建时候的 5 人增长到了 50 多人，其中员工有三分之一为外籍人士，公司氛围像一个快乐的国际大家庭。而在泰斯和林燕心中，虽然两人都不是成都人，但他们的公司与家庭都在成都，早就把自己当成了成都人。

从初来创业到搬进新家，他们在成都走过了匆匆八年。在这近三千天的岁月里，成都给予了这两个年轻人事业和家庭，也给予了他们归属感，这种归属感使得两个异乡人再没有了当年"独在异乡为异客"的孤独感，没有了举目无亲的踟蹰感，没有了"拔剑四顾心茫然"的无力感，成都已然是他们的第二故乡，他们的心灵福地，而由两人亲自创造的应用"熊猫博士"就像他们的另一个孩子。

对于"熊猫博士"的未来设想，泰斯希望能打造一个主题游乐场，这种游乐场的特点在于有更多的电子设备，更加吸引小朋友，他也希望是能基于更多虚幻现实等领先科技给孩子们带来不同的感官体验。为了达到预期设想，泰斯的公司目前正在制作一个关于"熊猫博士"的 3D 动画片，下个目标是将带有虚实互动 VR 技术的电子产品和实体紧密结合。

泰斯相信，在成都这个具有奇特魔力的城市里，开放性，科技性会让植根于此的"熊猫博士"走得更远，未来能够发展得更趋于成熟和完美。让我们一起祝福泰斯和他的"熊猫博士"。

The Panda and the Doctor

The year 2012 saw the popularity of a kid app named "Dr. Panda's Restaurant". It featured an adorable Panda Ph.D. wearing a regalia cap, who won the instant favor of children and their parents worldwide. A Chengdu-based software company is right behind the app, and its founder is a Dutchman named Thijs Bosma.

In 2008, Thijs came to Chengdu with his Chinese wife Lin Yan, and started their own business with the kid app "Dr. Panda's Restaurant". "Panda" means Chengdu, where the app originated, and "Dr." implies Thijs's idea of letting children learn through fun.

Pandas are the universally known national treasure of China, the image ambassador of the World Wildlife Fund (WWF), a flagship species for preserving the world's biodiversity, and also the highest-ranking "messenger" who has several times sent the greetings and best wishes of China to other countries. The usage of the panda image in their product testifies to Thijs and his wife's ingenuity and their deep attachment to Chengdu.

Meeting a Chinese Girl in Shanghai

Thijs was born in a small town near Amsterdam, capital of the Netherlands. Like any other small town in the world, it was plain, simple and unsophisticated. Here Thijs spent his uneventful childhood and adolescence.

In the eyes of his neighbors, Thijs was only one of the many ordinary boys who behaved themselves and did what they must do. Nobody had imagined that one day, this boy, after graduating from Rotterdam Business School, would launch a resolute exploration into a bigger world in a remote country—China.

In 2006, Thijs came to Shanghai alone. His first job was a tough one, which was in the marketing department of a Dutch company. However, as the saying goes, "no pain, no gain", Thijs earned his "first bucket of gold" here—a combination of an amount of money for future entrepreneurship, valuable interpersonal communication skills and experience in business. The most amazing thing for him was that in Shanghai he met the woman who was to become his beloved soul mate and partner in both his life and career.

Their story is very much like a romantic movie, where romance starts at the first sight and lasts a lifetime.

Lin Yan was Thijs's Chinese teacher at first. When Thijs saw her for the first time, the seed of love began to germinate in his heart. However, given that they newly met, Thijs decided to behave like a gentleman and kept his feelings to himself. As familiarity bred between them, they became close friends. However, their good times together were disrupted half a year later, when Lin Yan had to go to Europe for study. Routine emails and telephone calls became their only way of communication.

The feeling of missing someone out of sight was so torturing for Thijs! He was more sure about his feelings towards Lin Yan and, not restraining himself any more, he began to pour out his concern and love for Lin Yan through phone calls, while like a solid rock waiting for her to come back.

Love and time eventually transformed their teacher-student relationship.

In 2008, Lin Yan, upon her graduation, returned to China and tied the knot with Thijs. The two chose Chengdu to start their own business.

Entrepreneurship in Chengdu

Speaking of the reason why he chose Chengdu, Thijs grinned and said, "because there is the national treasure—pandas!" Chengdu used to be a completely strange city for Thijs, who only heard of its pandas. However, that unfamiliarity and even irrelevance between him and the city never proved to be a problem when he decided to come to Chengdu, the city with the Chinese national treasure in his eyes.

Though the whole idea seemed a bit whimsical, Thijs was actually never a rash person. He knew exactly why he came to Chengdu for business. The couple had seriously selected their candidates and done in-depth research about Chengdu. At that time, it was making headway in building itself into an international city, and it boasted a large population, which meant a labor force no less than the first-tier cities. And the most persuasive bonus was the cost of labor here was far lower than that of Beijing, Shanghai and Guangzhou.

Plus, Chengdu government was quite favorable to sci-tech innovation and offered many preferential policies. The city was home to over 50 institutions of higher learning, which had cultivated numerous software programming professionals and boasted a large pool of basic manpower. Carefully weighing his options, Thijs finally chose Chengdu. In 2008, when Thijs and Lin Yan set up their company, they agreed on its being positioned as a small but professional one. Their office was a rented room in a downtown office building. There were only five employees and the major business was game outsourcing.

Despite its small size, the company was a compact one, with each person fulfilling specific tasks and duties. As for the management of the company, Thijs and Lin Yan, were entrusted with clearly-divided responsibilities: Thijs, with abundant experience in business management, mainly dealt with external and legal affairs, as well as investor relations, while Lin Yan took charge of products and personnel management. Their prior working experience in Shanghai contributed to the company's smooth development.

That made Thijs gradually accustomed to the life of Chengdu, except for the stinging chilli peppers. Two years of living in Shanghai had acquainted him with the big context of China. By comparison he concluded that Chengdu is far slower-paced than Shanghai, saying that "if Chengdu is one in speed, then Shanghai would be two." Every time he returns to Chengdu from Shanghai, he would find himself landing in a much slower world, where his body and mind also ease their pace. In his own words, to be slow means there is time to buffer and to find more peace in the mind.

Chengdu, in comparison with many other cities, is always drawing people from far and wide with its spiritual uniqueness and variety of life. Its super inclusiveness could bring you insight into different styles of life, diverse cultures from across the globe and services of the highest quality. One thing is certain: Chengdu is making headway in going global.

During the early period of their entrepreneurship, Thijs and Lin Yan rarely had weekends. Their life was work. According to a calculation by Thijs, they stayed together for an average of 16 hours per day, and for six years up to now. The "seven-year itch" commonly known to marriages doesn't exist between them. Having experienced the hard times together during their entrepreneurship, they found that bearing hardship together could also equal happiness. The occasional sharing of a happy feeling and then an understanding smile in return could be a most enjoyable game between the two. There is a bond between them that has withstood the test of hardships and happy times, which makes their mutual communication barrier-free and their cooperation intimate and perfect.

Things began to change after they became parents. Lin Yan began to spend more time being a mother, while Thijs, burdened with work and family, found himself terribly busy. However, he was happy to be a husband and father, to bear the pressure and to work with his wife to keep their family and company going. Meanwhile, in the information age, the electronics industry saw a boom and digital products became popular. This proved a golden chance for Thijs's company to tap into a new sector.

"Dr. Panda's Restaurant" Launched

In 2012, Thijs's company launched its first game—"Dr. Panda's Restaurant", winning wide fame the moment it was placed in the App Store. The ensuing three years saw a "Dr. Panda" series totaling more than 20 games. Statistics showed that by 2015, the app had been downloaded over 40 million times worldwide, making Thijs's company the third biggest kids' game developer of the world only after Disney and Tocaboca, and also the biggest independent developer of paid kids' games.

Frequently asked by his customers about why he chose the image of the panda, Thijs simply tells them that, just as what is mentioned before, it is because his company is in Chengdu, the homeland of pandas, and pandas are the pride and symbol of the city. As an entrepreneur, Thijs has subtle, personal links with the adorable pandas, and he also wishes to introduce his beloved pandas to children and parents all over the world.

The "Dr. Panda" app provides kids with several open scenes and tools, which allows them to be the ruler of their own world. There are no rules, no points to score, and no traditional limitations to thinking. Children can give full play to their imagination, explore and make discoveries in the way they like. Parents also find that there are no wrong answers, nor the fear of losing, nor too much stress in the app, which meet their expectations.

On top of that, the "Dr. Panda" app also features a role-play pattern, open playing methods and highly expressive characters. Thijs wishes that through his games, children will not learn dead knowledge but rather get familiar with the world around them, such as the process of onboarding, the function of a hospital and the daily work of gardeners. All of this seemingly ordinary and common sense knowledge actually makes the game fun, plus there are all kinds of hidden treasures designed for kids to seek, who become quite proud of themselves by finding the treasures and then advance to the next phases of the game.

The learning potential of kids is inestimable, but only through easy and fun methods of learning can they best meet their potential. In the "Dr. Panda" games, there is no intentional teaching, but rather unconscious assimilation of knowledge and natural formation of good habits through the open role-play. Unquestionably, the primary concern of parents is their children's safe growth. For them nothing could be more soothing than a safe and trustworthy game for children. Thijs' "Dr. Panda" enables children to experience something beyond their age. For example, they could play a cook, a bus driver or a doctor in the game. With "Dr. Panda" and other cute animals presented, children have a safe and fun way to explore daily professions.

Thanks to the hard work of Thijs and Lin Yan, "Dr. Panda" has received wide attention and acclaim. The app is a most suitable one for kids, for it mainly consists of 3D presentations, cute animal cartoons, joyful music and simple rules. Among all of the kids' games in the market, "Dr. Panda" stands out for its high resolution of pictures, ingenious play and exquisitely-designed scenes.

What's most important is that it is also full of knowledge, greatly benefiting both children and parents. This is well demonstrated by its scores in the App Store and the users' comments. The most appealing thing about the "Dr. Doctor" series is that there are almost no words. A bit of guidance and interaction are all that would be needed if a kid wants to play. This make-things-easy design has won the app the official recommendation of the App Stores of many countries.

The Chengdu-based Company Going Global

In 2015, while "Dr. Panda" celebrated its garnering of 40 million downloads, Thijs moved his company to Laifushi Square. The size of the company had expanded from the original five employees to over 50, and a third of them were foreigners. It was like a big happy international family. As for Thijs and Lin Yan, though they were not from Chengdu, they had long viewed themselves as local Chengduers because of their life and career in Chengdu.

Eight years have flown by since they started their business here. The past three thousand days or so have endowed the couple with career success and a happy family, reassuring them about their future, and relieving their homesickness, loneliness, and feeling of loss and powerlessness. For them, Chengdu has become their second hometown and their spiritual shelter. The app "Dr. Panda" that they have created is just like another child for them.

Speaking of his plans for future, Thijs says that he will build a "Dr. Panda"-themed children's playground, where there will be electronic equipment that appeals to children. In addition, there will be various experiences for children brought about via cutting-edge technologies such as virtual reality. As a preliminary try, Thijs's company is currently making a 3D cartoon featuring "Dr. Panda", and its next goal is to bring virtual reality e-products into practical use.

Thijs believes that Chengdu, with its fancy appeal, openness and inclination towards hi-tech, will surely lead "Dr. Panda" further on its way towards perfection and success. Let's pray together for the most beautiful future for Thijs and his "Dr. Panda".

>> 索源（法国）

法国缔马农业公司中国西区总监

Sonia Suo, France

China Western Region Director of Timac Agro China

寻根之旅　农业之梦

有一座城市，它时尚而又历史绵长；有一座城市，它闲适而又生机勃勃；有一座城市，它市井而又气韵不凡；这座城市，便是成都。这一组组词汇看似矛盾，却又并不矛盾——老成都是历史悠久、安逸、平民化的，而新成都则是充满国际感、现代感的，发展速度令人惊艳。成都的高新区正是如此，这里高楼林立，现代化气息浓厚，象征着成都新的希望。高新区最为常见的，是脚步匆匆的行者，与街道上的车水马龙。每一栋写字楼都有无数怀揣梦想的人在各自办公室里为各自的目标奋斗着。

在高新区"天府新谷"科技创业孵化社区的法国缔马农业公司，眼睛闪烁智慧光芒的索源会用她并不足够熟练的四川话和她的同事们进行工作上的沟通，这个年轻女孩便是该公司的中国西区总监索源。

二十六年深深思乡情

索源虽是生在法国、长在法国，但她身上流淌的是纯正的中华民族血液，因为这位法语、英语流利但中文并不熟练的姑娘，是一位法国华裔。1990 年，索源出生在法国巴黎，孩提时代的索源常常因为自己和其他孩子的肤色不同而感到奇怪，而且她父母之间沟通常用的语言也和她常常听到的法语不同。随着自己慢慢长大，索源知道，自己一家人是中国人，而父母口中和大多数人不同的语言是汉语。人在异乡为异客，每逢佳节倍思亲。索源父母心中是常常记挂着故土的，他们也常给索源讲述有关家乡的故事。于是从记事起，索源就对"中国"这个遥远的东方国度产生了浓厚的兴趣，她从父母的讲述中知道了中国有着比法国辽阔数倍的疆土，有着悠久而灿烂的文明，有数不胜数的名胜古迹，还有她生活在中国重庆和成都的亲人们，而重庆和成都正处于魅力十足的中国西部。

中国的西部究竟是什么样？这个疑问在幼小的索源心中深藏数年，终于，在她快要迎来 5 岁生日的时候，父母带着她第一次乘坐飞机，此行的目的地是父母阔别 10 年的故乡重庆，这让索源激动不已。如今的索源已经记不清当年去过哪些地方，但初次到重庆时候的激动感觉却令她难忘。值得庆幸的是，索源父亲当年录下了她第一次到重庆时的视频，让她可以回忆儿时在重庆和亲戚们过生日的快乐时光，这短短几天的亲人团聚，便是她关于中国的最初记忆。

时光匆匆如白驹过隙，时隔 11 年，索源才终于第二次来到中国，而这次的目的地变为了成都。此次成都行，16 岁的索源和父母一起，看望了在成都居住的姑婆和许多亲友，她第一次品尝到了鲜美多汁的龙泉水蜜桃，见识了让人眼花缭乱的成都小吃，还在春熙路和锦里留下了快乐的身影。不过令索源印象最深刻的还不是这些，常听父母在家说重庆话的她，感觉成都人的口音非常有趣，而且成都这座城市比重庆更让她感到舒服和自在，重庆的节奏更快，人们性格更急；而成都的氛围更安逸，人们性格更温和，让她很是喜欢。

短短三四天的成都之旅，给少女索源留下了极其深刻的美好印象。也许就是从那时候起，索源就有了回到中国，留在成都的想法，这个故乡之梦，就这样久久萦绕在她的心头。

重游故地惊叹变化

2016 年 5 月，在与成都这座令索源魂牵梦绕的城市分别 10 年之后，她终于又回到了这里。这时的索源已经不再是个孩子,她的身份也不再是个游客,而是法国缔马农业公司的中国西区总监。她这次回到成都,除了重温旧梦,再叙故乡情,还肩负着更重要的工作使命,她要在这里实现她远大的人生理想。

时隔多年,索源变了,成都也变了,而且变化之大让索源十分吃惊。她没有想到,她印象中这座位于中国西部的城市会有着这样惊人的发展速度。索源一出机场就明显感觉到,这座城市和她当年见到的不一样了。这里的交通变得更加发达,高楼变得更加现代,环境变得更加优越,人们变得更加时尚,昔日里略显陈旧的城市,已然焕发出了强大的活力,变成了一座十分现代的国际化大都市。索源总是将成都比作美国的芝加哥,她深深觉得,成都和自己弟弟工作所在地芝加哥非常相像,一样的现代化,一样的蓬勃发展,她认为美国的发展中城市正是如此。尤其是成都的高新区,索源十分心仪高新区的区域规划,时尚的外表、合理的布局和便捷的交通都让她欣喜不已,毅然决定把办公场所选在了这里。

把法国缔马农业公司的西区总部开设在成都是索源的决定,这与索源第二次中国行所到城市是成都固然关系很大,但更重要的原因是成都这座城市的独特魅力。总公司关于西区总部的选址最初有两个设想,一是成都,二是昆明。但经过她和总公司的细致研究,认为四川是中国的一个农业大省,人口众多,市场前景不可限量,且成都与巴黎之间交通便捷,2015 年底就已开通了直飞的航线,成都的生活环境更加优越,是著名的宜居城市,再加上索源对成都的私人情感,选址成都便成了最佳选择。

在来到成都之前,索源的一些同事心中还存有担忧,他们担心成都是一个欠发展的城市,缺乏足够的人才资源,但他们很快就发现,所有的担忧都是多余的。万事开头难,作为一个刚刚建立的分公司,对人才的渴求非同一般，索源在各大招聘网站上发布了消息，也在成都各大高校展开了宣传，让她非常高兴的是，他们很快就得到了众多高素质人才的响应。这让索源意识到，成都是一块如此藏龙卧虎的宝地，在成都，人才的丰富程度和优秀程度完全不亚于中国的北京、上海等一线城市，她也由此更加坚信来到成都发展的选择没有错。

心系农业发展

作为一家有着60年历史的高级肥料企业，同时也是法国最大的肥料企业，法国缔马农业公司已在全球一百余个国家生根发芽，而中国这个巨大的市场还尚未得到有效开发。索源这次来到成都便是肩负着这一使命，她要让法国的先进农业技术和理念为更多的中国人所了解和接受，她希望公司产品能够为中国农业发展起到积极作用。索源公司研发的肥料和一般意义上的有所不同，这种肥料被称作植物营养产品，比传统肥料更加环保且不会破坏土壤的成分，使用起来也非常节省，可以更加绿色有效地提高农产品的质量和产量，若说是有机蔬果的好搭档也毫不过分。索源所在公司的法国研究中心专门成立了一个研发团队，研究中国西部的土壤情况，同时也分析中国西部的用肥情况和用肥水平，并在法国设计出最适合中国西部的产品。不久的将来，公司还会把工厂直接开在中国西部，届时将大大缩小工厂和农户之间的距离。

带领公司的同事们在成都奋斗，索源心中所想的不仅是创造财富，还有帮助成都乡亲们在农业方面取得更好的发展。索源曾亲自带领同事们前往位于都江堰的一家猕猴桃种植基地，在他们的技术支持下，那里猕猴桃的数量、品种和质量都达到了让索源满意的效果。与这家基地类似的农业基地在成都周边地区还有很多，如葡萄、草莓基地等，都一一得到了索源团队的关注和支持。保持城市高速发展过程中生态环境不被破坏，这样的目的，其实正是索源选择来到成都的初衷。索源把成都视作故乡，她热爱这片富饶的天府宝地，她想用自己所掌握的知识和技术为成都、为四川的乡亲们做一些力所能及的事情。

他乡却是心灵故乡

从巴黎坐飞机到成都需要 11 个小时之久，可是巴黎女孩索源和成都的心却是零距离。她亲切地把成都称作她的"心灵故乡"。

索源虽然有着法国国籍，并且生长在法国，但她内心深处是十分愿意以中国人自居的，这基于索源从小对中国产生的好奇和向往，也基于她骨子里对中国那种斩不断的情缘。所以，当她第一次踏上中国的土地，又当她第一次走进成都，她与成都命中注定的缘分便一次次得到检验。索源有不少亲戚依然生活在成都，其中有人是做水果生意，而她则是在著名的肥料公司工作，这本是个算不上巧合的巧合，也被索源看作是与成都的缘分。尽管才来到成都半年多，索源已经把自己当作成都人，时不时还会用不那么熟练的成都话和人们交流，她想努力学好这里的语言，从而与成都更加亲密。

从事农业行业的索源对自然环境有着强烈的兴趣，她对成都及周边的自然环境赞不绝口。在成都中心城区，虽然没有原生态的自然风光，但遍布全市的公园让人们无须出远门就能在美丽的环境中放松身心。再走得远一些，只需驱车数小时就可以投入大山的怀抱，美不胜收的风光更是宛如仙境。热爱运动的索源尽管工作忙碌，但她非常希望能在周末或节假日的时候继续去领略成都周边的秀美山水。一有时间，她和朋友们就会相约徒步登山，走走停停，为神奇的大自然而陶醉。成都附近的青城山、西岭雪山是索源常去之地，但索源不满足于此，她还把成都当作前往诸多名山大川的重要出发地，譬如她从成都出发前往四姑娘山的一次旅行，她打从心里认为，四姑娘山不仅无愧于"东方阿尔卑斯山"的美誉，而且完全胜过了法国的阿尔卑斯山，因为四姑娘山不仅比阿尔卑斯山的海拔高出了 2000 多米，气势更加雄伟，而且生态环境保护得很好，皑皑白雪圣洁美丽令人震撼，旅游设施的建设也更加完善。她的下一个目标是从成都出发去贡嘎山，那座 7556 米的主峰看起来遥不可及，但却和她对事业和理想的追求一样，她坚持认为只要勇于攀登，终能站在顶峰。

从事业到生活，出发点都是让索源深深眷恋着的成都。如今她的父母依然留在巴黎，男友也在巴黎，但她仍执意定居在成都。世间总有许多选择是冥冥中注定的，绝非三言两语能够解读，就如当年索源父母在 20 多岁的时候离开故乡赴法国，而索源则在 20 多岁的时候离开法国，选择定居"心灵故乡"——成都，这多么像是一个轮回。令人欣喜的是，索源准备邀请男友也来到成都，男友的父亲是一位中文不错的中国迷，且索源男友自己对中国、对成都也非常喜爱，这让索源对自己和恋人的未来信心十足。

索源坚信真正的爱情是不会被地理距离阻碍的。相信索源与她深爱的男友终究会上演一场"漂洋过海来看你"的故事，也祝福索源和她的另一半在未来的日子里，会携手在成都这座城市，看山看水，安享时光。

A Root-Seeking Journey, a Quest for Agriculture

There is a stylish city with a time-honored history. She breathes leisurely yet shines with vibrancy; she looks ordinary but boasts an unrivaled elegance. This city is Chengdu. The phrases used above sound contradictory, but as a matter of fact they are not. The old Chengdu, with a simple, comfortable life characteristic of its ordinary urban inhabitants, dates back thousands of years; the new Chengdu is international, modern, and developing at an amazing pace. The Chengdu High-Tech Zone is a case in point. Here skyscrapers sparkling with modernity are densely distributed on the landscape—they symbolize a new Chengdu. What one sees most in the High-Tech Zone are people coming and going amid the hustle and bustle at a hurried pace. Countless aspiring people are working towards their dreams at their offices in all the office buildings.

In Timac Agro, a French agricultural company in the "Tianfu Thinkzone" Startup Incubator Community of the High-Tech Zone, Sonia Suo's eyes sparkle with wisdom as she communicates with her colleagues on work in Sichuan dialect—a language she is still not proficient in. This young girl is Sonia Suo, the company's chief director of West China.

Twenty-six-year Long Nostalgia for Home

Though she was born and grew up in France, Sonia Suo has real

Chinese blood in her veins. This girl, fluent in French and English but not yet proficient in Chinese, is a French Chinese. In 1990, Sonia Suo was born in Paris, France. Young Sonia Suo was often puzzled that she had skin which was different from that of other children and that the language her parents used to communicate was not French, the language she was so familiar with. As she grew up, Sonia Suo came to learn that she had a Chinese family, and that the language spoken by her parents was Chinese, which was quite different from the language used by most people there. People living on foreign soil as guests think of their family with nostalgia during each festival. Sonia Suo's parents couldn't forget their homeland. They often told Sonia Suo stories about it. Since the day when she began to remember things, Sonia Suo had been developing a keen interest in the distant eastern country called "China". She learned from her parents' stories that China has a territory several times that of France, that it has a long and splendid civilization, and that it is home to countless scenic spots and historical sites. She also learned that she had relatives living in Chongqing and Chengdu, which are located in an amazing region called West China.

What is life like in West China? This question dwelt in the heart of young Sonia Suo for many years. Finally when she was about to turn five, her parents took her along on her first flight. The destination of this trip was her parents' hometown, Chongqing, which the couple left a decade before. Sonia Suo was extremely excited about the trip. Today, Sonia Suo doesn't remember where she went on that trip, but she does remember how excited she was when she first arrived in Chongqing. Fortunately, Sonia Suo's father kept a video clip of her first visit to Chongqing, which has kept alive her memory of the happy birthday party she spent with her relatives. This short several-day reunion with family is her first memory of China.

Time passes quickly like a white pony's shadow across a crevice. Sonia Suo came to China for the second time 11 years later. This time the destination was not Chongqing; it was Chengdu. On that trip to Chengdu, 16-year-old Sonia Suo and her parents visited her grandaunt and many other relatives and friends living in Chengdu. For the first time she tasted Longquan juice peaches, saw dazzling Chengdu snacks, and happily took a walk on Chunxi Road and Jinli Street. However, what impressed Sonia Suo most did not stop at these past moments. She used to hear her parents talk in Chongqing dialect at home. Chengdu dialect sounded funny to her. In addition, she found Chengdu more comfortable than Chongqing. Life in Chongqing was faster and people were more impatient; while in Chengdu life was more comfortable and people were milder. She liked this.

The short trip to Chengdu that lasted only three or four days left young Sonia Suo with a good impression. Perhaps it was then that Sonia Suo began to have the idea of returning to China and staying in Chengdu. This dream of a hometown lingered on.

Marvelous Change in Chengdu

In May 2016, Sonia Suo finally returned after a 10-year departure from Chengdu. This time Sonia Suo was no longer a child, and she came not as a tourist. She was chief director in West China representing the French agricultural company Timac Agro. She returned to Chengdu this time not only to revive an old dream and see her hometown, but also to fulfill a more important mission. She was going to pursue her ideals here.

Sonia Suo and Chengdu both have changed after so many years. The change in Chengdu was so drastic that Sonia Suo was surprised. She did not expect that the city in her memory would develop at such an alarming pace in West China. When Sonia Suo stepped out of the airport, she immediately felt Chengdu was no longer the city it used to be. Transportation was more convenient, tall buildings more modern, the environment better, and the people dressed in more fashionable clothes. The city which formerly had been slightly old-fashioned was now unleashing great potential and becoming a modern international metropolis. She always compares Chengdu to Chicago in the United States. She strongly believes that Chengdu is very similar to Chicago, where her younger brother works, because both of them are modern and vibrant. She believes these are what developing cities in the United States and Chengdu have in common. The Chengdu High-Tech Zone in particular has won the applause of Sonia Suo for its regional planning. She went into raptures about its stylish look, rational layout, and convenient transportation. She resolutely decided to locate her office building there.

It was Sonia Suo's choice to settle the West China headquarter of France's agricultural company Timac Agro in Chengdu. This certainly has to do with the fact that the destination of her second China trip was Chengdu, but the more important reason is the unique charm of this city. Initially, Timac Agro had two options concerning the location of its West China headquarters: one was Chengdu, the other was Kunming. However, after a thorough assessment with the head office, Sonia Suo confirmed that Sichuan was a major agricultural Chinese province with a large population and unlimited market prospects. The traffic between Chengdu and Paris is very convenient and direct non-stop routes were opened in late 2015. Chengdu as a famous livable city has a superior living environment. What's more, Sonia Suo is personally connected with Chengdu. As a result, Chengdu became the best choice.

Before Sonia Suo came to Chengdu, some of her colleagues worried that Chengdu was an underdeveloped city and lacked sufficient human resources. However, they soon realized such worries proved largely unfounded. All things are difficult before they are easy. The newly established branch had a huge appetite for talent. Sonia Suo placed advertisements on major recruitment sites, and mounted publicity campaigns at Chengdu's colleges and universities. Soon she gladly received quick responses from top-notch talent. Sonia Suo now realized that Chengdu was home to a wealth of undiscovered talents. Chengdu comes close to first-tier cities such as Beijing and Shanghai in China when it comes to the richness and excellence of talents. Since then, she has become convinced that the choice of Chengdu was the right path to future development.

My Heart is on Chengdu's Agricultural Development

As a 60-year-old advanced fertilizer company and the largest fertilizer company in France, Timac Agro has taken root in more than 100 countries around the world. However, the huge Chinese market has not yet been effectively developed. This time, Sonia Suo came to Chengdu to fulfill a mission. She wanted more Chinese people to learn about and embrace France's advanced agricultural technologies and ideas; she hoped the company's products would play an active role in China's agricultural development. The fertilizer developed by Sonia Suo's company is different from average fertilizers. This fertilizer is called "plant nutrition product", more environmentally friendly than traditional fertilizers and one that does not destroy the ingredients of soil. It is more economical and can effectively boost the quality and output of agricultural products in an environmentally friendly way. It is no exaggeration to say that it is a good partner of organic fruits and vegetables. The French research center of Sonia Suo's company set up a special R&D team to study the soil conditions in West China. At the same time, it analyzes the use of fertilizer and the levels of its usage in West China and has designed, in France, the most suitable product for West China. In the near future, the company will directly locate its facility in West China, which will greatly reduce the distance between the factory and farmers.

Working strenuously with colleagues in Chengdu, Sonia Suo thinks about not only creating wealth, but also helping fellow villagers and townsmen in Chengdu to achieve better agricultural development. Once, Sonia Suo personally led her colleagues to a kiwifruit plantation in Dujiangyan. Thanks to their technical support, the quantity, varieties, and quality of the kiwifruit there lived up to her expectations. There are many other similar agricultural bases in the surrounding area of Chengdu, such as those for grapes and strawberries, all of which have come to the attention of Sonia Suo's team and have been given support. Ensuring that rapid urban development does not do harm to the ecological environment is why Sonia Suo chose to come to Chengdu in the first place. Sonia Suo sees Chengdu as her hometown. She loves this fertile land, and she hopes her knowledge and technology can do something for her fellow villagers and townsmen in Chengdu and Sichuan.

An Alien Land has Become the Dwelling Place of the Soul

It takes up to 11 hours to fly from Paris to Chengdu, but there is no distance between Parisian girl Sonia Suo and Chengdu. She cordially calls Chengdu her "spiritual hometown."

Sonia Suo is French by birth and grew up in France, but deep in her heart she is willing to consider herself a Chinese. This is justified by her curiosity and longing for China that she had when she was young; it also derived from the profound bond between her and China. Since she first set foot on the land of China and first walked into Chengdu, her predestined close relationship with Chengdu has been tested again and again. Many of Sonia Suo's relatives still live in Chengdu: some of them sell fruits, while she works in a famous fertilizer company. This is no coincidence, but Sonia Suo regards it as her predestined relationship with Chengdu. Sonia Suo came to Chengdu just more than six months ago, but she already regards herself as a native. From time to time, she chats with people in Chengdu dialect—though awkwardly. She wants to learn the language better so that she can develop a more intimate relationship with Chengdu.

Sonia Suo engages in agriculture, and she has a strong interest in the natural environment. She keeps praising the natural environment in Chengdu and its surrounding areas. Downtown Chengdu has no pristine natural beauty, but the parks throughout the city allow people to relax in beautiful surroundings without having to travel far. Go further and you can throw yourself into the arms of mountains after just a drive of several hours. The scenery, which is a feast for the eyes, tends to give you the impression that you have entered a fairyland. Busy as she may be, sports-loving Sonia Suo very much hopes that she can continue to enjoy the beautiful scenery around Chengdu on weekends or during holidays. When she has time, she asks her friends to climb mountains with her on foot. She enjoys journeys to the magic of nature on which they walk and pause as much as they like. Qingcheng Mountain and Xiling Snow Mountain near Chengdu are often visited by Sonia Suo. But she is not satisfied with this. She sees Chengdu as an important place of departure for well-known mountains and rivers. After her trip from Chengdu to the Mount Siguniang, she thought it lived up to its reputation as the "Alps in the East" and outperforms the Alps in France because the Mount Siguniang is not only more than 2,000 meters higher than the Alps, it is also more magnificent. The ecological environment is kept in a good condition, and the sheer beauty of the white snow is awe-inspiring. Besides, the tourism facilities are better, comparatively. Her next goal is to depart from Chengdu for Gongga Mountain. The 7,556-meter peak seems out of reach, but just like how she sees her career goals, she insists that she can reach the peak as long as she is brave enough.

The starting point of both career and life has intimately connected Sonia Suo with Chengdu. Her parents and boyfriend are still in Paris, but she is determined to take up permanent residence in Chengdu. There are always many choices in the world that are destined in some way and are by no means limited in interpretation. Her parents left their homeland for France in their 20's, and Sonia Suo left France in her 20's and chose to settle down in her "spiritual home", Chengdu. This is exactly how life goes! The good news is that Sonia Suo will ask her boyfriend to come to Chengdu as well. Her boyfriend's father speaks good Chinese and is a fan of China. Sonia Suo's boyfriend is also very fond of China and Chengdu. She is confident about their future.

Sonia Suo is convinced that true love will not be blocked by geographical distance. We hope Sonia Suo and her beloved boyfriend will eventually stage a "go across the sea to see you" story. It is our benediction that Sonia Suo and her other half will work together, view mountains and rivers, and enjoy their time in Chengdu in the days to come.

>>> 郑赞美（韩国）
果汁品牌创始人

Jung Chanmee, ROK
Founder of a Juice Brand

90 后韩国美女蓉城创业创出新天地

　　成都国际金融中心 IFS，是当下成都著名的时尚聚集地。就在这处时尚聚集地的负二层，有一家不小的店面，醒目的招牌上写着"惠人芳"三个绿色的大字，清新的颜色显得很是别致。这是一家果汁专卖店，店内的装修更加清新，米黄色的墙壁，原木色的桌椅，文艺范儿的装饰，环境十分宜人。这样一家只卖鲜榨果汁的小清新风格的店，会有个怎样的老板呢？也许很多人都能猜到，这家店的老板一定是位女生，但可能很多人不知道，这位女生来自韩国，而且是一位非常年轻的"90 后"。

　　没错，就在这家小清新的店里，在浪漫的乐曲中，一位长发飘飘、面容清秀、衣着精致的美女每天会迈着优雅的步伐来到店内，对店内的服务人员和客人们都报以甜甜的微笑。她便是"惠人芳"果汁店的"90后"韩国老板郑赞美。

一次旅行　改变人生

　　出生于 1990 年的郑赞美笑容清纯，看上去像个大学生，但她却已经是连锁果汁店"惠人芳"的老板，"年轻有为"这个词用在她的身上丝毫也不为过。郑赞美长相甜美可爱，颇有韩剧女主角的味道，再加上她会说一口流利的普通话，难免让人觉得她是一个韩范儿的时髦中国女孩，然而实际上，她不仅是个土生土长的韩国首尔人，而且来到中国的时间也并不算久。

韩国与中国相邻，所以很多韩国人都会把中国作为他们心仪的旅行目的地，郑赞美也不例外。2013 年，23 岁的郑赞美刚刚从高丽大学毕业不久，决定和父母一起来到中国旅行。不过郑赞美没有像大多数韩国人那样，选择去北京、上海、广州等一线城市，而是选择来到成都。从未到过中国的郑赞美对中国的了解不多，对成都的了解也仅限于电视、网络上的只言片语，但她记得曾经听说过，成都是个美丽且休闲的城市，还是大熊猫的家乡，所以她决定把成都作为她在中国的第一站。当年的她一定没有想到，这个看似平常的决定，居然改变了她的人生。

当郑赞美经过 4 个小时飞机的长途跋涉抵达成都，原本疲惫的她走出机场看到成都这座城市之后，瞬间就兴奋了起来。成都留给郑赞美的第一印象是"干净"。她看到成都宽阔的街道几乎一尘不染，车辆和行人都井然有序，一幢幢高楼充满时尚感，这分明是一个国际大都市啊！比郑赞美想象中更加美好的画面，让她对此次成都之行充满期待。

这趟旅行的时间并不充裕，郑赞美和父母一起逛了久闻大名的春熙路，热热闹闹的繁华商场和丰富多彩的美食给郑赞美留下了深刻印象；他们去了国际化的桐梓林片区，便捷的交通和现代化的社区让郑赞美心生向往；他们体验了九眼桥的酒吧文化，悠扬的民谣、动感的电音都让郑赞美赞叹不已……那一次旅行后，成都的休闲、时尚、舒适和满满活力，给她留下了难忘的印象。同时，她也发现，成都年轻人对"韩流"非常感兴趣，韩国文化在成都的餐饮业有着不小的市场，并且年轻人越来越喜爱绿色、健康的生活方式。

短暂的成都之旅令郑赞美意犹未尽。她还想再次来成都旅行，却又不甘于仅仅旅行，她觉得成都这个美丽的城市有着不可限量的前途，这闪烁着光芒的未来让她情不自禁地想要与成都真正结缘。在与做贸易的父亲商量后，郑赞美滋生了来成都创业的想法，她考察了首尔的餐饮市场，发现健康又美味的鲜榨果汁越发流行，预测这一潮流势必会传到成都，那何不亲自把它引入成都呢？于是，2014 年，郑赞美再次来到成都，这次的她不再是一个游客，而是一名青年创业者，她决定把未来的赌注押在令她一见钟情的成都。

韩国风格　成都味道

2014 年情人节前一个月，郑赞美辛劳筹备的"惠人芳"果汁店正式开业了。她坚信，正在飞速发展中的成都有着数不胜数的机会，其中必然有一个机会属于自己。对春熙路有着深刻印象的她，决定把自己的第一家店开在春熙路商圈的 IFS，她相信这家年轻人十分喜爱的时尚商城是她施展才能的最佳空间。

初步实现了成都创业计划的郑赞美踌躇满志，却没想到很快就遭遇了寒冰。由于前期准备略显仓促，而且把开店时间选在了临近春节的时候，郑赞美的新店遭遇了招不到店员的尴尬。她很懊悔自己没有做好功课，没有掌握中国传统文化，不知道春节在中国人心中的重要意义，韩国的春节只放假三天就已经是最长的假期，这次始料未及的挫折让她更加清楚中韩文化的差异性。

在充分考虑清楚这一差异性之后，她试图利用中韩文化的差异来为自己创造市场。IFS 的"惠人芳"果汁店是郑赞美的第一家店，她在其中倾注了无数的心血。店内的装修走的是韩式路线，请了韩国设计师亲自操刀，米黄色、绿色的搭配让店内看起来温馨又休闲。店面风格很韩范儿，饮品更是韩范儿。"秘密花园""金三顺""继承者""星星的你"……郑赞美店里的果汁名字大多都取材于知名韩剧，因为她了解到了韩剧在中国年轻人中的流行，也了解到中国人对韩国文化的浓厚兴趣，所以萌生了这一独特的创意。

为了尽快打开成都市场，郑赞美和父亲不辞辛劳四处奔走宣传，他们曾经一同在成都的大街小巷发宣传单，曾挨家挨户向各种果汁店推介他们代理的韩国原汁机，并免费提供机器让果汁店使用。然而父女两人的力量终是有限的，推广的效果并不尽理想。生意的转机来自于2014年在成都举行的中国西部国际博览会。

在展会上，漂亮的郑赞美穿着华丽的韩国传统服饰，用韩语向来宾们问好，不失时机地向客人们介绍她的产品，吸引了很多目光，展示效果出乎意料得好。于是郑赞美不放过任何大型的展会、沙龙与供货商、顾客多次"亲密接触"，她美丽的身影和新创的品牌就这样逐渐为蓉城商家和百姓所知晓。提高品牌知名度还远远不够，郑赞美还要牢牢抓住成都人的胃。在每次销售的过程中，郑赞美总不忘询问顾客口感，她了解到成都人喜欢果味胜过蔬菜味，就立即调整配方，又在一些饮品中加入成都人喜爱的火龙果、山楂等，就这样逐渐赢得一批批回头客。

分享经验　共同创业

看似娇弱、文静的郑赞美，凭借着吃苦的精神、强大的内心和聪明的头脑，在春熙路商圈站稳了脚跟。小有名气的"惠人芳"果汁店收获了可喜的业绩，周末大概每天能售出400~500杯果汁，工作日一天能售出150~200杯果汁，单单凭借着各式各样的鲜榨果汁，郑赞美就可以月入20万，这让她非常欣喜，也非常庆幸自己当初来成都创业的选择。

郑赞美在成都收获了财富，也收获了名气。就在2016年底，她受邀在锦江宾馆参加由国家科技部、四川省政府、韩国未来创造科学部共同主办的、主题为"创新创业·合作共赢"的第六届中韩科技创新论坛，这一论坛围绕"中国十三五科技创新发展的有关考虑""韩国创造经济政策""共享经济与创新治理""打造创新创业一流环境、建设中国西部科技中心"等多个话题展开讨论。

参加论坛后，郑赞美对自己的未来更加信心十足，她相信依靠着成都市政府对创业的支持与关注，像她这样的外国创业者今后将有更多的发展机会。2016年4月，郑赞美还曾受邀参加了"创业天府·菁蓉汇"首尔专场活动，并作为韩国在蓉创业者代表在活动中发言。郑赞美向来宾们分享了她在成都的创业经验以及创业经历，鼓励广大韩国企业和青年创业者到成都创新创业。

在郑赞美的身上，与名利一同而来的不是骄傲自满，却是社会责任感。自从被央视报道之后，郑赞美的店里就偶尔会有些"特别的"客人，他们走进店里不是为了喝果汁，而是向郑赞美请教创业经验，郑赞美也从不吝啬于此，而是大大方方地和他们分享。其中有一位耄耋之年的老爷爷让她印象深刻，老爷爷在店内找到她并感谢道，她的故事启发和鼓励了自己正在创业的孙子，郑赞美惊讶又感动。

于是郑赞美想，既然成都的人们喜欢她的故事和经验，那何不与更多的人分享呢？于是，郑赞美在位于成都菁蓉国际广场的中韩创新创业园内开设"惠人芳"新店时，专门设立了一个面向成都年轻人的创业交流、培训场所，可供创业青年学习韩国的文化、服务、经营模式等，并有意在未来打造出一个小规模的蓉城90后创业团队，帮助更多和她有着同样理想的创业青年。

心仪之城　成功之都

从2014年至今，郑赞美定居成都已有三年，这座充满机遇的城市已经成为她生命中不可分割的一部分。郑赞美如今已经实现了自己创业梦的第一步，从IFS第一家店开始，她陆续拥有了5家店铺，同时开辟了面积达350平米的创业青年培训广场。不断扩大的事业版图让郑赞美每天既忙碌又快乐。

上进的郑赞美并不满足于眼前的 5 家店，她还有着更远大的目标——在成都拥有 200 家店。2010 年，成都被联合国教科文组织授予"美食之都"的美誉，餐饮业在成都发展兴旺，成都市政府敞开大门欢迎外籍创业者来成都创业发展。目前，成都市"创业天府"行动计划正在如火如荼地开展，按照计划，成都将建设成为一座"创业之城，圆梦之都"，这成为了外籍创业者创造财富的绝好时机。

随着成都国际化水平的提升和创业氛围的增强，越来越多外国人看好在成都投资创业，其中自然就包括郑赞美。成都的市场对于大多数外国人来说依然是新鲜的市场，其发展空间和市场潜力大得令人惊喜。成都人注重休闲养生和生活品质，在忙碌工作的时候依然懂得忙里偷闲地享受生活，这便是她的果汁生意生存、红火的关键原因之一。

成都安逸的气质不仅为郑赞美提供了商机，也让她真心热爱这座城市，她甚至认为成都比她的家乡首尔更胜一筹。住在桐梓林的她，最喜欢每天坐地铁上班，因为她喜欢成都优质的公共交通。乘坐地铁去吃成都美食，则更是一大乐趣，火锅、串串、麻辣香锅都是她的最爱，如今的她已然像是个无辣不欢的成都妹子。

郑赞美还在成都结交了许多新朋友，大多是相识于果汁店里的成都人，从顾客变成了朋友，这让她十分快乐，免除了思乡之苦。郑赞美现在一年只会为了掌握最新的市场潮流而回首尔四五次，其余时间全部在成都度过，她的家人也和她一起生活在成都。

"九天开出一成都，万户千门入画图。草树云山如锦绣，秦川得及此间无。"1300 多年前，诗仙太白盛赞成都是独一无二的人间天堂，1300 多年后，韩国创业者郑赞美认为成都是她无可取代的第二故乡。她已然习惯了这座城市，习惯了成都的生活方式，甚至习惯了用中文和人们聊天，偶尔还会向朋友们学一学成都话，日子过得有滋有味。这个机遇与快乐并存的地方，她只能越来越爱。

Post-90s South Korean Girl Launching a Successful Business in Chengdu

On floor B2 of Chengdu's International Finance Square (IFS), a famous fashion center, there is a store of considerable size, with an eye-catching sign saying "Huirenfang". The three big green Chinese characters look fresh and fancy. It is a juice store. Step inside and you will find it even more refreshing and cozy, with beige walls, burly wood tables and chairs, and artistic decorations. Who is the person running such a stylistic juice store? Many people may have guessed the owner is a girl. But very few would expect that she is from South Korea and is a member of the post-90s generation.

Along with the romantic music, there she comes, a long-haired, nice-looking and delicately-dressed young lady. She gracefully walks in her shop every day and greets her employees and customers with sweet smile. She is the boss of "Huirenfang" Juice Store—Jung Chanmee.

A Life-changing Journey

Born in 1990, always wearing a teenage-like smile, Jung Chanmee looks like an ordinary university student. But in fact she has already been a boss of a chain of Huirenfang juice stores. "Promising" is exactly the right word for her. Looking as sweet and cute as a Korean drama heroine and speaking fluent Chinese, she is very likely to be assumed as a fashionable Chinese girl crazy about Korean culture. However, the truth is that she was born and bred in Seoul, ROK. And she hasn't been here long.

As a neighbouring country of ROK, China has always been a favourite destination for many Korean tourists. Jung Chanmee is no exception. In 2013, 23-year-old Jung Chanmee, who was just newly graduated from Korea University, planned a sightseeing tour to China with her parents. But unlike most South Koreans who chose first-tier Chinese cities like Beijing, Shanghai and Guangzhou, they came to Chengdu. Prior to the journey she knew very little about China and her only perception of Chengdu was only some penny knowledge from TV and the internet. But she heard that Chengdu is a beautiful, leisurely city and also home to pandas. And this made Chengdu her first stop in China. By the time she would have not expected such a seemingly ordinary decision would change her life.

After a four-hour long flight, Jung Chanmee arrived in Chengdu. She got refreshed and excited the minute she walked out of the terminal. Her first impression of Chengdu was "clean". It is an international metropolis with broad streets that are almost spotless well-organized vehicles and pedestrians and stylistic tall buildings. It was far more charming than she had expected. She was certainly excited about her tour afterwards.

It wasn't a long trip. But Jung Chanmee and her parents still managed to visit Chunxi Road, a place they had heard so much of. The bustling shopping malls and a wide variety of snacks greatly impressed them. They also went to Tongzilin, an international residential block where she was fascinated by the convenient transportation and modern-style communities. They also toured Jiuyanqiao, the bar district in Chengdu, and were amazed by the beautiful folk music and dynamic electronic music. Chengdu became deeply imprinted in

Jung Chanmee's mind as a leisurely, fashionable, comfortable and energetic city. Meanwhile, she also discovered that Korean culture was quite popular with young people here. To some extent, Korean culture has some influence on the catering market. Young people here were seeking greener and healthier life styles.

The journey was so short that Jung Chanmee wanted to come to Chengdu again, but not just as a mere tourist. Seeing great business potential in Chengdu, she was considering taking a real step that would closely link her with Chengdu. After consulting her father, who worked in the trade business, Jung Chanmee planned to start her own business in Chengdu. Through investigation of the catering market in Seoul, she found that the delicious fresh fruit juice is in line with the healthy trend that could definitely find its way to Chengdu. Then why not bring it there right now? Hence in 2014, Jung Chanmee came to Chengdu again. This time she did not come as a tourist, but as a young entrepreneur who bet her future on the very city she loved at first sight.

South Korean Juice with Chengdu Flavor

A month prior to Valentine's Day, 2014, after tireless preparation, Jung Chanmee's Huirenfang Juice Store was finally opened. She firmly believed that among the numerous opportunities brought by Chengdu's skyrocketing development, there must be one for her. She decided to open her store in Chengdu IFS shopping district beside Chunxi Road, a road that had deeply impressed her. She was convinced that this fashion mall popular with young people would be perfect for her juice business.

Riding high in her initial stage of entrepreneurship, harboring ambitious plans, Jung Chanmee, however, was greeted not by customers as she expected, but by a severe setback. Her tight schedule had forced her to open the store around the Spring Festival in China, when employees were nowhere to be found. Seized with remorse, she reflected upon how careless she was to forget the importance of traditional Spring Festival to Chinese people. In South Korea, the Spring Festival lasts no longer than three days. But things are different here in China! After this unforeseen setback, Jung Chanmee began to pay more attention to the differences between Chinese culture and South Korean culture.

Setbacks could also be a blessing in disguise as later on Jung Chanmee's growing business was largely attributed to those differences. The Huirenfang Juice Store in IFS was her first store, in which she poured relentless efforts. She invited South Korean designers to take charge of the decoration work, and the store finally came out as a warm and cozy place in Korean style with beige and green as main colors. The names of the juices were Korean too, all based on well-known Korean TV series. Jung Chanmee noticed the popularity of Korean TV series among Chinese young people and their keen interest in South Korean culture. Hence she came out with this creative initiation.

To seek instant access in the local market, Jung Chanmee and her father went about promoting their store, handing out flyers on the streets, and going door-to-door to promote juicers to juice stores, offering free trials. However, a team of only two proved deficient and they didn't get the results they wanted. Their turning point came from the 2014 Western China International Fair held in Chengdu.

At the exhibition, fabulously dressed in traditional Korean clothes,

Jung Chanmee greeted guests in Korean and seized every opportunity to introduce her products. The promotion attracted wide attention and proved very successful. After that, Jung Chanmee became a regular guest at large exhibitions and salons. Therefore she could communicate with vendors and customers face to face. Gradually, her brand, along with her beauty, became known by businesses and people of Chengdu. However, the success of her branding was far from enough for Jung Chanmee who was also trying hard to cater the appetite of her Chengdu customers. In her store, she would always ask her customers about how they liked the taste of the juice. After learning that Chengdu people preferred fruit flavors to vegetable flavors, she instantly changed her recipe, adding the commonly favored pitaya and hawthorn to her drinks. This has gradually won her a large group of regular customers.

Sharing Entrepreneurship Experiences to Encourage More to Come on Board

Hard-working, tough at heart and smart in mind, the delicate-looking and gentle girl Jung Chanmee came to take root among Chunxi Road businesses. Her "Huirenfang" juice store, which has garnered a reputation, brought her encouraging revenue with 400 to 500 cups of juice sold per day on weekends and 150 to 200 cups sold per day on workdays. The wide-ranging juices alone won her a monthly income of 200,000 RMB, which proved quite soothing and made her more certain about her choice to start her business in Chengdu.

Fame came along with wealth to Jung Chanmee. At the end of 2016, she was invited to attend the 6th China-South Korea Science and Technology Innovation Forum themed as "innovation, entrepreneurship and win-win cooperation" jointly hosted by the Ministry of Science and Technology of the People's Republic of China, the People's Government of Sichuan Province and the Ministry of Science, ICT and Future Planning of the Government of South Korea. The forum touched on topics such as "considerations concerning China's 13th five-year sci-tech innovation development," "policies regarding South Korean creative economy," the "shared economy and innovative governance" and "foster first-class environment for innovation, entrepreneurship and establish sci-tech center in Western China".

After the forum Jung Chanmee was even more confident in her future. She firmly believed that with the governments' supportive policies and initiatives at hand, foreign entrepreneurs like her would be able to embrace more favorable opportunities. In April 2016, Jung Chanmee was invited to attend the Seoul-themed section of the "Venture Tianfu·Jingronghui" campaign and made a speech on behalf of South Korean entrepreneurs in Chengdu, sharing her entrepreneurial experiences and encouraging more Korean companies and young talents to come to Chengdu to start their business.

Jung Chanmee was never befuddled by her success. Instead, she felt a deeper sense of social responsibility. Immediately after a coverage by CCTV, her juice store began to have "special" customers occasionally, who stepped in not for the juice, but for entrepreneurship counseling. Jung Chanmee would hold nothing back and tell them all she knew. She still remembers an old man in his eighties who came to thank her. Her story inspired his grandson, who was also an entrepreneur. Jung Chanmee was surprised and touched.

Then an idea came to her: since people in Chengdu liked her story, why not share it with more people? So when she was planning another "Huirenfang" juice store at the Sino-Korea Innovation & Entrepreneurship

Park in Chengdu Jingrong Global Startup Hub, she went out of her way to set aside a room for entrepreneurship counseling for young people in Chengdu. Young entrepreneurs are also able to learn about Korean culture, business patterns of Korean enterprises and exchange ideas. She is also thinking about building a small post-90s entrepreneur team in Chengdu in the future to offer help for young people like her.

The City of Success and the Second Hometown

Jung Chanmee has been in Chengdu for nearly three years, and since 2014 this promising city has become an integral part of her life. She has now achieved the first step of her entrepreneurial dream. Starting with the first IFS store, she now owns five stores and an entrepreneurial youth training plaza covering an area of 350 square meters. The growing business landscape keeps her tied up but joyful at the same time.

However, five stores are not enough for Jung Chanmee. She has a more ambitious goal to have 200 juice stores in Chengdu. In 2010, Chengdu was awarded the title of "Gastronomy City" by UNESCO. The catering business has been thriving in Chengdu. And Chengdu has opened its door to foreign entrepreneurs. Currently, the "Venture Tianfu" campaign is in full swing, according to which Chengdu is building itself into a "city of entrepreneurship and a capital of success". This would be a golden opportunity for those with dreams from abroad.

As Chengdu goes global and its entrepreneurial climate gets better, an increasing number of foreigners, including Jung Chanmee, have become more optimistic about investing and starting business in Chengdu. For most of them, Chengdu is still a fresh market with astonishing potential. People in Chengdu stick to a leisurely lifestyle and care about quality of life. They know how to enjoy life even during busy days. And that is the very reason Jung Chanmee's store survives and grows.

The leisurely style of Chengdu has not only created business opportunity for Jung Chanmee, but also made her more obsessed with this city. She even thinks Chengdu outshines her hometown Seoul. She loves to commute by subway every day from her living place in Tongzilin to her store. She loves the good public transport in Chengdu. Taking subway to hunt for food is another fun pastime for her. Hotpot, hot and spicy kebab and spicy incense pot are her favorites. She is almost a chili-addicted Chengdu girl now.

Jung Chanmee has made a lot of new friends in Chengdu, many of which are her customers. They play a big role in her happy life, largely relieving her homesickness. Seoul for her now is only a place to return to four to five times a year for her market research on the latest trends. She and her family now all live in Chengdu.

Over 1,300 years ago, Li Bai, the genius poet, wrote in a poem that Chengdu is an unrivaled paradise on earth. His poem reads:"Out of God's hand Chengdu was carved, into the canvas thousands of homes adorned."1300 years later, Jung Chanmee, the South Korean entrepreneur, views the city as her second hometown. She has got quite accustomed to the city. She even uses Chinese in daily conversation and occasionally picks up some Chengdu dialect from her friends. She is enjoying her life here and loves more and more of the city that vibrates with opportunity and happiness.

教・学在成都

>>> 裴德乐（古巴、美国双国籍）
电子科技大学教授

Pedro Antonio Valdes Sosa, Cuba/USA
Professor of University of Electronic Science and Technology of
China

追寻先辈足迹的共产主义者

有人说爱上一个人，恋上一座城。大多数时候，我们不会无缘无故地喜欢上一座城市，这其中可能是有独特的回忆，或是不舍的挚友，或是爱上的人。

同许多外国友人因为爱情来到中国不同，对于裴德乐来说，朋友的"忽悠"是留下来的关键所在。挚友追随着爱情的脚步，远涉重洋来到中国，来到成都，这让裴德乐百思不得其解。在与好友的一次次聊天中，裴德乐总是试图说服老友回国，事与愿违，每一次都让老友将话题引入这座城市的人文、故事、饮食、民情，在交谈中，裴德乐对这座陌生城市越来越了解，一开始是一点点，友人说，他听，其中关于革命烈士的那些故事越来越引他入胜，深深吸引了他。最后，在朋友的大力"忽悠"下，裴德乐来到了成都，试图一探究竟，揭穿老友的假面具。然而事与愿违，最终，裴德乐误入蓉城不忍离去，短短的相处，让他深深地迷恋上了这座城市。

由于这一点，裴德乐常常自嘲："你看吧，交个靠谱的朋友还是有必要的。"幽默风趣的言谈举止，一下就拉近了这位外国人与成都这座城市的距离。

追随先辈的足迹

一脸白色的络腮胡，高大的身躯，还有爽朗的笑声，电子科技大学中国——古巴神经科技转化前沿研究联合实验室里面总是活跃着特约教授裴德乐的身影。路过实验室的人，往往能和他交流两句，短短的交流，他就会很满足。客观讲来，裴德乐可谓是一位标准的学霸。1950年3月，裴德乐出生在美国。21岁，他考入古巴哈瓦那大学学习数学。而后，他又分别攻读了医学博士和哲学博士。他的科研道路并没有因为拿到两个博士学位而终止，反而仍在继续。1978年，他到美国的纽约大学攻读博士后。2011年，他成为古巴国家科学学位委员会的科学博士——这是一个终身成就奖性质的学位，约每300位博士中才能产生一位，以表彰他作为所在科学领域的奠基人。

裴德乐来自古巴，一个革命者的故乡，作为一名忠诚的共产主义者，他总是跟朋友打趣："我也是共产党员哦！"在学校里面，他独特的外形为电子科技大学平添了几分特色。

那些过往的岁月，对于裴德乐来说或许是最好的念想，他每天在实验室带领着来自世界各地的研究生们为了改善人们的健康状况而工作着。

在父辈和导师的影响下，裴德乐崇尚正义，抵制一切邪恶。他父辈那一代，有人为了正义与真理而战，有人奋起抗争，终成古巴革命的领导者之一；有人积极外交，成为中华人民共和国成立后受到毛主席和周总理第一批接见的外国友人。尤其对他影响深远的，是他的导师。现在裴德乐和自己的双胞胎哥哥都为古巴的国家神经科技转化研究所工作。"我自己走上这条科学研究的道路，更多的受到导师的影响。"他的导师是一名犹太人，家人均被纳粹杀害，终身致力于科学研究。而裴德乐就追寻着父辈的足迹来到中国，希望可以用自己的科研去为世界的美好做出贡献。

人对于理想和信仰的忠诚，或许就是需要一代又一代的传承，如果没有机会去为自己所崇尚的理想和信念奋斗，人就不为人，人生也就变得寡淡无味。"为共产主义奋斗"这句很多人从小熟悉的口号，是古巴人裴德乐愿意信仰并愿意为之奋斗的动力。延续祖辈的意志，在新时代新格局下传承着，是多么难能可贵。有时候，我们不得不承认，裴德乐绝对算得上一位值得钦佩的、高尚的外国友人。

裴德乐最早选择的是自己父辈们来过的城市——北京，他作为中国科学院的特邀嘉宾，多次来访中国。匆匆的人群、忙碌的人们给他留下太深的印象。他总是感觉生活不应该是这样的，直到 2011 年，裴德乐第一次来成都参加一个会议，他被这座城市深深迷住了，他发现这里才是他梦想的生活地。那之后，裴德乐受邀成为电子科技大学的特邀教授。从起初的每年短暂教学到现在的常驻联合办学，他与这座城建立起了不解之缘。

裴德乐追寻着先辈的足迹来到东方，并且把这段足迹进行了延伸，从中华大地的北方延伸到了西南。裴德乐教授在自己的办公桌上摆放着卡斯特罗的相片，始终督促着自己牢记身为一名共产主义者的任务和信念。

闲适生活中享受每个细节

战争年代，在战火硝烟面前，任何力量都是那么薄弱，那么不堪一击，前一刻你看到的人还在铿锵有力地谈救国，转瞬就可能化为灰烬。也许，裴德乐就是这样的革命者，初识觉得他风趣淡然，长久交往才能品出他浓郁的醇香。他因为知晓生活的来之不易，所以愿做生活中的有心人。

裴德乐生命中的大多数时间在古巴，每次电子科大银杏树叶飘落的时刻，他总会想起哈瓦那的郊外是否也有落叶。庆幸的是，裴德乐的爱人和他一起也在电子科技大学帮助学生们做科学研究，有爱人的陪伴在侧，心也随之宁静下来。

中国人常说：民以食为天。每个人到异乡总是会害怕饮食的不便。裴德乐之所以喜欢成都还有一个很重要的原因，就是成都的饮食是以米为主的。裴德乐在古巴的主食喜欢吃红豆配米饭，而成都的餐桌上，米饭是每顿餐的必备品，这个共同点让他倍感亲切。爱喝咖啡的裴德乐来到中国之后，渐渐地爱上了中国的茶，尤其是清雅的绿茶和醇香的苦荞，更是成为了他杯中的常客。

每每到约朋友吃饭的时候，裴德乐总是会不自觉地选择成都代表性美食——火锅。裴德乐夫妇二人很享受和三五朋友端坐在铺满辣椒的火锅旁等待着食物熟透的感觉。有时热辣，有时淡然，就如裴德乐有时也喜欢在冬日的阳光中，手持一卷书在林中静读，在他看来这很有一种中国儒雅士绅的风范。

裴德乐夫妇就住在电子科技大学旁边的小区，或是傍晚，或是周末，夫妻两人总是会牵手上街去散步。不同于中国人的腼腆和羞涩，裴德乐夫妇总是毫不介意地、大方地秀出自己的恩爱。行走在被万年青和不知名树木包围的人行道，来来往往的行人，或是背着书包放学懵懂无知的孩童，或是哼唱着川腔姗姗独行的老人，或是手提公文包归家的白领，抑或是买菜归来的主妇，总会亲切地和他们打招呼。

浅浅的一个微笑，简单的一声问候，却是这座城市给裴德乐最好的礼物。裴德乐常常坦言，他走过很多国家，去过很多地方，没有一座城市让他感觉到如成都般温暖，总有一些陌生的人让他感觉到这座城市的温度。这些路人中，裴德乐有些时候听不懂别人的"你好"，他就用西班牙语跟别人打招呼。双方似乎都不太明白对方在说什么，但即使别人听不懂也都会很开心地对他笑，他能感受到人们对他的热情。虽然语言不通，但在传递感情这件事儿上，文字和声音往往都变得不是那么重要了。一颦一笑，眼神交错中，你的姿态和眼神，已经传递了所有的情感。

他的古巴，也是如此——如此热情。

在裴德乐的心里还埋藏着自己的一个愿望，或许是一个想法，他希望成都人能够教会古巴人吃辣椒，因为川菜的辣味给他留下了太深的印象；古巴人应当教成都人跳舞，希望可能在街头的拐角处看到大家翩翩起舞活力四射。我们也希望裴德乐的这个梦想可以实现。如果让他将中国和古巴，成都与哈瓦那相对比，在成都，有可能每天早上被小区里面娘娘们搓麻将的声音吵醒。

裴德乐现在对四川麻将产生了浓厚的兴趣，可能在不久的将来，我们就会看到在电子科大的茶馆里，裴德乐教授带着夫人和一桌外国朋友在打四川麻将，画面生动得让人有些不敢想象。

桥都坚固隧道都光明

信仰的价值就在于它能够给人带来"绝对意义上的安全感"，唯有如此，人们才会愿意坦然接受。当你拥有一个专一信仰的时候，你就会很坚定，有动力，敢于为之付出努力，而当你没有信仰的时候，往往什么都变得无所谓，你甚至会觉得仿佛思考都是在浪费心思。

在所有学生和同事眼中，裴德乐教授是一个"怪人"。我们常说：术业有专攻，希望个人可以在一件事情或者一门学科上努力。然而裴德乐就像是一个异类。他做的是科学研究实验，但是却热衷于所有的读物。而且在读书这件事情上，他显得很杂食，除了自己的学科外，他偏爱于文学、诗歌、歌剧等读本，谁让他是哲学博士呢？当你在电子科技大学中国——古巴神经科技转化前沿研究联合实验室中发现英文版的《西游记》或者《红楼梦》之类的著作，肯定是裴德乐的。作为古巴较出名的科学家之一，也是世界上脑科学的前沿专家，在同事眼里，裴德乐还有着极其可爱的一面。几个月前，裴德乐走在街上遇到一条流浪狗，听着小狗充满渴求的叫声，他的心瞬间融化了。他把小狗带回家，此后便如影随形，甚至抱着小狗到实验室办公，也成为了一道风景。

他把自己的时间献给了书籍、科研与爱。所有相识的人都会惊异于他的阅读量。读书的人，思想比较通透，面对不能依靠抱怨来解决的事，他往往会选择比较有素质的回应方式。平时有人面临种种困境向裴德乐求教，他一般会用自己的行为告诫着身边的朋友，无论面对什么，都要积极而有修养地对待它。这才是一位成熟的人应有的素质。

说起往事，裴德乐最难忘的是他10岁时候自己阅读《白求恩传》，那让他第一次了解到世界上有中国这样一个国家。幼时的印象总是难以磨灭。在随后的阅读生涯中，他从安娜·路易斯·斯特朗的文本中进一步了解到了中国。他当时就在设想，若是哪一天，中国特别需要他，他就会来到中国。语言总是在不经意间就变成了现实，就像是裴德乐教授在现在中国的工作，他认为中国的科研需要他的帮助，自己便义无反顾前来帮助。谁能知道这竟然圆了他少年时的一个预想呢？而今，他很高兴在中国这样的一个国家去进行自己的科研。

他走过大山和大海，跨国千难和万阻，来到了幼时读本上的领土，追寻着父辈的足迹，承载导师的信念，把无国界之分的科研带给需要的人。银杏飘落，穿过一栋栋教学楼，牵着妻子的手，微笑着打着招呼，白色胡须上的面容坚毅，这都是裴德乐对成都最深沉的爱恋。

A Communist Following in Ancestral Footprints

Some say if you love someone, you will fall in love with her city. Normally, we love a city for good reasons. It may be a unique memory, a close friend, or a loved one.

Unlike many foreign friends who came to China because of love, Pedro stayed primarily because of the "enticing" of friends. His best friend went all the way across oceans to Chengdu, China, in pursuit of love. This baffled Pedro. While chatting with friends, Pedro tried to persuade his old friend to go back to their own country, but it was in vain. The friend would always switch the conversation topic to history and culture, stories, cuisine and the daily life of this city. During these conversations, Pedro got more familiar with this alien city. The friend talked, and he listened. The stories about revolutionary martyrs had increasing appeal for him and he was impressed. As a result of the vigorous "enticing" of the friend, Pedro finally came to Chengdu to check if his friend had lied to him by telling fake stories. Contrary to his expectations, Pedro strayed into Chengdu and was reluctant to leave in the end. A brief encounter led to a deep affection for the city.

When asked, Pedro often jokes about himself: "See, it is important to have reliable friends." Humorous manners have shortened the distance between this foreigner and the city of Chengdu.

Following the Footsteps of Ancestors

With large white whiskers, a tall figure, and hearty laughter, Professor Pedro is always on the run in the China-Cuba Joint Lab of Cutting-Edge Research into Neuro Technology Transformation at the University of Electronic Science and Technology of China. Anyone passing the laboratory has the opportunity to talk to him. Even short exchanges will make him satisfied. Objectively speaking, Pedro is a straight-A scholar through and through. Pedro was born in the United States in March of 1950. At the age of 21, he was admitted to Havana University in Cuba, majoring in mathematics. Then he went on to study medicine and philosophy as a doctoral candidate. Obtaining two doctorates did not mean the end of his research career. He continued instead. In 1978, he went to New York University for postdoctoral research. In honor of him as the founder of the field of studies he was involved in, the Cuban National Committee for Science Degrees named him Doctor of Science in 2011—a degree comparable to a lifetime achievement award that is conferred to only one out of about 300 PhDs.

Pedro is from Cuba, a country of revolutionaries. As a loyal communist, he always jokes with friends: "I am also a communist party member." His striking features are an elegant silhouette on the campus of UESTC. Later, people who knew him and those who did not came to know that an old Cuban communist was working in one of the laboratories at the University of Electronic Science and Technology of China.

Those passing years may be the best memories for Pedro, who leads graduate students from around the world and works to improve people's health every day.

Under the influence of his elder generation and mentors, Pedro is an advocate of justice and an opponent to all evils. Some of his elder generation fought for justice and truth; some fought for liberation and eventually became part of the elite group leading the Cuban Revolution; some actively conducted diplomacy and became the first group of foreign friends whom Chairman Mao and Premier Zhou met with after the founding of the People's Republic of China. His supervisor, in particular, had a far-reaching impact on him. Now Pedro and his elder twin brother both work for the National Institute of Neuroscience Transformation in Cuba. "I embarked on the path of scientific research out of the influence of my supervisor." His supervisor is a Jew, whose family were killed by Nazis and who dedicated all his life to scientific research. Pedro came to China to follow in the footsteps of his predecessors, hoping his research could add to the beauty of this world.

Commitment to ideals and beliefs need to be passed on from one generation to another. Without the opportunity to fight for the ideals and beliefs that they advocate for, people would no longer be humans and life would become dull. "Fight for the cause of communism" is a slogan that many people were familiar with when they were young. It is what Cuban Pedro believes in and what motivates him to fight for his beliefs. It is commendable to inherit the will of our ancestors and to pass it on in this new era of new conditions. And we cannot deny that Pedro is an admirable and honorable foreign friend.

The first city Pedro chose was Beijing, where his parents' generation once visited. He visited China many times as a special guest of the Chinese Academy of Sciences. The busy people who came and went left a deep impression on him. He always felt that life should not be like this. It was not until 2011 that Pedro first came to Chengdu to attend a conference, during which he got fascinated by the city and found it was the place he had dreamed of living in. Later, Pedro was appointed as a guest professor at the University of Electronic Science and Technology of China. Initially, it was only a short-term teaching program. Now he has become part of a permanent joint education program. A closer bond with the city has been developed.

Pedro came to the orient in pursuit of his ancestral footsteps, but he went further than that. He did not stop in northern China and went all the way to the Southwest. Professor Pedro placed a photograph of Castro on his desk to remind himself that as a communist he had a mission to fulfill and a belief to hold on to.

Enjoying Every Detail of a Relaxed Life

In wartime, everything seemed powerless and vulnerable against gunpowder. A minute ago people you saw passionately talking about fighting for their country may turn into ashes in the blink of an eye. Pedro is perhaps such a revolutionary. Your first impression of him might be that he is a humorous person. Long-time contact will eventually unveil his fiery passion for revolution. Deeply aware of this hard-won happy life, he wants to be someone with high aspirations and a strong sense of responsibility.

Pedro spent most of his life in Cuba. When the ginkgo leaves start falling on the campus of UESTC, he will always think of the fallen leaves on the outskirts of Havana. Fortunately, Pedro's wife is together with him helping students do research at UESTC. Accompanied by his wife, Pedro's heart nestles.

"Food comes first," the Chinese often say. Everyone on foreign soil worries about the food there. This is another important reason why Pedro likes Chengdu. Rice is the staple food here. And his staple food in Cuba is red beans with rice. This shared preference has shortened the distance between him and Chengdu. Pedro loved coffee before gradually falling in love with Chinese tea after his arrival in China. Refreshing green tea and mellow buckwheat are frequent visitors to his cup.

When Pedro invites friends to come over for dinner, he always opts for hot pot—a representative delicacy of Chengdu. Pedro and his wife enjoy the time when they sit upright at the table with a couple of friends, watching ingredients boiling in a pot full of chilies. Life here is sometimes hot, sometimes mild. Pedro likes reading in the quiet woods on a sunny winter day. In his view, it is a style typical of Chinese gentlemen.

Pedro and his wife live in a community near UESTC and often take walks, hand in hand, on the street at dusk or on weekends. Unlike Chinese people who tend to conceal their true emotions, Pedro and his wife show their love in public places, not caring what people might have to say. Walking on a sidewalk shrouded in evergreens and anonymous trees, Pedro is warmly greeted by pedestrians coming and going—children carrying school bags on their way home after school, an elderly humming Sichuan folk songs while tottering along, white-collars heading home with briefcase in hand, and housewives returning home from the food market.

A smile or a simple greeting is the best gift to Pedro from Chengdu. Pedro admits that in his heart Chengdu is the warmest of all the countries and places he has ever traveled to. There are always strangers who touch him with the warmth of the city. When Pedro fails to understand the greeting "hello" that some people call out in Chinese, he returns the greeting in Spanish.

Neither side seems to understand what the other side says. But he always receives a happy smile even if he is not properly understood. He can sense the passion that people have for him. Language may be a barrier, but the actual words and sounds uttered don't seem to matter when it comes to the exchange of emotions. Your posture and the expression in your eyes say everything about your attitude and emotions when you smile and look at each other.

The same goes for his hometown in Cuba—a place as friendly as Chengdu.

Deep down Pedro has an idea. He hopes the people of Chengdu will help Cubans to adapt to food with chilies because, for him, the spicy taste of Sichuan dishes is impressive. He also hopes Cubans could give lectures on dancing in Chengdu and that someday he may see Cuban dances at street corners. Hopefully, his dream will come true. When asked to compare China with Cuba or Chengdu with Havana, he says the neighborhood aunties and grannies playing Mahjong are likely to wake you up early in the morning.

Pedro now has a keen interest in Sichuan Mahjong. Perhaps in the near future, we will see Professor Pedro and his wife playing the game with some foreign friends at a Mahjong table in a teahouse at the University of Electronic Science and Technology of China. That would be such a wonderful scene.

Bridges are Strong and Tunnels are Bright

The value of faith is that it gives people "a sense of absolute security". When you uphold one particular faith, you are determined, motivated, and prepared to make an effort for it; when you don't, everything becomes irrelevant, and even thinking would be a waste of time.

In the eyes of his students and colleagues, Professor Pedro is a "freak". "There is expertise involved in every profession". By this we mean an individual is supposed to be hard at work on a subject or job. However, Pedro looks entirely different from the rest of us. He engages in scientific experiments, but is keen on a wide array of books. And he seems "omnivorous" when it comes to the choice of books. In addition to his own subjects, he likes literature, poetry, and opera—exactly what a Doctor of Philosophy would be fond of. If you find an English version of The Journey to the West or A Dream of Red Mansions in the China-Cuba Joint Lab of Cutting-Edge Research into Neuro Technology Transformation at the University of Electronic Science and Technology of China, it has to be Pedro's. As one of the most famous scientists in Cuba and a world-leading expert in brain science, Pedro is an adorable man in the eyes of his colleagues. A few months ago, Pedro saw a stray dog while walking on the street. The plaintive cry of the puppy melted his heart. He took the puppy home and later it followed him everywhere like a shadow. He even took the dog to the lab—a much talked-about topic among his colleagues.

He spends all his time on books, research, and love. All of his acquaintances are amazed at how extensively he reads. Men of letters think wisely. They maintain high moral standards when faced with problems. When people locked in the grip of trouble ask Pedro for help, he usually replies with his own actions. "Regardless of what you face, cope with it vigorously and in the meantime maintain a high level of moral standards," says he. This is the ethical standard that a wise man is expected to uphold.

Speaking of past events, the most memorable thing for Pedro was the

Biography of Bethune he read about at ten. It was the first time he learned about China. Childhood memories are always indelible. As he continued reading, he knew more about China from texts by Anna Louise Strong. And he even imagined coming to China one day when China needs him. Words become reality before you know it. Professor Pedro now works in China and he thinks he can offer some help and play a part in scientific research. No one would have anticipated that his childhood dream would come true. Now, he is very happy to conduct his own research in a country like China.

As gingko leaves flutter in light breeze, white-bearded Pedro walks by rows of classroom buildings, holding hand with his wife, and greets people with smile. Following the footsteps of ancestors and carrying with him the faith of his supervisor, Pedro went all the way across the oceans to the place he read about during childhood, bringing his science research to those who need them.

>> 尼格尔（英国）
幼儿教育专家

Nigel Jones, UK
Child Education Expert

来了就不想走的"洋爸爸"

尼格尔是一位专门从事幼儿教育的英国人，在来到成都之前，他辗转于世界各地从事教育工作，和他交谈总能有颇多收获，每次聊天就像同多年未见的老友在深夜里彻谈。在交流中，尼格尔会叙述他走过的千山万水，讲述他经历过的海角天涯。在尼格尔去过的地方，有温暖、有疯狂、有坚守、有执拗，甚至连无聊都显得那么真实。直到他来了成都，被这座城市所吸引，最终停留在这里，生根结果，安家此处。回首曾经的一切，尼格尔总是微微一笑，他此前所有的经历或许都是在为更好地遇到成都而做的准备。

逃不掉的成都教育缘

尼格尔作为一位地道的英国人，绅士风度十足，举手投足间隐隐透着股贵族气，成熟稳重的气息一览无余。尼格尔自己坦言，要是几年前来到中国时没有遇到成都，他应该现在还一直在路上，在不同的城市间漂泊。在台湾工作时，他对中文产生了极其浓厚的兴趣，之后辗转北京系统地学习中文，中国博大精深的文化使得尼格尔在学习过程中越发痴迷。中国的美食，中国的美景，中国的美酒，乃至中国的美人，无一不是让他着迷的理由。

北京、上海、长沙、湘潭、云南这些城市都留下了他的脚步，最终他选择停驻在这座众人皆知、来了就不想走的城市——成都。对于尼格尔而言，更加准确地说，成都是一座来了就走不掉的城市，正如他常常挂在嘴边的说辞：妻子、孩子、房子都在这座城市，这座城市里有了他的家。他深爱这座城市的人，他们友好善良；他也爱这座城市的每一处景色，它们艳丽动人，这里不仅留住了自己的人，也留住了自己的心。

成都是除了自己家乡外，尼格尔停留时间最长的城市。2000 年，他初识这座城市的时刻，成都还像是个情窦初开的少女，并没有太多的异国人士探访它。尼格尔是在一碗豆花的温度中认识蓉城的。乳白色的豆腐花，和红艳艳的辣椒蘸酱让当时的他感觉有些不知所措，一直到现在习惯了"无辣不欢"的饮食。成都让这位异国的大男孩成长起来，他总是会在走过九眼桥的时候怀念起刚到成都的岁月。

那时候酒吧一条街还不似现在这样繁华热闹，夜晚的滨江路边也没有如此多的街头卖唱艺人，尼格尔曾经租住的四合院也不复存在。虽然成都已经改头换面更加繁华热闹，不似当年般青涩懵懂，可住在这里的尼格尔依旧钟爱着这里的一切。他用一个外国人的视角观察着这座城市的变迁，他喜欢这座城慵懒又不失活力的状态，他热爱这里教会他生活的人们。

如今的尼格尔身处教育行业。尼格尔做教育不是为了在成都找一份相对工资高的工作而做，更不是头脑发热一时兴起。从 1994 年的暑假到今天，他已经在教育这条路上走了快 23 年了。最初尼格尔是在假期作为志愿者去捷克的工厂做义工。一次机缘巧合，幼儿园的授课老师生病无法给孩子们正常上课，学校负责人让他代替老师上几天课。从那一天起，他似乎找到了自己更加喜欢的东西——幼儿教育。他愿意花时间和精力与孩子们待在一起，去探索孩子们世界里的美好，去交流倾听孩子们对世界的认知。

也正是出于这份爱和喜欢，一位学计算机的男生最后却成了一名幼儿教育工作者。事实上，这颠覆了人们对学计算机乃至整个工科男的印象，那种传统的呆板，不善交流，不喜欢吵闹，喜欢宅在自己世界里的工科男似乎已经成为了过去。我们所看到的尼格尔，是细心、耐心、有爱心的大哥哥形象。这样的热爱，这样的性格，最终使得尼格尔和教育结下了不解之缘，并一直走到了现在。

外国老师眼中的中国幼儿教育

杨绛先生在谈到"什么是好的教育"时曾说到："好的教育首先是启发人的学习兴趣、学习的自觉性，培养人的上进心，引导人们好学和不断完善自己。要让学生在不知不觉中受教育，让他们潜移默化。"尼格尔不知道杨绛先生是谁，但真理总是相通的。尼格尔辗转这么多个国家，他发现中国的教育方式确实和国外的教育方式有一定区别，但核心却都是一样——爱孩子。相对而言，中国的家长比外国的家长更加细心。尼格尔凭借自己在中国多年的教育经验和跟家长接触的经验感知到，中国家长喜欢想得很多很细，去帮孩子规划一些框架或者路线，可能从几岁就规划到了二十几岁，而外国家长则不会有这样的想法，他们会遵循孩子的意愿，看孩子更喜欢什么从而鼓励孩子去探索。

谈到幼儿教育，尼格尔可算得上是资深元老。然而尽管在幼儿教育领域工作如此多的年头了，尼格尔仍然能够保持初心，去探索真正的中西合璧。这不只是口号或是标语，尼格尔希望能够让孩子们更自由、更快乐地进行学习，在学习中找到自己的兴趣所在，潜力能够被激发出来。

作为教师的尼格尔，总是奔波在成都各个金苹果幼儿园之间，面对"不让孩子输在起跑线上"这样的话语他也表示非常能够理解。他认为父母不用太担心自己的子女落后，有时候把孩子的未来看得简单一点，让未来就掌握在他们自己手中未必不是一件好事，父母应该鼓励并相信自己的孩子，让孩子们从小就有"自己去创造"的概念。从尼格尔的角度讲，他自己作为一名身处成都的西方人，又身为幼儿教育从业者，内心是非常希望自己能够真正把教育做好，真正推动中西教育的融合，真正找到中西教育的契合点。

教育是一个国家的希望和民族复兴的起点。走过天南海北，停留在中国，驻足在成都，尼格尔看到过太多国家的教育现状，也体验过太多地方的教育方式。尼格尔从事的是幼儿教育，他认为这种最基础的教育是奠定一个孩子成长的必需环节。不管是语言天赋的开发还是逻辑智力的引导，都将影响一个孩子一生的成长。他常常惊异于中国教育体系的完备和严谨。

为了给孩子们更好的教育，他曾经完整阅读过中国小学教育的全部提纲和教材，他认为这种课本的设定是科学和合理的，并且能够引领孩子的健康学习。尼格尔常常会站立在办公室的落地窗前，思考着自己如何才能真正的把中西方的教育模式融合到一起。毕竟在每一个国家都有自身的不同情况，如果只是简单地复制国外的教育模式，难免会"水土不服"。

工科生出身的尼格尔，有着严谨的思维模式和高效的办事作风，他热爱着自己的工作，热爱和孩子们在一起的感觉。不管是以前做老师，还是现在做管理，尼格尔一直坚持亲自到孩子们中间去体验教育的真实感受。只有实践才是检验教育方法的唯一标准。虽然就现在来看，金苹果幼儿园在成都已经具有了一定的知名度，然而作为管理者的他仍然在不停地探索和创新着教育方法。他常常会告诉身边的朋友，做一名老师是十分幸福的事情。当所有孩子天真甜蜜的笑容呈现在你的面前，你会感觉这就是上帝给你最好的礼物。他有着不同的肤色，但却有中国古人说的"爱人"之心，他希望能够用自己的工作和努力为孩子们带去真正的快乐。

洋女婿的中国式生活

　　最美的邂逅就发生在成都。在这里，尼格尔和妻子相遇、相知、相爱。目前已经是两个孩子父亲的他有着自己幸福甜蜜的小日子。因为始终坚持自己的幼儿教育理念，很多朋友会担心尼格尔和妻子之间在孩子的教育问题上会产生分歧，但事实上恰恰没有。自从尼格尔的两个小宝宝出生以来，他的休息时间就全部奉献给了自己的孩子。

　　就像是同事和朋友眼中看到的那样，尼格尔白天上班，他的工作是和孩子们在一起，晚上回家也是和孩子们在一起，一整天他都是一位老师也是一位父亲。由于妻子工作时间比他长，大多数时候都是他来带孩子。他常说陪伴是孩子们成长过程中必不可缺的，他也实实在在喜欢跟孩子们在一起。尼格尔和妻子之间就孩子教育的问题，基本没有分歧，他们希望孩子们在自由中找到自我。

　　在学校里，尼格尔是一名老师，一名管理者；在家庭中，尼格尔是一位丈夫，一名好爸爸。或许是因为幼儿教育工作的原因，他最明了孩子是需要陪伴的，所以他总是把自己所有的业余时间留给孩子。每每面对学校组织的家庭手工作业、亲子游园活动等事务，他会表现出异常的兴奋。他耐心、亲昵地陪着孩子做手工、玩游戏，用称职爸爸来形容他再恰当不过。有时候他听说有家长借口工作太忙没有时间参加亲子活动，尼格尔的神情会有些落寞，他无法理解有什么事情是比陪自己的宝贝更加重要的呢？

　　在他的眼中，孩子就是父母的一切。尼格尔对待自己的孩子不同于中国的父母，他从来不会为孩子去规划长久的未来。他总是告诫身边的年轻父母，孩子的未来是他们自己的，父母的规划有时候只会产生阻碍的作用。我们常常会把自己未实现的梦想、未完成的事业寄托到孩子的身上，可是从而不会真正的去询问孩子的需求。该来的总会来，孩子自己规划的未来才是真正属于他们自己的。

在常人的眼中，外国人的生活总是井井有条，对于他们而言，亲情这个词，可能最重要的就是和自己的父母、妻儿和兄弟姐妹之间的情感。面对中国式家庭关系，很多外国人会感觉头疼，但在尼格尔这里却变成了一件很有爱的事情。妻子的亲戚朋友让他感受到了中国式关系里大家庭的温暖，大家都坦诚相待，相互帮助，亲情味道浓郁，给他温暖温馨之感。

但是尼格尔还是无法理解，为什么中国的家长总是喜欢为子女做事情。在他的概念中，孩子成家立业之后，父母回家看孩子，理应是孩子为父母做饭、洗衣服等，让父母休息。可是在他岳母到访的时刻，总是争抢着做家务，尼格尔十分不赞同这样的做法。在某种角度讲，他可谓是一名孝顺的"女婿"。有些时候，当岳母在家中小住的时候，尼格尔总会自己亲自做所有力所能及的事情，让老人得到休息。

漫步成都的大街小巷，尼格尔发现定居在成都的外国人越来越多。在春熙路、宽窄巷子等闹市区，随处都能看到外国人与成都人一道逛街、购物、品尝小吃、喝盖碗茶；在成都的各色火锅店里，也能找到不同肤色的外国人在大快朵颐。坦率地讲，这样一座悠闲自在的城市并不是从未让尼格尔产生过想要离开的念头，然而爱情、亲情将他留下了。尼格尔常常希望成都的涉外公共服务不断提升，因为他将会带着自己的爱情和事业，继续在成都生活下去，继续为成都的教育做出一个国际友人的贡献。

A "Foreign Dad" that Never Wants to Leave

Nigel is a preschool education specialist from the UK. Prior to Chengdu he had undertaken several educational jobs around the world. Talking to him is always fruitful, like a hearty late night talk to a long-lost friend from old times. Nigel reflected upon his journeys across the world. There were warmth, craziness, persistence, stubbornness and even boring things. But all is real. His life of drifting did not end until he came to Chengdu. Attracted and enchanted, he decided to settle down. Looking into the past, perhaps everything was right there to prepare him for a better encounter with Chengdu.

His Predestined Educational Mission in Chengdu

As a typical British, Nigel holds an air of gentility with noble bearing and looks very mature. He confesses that if Chengdu had not intercepted him during his journey to China several years ago, he might have still been drifting between different cities. He got extremely interested in Chinese when he was working in Taiwan. Later he went to Beijing for a systematic study of Chinese, during which he got even more obsessed with the profound Chinese culture. The food, scenery, and wine culture and even the Chinese beauties, all made him fascinated.

He has been to Beijing, Shanghai, Changsha, Xiangtan and Yunnan. But he finally settled in Chengdu, the well-known city that people would never want to leave once they come. More precisely, for Nigel, it should be "a city that one could hardly get rid of". As he often mentions, his family, wife and children are all in this city. He loves the city for its kind people and its ever-present scenery. They captured his heart and soul.

His stay in Chengdu has been the longest besides his hometown. In 2000, when Nigel first set foot in the city, Chengdu was like a teenage girl behind the veil, rarely visited by foreign people. For Nigel, his intimate ties with the city began with a bowl of Tofu pudding. The milky bean curd jelly combined with hot chili sauce almost petrified him. But who could have imagined that he would become a chili-addict one day? Chengdu saw him grow up and even today, whenever he passes Jiuyanqiao, Nigel will always recall his first nine months in Chengdu.

The bar street back then was much quieter. The nightly riverside roads were yet to be dotted by street artists. And the courtyard he rented no longer exists. Today's Chengdu, entirely renovated, has been much busier and nothing like its old self, but Nigel still loves the city. Watching the city grow, he has been attached to its casual vivaciousness and its people who have taught him the very truth about a happy life.

Working in education, Nigel didn't choose his job because of the high wages nor did he get into it on a whim. He has spent almost 23 years in education ever since he worked as a volunteer in a Czech factory during his summer vacation in 1994. A teacher of the kindergarten was on sick leave, and the principal asked Nigel to take the place. It was not until then that he finally found his real calling: preschool education. He just loved spending time with kids and exploring the beautiful world together with them and listening to their cute sayings about the world.

Out of love and affection, a computer science graduate ended up as a preschool teacher. And this has subverted the dogmatic, stiff, unsociable, silent and otaku impression people have on those who study computer science or many other engineering disciplines. He is a whole new type: considerate, patient and caring just like a big brother. Such a temperament combined with his love for education has finally led him to his predestined educational career till now.

Chinese Preschool Education in the Eyes of a Foreign Teacher

Yang Jiang, a famous Chinese writer, once said: "Good education is about igniting a child's interest in learning, motivating spontaneous learning, cultivating students' aspirations to learn more and improve themselves, and letting positive affitudes and moral mind unconsciously grow up in them." Nigel doesn't know Yang Jiang, but the truth is always universal. His previous journeys around the world made him aware that Chinese education is different. But there is one thing in common—love for children. Comparatively speaking, Chinese parents are more attentive. Nigel finds from his teaching experience and communication with Chinese parents that Chinese parents tend to get down to very specific things and make guidelines or plans for their children. They start planning when the child is still a toddler and extend to his or her twenties. However, parents in other countries never have such a thought. They just follow their children's inclinations and encourage them to explore whatever they like.

Nigel could be counted as a senior expert when it comes to preschool education. Despite a very long period of working in preschool education, Nigel still remains true to his initial aspiration to seek combination of Chinese and Western education. It is not a token aspiration. Nigel has always wished that his children can learn freely and happily and find their real interests in the process and finally have their potential fully released.

As a teacher bustling through several Golden Apple Kindergartens, Nigel says he quite understands the Chinese parents' fear of "losing at the starting point". He encourages parents to take it easy and not to worry about their kids' future too much. To make things simple and let the children control their own life is not a bad thing. Parents should encourage and trust their children, and inject into their mind the concept of "self-creation" when they are young. As a western preschool education practioner, Nigel sincerely wishes to serve his duty well in education, in boosting the integration of Chinese and Western education, and in finding the very connection between the two.

Education is a nation's hope and a starting point for its rejuvenation. Having seen different education systems in many different countries, Nigel holds that basic education can be decisive to children during their formative years. Whether it is language acquisition, or cultivation of logical thinking, basic education will influence a child's whole life. And he is surprised by the compact and rigorous Chinese educational system.

To perform his work better, he once went through all the teaching guidelines and textbooks of Chinese primary education. He concluded that the whole design was scientific and reasonable, and would contribute to good study habits. Nigel is often found standing in front of the French window at his office, reflecting on how he can truly bring together Chinese and Western education. Since each nation has its own conditions, simple copy and paste would only result in incompatibility and disaster.

As an engineering graduate, Nigel is rigorous in thinking and efficient at work. He loves his job, and loves being with children. Whether being a teacher or a manager, he insists that real education should only present itself among children and only practice can tell whether a teaching method is good or not. For the time being, Golden Apple Kindergarten has won some good recognition, but as a manager Nigel never stops exploring new teaching methods. He often tells his friends that being a teacher is the happiest thing. When the kids stand before you with their cute, sweet smiles, you see the best gift from God ever. He is a foreigner on the outside, but inside he has a "loving heart". And he is always hoping to bring children more happiness through his hard work.

Living like a Real Chinese

Chengdu also witnessed the happiest moment for Nigel. He met and fell in love with his wife in Chengdu. He is a father of two now, living his simple but happy life. Due to his insistence on his own preschool educational theories, Nigel's friends used to worry that the couple might have conflicts regarding children's education. But in fact they did not. Ever since the birth of his two children, Nigel has dedicated all his spare time to them.

As is often seen by his colleagues and friends, Nigel works with kids in the day. After work, he returns home and spends time with kids. For the whole day he is a caring teacher and then a caring father. Since his wife is busier, Nigel is the one who takes care of his two children most of the time.

He usually says that companionship is essential for the development of children and he genuinely loves being with children. There is basically no big difference between Nigel and his wife about their children's education. Both of them agree that children should find their own way.

At school, Nigel is a teacher and a manager. At home, he is a good husband and father. His work possibly teaches him that children actually need companionship the most. Hence he gives all his spare time to his children. Whenever child-parent handcraft homework is assigned or a child-parent activity is organized by the school, this dedicated father will get exceptionally excited and perform his duty in a most patient and affectionate way. "Responsible" would be a perfect word for him as a father. Sometimes he might get a little downcast and sad when he hears that some parents miss the child-parent activities and place something else on the top rather fhan their children because they are too busy. He can't understand and accept it.

In Nigel's eyes, children are the world. However, unlike many Chinese parents, he never makes long-term plans for his children. He often reminds young parents that children are their own masters. Parents' over-involvement might end up an obstacle for their future. It's common for parents to burden their children with their unaccomplished dreams, while children's real needs are neglected. What Will be Children's future should be mapped by themselves.

Family life of foreigners seems simple and direct in the eyes of Chinese people. For foreigners, family is limited to parents, wife, children, brothers and sisters. The Chinese families, typically larger in size and more complicated, might have caused many foreigners headache. But Nigel finds it a real loving thing to meet members of a big family. It is filled with warmth, sincerity, mutual support and affection.

But it still puzzles Nigel that Chinese parents keep doing things for their children. In his opinion, when children grow up and build their own family, it should be children who handle things such as the cooking and laundry when parents come to visit and parents should rest themselves. However, whenever his mother-in-law visits, she takes care of all the housework, which Nigel completely disagrees. He is the kind of dutiful "son-in-law" who will always do what he can to let his mother-in-law relax and rest. He is truly a model son-in-law.

Take a walk around Chengdu, and you would see an increasing number of foreigners settle in Chengdu. In downtown areas such as Chunxi Road, Wide and Narrow Alley, a lot of foreigners are strolling, shopping, eating or drinking covered-bowl tea with locals. You may also see people of all colors enjoying their feast at hotpot restaurants. Frankly speaking, once in a while the idea of leaving this leisure city would flash across his mind. But love and family made him stay. He wishes further improvement of Chengdu's foreign services. He would carry on with his life and career in Chengdu, and contribute to the development of early childhood education in Chengdu as a foreign friend.

>> 艾瑞克（德国）
文化公司创始人

Erik Ackner, Germany
Founder of a Culture Company

穿行在文艺圈的西洋自行车 "骑士"

有人说，成都总是由内而外散发着一种神秘的魅力，似乎可以让人看见无数的可能，吸引着人们情不自禁地去探索，去爱它。譬如，暮色中的成都小通巷，行人寥若晨星，干净的灰色街道上只有银杏叶静静躺在那里，像是等着被谁拾起，开始一段新的故事。安安静静的道路两侧，是低矮的小房子，每一间都是被装修得别具韵味的小店，或点着暖黄色的灯，或挂着彩色流苏的门帘，或摆着小巧的盆栽，给这条巷子增添了许多温馨。

在这样情调别致的小巷里选一家最温馨的小店等人，一定会忘记时间的流淌。这条小巷是来自德国的艾瑞克平日与朋友见面的常选之地，他喜欢骑着自行车穿行于这样安静的巷子。

骑车两天去看大熊猫

要说什么是成都的标志，或许你能想到不少词语，但其中一定少不了 "大熊猫"。憨态可掬的大熊猫是中国的国宝，也一直为成都 "代言"，无数外国友人的梦想都是来中国、来成都亲眼看看大熊猫，艾瑞克也是一样。此前生活在故乡德国柏林的时候，艾瑞克就对大熊猫充满了向往，电视新闻里看到的圆滚滚的黑白色小精灵深深抓住了他的心，所以来到成都后，艾瑞克果断把看大熊猫列入自己的计划。

那么，在哪里可以看到大熊猫呢？也许你会回答 "熊猫基地"。但对于艾瑞克而言，成都大熊猫繁育研究基地远远不能满足他想看大熊猫的欲望，他还想要亲眼看看大熊猫生活的自然环境，感受人与自然和谐相处的氛围。想了就立即做，在去过熊猫基地之后，艾瑞克制订好计划，决定骑自行车去卧龙看大熊猫。2016年国庆节期间，艾瑞克与女友骑自行车完成了一次成都—卧龙之旅，尽管事后回忆当时，两个人都疲惫到极点，但他们总是会因为那次尝试而感到骄傲。艾瑞克对他骑车去卧龙没有一丝后悔，在他看来，骑车去旅行是对自己的一种挑战，而且骑车可以更细致地欣赏沿路的风景，可以随时休息，品尝沿途的美食，这真是一件再快乐不过的事呢。

践行和推广健康生活

2010年，作为交换生的他来到了西南财经大学，在光华校区学习了半年国际贸易专业后便返回德国，而后在2011年10月，艾瑞克作为实习生又一次来到成都，在一家环保公司担任公司负责人助理。尽管这次实习的时间十分短暂，但艾瑞克敏锐地觉察到了成都的良好发展前景。2014年10月，艾瑞克第三次来到成都，正式实践他在柏林经济学院与西南财经大学的合作项目，开始了他在成都的创业生涯。

从那时至今，艾瑞克出行都会首选自行车。不管是在白果林办公的时候，还是在红星路办公的时候，他总是会骑上一辆自行车，一天骑行超过20公里，已然成为了他的日常健身方式。骑自行车出行是艾瑞克最爱的出行方式，能骑车的时候，艾瑞克一定是自行车解决出行问题。骑车穿梭在成都的大街小巷，去谈工作，去会朋友，都让他感觉十分惬意，也让他对成都的道路了如指掌，成了外国友人圈儿里的"活地图"。

其实，艾瑞克在成都还有了一个特别的小圈子，圈内都是成都的骑行爱好者，他们每周五定期举行夜骑成都的活动，有着共同爱好的朋友们聚在一起，各自骑上最爱的自行车，成群结队地一同骑上成都的街头，探寻不曾看到的美景，探寻最新的潮流，探寻最隐秘的美食，探寻这座城市的灵魂深处。

除了骑自行车之外，艾瑞克还有不少健身爱好。他在成都办理了不止一家健身房的会员卡，结束了一天的忙碌工作后，他总会骑车去健身房释放工作压力，用一身淋漓汗水，让一天的生活更充实。武术、游泳、搏击、排球、篮球也是艾瑞克的最爱。

最近，艾瑞克正痴迷于武术，偶然的一次机会，让艾瑞克与这一独特的"中国功夫"结下不解之缘。在一位美国朋友的推荐下，艾瑞克加入了一家八宝街附近的武馆，开始学习自卫防身术，这对于有一定的拳击和太极基础的他来说，并不算很难，所以他学得格外起劲。艾瑞克计划在学习一两年自卫防身术之后，再学习更有难度的"中国功夫"。

正是出于自己对运动、对健康生活的热爱，艾瑞克的公司致力于把健康的生活方式在成都推广。艾瑞克与他的合伙人长期在成都长期坚持推广"绿色星期一"公益活动，这项活动提倡人们通过低碳的生活方式来让生活环境得到改善，并实现全社会的可持续发展。艾瑞克由衷希望，成都这座他热爱的东方城市，可以越来越好。

成都是梦实现的地方

艾瑞克热爱成都，不仅仅是因为成都的山水、人文、美食，最为重要的是，艾瑞克坚信，成都将会是他实现梦想的地方。在成都实习期间，艾瑞克就打定了主意要在成都奋力打拼，因为他觉得，成都的经济发展前景非常好，许多行业在成都都能得到快速有效的发展，比如金融行业、电子竞技产业等，都有着良好的发展势头。与此同时，成都周边的高科技产业也越来越多，许多新的公司、新的创意得以被"孵化"，许多年轻人在成都都能很好地施展自己的才华。如此种种，都让艾瑞克对自己在成都的未来充满信心。

事实证明，艾瑞克的判断没有错。2014年来到成都创业后，艾瑞克主要从事活动策划类工作，头脑灵活的他，总能有令人眼前一亮的好创意。2016年6月，艾瑞克与法国总领馆合作，推出了盛大的法国夏至音乐节，在成都的恒大广场、凯德天府、I BOX创意园区和泰合索菲特万达大饭店4个场地各举办一场盛大文艺主题活动。

这次的法国夏至音乐节群星闪耀，法国驻成都总领事馆请到了众多高人气的法国乐队以及欧洲其他国家的乐队，许多成都本地的优秀乐队和音乐人也参与进这一国际文化盛事之中，国内外的乐手们通力合作，互相切磋，各自惊叹于对方独特的艺术造诣。有法国乐手在与成都乐队合作后欣喜地告诉艾瑞克，他第一次知道成都本土有着这样优秀的乐队，这样有生命力的音乐文化。

成功的音乐节离不开观众的热情支持，那次法国夏至音乐节完全免费，尽管只有短短一天，却得到了约5000名成都市民的积极参与，4场活动各自有着不同的主题，各自吸引到喜爱不同音乐类型、不同乐队的成都音乐爱好者们，纯正的欧洲音乐文化和地道的成都音乐文化就这样在系列活动中碰撞出绚烂的火花。而这，引发了艾瑞克的更多灵感，他想要让他祖国德国驻成都的总领事馆也一同参与，把德国的音乐文化在成都推广。

在艾瑞克的事业版图上，还有着更丰富的内容。艾瑞克和英国商会合作，在成都推出了英国日和全球公民日，还把正流行于全球的"创业周末"引进到成都，专门帮助像他一样决心创业的成都青年，为创业者或创业团队提供创业经验和发展建议。近期，艾瑞克开始了一个名为"SHIFT"的项目，顾名思义，这一项目是希望人们转变生活态度和生活方式，提倡绿色健康生活，普及健身、营养等相关知识。不少成都的健身教练已经参与到这一项目中，他们将致力于改善成都市民的生活和身体健康。

从 2010 年的学生，到 2011 年的实习生，再到 2014 年至今的创业者，艾瑞克在成都的身份发生了不小的改变，生活、圈子、眼界也发生了不小的改变，这些改变让他更加渴望在成都做出一番事业，同时也为成都的发展献出一份力量。艾瑞克把成都日新月异的发展都看在眼里，他认为，现在不仅仅是中国，全世界的目光都注意到了这座城市，成都的国际地位日益提升。

在这样的大背景下，艾瑞克自然也是倍加珍惜时机和环境，在更好地规划着自己的职业发展方向。他计划先把公司在成都发展壮大，然后逐渐扩展到成都周边的德阳、绵阳等城市，深入推进他的"SHIFT"项目，成都、四川乃至中国的市场空间都将是他的翱翔之地，他相信两三年后的自己，将能实现这一梦想。

跟成都女友学做菜

工作上，艾瑞克雷厉风行，敢想敢做，充满事业心；而生活中，艾瑞克则是一个温柔体贴又居家的好男友。说起女友，艾瑞克一脸甜蜜，幸福之情溢于言表，再加上心爱的女友是成都本地人，更是令他倍感骄傲。

艾瑞克与他的成都女友在一起已经两年了，和他在成都创业的时间几乎一样长，他与女友相识的经历也与他在成都的工作息息相关。2014年圣诞节，刚来成都不久的艾瑞克策划并组织了一个圣诞活动，这次活动上，和他的一个德国朋友同行的一位中国女孩引起了他的注意。

黄皮肤黑眼睛黑头发的她，有种东方女性特有的温婉气质，尤其是笑容格外明媚，令艾瑞克一见钟情。再加上她说着一口流利的英语，交流起来没有丝毫障碍，让艾瑞克感觉十分自在。从那一晚开始，艾瑞克就对这位可爱的成都女孩展开了热烈的追求，有情人终成眷属。

2016年春，回德国办签证的艾瑞克带上女友同行，他很高兴亲朋好友都欣然接受了这个成都女孩，也很高兴自己获得了女友家人的认可。艾瑞克的成都女友比艾瑞克年长6岁，并且在上一段婚姻中有了一个6岁的女儿，这让只身在异国他乡的艾瑞克获得了更多的关怀和家的温暖。

贤惠的女友经常会为艾瑞克洗手做羹汤，一道道精致可口的成都小菜，让艾瑞克乐不思蜀。在女友的指导下，艾瑞克甚至也开始学习做川菜，他非常骄傲地说，自己已经学会做自己最爱的菜——鱼香茄子，而且凉拌黄瓜、包饺子也不在话下。女友一边教他，一边教女儿，艾瑞克幸福得像个孩子。有空闲的时候，他会和女友一起下厨，合作几道绝无仅有的"中西合璧"的菜肴，制造专属于他们二人的浪漫。

艾瑞克不仅跟女友学做川菜，还跟着女友游览了成都的许多风景。土生土长于成都的女友，对成都的一草一木了如指掌，带着他去武侯祠瞻仰诸葛孔明，去草堂品味诗圣杜甫，去文殊院焚香祈福，还去浣花溪公园坐在静静的湖水边，遥望飞鸟来来去去，近看人群熙熙攘攘，在惬意的清风中，细细体会成都的安逸和美好。

对于28岁的艾瑞克来说，未来的路还有很长。对于未来，艾瑞克已经有了规划，他计划在三年内实现他推广"SHIFT"项目的理想，但更重要的是，他想要和心爱的成都女友相守一生。在他们身上，"执子之手，与子偕老"这样单纯而美好的心愿早已打破了国界的限制，而和谐包容的成都也必将会成为他们美满小家庭的温暖大港湾。

A Western Cycling "Knight" in Chengdu

Some people say Chengdu exudes a mysterious charm from the inside, presenting endless possibilities and inviting spontaneous attempts to explore: Xiaotong Lane at dusk, for example, sparsely dotted by passengers, hold onto their spotless, gray streets. The fallen ginkgo leaves, which lie there silently, hoping to be picked up for a whole new journey. The low storefronts flanking a peaceful lane, are all uniquely furnished: some lighted in a warm yellow, some decorated by curtains made of colored tassels, and some fresh with small potted plants, all making the lane warmer still.

Picking a warm place in a tasteful lane and waiting for someone, what comes next might be so nice that time itself might be forgotten. The lane is one of the most frequent hangout places for Erik and his friends. He loves cycling around on the placid path.

A Two-day Cycling Trip for Pandas

As to the question "what is the symbol of Chengdu", you may think of many possibilities. Among them there must be "the Pandas", who have always been an adorable national treasure of China and Chengdu alike, attracting numerous foreign tourists with one goal in mind: coming to China to see those pandas for themselves. So it is with Erik, who, even when he was in Berlin, Germany, had got intrigued with those black-and-white creatures on the TV news. So as soon as he was in Chengdu, Erik wasted no time in placing seeing pandas on his to-do list.

So what's the best place to see pandas? An immediate answer would be the Chengdu Research Base of Giant Panda Breeding. However, in Erik's eyes, this place is far from enough, for he wished to see pandas living in nature and experience the harmony between man and nature. His thoughts were soon put into action. After a trip to the breeding base, Erik made a plan to cycle to the Wolong National Nature Reserve, where he could see pandas as he originally wished. During the National Day Holiday of 2016, Erik, along with his girlfriend, managed a cycling trip from Chengdu to Wolong. Though it was an extremely grueling trip, they were proud of it. In addition, Erik has no regrets, for he insisted that cycling trip was an exciting challenge. Moreover, he could view the scenery more closely, rest at will and taste delicacies along the way. What could be happier than that?

Practising and Promoting a Healthy Life

In 2010, he came to the city for the first time as an exchange student at Southwestern University of Finance and Economics and returned to Germany after half a year of study of international trade at the Guanghua campus. Then in October 2011, he came again, this time as an intern assistant of the head of an environmental protection company. Though brief, this period showed great prospects of Chengdu to the discerning and sensitive Erik. So in October 2014, he came to Chengdu for the third time, officially implementing a cooperative project between the Berlin School of Economics and Southwestern University of Finance and Economics, and kicking off his entrepreneurship in Chengdu.

From then on, he has made cycling his No. 1 transportation choice. Whether it is to his Baiguolin office or the one on Hongxing Road, he will hop on his bicycle and, as if it were a workout routine, ride for more than twenty kilometers every day. Cycling is his favorite means of transportation, and so as long as that's possible, he would never consider any other alternative. Travelling through Chengdu on his bike to business and private meetings is the most enjoyable thing for him. And there is a bonus: he has gotten so familiar with the roads of Chengdu that he is even nicknamed the "walking map" by his foreign friends.

Erik is also a member of a special circle that consists of cyclists from Chengdu. Each Friday they will hold a nightly cycling tour where people united by their common interest, get together, hop on their favorite bicycles, and engage in a group street search for beauty that's usually obscured, for the latest trends and for the most secret good food, exploring into the very depth of the city.

Apart from cycling, Erik is also a fan of workouts. He is a member of more than one gym in Chengdu. After a day's busy work, his way to relieve stress is to work out: to enrich his life with sweat. His favorite options include martial arts, swimming, sparring, volleyball, and basketball.

Recently, Erik has become intensely interested in Chinese martial arts, a sport to which he was quite incidentally introduced. Currently, upon the recommendation of a friend from the US, he is learning self-defense techniques at a martial club near Babao Street, which, thanks to his previous study of boxing and Tai Chi, has proven not that difficult, and thus thrilling. Erik plans to learn the higher-level "Chinese Kung Fu" after one or two-year study of self-defense techniques.

It is out of his own love for sports and a healthy life that Erik extends a healthy lifestyle to the whole city through his company. He and his copartner have long been promoting a pro bono program named "Green Monday" across Chengdu, which aims to improve the environment by leading a low-carbon life, and to realize sustainable development of the whole society. Erik sincerely wishes that Chengdu, the Eastern city he loves so much, can become better and better.

Chengdu Makes His Dream Come True

Chengdu appeals to Erik not merely for its scenery, culture and food. What's most important for Erik is that in Chengdu his dreams can come true. Even as early as when he was an intern in the city, he had made his mind to establish his own career in Chengdu, a city that he believed had a promising future for its economy and would witness a boom in many industries, such as finance and e-sports. Indeed, more and more hi-tech companies are springing up around the downtown area, and a number of start-ups and creative ideas are incubated, while many young people have thereby found their callings here. All of these auspicious signs have made Erik even more confident in his future life in Chengdu.

And he is proved to be correct. Starting his career in Chengdu from 2014, he mainly engages in designing all kinds of promotional activities. With a resourceful and active mind, he always has amazing ideas. In June 2017, Erik and the Consulate General of France in Chengdu jointly held the French Summer Solstice Music Festival, also a combination of four grand art activities respectively hosted at Chengdu's Evergrande Square, Capitaland, I-BOX Creativity Garden and Sofitel Chengdu Taihe.

The event gathered a huge lineup of musical stars. The Consulate General of France in Chengdu invited the most popular bands from France and some from other European countries to attend this grand international festival, which also attracted a large number of excellent local bands and musicians. The musicians were thus given a chance to know, to cooperate with and to be amazed by each other. A French musician, after a co-performance with Chengdu bands, got so excited that he told Erik that he had never imagined that there could be such amazing bands and such lively music in Chengdu.

The success of the music festival couldn't have been achieved without the enthusiastic support of the audiences. Free-of-charge, it was attended by about 5,000 Chengdu citizens in only one day. Its four sub-activities with four different themes proved popular with their respective target groups who had different tastes on musical types and bands. When pure European music met Chengdu local music, a miraculous auditory splendor was created. This inspired Erik, who decided to further join hands with the consulate general of his home country Germany in Chengdu and to promote German music across Chengdu.

Erik's work is much more than that. He once worked with the British Chamber of Commerce Southwest China and launched the UK Day and the Global Citizenship Day in Chengdu. He also introduced the globally trendy "Startup Weekend" to Chengdu, helping young people like him with entrepreneurship aspirations and providing experience and advice to startups. Very recently, Erik initiated a program called "SHIFT", which, as its name implies, is meant to make people change their attitude towards life and their lifestyle by promoting a green, healthy life and providing a broad education on fitness and nutrition. So far a group of fitness coaches have joined in this undertaking that aims at the improvement of Chengdu citizens' life and health.

From a student in 2010, to an intern in 2011 and then an entrepreneur in 2014, Erik's identity in Chengdu has changed drastically, and so does his life, social circle and horizons, which have encouraged him even more to carry on with his pursuit of real achievements and doing something for Chengdu. Noticing the city's rapid development, Erik holds that Chengdu, drawing the attention of the whole country and even the entire world, is becoming more internationally influential.

Within this context, Erik found it natural to be grateful and to try to make all things work in favor of his career. Currently, he plans first to expand his company in Chengdu, then taps into neighboring cities like Deyang and Mianyang and also further promoting his "SHIFT" program. In his eyes, Chengdu, Sichuan and even the entire China are all possible markets for his business in two or three years, and he is confident about that.

Learning Cooking from His Caring Girlfriend

At work, Erik is resolute, ambitious and aggressive, while in private, he is a gentle, tender and caring boyfriend. Speaking of his girlfriend, he is all smiles and could hardly conceal his happiness, which is tinted by a sense of pride upon the fact that she is a local Chengduer.

They have been together for two years and the time is as long as his entrepreneurship. They first met because of work. During Christmas of 2014, Erik, still new to Chengdu, planned and organized a Christmas party, which turned out to be the matchmaking event, for it was at this party that the girl, who came with his German friend, caught his attention.

A typical Oriental girl was she, gentle, with yellow skin, black eyes, black hair, and most charmingly, a bright smile. It was a first-sight love story on Erik's part. What's more amazing was that the girl spoke fluent English, ensuring very smooth communication, putting Erik at ease. He began to woo her passionately soon after that, and finally, they had their happy ending.

In the spring of 2016, Erik brought his girlfriend along with him during his trip back to Germany for visa business. To his great joy, the girl was warmly accepted by his family and friends. And they wished them all the best. Erik's girlfriend is six years older than him and has a daughter from her last marriage. She gives homely care and warmth to the lonely Erik, far away from his homeland.

The caring girl makes soups or delicious Chengdu dishes for Erik, largely relieving his homesickness. He has even begun to cook Sichuan food by himself and likes to flaunt his achievements: eggplant with garlic sauce, his favorite dish, cucumbers in sauce, and even dumplings. Usually, he receives cooking lessons from his girlfriend along with her daughter, and whenever this happens, Erik is as happy as a kid. If time allows, Erik and his girlfriend sometimes cook together, make both Western and Chinese food, and create a most romantic world for themselves.

Erik's girlfriend is not only his cooking master, but also his tour guide in Chengdu. Born and bred in Chengdu, the girl knows Chengdu like the back of her hand. She gives Erik such beautiful tours around Chengdu: gazing upon the statue of Zhuge Liang with reverence at the Wuhou Temple, remembering the Poet Du Fu at Du Fu's Thatched Cottage, burning incense and praying at Wenshu Monastery, or sitting beside the peaceful lake of the Huanhuaxi Park, with birds hovering overhead, crowds bustling around, breezes caressing their faces, and feeling beauty and leisure exuding from each pore of the place.

The twenty-eight Erik has a long way to go. But he has already made clear plans, such as making his "SHIFT" program operational in three years, and what's more important, marrying his girlfriend. The pure, beautiful wish of finding the right person and living happily-ever-after transcends national boundaries. Better yet, Chengdu, harmony-oriented and inclusive, is sure to harbor them like a big warm house.

>> 江喃（美国）
"斜杠青年"

Jonathan Kott, USA
A "Slash Youth"

让成都遇上西雅图

玉林，是成都著名的美食聚集区。在玉林路的南街，一家装饰古朴的火锅店门庭若市，门口的人形立牌也十分抢眼。走进店内，香气袅袅，令人垂涎欲滴。环顾四周，大厅被分成许多小隔间，每个都被装饰的具有浓浓的四川风。远处飘来几句纯正的成都话，走近，一个蓝眼睛高鼻梁的老外正热情地招呼着客人。"嗨哥，过来喝一杯噻。""要得！马上哈！"此时的老外正在给服务生交代店内事宜："火锅味道一定要巴适，质量一定要过关。"这位操着正宗成都话的老外就是这家店的老板，名叫江喃，大家都亲切的称呼他为"喃哥"

江喃出生于美国西雅图，来成都已经有 19 个年头了。当时，他还是一个叫 Jonathan 的小伙子。从美国西雅图一路"飞"到成都的 Jonathan，对这个向往已久的地方，期待不已。当时的双流机场并没有现在这样的规模，成都二环之外全都是田坝坝。可对这个身高 1.87 米、满头金黄鬈发的"老外"来说，这里的一切都是心中期待的样子。

因为喜欢道教、佛学，Jonathan 给自己取了个好听的中文名字：江喃。"江"与英文名中 Jon 相近，且他崇尚的道教文化重视"水"。而"喃"的意思是自言自语，慢慢说，他就是这样练成都话的。而且佛教文化常常用"喃"，代表着循序渐进不急不躁的人生态度。

江喃第一次来到成都，是 1998 年 1 月，作为交换生来到四川大学进行阶段性学习。选择来成都上学的理由很简单，因为从小受父母的影响，他喜欢吃辣，对成都的第一印象，就是这里的"辣"。半年的学习，让江喃渐渐爱上了这座城市。

在美国完成大学学业后的江喃，于 1999 年再次回到成都，因为这里有他放不下的生活，还有他心心念念的成都历史文化、人文风情、美景美食等。

再次踏进这片土地，江南没有直接学习汉语普通话，反而把兴趣放在成都方言上。被成都方言吸引的他，喜欢去各个老茶馆，跟地道的老成都人聊天。那段时间，他上午去茶馆喝茶，与成都本地的老年人学习成都话，吃完午饭后继续来茶馆，听他们聊天。

正是这种特殊的学习方式，让江喃的成都话突飞猛进。他身边的朋友都说，跟江喃摆龙门阵是最巴适的，因为他那一口地道的成都话听起来让人感到尤为亲切。每次说话，总会带上一些特有的成都人才会用的字眼"嗻""嘛""喃"。"等一呵儿""咋个回事嘛""要的欢""安逸""巴适惨了"等四川话四六级的基本词汇，这些外地人轻易掌握不好的词在江喃那里总是能够信手拈来。

江喃曾说，他眼中的成都有三美：美食、美酒、美景。

珍馐之选

近 20 年的成都生活，让江喃不仅练就了一口地道的方言，还和川菜结下了不解之缘。其实当时在美国读大学时，江喃的研究方向是中国文化。他来中国当交换生时有两个学校可以选择，一个是四川大学，一个是中山大学，因为四川有自己爱吃的辣椒，于是他毫不犹豫地选择了成都。

因为美食，江喃留在了成都，后来参加《辣王争霸赛》，吃了 50 几根朝天椒的江喃一战成名，有了"四川辣王"美誉。也因为这张"好吃嘴"，江喃慢慢混出了名气，干脆当上了美食节目的主持人。

做美食节目期间，江喃也尝遍了四川美食，用他自己的话说："吃过许多的火锅，却对成都的火锅情有独钟。"他还仔细研究成都火锅与重庆火锅的区别：重庆火锅猛烈、干辣，成都火锅不仅辣而且又香又麻。

江喃是一个不折不扣的"吃货"，在他眼中，"辣"是刺激，"麻"是鲜香，麻与辣是一种奇妙的组合，它们的相遇使味蕾与神经发出电光火石般的碰撞。

凭借着对成都火锅透彻的研究以及对健康饮食的追求，江喃决定开一家地道的成都火锅店。经过了几个月的试锅，江喃渐渐探索出了自己的火锅底料配方。每天下午，店员们会将一大麻袋的红辣椒，放入特制的大铁锅，小火微炒，待表面些许焦脆，并散发出香辣味，再放入簸箕里凉凉，入夜，抓上一大把往亮澄澄的汤中一撒，香辣味与汤底相融，整个城市笼罩在浓郁的火锅辣味里。

吃完火锅后，来上一杯淡淡的苦荞茶是最合适不过的了。江喃对中国的茶文化亦是非常迷恋。周末，他会到茶馆里喝茶聊天，在他的家中也收藏着几套精美的茶具。每当有人来家里做客，他会给客人展示自己娴熟的泡茶手艺。壶托在他的手指尖，轻巧得如一张薄纸，左手中指按住壶钮，水流悠然而下。一枚枚芽叶缓缓潜沉至杯底再渐渐浮出，顺着水流的方向摇曳飘送，三沉三浮，茶叶微卷，就像是捏起的小皱褶。

每年江喃都会带着火锅底料和他珍藏的茶叶回到西雅图，和家人一起吃一顿地道的火锅。同样"无辣不欢"的父亲，曾开玩笑地对江喃说："如果不带火锅底料就不要回来了。"可见这一家人对成都美食的喜爱，也难怪江喃打算把地道的火锅开回西雅图，来个真资格的"成都遇上西雅图"！

宴酣之乐

"酒逢知己千杯少"，江喃和朋友们在一起时，总会小酌两杯。酒是人类生活中的主要饮料之一，中国制酒，源远流长，品种繁多，名酒荟萃，享誉中外。白酒是中国人饮用的主要酒类，渗透于整个中华几千年的文明史中，从文学艺术创作、文化娱乐到饮食烹饪、养生保健等各方面，酒都占有重要的地位。成都的酒文化也有着悠久的历史，老东门大桥外的水井坊，是一座元明清三代川酒老烧坊的遗址，又被称作世界上最古老的酿酒作坊。

来成都之前，江喃从未品尝过白酒。可如今他不仅喜欢喝白酒，啤酒更是深得他心。被誉为"液体面包"的啤酒，在人们的日常生活中起着不可替代的作用，有了它人们的生活变得丰富起来。

江喃说，随着经济的发展，成都的精酿啤酒文化日益流行，人们越来越追求健康，追求品质。喝酒，不再是一种应酬，而是一种享受。

秀丽风光

当然，江喃除了吃，还有另外一个爱好就是摄影。来成都的第二年他就在这里安了家，一有空闲就出去摄影，拍成都的古树、古街和古镇。2005 年，江喃的摄影文化交流公司在美国开业，他准备将所有作品展现在自己的同胞面前，让美国、让世界认识中国、了解成都。

刚从四姑娘山拍摄回来的江喃，对那里的景色赞不绝口。其实，在这里生活的十几年里，他早已踏遍四川的大小山川，领略过无数的秀丽风景，都江堰、青城山、峨眉山等早已布满了他的脚印。不同的时节去不同的地方，一本书、一杯茶、一个人，将这青山碧水拥入怀中，足矣。

雾气迷蒙，水天一色。高山，是那么巍峨而高耸，湖水，是那么清澈而透亮，心境，是那么悠闲而自在。

"你站在桥上看风景，看风景的人在楼上看你。明月装饰了你的窗子，你装饰了别人的梦。"江喃将他看到的风景留住了，每到一处，就将那里的人文风情刻在了相机里，装进了心里。四下无人的街头，他能够欣赏；人头攒动的闹市，他也能记录。在他的眼里，每个角落都有独特的美，即使是墙边不起眼的小草，他也能发现其顽强的生命力。

旅行，就是在地图上的一个点，留下自己的脚印，然后慢慢回忆和品味。旅行，就是体验不同的地域文化，风土人情，那里有着别样的生存方式，有着别样的人生所构成的多姿多彩的文化。

或许，这就是江喃眼中旅行的意义吧。

江喃说，成都是他见过变化最快的城市。"我刚来那哈儿，成都没得三环的，二环以外全是田坝坝。"江喃的方言总是逗得人忍俊不禁："还有那哈儿成都的楼房都只有三四楼，最多就是五六楼嘛，哪儿像现在哦，那么多电梯公寓。当时买房买一整栋就好了。"

确实，世纪之交时的成都，陈旧、古朴，却又蕴含着一股躁动，房子就那么一点高，楼宇稀稀落落，路窄人瘦。那时的双流机场也还很小，二环路外还是郊区，三环外，还可以种瓜种豆种油菜。在江喃的记忆中，那时的川大和成都科大还没有合并，两校间有条文化路，路上有许多美食和茶馆，深受两校学生的欢迎。但那时的成都远没有如今繁华。

现在的成都，高楼如雨后春笋般密密麻麻地拔地而起。太古里、IFS的建立，成都在形成一个又一个的商业圈。车辆如流的街道，人影拥挤。每一张缀满青春容颜的脸上，都是激情，都彰显着每一个生命的活力。

见证了成都的飞速发展，江喃最喜欢的是成都与重庆之间的高铁，因为对于游走在两个城市工作的他来说，高铁是最便捷的交通工具，"中国的高铁技术比美国先进多了"。

不过，他也偶尔会吐槽，比如当前大热的共享单车。"有一天我从重庆回成都，已经很晚了，就想骑车回家。扫码后要注册，可是我是外国人，要注册护照信息，我等了很久，直到第二天上午10点才收到注册成功的信息，可那时候我已经把APP卸载了。"

其实江喃很喜欢骑车，从小是参加山地车比赛长大的。江喃说，骑车是一种有氧运动，骑在车上你会感觉十分自由且畅快无比。在江喃心中，自行车不再只是一种代步工具，更是愉悦心灵的方式。来到成都后他也没有放弃这个爱好，一有空就骑车环游，成都周边的大大小小山地都留下了江喃的身影。

除了骑车，他也酷爱跑步。在奔跑的过程中，听着鞋子摩擦地面的沙沙声，感觉细细密密的汗珠一点点沁满额头，然后放任汗水在背上静静地流淌。沐浴着清晨的第一缕阳光，贪婪地吮吸着青草的芳香，感受着露珠的生机，给生命添一抹亮丽的色彩。跑步是一个过程，一个享受的过程。

2016年3月，江喃第一次参加马拉松半程比赛，二十多公里的路程，有欣喜愉悦，也有疲惫困顿，每跑一步每过一段都是不同的风景，每个足迹都被汗水浸染，每一次都是人生的历练。

比赛至少半年前，他就开始做准备工作了。"LSD"，长距离慢跑是他最常用的训练方法，他每周坚持跑步十公里以上，即使成都的夏天烈日炎炎，他挥汗如雨，却仍然不放弃。他说，人生就像一场马拉松，不在于跑得快，而在于跑得远。

江喃前几年还拜了巴蜀笑星李伯清为师，拜师学艺后便搞了一系列演出，不少人开始称他"成都大山"。江喃笑着说："我不是大山，大山只有一个，江喃也只有一个。我学习的目的是为了宣扬巴蜀文化。"

现在，这个美国小伙子走到大街上早已是个名人。"让我感到变化最大的是，刚来的时候，路上碰到的行人看到我，隔到多远就会像看到啥子稀奇一样喊：'快看，老外！老外！'让我觉得自己像个异类一样。现在，我走到街上，大家都笑着喊我'喃哥'，还多热情地跑过来和我摆龙门阵，让我觉得自己变成了一个真正的成都人，越留越不想走了。"从这一点看来，成都的魅力似乎一点都不输西雅图，不是么？

When Chengdu Meets Seattle

Yulin is a famous gourmet block in Chengdu. In the southern part of Yulin Road, a rustically decorated hot pot restaurant with an eye-catching poster at the door is crowded with customers. Walk inside and you'll sense the tempting aroma that makes your mouth water. Look around and you will find the restaurant divided into many small and enclosed areas, each showcasing a strong Sichuan decorative style. Someone's greeting guests in Chengdu dialect. Getting closer you'll see a foreigner with blue eyes and a high nose. "Brother Nan, come and have a glass of wine." "On my way!" He is giving directions to the waiters: "The taste of the hot pot has to be the best and the ingredients have to be of top quality." This foreigner, who speaks authentic Chengdu dialect, is the owner of the restaurant. He is Jonathan Kott, affectionately called "Brother Nan" by locals.

Jonathan was born in Seattle, USA, and has been in Chengdu for 19 years. At that time, he was still a young man named Jonathan, who "flew" all the way from Seattle in the United States to Chengdu, a city he had been longing for. Shuangliu International Airport was much smaller at the time. Crop fields were everywhere outside of the second ring road of Chengdu. For this 1.87-meter-tall "foreigner" with golden curly hair, everything here was what he had hoped for.

Obsessed with Taoism and Buddhism, Jonathan named himself Jiang Nan. "Jiang" means river. It sounds similar to the English pronunciation of Jon.

And Taoism, his favorite, greatly values water. "Nan" means talking slowly to oneself. This is how he learned Chengdu dialect. "Nan" is also frequently used in Buddhism and it represents a gradual and patient attitude to life.

Jonathan Kott first came to Chengdu in January 1998 as an exchange student at Sichuan University for a short-term study. His reason to study in Chengdu was simple. Influenced by his parents, he loves spicy food. His first impression of Chengdu was "spicy". After six months of study, Jonathan gradually fell in love with this city.

In 1999, after the completion of his university study in the United States, Jonathan Kott returned to Chengdu because of the life, history, culture, customs, beauty, and delicacies of this city.

When he once again set foot on this land, Jonathan did not go for Mandarin Chinese. He was keen on Chengdu dialect. Obsessed with Chengdu dialect, he liked to visit old teahouses and chat with the locals. During that time, he went to the teahouse in the morning to have tea and picked up the dialect from the elderly in Chengdu. After lunch, he went back and listened to their conversations.

It was this unique way of learning that has allowed Jonathan to make great strides. His friends say that it is always a pleasure to chat with Jonathan because his authentic Chengdu dialect sounds particularly cordial. Whenever he speaks, he uses modal particles such as "sai", "ma" and "nan", which are known by locals. Jonathan has a considerably large vocabulary of Chengdu dialect. He has been even well-versed in some expressions that are difficult for people from other parts of China.

Jonathan Kott once said that in his view Chengdu has three most precious things: food, alcohol, and scenery.

Delicions Food

Nearly 20 years in Chengdu has not only enabled Jonathan to speak fluent Chengdu dialect, it has also forged close ties between him and Sichuan cuisine. In fact, when studying in the United States, Jonathan majored in Chinese culture. Before coming to China as an exchange student, he had two options: Sichuan University and Sun Yat-Sen University. Sichuan had his favorite chilies, so he chose Chengdu without hesitation.

Jonathan stayed in Chengdu because of delicious food. Later he participated in the "Spicy King Tournament", and was immediately known for eating over 50 pod peppers. He won the title "Spicy King of Sichuan". Also, because of this "greedy mouth", Jonathan gained recognition and became the host of food shows.

Jonathan tasted all of Sichuan's delicacies when he hosted food shows. In his words: "I have eaten a lot of hot pot, but fallen in love only with Chengdu hot pot." He also studied the difference between Chengdu hot pot and Chongqing hot pot: Chongqing hot pot is of strong spicy flavor, while Chengdu hot pot is not only spicy but also fragrant and pungent.

Jonathan is a total "foodie". In his eyes, "spicy" means excitement, "pungent" means fragrance. They are a wonderful combination and their encounter stimulates taste buds and nerves.

As a result of his thorough study of Chengdu hot pot and his pursuit of a healthy diet, Jonathan decided to open an authentic Chengdu hot pot restaurant. After several months of tests, Jonathan figured out his own hot pot recipe. Every afternoon, a big sack of red peppers would be put into a special large iron pot and then fried over small fire until the surface becomes slightly crispy and emits spicy flavor. Then they are placed in a dustpan to cool. At night, add some of these cooled down chili into the shiny soup. The chili flavor blends with the soup, and the whole city is shrouded in a strong spicy fragrance.

A cup of buckwheat tea after hotpot is perfect. Jonathan Kott is also quite obsessed with Chinese tea culture. On weekends, he will chat in the teahouses, and has several beautiful tea sets at home. Whenever a guest comes, he will show them his masterful tea making skills. The jug holder at his fingertips is as light as a thin piece of paper. When his left-hand's middle finger presses the jug button, water flows down leisurely. Tender tea leaves slowly sink to the bottom of the cup and then gradually emerge, dancing to the ripples in the cup. After sinking and surfacing three times, tea leaves would get slightly curled, like small wrinkles.

Every year, Jonathan goes back to Seattle with some hot pot ingredients and tea that he has collected. It is a good idea to eat authentic hot pot with family. His father also likes spicy food. He once joked: "Never come back without hot pot ingredients." How this family has loved Chengdu food! No wonder Jonathan plans to open an authentic hot pot restaurant back in Seattle. That'll be a real scenario of "Chengdu meets Seattle"!

Wonderful Alcohol

"Even a thousand shots will not suffice when drinking with congenial friends." Jonathan will always have a few shots when he is with friends. Alcohol is one major beverage in human life. With a long history and a wide variety, Chinese Alcohol is famous at home and abroad. Spirits are one of the main drinks consumed by the Chinese people, and they have penetrated the entire Chinese civilization for thousands of years. Spirits play an important role in everything from literary and art work to cultural entertainment, cuisine, and health care. Chengdu's alcohol culture also has a long history. Swellfun beyond the old Dongmen Bridge is the site of an ancient Sichuan spirits brewery that dates back to the Yuan, Ming, and Qing dynasties. It is also known as the oldest alcohol workshop in the world.

Before coming to Chengdu, Jonathan had never tried Chinese spirits. But now not only has he fallen in love with Chinese spirits, he has also been obsessed with Chinese beer. Known as "liquid bread", beer plays an irreplaceable role in the people's daily life. It has enriched our life.

Jonathan said that with the development of the economy, craft beer culture has become increasingly popular in Chengdu. People have begun to seek healthy lifestyle and quality of life. People no longer drink purely for the sake of business or courtesy, but also for pleasure and enjoyment.

Beautiful Scenery

In addition to seeking good food, Jonathan has another hobby, photography. He took up residence in Chengdu the second year after arrival. Once he has spare time he likes to go out for photography, taking pictures of ancient trees, streets and towns. In 2005, Jonathan started his photographic cultural exchange company in the United States. He intended to show all his works in front of his own countrymen so that the United States and the world would get to know China and learn about Chengdu.

When Jonathan came back from Mount Siguniang, he kept mentioning its beauty. In fact, he has been to Sichuan's vast mountains and rivers and enjoyed countless beautiful landscapes since he came over 10 years ago. He has left footprints in Dujiangyan, Qingcheng Mountain and Mount Emei. He went to different places in different seasons. A book, a cup of tea with beauty of the green mountains and blue waters, there's no need to ask for more.

Amid mist, the waters and skies merge in one color. Towering mountains, clear lakes, and a quiet state of the mind—one couldn't be cozier.

"On the bridge you enjoy the view. Up in high lands sightseers look at you. The bright moon lights your window a gleam. You shine in other's dream." Jonathan has managed to keep the scenery he has seen stay. Wherever he goes, he records history, culture and customs on his camera and puts them into his heart. He finds beauty on empty streets, and he captures the crowded downtown area on camera. In his eyes, every corner has it's unique beauty. Even the grass at the foot of a wall reveals infinite vitality.

Travel means leaving your footprints on a point on the map and then recalling the precious moments. Travel means experiencing different regional cultures and customs. You can always find a different way of life and a colorful culture.

Perhaps that's what traveling is all about in Jonathan's eyes.

Jonathan Kott said Chengdu is the fastest changing city he has ever seen. "When I first came to Chengdu, it did not have the third ring road. Fields were seen everywhere outside of the second ring road." Jonathan's dialect is always amusing. "At that time, buildings in Chengdu had only three or four floors. The highest building had only five to six floors at most. Well, there are many elevator apartments now. I should have bought a whole building at that time."

Chengdu was really outdated and old at the turn of the century. But it had a hidden restlessness. The houses were low and the buildings were sparsely scattered on a landscape of narrow empty streets. At that time, Shuangliu Airport was very small. Outside of the Second Ring Road was sheer wilderness. You could grow crops outside the Third Ring Road. In Jonathan's memory, Sichuan University and Chengdu University of Science and Technology were not yet merged. There was a cultural road between the two universities with many delicacies and teahouses along the road. They were greatly welcomed by students from both schools. By then Chengdu was far less prosperous.

Today, high-rises are springing up like mushroom. Taikoo Li, IFS— business districts are emerging in big numbers. Vehicles flood into the streets. Wherever you go, you see energetic people full of vitality and passion.

Jonathan Kott has witnessed the rapid development of Chengdu. He is particularly obsessed with the Chengdu-Chongqing high-speed rail. That is the most convenient means of transport for people working in two cities at the same time. "China's high-speed rail technology is far more advanced than that of the United States."

However, he occasionally lashes out at things that he does not approve of, such as bike sharing, which is a very hot topic nowadays. "One day I came back to Chengdu from Chongqing. It was already late and I wanted to go home by bike. Passport registration is required after QR code scanning because I am a foreigner. I didn't receive the confirmation until 10 am the next morning. I had already uninstalled the app by then."

In fact, Jonathan likes cycling and has continued to participate in mountain cycling competitions since he was young. Jonathan Kott said cycling is an aerobic sport and when you ride a bike you feel free and fantastic. For Jonathan, bicycles are no longer just a means of transport; they are also a way to delight the soul. He did not quit this hobby after his arrival in Chengdu. Whenever he has time, he cycles and leaves his footprints on the hills around Chengdu.

In addition to cycling, he loves running too. When running, he hears the rustle of his shoes rubbing against the ground; he feels the tiny beads of sweat coming up little by little on his forehead; and he feels the sweat quietly pouring down on his back. He bathes in the first wisp of sunshine in the morning; breathes in the fragrance of the grass and feels the vitality of dewdrops. Running is such an enjoyment.

In March 2016, Jonathan participated in a half marathon competition for the first time. It was a journey of more than 20 kilometers. There were joys as well as exhaustion. He saw different views along the way. Every step was soaked in sweat and was a test of his perseverance.

At least six months before the game, he began to prepare. "LSD", or long distance jogging, is his most commonly used method of training. He runs more than 10 kilometers per week, even during hot summer days in Chengdu. He sweats and toils but never stops. He says life is like a marathon. Speed is not what matters but perseveranceis.

A couple of years ago, Jonathan was a student of Sichuanese comedian Li Boqing. After the apprenticeship ended, he participated in some performances and many began to call him "Chengdu Dashan". Jonathan Kott said with a smile: "I am not Dashan. Dashan is unique and I am unique. The purpose of my study is to promote Bashu culture."

Now this young American is already a celebrity. "The biggest change I've felt is that when I first arrived, the pedestrians I met on the road would shout 'Look, foreigner! Foreigner!' as if they found something extremely unusual. I felt like an alien. Now, everyone on the street smiles and greets me with 'Brother Nan', and some even come all the way to chat with me. Now I feel like I'm a local. The longer I stay, the more reluctant I am to leave." Chengdu is no less attractive than Seattle, is it?

乐·享在成都

>> 董威廉（荷兰）
荷兰贸易促进会成都代表处首席代表

William van Tongeren, the Netherlands

Chief Representative at Netherlands

Business Support office (NBSO) Chengdu

来到成都　得偿所愿

　　不同于冬暖夏凉的荷兰，这里没有蜿蜒到天边的海堤，这里没有随处可见的风车，这里同样也没有芬芳诱人的郁金花香。在成都这座城市看到的是芙蓉锦绣花开暖，看到的是蓉城细雨恋过客，看到的是银杏叶落满城金。

　　在成都锦江区东御街非常繁华的一段路上，有一座大厦格外显眼。来自荷兰的董威廉就在这里工作。从 2016 年起作为荷兰贸易促进会成都代表处首席代表，他有大半的时间会在这里见客人、聊生意，或者是做一些别的事。然而不论做的是什么事，他都乐在其中，用他的话讲，他享受成都生活的每一个瞬间。

用最快的速度适应成都

　　如果你见到董威廉，便会发觉他是一位极亲切又妥帖的绅士，似乎与网络资料中显示的内容不太一样。资料中，有时董威廉是极其正经又严肃的。作为首席代表的他，总是西装革履地游刃于各大宴会之间。有时的董威廉，是个纯粹的语言高手，精通英文、中文和荷兰语，还能熟练地使用日语、德语和法语。总之董威廉有一种能力，可以让每一位和他交往过的客人，都能被他的干练所吸引。他与人交谈时，总是讲着一口流利的英文，握手时从来不用力却又礼貌非常……他总是喜欢穿极简单的纯色衬衣，衬得他白皙的皮肤更白了，金发碧眼，眼睛深邃，他本人非常爱笑，不是含蓄一笑，而是每到激烈讨论时都会爆发出阵阵大笑，在座的人无一会被他的爽朗和亲切打动。

最令人印象深刻的是他的一口流利中文。除了能进行日常的对话之外，他还能分清平翘舌和四种声调，不知这在外国人里算不算是出色，毕竟连很多成都人讲话时都会分不清平翘舌。谈到有关于自己"出神入化"的中文能力，他显然有些害羞，但同时表示他不太接受语言天赋这个说法。他时常听别人夸赞他的中文好，又或者是说他学语言特别有天赋，云云。但是他背地里究竟花了多少时间，又有谁知道呢？在学中文这件事上，董威廉其实付出了大量时间和精力，早在荷兰读大学时，他就花了两年时间深入学习中文，而后又到北京语言大学进修一年，这一切奠定了他说一口流利中文的基础，但彼时，他还不知道自己会有一天去中国生活工作。现在看来，董威廉当初选择中文似乎是对了，因为缘分使然，他竟然来到中国成都开始他人生中的一段重要历程。

许多外国人到成都之后面临的第一个问题就是饮食差异，但这个问题在董威廉身上不存在，对于成都饮食的辣，董威廉显然适应得非常好。他平常就比较喜欢吃辣，最喜欢吃的是肥肠粉，他总是会告诉自己的朋友肥肠有一种很特别的味道。他也可以接受脑花，只是觉得味道一般，跟豆腐差不多，与肥肠比少了一种好吃的味道。董威廉对于自己喜欢肥肠，无惧脑花的特殊饮食爱好，表现得十分镇定，就如同在谈论今天的天气一样。可是天知道，这两种特殊的食物连许多本地人也不一定能吃得惯。用董威廉自己的话来说，在某种程度上，自己可以算是一位资深的成都"吃货"，而成为一名合格成都"吃货"，对他来讲也是件幸福的事，毕竟这样容易让他感觉到自己离成都这座城市更近了一步。

成都是座令人好奇的城市

这个眼睛深邃的外国人，总是非常乐意和他人分享自己内心的一些东西。董威廉为自己列有一份"Bucket list"，中文叫"遗愿清单"，内容是他去世前一定要做的事，一定要去的地方，等等。然而对于他来说，来到成都，这份"Bucket list"实现的可能性便大打折扣，因为对成都的眷恋让他不忍离开这座城市去做其他的事情。有一部摩根·弗里曼主演的电影，也叫作《Bucket list》，电影讲的是得了癌症的两个老头在临死之前完成他们的心愿单，所以电影除了"遗愿清单"这个译名，还有另外一个译名"一路玩到挂"。中国人从不会随意地谈论自己的生与死，因为几乎所有人对于死，都是畏惧的。除了一些年老的人会逐渐考虑到自己的身后事，年轻人是真没有心思去关注"死"之前要做些什么。但西方人不一样，他们异常坦然地规划着死之前一定要做什么事情。董威廉就不畏惧死亡，他总是开玩笑，说他就算在成都安息也是个不错的选择。虽然这样的话听起来不那么吉利，但这也让人充分感受到董威廉对成都是真爱吧？他也为生活在成都的自己列了这样一个清单：宽窄巷子、锦里、琴台路，这些地方第一次来的人都会去，还有洛带古镇，这里好玩的特别多，而他也会带他初到成都的外国朋友们去这些地方。

到成都工作生活的时间还不满一年，但是对于董威廉来说，这不足一年的时间已经让他感受到，他一直都在变化当中，变得越来越像成都人。譬如说他在出行方式上的变化，刚刚来到中国的时候，他一般选择的交通方式是公交、地铁或者出租车，但是现在他又学会了一样，就是软件叫车。他甚至能在滴滴的各种功能中熟练切换，因工作需要去接荷兰商人的时候可以预订 7 座的商务车、不小心忘记了护照却又不得不去外地可以求助顺风车，俨然一副"我是本地人"的表情。

工作让他焕发新生

　　说起董威廉与成都的缘分，颇有几分命中注定的意味。早些年，董威廉在鹿特丹学习中文时，就一直想找一个机会到中国工作。曾经他在中国的联络人，也是他现在的同事，给他提供了一个工作机会，而工作地点就是在成都。在来到成都之前，有很多朋友给他推荐过成都这座城市，说这里空气湿润、气候适宜、食物美味、人也热情，经济发展得也不错。董威廉自己倒是没有太多顾虑，凭借着自己的一腔热血，义无反顾的来了自己梦寐以求的工作地——成都。

　　来到成都后的这份工作让董威廉十分满意。荷兰贸促会主要是为荷兰的中小企业提供服务，同时也帮助成都的中小企业走出国门。作为荷兰贸易促进会成都代表处首席代表，董威廉虽然会在工作中遇到各种各样的难题，每天都会遇见不同的人，每一天都会遇到诸多挑战，但是他坚信办法总会有的，他始终在用自己的努力和真诚为中外企业服务，因为他能深刻感受到，他现在做的工作是对中荷两国都有好处的，是能够实实在在的帮助中荷两国商人的。就是这样的一个信念，让他感觉无论工作多么辛苦都值得。很多时候，他能够收获别人的笑容和感谢，也让他更加肯定了了自己的价值所在。

　　也许这种挑战自我的性格和他以前的工作经历有关。董威廉曾经在新加坡从事金融方面的工作，主要负责的是原油石油的买卖等，大部分时间都在和数字、屏幕、资料打交道，这些东西都是冷冰冰的，没有与人相处的真实感。而对于董威廉自己来说，他更喜欢和人交往，喜欢与人相处，而不是数字或者屏幕。所以在成都的这份工作就显得格外适合他，而他也确实做得很出色。就在 2016 年底，成都荷兰日活动顺利举行，董威廉所在的荷兰贸促会成都代表处作为该活动的主办方之一，联合了近 20 家荷兰企业，在成都远洋太古里地铁广场以"游园嘉年华"

的形式，让成都市民全方位体验荷兰生活，更携手 IF 艺孚时尚艺术，邀请成都本土设计师，买手店、商业综合体负责人等时尚界人士，共同举办交流活动，让荷兰时尚设计无缝对接成都市场，为成都与荷兰的时尚交流开拓新的尝试与模式。

因为找到了喜欢并为之奋斗的事业，董威廉的空闲时间明显变得很少。他每一天的时间都安排得很满。作为荷兰贸易促进会成都处首席代表，做每一个项目前，他一定会亲自去考察、去核实。只有这样踏踏实实地工作，当别人问起他成都任何一处的情况，他才可以讲述得头头是道。

荷兰是心之所系

当然，董威廉也有不专心工作的时候。闲暇之余，他会经常思念自己的家乡和亲人。作为一个孝顺的儿子，以往每年的圣诞节他都一定要回国跟父母一起过。就跟中国人的守岁一样，他对父母的爱也是如此深沉。因为他的爸爸妈妈退休了，平时也非常想念威廉，希望儿子能陪在他们身边。所以，即使每一天都恨不得掰成 48 小时用的董威廉，也一定会腾出圣诞节的时间陪伴父母。有趣的是，他还会经常调皮的扳着指头认真数数自己回荷兰的次数。在董威廉看来，在荷兰家中，同父母一起过圣诞节，是令他倍感温暖的事情。

董威廉的家乡不是荷兰那些著名的大城市，而是荷兰的一座名叫豪达的小城。那里盛产一种奶酪，品相上等，口感甚佳，畅销世界各地。董威廉经常会向周边的朋友推荐一些荷兰很适合旅游的景点。第一次去荷兰的人可以去大城市，类似于鹿特丹、阿姆斯特丹等，但在董威廉看来，如果想要来一场特别一点的旅行，可以选择去羊角村，这个小镇四面环水，雾气缭绕，一栋栋极具欧式风情的小屋就矗立在河水的中央。

当谈起旅游时，若不是你能看到他一身西装革履，还以为是一名拿着导游旗的小贩在向游客推销景点。

成都让他遇到良眷

如今，董威廉不只喜欢上了成都这座城市，他还喜欢上了一位成都女孩。董威廉口中的她符合自己现阶段对于爱情的一切幻想，她会讲一些英文，有一些国外生活的经历，同时还聪明、美丽、体贴。如果有时间，他们会在入夜时分到成都的街头走一走，聊一聊白天发生的故事和见过的人。有时他们还会结伴去城北一个叫 Wonderland 的地方，董威廉很喜欢在那里打乒乓球和台球。来到成都，他喜欢上了和女朋友一起去 KTV，谁也不会想到，这个荷兰人，唱得最拿手的竟然是刘德华的歌。

如今，董威廉已经逐渐习惯了这座城市华灯初上的喧嚣，空气中弥漫着的火锅味儿，老茶馆里一盏茶可以眯一个下午的安逸日子。如今，他让我们知道荷兰除了阿姆斯特丹和鹿特丹，还有一个叫羊角镇的人间仙境。他也让我们知道，一个外国人想要在陌生的中国城市生活和工作，要遭遇多少的新奇和挑战。

成都，对于董威廉而言，既是工作所在的城市，又是最令他感到温暖的城市。因为在成都，有他志同道合的朋友，有他温柔缱绻的爱人，当然，还有他的梦想在这里生根发芽。

A Fruitful Life in Chengdu

Unlike the distinctly seasonal Netherlands, and without the endlessly meandering seawalls, the ever-present windmills, or the tantalizingly fragrant tulips, Chengdu presents a unique look that consists of blossoming hibiscus flowers in the spring, rainy days in the summer and golden carpets of ginkgo leaves during the cold seasons.

Along the busy Dongyu Street, Jinjiang District, Chengdu, lies a striking building where our hero today—William van Tongeren—works. Since 2016, as the chief representative of the Chengdu Representative Office of the Netherlands Council for Trade Promotion (NCH), William spends most of his time meeting guests in this building, talking about business or handling other affairs. The truth is that, whatever he does here, he just loves it. In his own words, he is enjoying every moment of his life in Chengdu.

Do as the Romans Do

Everyone finds William a very amiable and decent gentleman when sees him in person. While, in striking contrast, his online image is rather serious. This chief representative of the NCH, decently attired, makes his way through one banquet after another with ease. Sometimes, he turns into a language genius, an expert of English, Chinese and Dutch, and a proficient speaker of Japanese, German and French. In general, there is a kind of professionalism in William that appeals to everyone who has met him. He speaks fluent English and shakes hands with people with appropriate strength. He wears a simple solid-color shirt, which makes his complexion even fairer. With golden hair and deep blue eyes, he is easy to laugh—not with gentle smiles, but with violent fits of laughter that punctuates intense discussions. Everyone's infected by his cheerfulness.

The most impressive thing about him is his fluent Chinese. Not limited to daily talks, he explores still further to distinguish between blade-alveolar and cacuminal and among the four Chinese tones. It is amazing, given that even a lot of Chengduers have difficulty in separating blade-alveolar from cacuminal. He becomes shy when his Chinese is praised as "superb", declining the "title"as a genius in language. Praise on his Chinese or his gift for language learning is lavish, but not many know how much effort William has made for his Chinese study. For him, Chinese learning has always been time-and-energy-consuming. He first spent two years on it at university in the Netherlands, and then he further studied the language at Beijing Language and Culture University for one year, which laid the foundation for his fluent Chinese later on. But he never imagined that he could work and live in China one day. As if designed by fate, his Chinese finally served its purpose when he came to Chengdu and kicked off another new chapter of his life.

New-coming foreigners in Chengdu might easily get frustrated by food. But for William that is never a problem. He naturally takes to the spicy food in Chengdu. Normally a spicy-food fan, he loves Pig's Large Intestines with Noodles the best. The pigs' large intestines, as he tells his friends, have a very special flavor. And the Roasted Pig Brains is also OK for him, except that it is mediocre in taste, kind of like beancurd, and less delicious than intestines.

William is very calm when showing his delight for the pig's intestines and acceptance of pig brains as food, as if he were just talking about the weather. And to think that even the locals sometimes abhor these two "special delicacies", he is, in his own words, a sort of qualified "foodie", which is a happy thing for him, since this brings him much closer to the city.

A City Worth Exploring

This foreign guy with deep blue eyes never minds opening his heart and sharing his innermost thoughts. He has made himself a "Bucket List", meaning "a list of things that one wishes to do and places one must go to before death." However, possibilities for carrying out his list might be hugely reduced here in Chengdu, for he could hardly bear leaving the city. There is also a movie called "Bucket List", starring by Morgan Freeman, which tells a story of two terminally-ill old men carrying out their lists of wishes. Hence there is another Chinese name for it: "Playing until Death". Chinese people may not speak of death at ease, for death haunts us all. Chinese youth rarely think about their wishes before death, and only a few of the elderly have to come to consider it. But Western people are different. They plan things that have to be done before death with a light heart, as is seen in William, who is fearless of death, and jokes it around, saying that it is not bad to rest forever in Chengdu. Ominous as it might sound, his love for Chengdu is undeniable. He has also made a list of his favorite hang-outs: Kuanzhai Alleys, Jinli Street, Qintai Road, etc., all worthy of a second visit. There is also the ancient town of Luodai, boasting a large number of fun places. This is the list he refers to when he shows his newly arrived friends around Chengdu.

Though one year has hardly passed since he came to Chengdu, William says that this period of time is quite enough for him to change into another person, a real Chengduer. For example, he used to depend on buses, subways or taxis, but now he has another choice—the e-hailing apps like didi, which offers him flexible alternatives: a seven-seat commercial vehicle to pick up business guests from the Netherlands, or didi carpooling under emergency circumstances when he loses his passport but needs to go to other places. He is so familiar with this kind of stuff as if he were a local.

The Invigorating and Inspiring Job

The story between William and Chengdu is kind of predestined. As early as he was learning Chinese in Rotterdam, he had been dreaming of working in China. Then someone in China, now his colleague, contacted him and offered him a job in Chengdu, a city which had already been recommended to him by several of his friends. For William, it was humid, climatically comfortable, with delicious food, friendly people, and good economy. Without thinking too much about how things will be, William, armed with enthusiasm and ambition, wasted no time in setting out for his dream workplace: Chengdu.

The job proved satisfying. NCH mainly serves small and medium-sized enterprises from the Netherlands, as well as those from Chengdu who wish to go global. As the chief representative of NCH in Chengdu, he never spends a day without being challenged by all kinds of problems and people. But he firmly believes in the possibility of solutions and makes endless efforts to serve the enterprises with sincerity, for he could feel that what he does is beneficial for both China and the Netherlands, and he is offering solid help to their businessmen. Such a faith justifies all his efforts, however weary he is. Sometimes even a smile or a "thank you" in return gives him enormous reassurance and encouragement.

His fearlessness of challenges is perhaps linked with his former working experiences. William used to work in finance in Singapore. There he took charge of crude oil transactions, spending most of his time with icy cold figures, computer screens and documents, which completely alienated him from the warmth of the human world. That was a disaster for William, who loves to spend time with people, rather than rigid figures or screens. So when he met with this job opportunity in Chengdu, it just clicked, and he does do a good job. At the end of 2016, the Day of the Netherlands in Chengdu was successfully held in the subway square of Sino-Ocean Taikoo Li Chengdu, with NCH as one of the hosts gathering close to 20 companies from the Netherlands. The garden carnival offered Chengduers a chance to experience life in the Netherlands at all metrics. It also joined hands with IF Fashion Art and invited local fashion personages, including designers, select shops and heads of commercial complexes, to attend art exchanges that were meant to boost a seamless synergy between Netherlands fashion design and the Chengdu market, and launch new efforts and new models for the fashion-themed communications between Chengdu and the Netherlands.

Convinced that it is his calling, William throws himself into his work such that his leisure time is drastically reduced, with a full schedule every day. As the chief representative of NCH in Chengdu, he never kicks off a project without a beforehand inspection and check by himself. Only by making every step of his work solidly reliable can he make the most persuasive remarks on the details of Chengdu.

Homeland, Far in Distance yet Close at Heart

Of course, work is not everything for him. Leisure time often sees William terribly missing his family back in the Netherlands. As a good son, he deeply loves his parents the way Chinese children do, and makes sure that each Christmas is a time of family reunion. His parents are both retired, longing for his company. Crazily busy as he is, William is sure to spare time for the Christmas reunion. Like a naughty boy, sometimes he will pretend to figure-count the times of his return to the Netherlands. Christmas with his parents back in his home country is a real warm thing for him.

William's hometown is neither so famous nor large. It is a small town called "Gouda", which produces an upscale kind of cheese that sells well worldwide for its fantastic taste. William sometimes acts as a warmhearted travel guide to his friends who wish to visit the Netherlands. He recommends large cities like Rotterdam and Amsterdam for first-time visits. But for the unique experience seekers, he names Giethoorn, a small town surrounded by waters, with fog swirling and wreathing all around, and typical European-style cabins standing in the center of the rivers. He is such a devoted speaker when talking about tourism that, if not for his decent dress, you might mistakenly take him as a hawker waving his tour-guiding flag and selling tourist attractions at first sight.

Love in Chengdu

William now is not only attached to the city Chengdu, but has also fallen in love with a Chengdu lady. In his eyes, she is all he could currently dream about love: she speaks good English, once lived abroad, and she is smart, beautiful and considerate. Sometimes they will take night walks on the streets, sharing their daytime experiences. Sometimes they will hang out at a place called "Wonderland", where William enjoys playing table tennis and billiards. He also has developed a hobby of singing karaoke with his girlfriend, and to think that this man from the Netherlands should make the best covers of the songs by Andy Liu, a very famous Hong Kong singer, is simply amazing.

William is now used to the nightly bustle of the city, the ever-present flavor of hotpot, and the ease of taking his time in a tea house for a whole afternoon. Thanks to him, we know that apart from Amsterdam and Rotterdam, there is a fairyland called Giethoorn, and could get a glimpse of the incredible and challenging life a person leads in a strange city and a strange country.

For William, Chengdu is not only a workplace, but also a place that warms his heart, for here live his best friends, his beloved girlfriend, and of course, his dream that is germinating and blossoming.

161

>> 安东尼奥·威利（瑞士）
艺术家

Wiley Antonio, Switzerland
Artist

从成都开始的艺术人生

2012 年夏天，安东尼奥·威利游历中国名山大川时途经成都，在一辆出租车上，他做了一个决定：留在成都。"没有原因，只是当时突然的一个念头。"如同是一个艺术家天生对自由的向往和追求，安东尼奥跟随着自由的脚步最终落地成都。

苏黎世工程师

安东尼奥·威利出生在瑞士第一大城市苏黎世，爸爸是当地的一名律师，母亲是一名教师。在安东尼奥小的时候，爸爸很希望他长大后能在这个以银行和精密机械工艺闻名世界的城市里当一个工程师，由于父亲时常在他耳边如此提及，从五岁开始安东尼奥也一直认为自己长大以后会是个工程师，尽管当时安东尼奥甚至并不知道"工程师"这个词到底意味着什么。

然而未来并没有随着父亲的愿望发展。从中学开始，安东尼奥逐渐对艺术着了迷，绘画、摄影、音乐都是他所热爱的，他在一次画展上看到了一种特别的绘画，那是一种厚涂法的绘画。不知何故，他对此手法一见倾心，并由此萌生要做一个画家的念想。但在当时，由于时间的限制，他更多的是在做一些摄影，经常会帮学校的活动拍照，还因此获得一定的收入。

中学毕业后，对未来感到迷茫的安东尼奥最终选择去学习工程，然而学科的枯燥让爱好自由的安东尼奥日渐感觉难以继续，开始时还能每一个礼拜去一次，后来两周去一次，之后去的频率越来越小。学习工程的第二年，安东尼奥斩钉截铁地跟爸爸说"这并不是我想要的"，而后便告别了这个儿时便被安放的志愿。

后来的日子里，因为偏爱旅行又会摄影，安东尼奥便找到了一份游轮摄影的工作，接下来的两年，安东尼奥开始了在海上漂泊的日子，加拿大、阿拉斯加、墨西哥、加勒比海、地中海、黑海……每一处都在他的足迹和影像中被记录。

北京中国女孩

安东尼奥第一次来中国是在 1999 年，那时候他还在读高中，在一个假期旅游中，他和朋友一起先是去了俄罗斯，随后辗转来到北京。初次来中国，像很多普通外国游客一样，他特地去看了长城、故宫、天坛等闻名于世界的景观。其中他对天坛的印象最深刻，因为独特的建筑风格和色彩令他感到赞叹。但这次短暂的旅行仅仅维持了三天，他便返回了家乡。

在这之前，安东尼奥对中国的最大的兴趣是"功夫"和道教。而也正如同他钟情的道教，似乎冥冥中自有注定，毕业以后漂泊了两年之后，2007 年，他独自一人再次来到北京，并决定长住一段时间。初到异国他乡的日子不容易，安东尼奥还记得当时的窘态，当时他订了一个叫"西方公寓"的酒店，和游轮工作时所住酒店条件的落差使他感到十分失落，对自己能否长久待下去也充满了疑问，直到认识了现在的妻子——中国女孩章玉莲。

来北京的第二个星期，安东尼奥在北京秀水街第一次见到了章玉莲。"她的笑很特别，我第一眼便记住了。"尽管当时，章玉莲并没有留意到这个陌生又普通的外国男子。后来，奥东尼奥想尽办法递了一个邀请函给章玉莲，里面写上了自己的联系方式和地址，邀请章玉莲参加在自己的公寓举行的一个 party。

让他感到失望的是，聚会当天章玉莲并没有如期而至。当时安东尼奥的感觉便是："或许就这样了。"但是一星期后，他忽然收到了一个短信，是章玉莲发的，内容是解释当天是因为确实有事走不开便没有去。安东尼奥耐心地回复说没关系，并向章玉莲再一次发出了邀请，于是在一个咖啡店，安东尼奥与章玉莲开始了第一次约会。

成都道

2008 年，安东尼奥和章玉莲在一次旅途中，初次来到成都。"当时因为来得比较匆忙，对成都的印象并不深。"他也并没有想象过之后会在这里生活。那次旅行他们还去了昆明、福州、南京、厦门等城市，回到北京以后，安东尼奥还是觉得北京更适合自己一些。

直到 2010 年，由于对中国道教的向往，安东尼奥去了趟武当山，在山上的日子每天练气功、打太极，安享其中。三个月后，山上的师傅却告诉安东尼奥说："缘分到了，你要走了。"于是，安东尼奥动身离开去寻找下一个缘分。

第二次与道教的结缘是发生在两年以后，这一次，安东尼奥的目标是位于成都近郊的鹤鸣山，在途经成都时一辆出租车上，安东尼奥突然涌出一种感觉："我们留在这里吧，我要在这里画画。"他对同行的女友章玉莲说。"没有原因，只是当时突然的一个念头。"如同是一个艺术家天生对自由的向往和追求，安东尼奥跟随着自由的脚步落地成都，这一落地便是六年。

蓝顶艺术村

成都三圣乡附近的蓝顶艺术村，作为成都标志性的艺术区之一，吸引着诸多艺术家在此驻留。然而对于外国艺术家安东尼奥来说，在6年前，他还算是个"异类"。

初来成都的几天，安东尼奥在酒店了解到，当时在成都有两个艺术区，分别是双流的"浓园"（浓园国际艺术村）和三圣乡附近的蓝顶艺术区。因为距离蓝顶较近，安东尼奥便先动身前去，多次辗转后，在荷塘月色，一片竹林旁的一所老房子吸引了安东尼奥，这栋看似普通的二层楼砖瓦房，让安东尼奥很兴奋："我最中意二楼的阳台，坐在这里喝茶聊天很享受，和妻子在一起，我觉得很浪漫，当时看到这个阳台我就走不了了，决定住在这里。"

住下的前几个月，安东尼奥没有什么朋友，平时业余活动也不多，基本上都是待在工作室画画。经常的状态便是从早上五六点开始起来创作，一直到下午两三点，饥饿感涌遍全身时才停下来，吃点食物补充能量，然后继续画画。"那个时候我没什么事，觉得自己需要多画，那就随自己的心意画吧。"

"以前我爱摄影，照片可以记录我看到的风景。但我现在觉得绘画才是真的创作，它可以呈现现实中看不到的东西，也可以把摄影积累的素材放在同一幅画里组成新的故事。每天我都会有很多想象和思考，这是用镜头无法记录的。"安东尼奥如此解读他与绘画的缘分由来。

在安东尼奥的作品中，经常展现出多元化视觉艺术，这改变了成都观众对油画的理解。安东尼奥回忆，自己受到的艺术影响最早是17岁时参观博物馆看到的一幅凡·高作品，那幅画就不是传统油画，大量的颜料使用，让这幅凡·高作品"立体"起来。这个偏好使得安东尼奥对于绘画质地特别看重，他也逐渐形成了自己标签般的绘画风格，即极

"厚"的绘画。最厚处可达六七厘米，以至于他的画作无法重叠安放，不然画面纹理就会有所损坏。因为太厚，其画框背后须以木板加固，不然画框会承受不起。"我不知道世界上还有没有更'厚'的绘画，至少就我所见，这算是最'厚'的画作了。"

在他创作的油画作品《荷花》中，安东尼奥并没有像中国艺术家那样以常用的45度视角创作，而是俯视，这样出来的效果荷花变成了"平面视角"，反倒让人耳目一新。"我的作品里有很多中国符号，比如有很多山水，我承认，中国画对我的创作有影响。"安东尼奥回说，比如张大千的泼墨画就让他很感兴趣。

在这段时间，安东尼奥的艺术也得到了成都艺术圈的关注，在蓝顶美术馆的一个展览中，他认识了成都艺术名家许燎源，表达了想在成都画画的想法，竟立刻得到许燎源的热情回应。很快，许燎源现代艺术博物馆里专门开辟了一块空间，为他举办了展览，许燎源还亲自当导览员，向观众介绍安东尼奥。"这里的很多艺术家，都对我非常友善，我感觉这个地方很热情、包容，接纳我。"

成都著名画家何多苓是安东尼奥另一个"贵人"，他看了安东尼奥作品后评价："这一看就不是中国人画的，但又受中国文化影响。"何多苓说，这种介乎东西方之间的艺术创作表达方式，是成都这座包容性极强的城市所需要的。受到了许燎源、何多苓等本土艺术大家的肯定，大大增强了安东尼奥的信心，同时也让他对成都有了更深的好感。在这个城市，安东尼奥也开始逐渐感受到了一种"归属感"，虽然身处异国他乡，但家的感觉越来越浓。

扎根生子

这些年，安东尼奥一直保持一种随性的感觉。他曾为随性而放弃了成为一名精密机械工程师的体面工作，做一名"不务正业"的画家。仍然是因为随性，他去游轮上做了一名摄影师，去了俄罗斯，然后又来到了中国，再到去武当山静修了好几个月，最终辗转来到成都，并在这里定居，正式成为一名职业画家。所有有时候，随性也是一种缘分指引。

两年前，由于绘画的需要，他的工作室从荷塘月色搬到了蓝顶艺术村附近一所稍大一些的公寓里。二楼为住处，一楼则为画室，画室里整齐排列着安东尼奥的作品，简陋的房间里配备了除湿机和照灯。荷花、熊猫、山水抽象画，还有少数人像，这些作品的灵感都是他在成都生活过程中获得的。最显眼的位置摆放着几幅已经完成的荷花图，荷花与荷叶都是立体的，好像生长在纸上，有着风格独具的效果。他画荷花，是因为太太的名字中有个"莲"字，而这里恰好也有个荷塘，"真的是缘分"。来三圣乡后，他画的第一幅荷花便送给了太太章玉莲，这幅画一直挂在他俩的卧室，素雅的荷花是他们爱情的象征和成都记忆。

安东尼奥说自己去过至少50个国家和地区，他认为生活就是为了寻找刺激和灵感，但没有一个地方像成都这样，给他想要安定的感觉，成都很有生活气息，每个人都很nice。在安东尼奥看来，成都是最适合体验和感受东方性的城市。"这种东方性是有别于西方艺术的一种东西，是灵魂深处的感受"。如今，安东尼奥在成都沉淀自己，他的心该是如他理想中一般清净。

对于安东尼奥来说，成都是他的福地，既吸引了他，又给了他安家扎根生活的理由。安东尼奥的母亲曾经专门从瑞士来成都看他，当这位母亲看到自己的儿子融入成都生活时，她真心为儿子感到幸福。这种幸福情绪传递给安东尼奥，并被安东尼奥传递给他的下一代，他和太太有了爱的结晶，他们的女儿来到了这个艺术氛围浓厚、满满都是爱的家庭，来到了他们安在成都的家。

如今安东尼奥这样描述自己一天的生活状态：怕吵醒孩子，早上一般不会太早起，大概八点多，起来吃过早餐后便开始画画，下午的时候会带着妻子和孩子在蓝顶艺术村附近随便走走，到了晚上常常会和朋友一起吃饭聊天。最近他开始经常活跃于成都的艺术圈，不止绘画，在策展和一些公益活动中都能见到安东尼奥的身影。由于名气越来越大，他最近还接了一些小业务，偶尔要出差。繁华终归只是表象，安东尼奥内心深处还是更向往妻女在侧的闲适生活，他愿意更多地去为家庭尽责，做一位好丈夫、一位好父亲。

也许未来是否一直生活在成都还是未知之数，但是对于安东尼奥而言，当前在成都的生活宁静且有序，平实又幸福，既然缘分在成都，那么维持这种不错的状态又有什么不好呢？

An Artistic Life Starts in Chengdu

In the summer of 2012, when Wiley Antonio was visiting well-known mountains and rivers in China, he came across Chengdu. While in a cab touring the city, he made a decision—to stay in Chengdu. "There was no logical explanation for that, just a fresh idea." An artist has an in-born aspiration for freedom. And that's what motivated Antonio to eventually get settled in Chengdu.

An Engineer from Zurich

Wiley Antonio was born in Switzerland's largest city, Zurich. His father was a local lawyer; his mother was a teacher. When Antonio was young, his father wanted him to be an engineer in this city known for its banking and precision machinery. As his father often mentioned this to him, Antonio had always considered himself an engineer-to-be since he turned five, though he did not really know what the word "engineer" meant.

However, his future development ran counter to his father's expectations. Antonio became obsessed with art since high school. Painting, photography, and music were his favorites. He learned about a special painting—impasto—at a painting exhibition. Somehow, he was intrigued by this technique at first sight and began to entertain the thought of starting an artistic career. Constrained by limited time, he was more involved in photography, taking pictures of campus activities and making money.

After graduating from high school, Antonio was at a loss as to what to do in the future. He chose engineering in the end. The subject came across as boring. Antonio, who preferred freedom, found it increasingly difficult to continue. At the beginning he went to class every week, then once every two weeks. His attendance fell as time went by. In his second year of engineering studies, Antonio said firmly to his father: "it's not what I want." With that, he said goodbye to the arrangement that had been pre-made during his childhood.

Later, Antonio found a job as a cruise ship photographer since he liked traveling and was good at photography. During the following two years, Antonio drifted in the oceans. Canada, Alaska, Mexico, the Caribbean, the Mediterranean, the Black Sea... his footsteps in all of these places were captured in his camera.

A Chinese Girl Encountered in Beijing

Antonio first came to China in 1999, when he was still in high school. During a holiday tour, he first went to Russia with his friends and later, ofter taking pauses here and there on the trip, arrived at Beijing. Like many foreign tourists who came to China for the first time, he specifically went to see the Great Wall, the Forbidden City, the Temple of Heaven, and other world-famous tourist attractions. He was most impressed by the Temple of Heaven, with its unique architectural style and dazzling colors. However, he returned home immediately after this three-day short trip.

Prior to this, Antonio's greatest interest in China had been "Kung Fu" and Taoism. Just as his beloved Taoism preaches, "like it or not, fate is predestined." He wandered about for two years after graduation, and once again came to Beijing alone in 2007. He had decided to stay for a longer time. The first days in a foreign country were not easy. Antonio still remembers how embarrassed he was. He checked in the "Western Apartments" hotel, only to find that it barely came close to the hotel he stayed when he was working on board the cruise ship. Disappointed, he wasn't sure if he would be able to stay long until he met Chinese girl Zhang Yulian, who is now his wife.

During his second week in Beijing, Antonio encountered Zhang Yulian on Xiushui Street. "Her laughter was very special. I was impressed." However, Zhang Yulian did not find anything special about this unfamiliar, ordinary foreign man. Some time later, Antonio tried every means possible to send an invitation to Zhang Yulian, enclosed with his contact information and address. He wanted Zhang to attend a party held at his apartment.

To his disappointment, Zhang Yulian did not show up. Maybe that would be the end of it, Antonio thought. A week later, he received an unexpected text message from Zhang Yulian explaining her absence that she was held up the day of the party. Antonio replied that it was OK and once again invited Zhang to come over. At a coffee shop, Antonio and Zhang Yulian started their first date.

Chengdu and Taoism

During a trip in 2008, Antonio and Zhang Yulian first came to Chengdu. "I was not particularly impressed by Chengdu because I was in a hurry." He did not have the faintest idea that he would live here. During that trip, they also went to Kunming, Fuzhou, Nanjing, and Xiamen. Back to Beijing, Antonio felt Beijing was a more suitable place for him.

In 2010, Antonio's interest in China's Taoism drew him to Wudang Mountain. He practiced Qi Gong and Tai Ji on the mountain and quite enjoyed it. Three months later, Antonio's master told him, "this is the end of it. It is time for you to leave." Antonio left and went on a journey to his next stop.

His second contact with Taoism came two years later. This time, Antonio's destination was Heming Mountain on the outskirts of Chengdu. On impulse, Antonio said to his girlfriend Zhang Yulian while in a taxi passing Chengdu, "Let's stay. I want to go on painting here." "There was no logical explanation for that, just a fresh idea." An artist has an in-born aspiration for freedom. Antonio came to Chengdu exactly in quest of that. Now it has already been six years since his arrival.

Blueroof Art Village

Blueroof Art Village near Sanshengxiang, one of the iconic art districts in Chengdu, draws many artists. However, foreign artist Antonio was considered a "freak" six years ago.

During the first few days after arrival, Antonio learned from the hotel that there were two art districts in Chengdu at that time: the "Nongyuan Garden" (Nongyuan International Art Village) in Shuangliu and the Blueroof Art Village near Sanshengxiang. The Blueroof Art Village was not far from the hotel, so Antonio decided to pay his first visit there. An old residence by a bamboo grove in Lotus Pond attracted Antonio's attention at the end of multiple visits. Antonio was excited about this seemingly ordinary two-story brick building, "I was most interested in the balcony on the second floor. It would be immensely romantic to drink tea and chat with my wife here. I was unable to move my steps after I saw it. I decided to stay."

During the first few months after he moved in, Antonio did not have any friends, nor was he involved in other activities. He spent most of his time drawing pictures in his studio. He usually got up and began to work at five or six o'clock in the early morning to two or three o'clock in the afternoon. He wouldn't stop until he felt hungry. He would eat something to regain energy and then continue to paint. "At that time, I had nothing else to do. If I felt I needed to draw more pictures, I would go ahead as long as it pleased me."

"I used to love photography. Photos enabled me to keep a record of the scenery I saw. But now I think painting is real creative work when compared to photography. It presents things that cannot be seen in reality. It tells a new story by bringing together in one piece of work the materials accumulated in photography. I imagine and think a lot every day. The lens cannot capture this." This is how Antonio interprets his encounter with painting.

Diverse visual arts are often displayed in Antonio's works. They have changed Chengdu audience's understanding of oil painting. Antonio recalls that he was first influenced by art when he saw a work by Van Gogh in a museum at 17. It was not a typical painting. Van Gogh's brilliant use of paint gave a "three-dimensional" look to this work. Antonio's preference for this type of painting underlies his focus on the texture of a painting, and he gradually developed his own signature painting style—"thick" painting. His painting can be as thick as six or seven centimeters. They are too thick to be stacked up or the lines and patterns would be damaged. And the painting is so thick that the picture frame must be reinforced with planks of wood. Otherwise it will not be able to carry the amount of weight. "I do not know if there are 'thicker' paintings. As far as I can see, this is the "thickest" painting in the world."

In his painting "Lotus", Antonio does not adopt the 45-degree angle of view as Chinese artists usually do. Instead, he adopts a bird eye view that presents a lotus in a top-down perspective. "There are many Chinese symbols such as mountains and rivers in my paintings. I cannot deny that traditional Chinese painting has influenced my work." Antonio is very much interested in Zhang Daqian's splashed-ink landscapes.

During this time, Antonio's art draws the attention of Chengdu's art circles. In an exhibition at the Blueroof Art Gallery, he met Xu Liaoyuan, an art celebrity of Chengdu to whom he expressed his wish to pursue an art career in Chengdu. Xu Liaoyuan's response was enthusiastic. Soon, Xu Liaoyuan Museum of Modern Art offered him a special space where he could hold an exhibition. Xu Liaoyuan personally introduced Antonio and his work to the audience. "Many of the artists here are very kind to me. This city took me with great enthusiasm and understanding."

He Duoling, a famous painter in Chengdu, is another man who has offered Antonio great help. "This is obviously not a Chinese painting, but Chinese culture has left a mark on it," he commented after seeing the exhibition. He Duoling said Antonio's art expression is something between the east and the west and is exactly what an inclusive city like Chengdu needs. The recognition by local artists like Xu Liaoyuan and He Duoling greatly enhanced Antonio's confidence. At the same time, his love for

Chengdu grew intenser. Antonio began to feel a real sense of belonging in this city. This is foreign soil, but the breath of home gets stronger with each passing day.

Taking Root and Having Children

Antonio has been following his heart all these years. To follow his heart, he gave up on a decent job as a precision mechanical engineer and practiced what was not expected of him—painting. To follow his heart, he worked as a photographer on a cruise ship, went to Russia and then came to China. He spent several months meditating on Wudang Mountain, and eventually arrived in Chengdu, where he settled down and became a professional artist. Sometimes, following your heart is following the guidance of your destiny.

Two years ago, as required by the painting work, he moved his studio from the Lotus Pond to a slightly larger apartment near Blueroof Art Village. The second floor is where he lives and the first floor is where he works. Antonio's works are neatly arranged in the shabby studio equipped with a dehumidifier and an illuminator. Lotuses, pandas, abstract landscape paintings, and some portraits—he draws inspiration for these works from his life in Chengdu. Some completed works of lotus occupy the most prominent positions in the studio. The unique lotuses and lotus leaves are three-dimensional as if they grew on the paper. He paints lotus flowers because his wife's name ends with the word "lotus". And a lotus pond happens to be here. "It is really fate." The first lotus painting he drew after coming to Sanshengxiang was dedicated to his wife Zhang Yulian. It hangs in their bedroom. The unadorned elegant lotus flower symbolizes their love and their memory of Chengdu.

Antonio says he has been to at least 50 countries and regions. He thinks life is about excitement and inspiration, yet no other place has ever given him a sense of stability except Chengdu. Chengdu is lively and bustling, and everyone is nice. In Antonio's opinion, Chengdu is the ideal city for experiencing and feeling the charm of the East. "This oriental charm is different from Western art. It is what you feel deep down." Antonio is immersing himself in Chengdu. His heart should be as pure as he has hoped for.

For Antonio, Chengdu is a place of happiness, as it drew him here and gave him a reason to take root and have a family. Antonio's mother once came all the way from Switzerland to Chengdu to see him. When she found her second son had woven himself into the life of Chengdu, she felt very happy. Antonio inherited this happiness and passed it on to his next generation. His daughter, the pledge of love, was born to this family full of art and love built by Antonio and his wife in Chengdu.

Today, Antonio describes his daily life as follows: afraid of waking up the child, his day starts late at around 8 a.m. He then begins painting after breakfast. In the afternoon, he takes a casual stroll around the Blueroof Art Village with his wife and child. At night, he has dinner with friends and chats with them. He has been active in Chengdu's art circles recently. In addition to painting, he is also involved in curations and charity events. Increasing popularity has brought him business opportunities. He occasionally goes on a business trip to deal with small business. It is good to have a flourishing business. Deep down Antonio longs for a life of leisure together with his wife and daughter. He is willing to do more for the family. He wants to be a good husband and a good father.

It is still unknown if they will live in Chengdu all their lives. For Antonio, life in Chengdu is quiet, orderly, simple, and happy. Since he has now nestled in Chengdu, what's so bad to stay here a while longer?

>>> 葛大卫（法国）

东风神龙汽车有限公司成都工厂副厂长

Jerome David Guirsch, France

Assistant Director of Chengdu Plant of Dongfeng Peugeot Citroen

Autombile Company Ltd.

缘定成都

　　成都，是一个神秘而诗意的城市。几千年前的金沙文明，是古蜀人智慧的结晶，静静地诉说着古老的智慧……武侯祠中，诸葛亮在悄悄地感叹成都的美；杜甫草堂，虽然简陋，却给了杜甫一个温暖的港湾。

　　生活在法国的葛大卫，在他少年时就已经从地图上看到过这个中国西部的城市，虽是地球上的一个小点，却让他对成都充满了好奇。有时是"晓看红湿处，花重锦官城"，有时是"九天开出一成都，万户千门入画图"，有时是"窗含西岭千秋雪，门泊东吴万里船"……诗人笔下的成都，现在究竟是什么样的呢？

　　直到 2015 年，公司领导问葛大卫是否愿意到成都任职，他陷入了沉思：四川有着悠久的历史文化，丰富的自然资源，而且是中国西部最发达的省份，而成都作为四川的省会，有着天时地利人和的巨大优势，他找不到理由拒绝这个选择。就连妻子听说要去成都生活时，都满心欢喜，因为她早已听说这里是美食之都，是中国美食的精髓所在之地。于是，举家前往。葛大卫与成都的缘分，就从那时开始了。

爱上巴蜀韵味

　　同许多在成都的外国人一样，葛大卫居住在桐梓林，那里有许多外国人，还有专门为外国人而开的酒吧、餐厅，为他们的生活带来了便捷，也是在那里，他交到了来自世界各地的朋友。但他却就被成都人本身的魅力所折服："求知欲""淳朴"，是他对成都人的认知；"笑意满满""热情好客"是成都人带给他的感受。当年陆游的那份"莫笑农家腊酒浑，丰年留客足鸡豚"之情，也让初到成都的葛大卫感同身受。

成都最吸引葛大卫的一点，是这座城市并没有因为时髦，而失去了它传统的那一面。成都历史悠久，有"天府之国""蜀中江南""蜀中苏杭"的美称。成都有被誉为"世界水利文化的鼻祖"的都江堰，是全国著名的旅游胜地；蜀绣、蜀锦、川剧、茶艺都是成都文化非常重要的组成部分。成都小吃风味独特、品类繁多，令人垂涎。走进成都，总能让人不由得去品味历史，去感受特别的"巴蜀文化"。

而且，成都地处长江上游岷江水系的成都平原，这里水源丰富，使得这座城市有了特别的灵动韵味。像那些小河流水一样，这里的人们生活节奏相对缓慢，没有一般大都市那样的匆忙和急躁，更多的只是闲散与从容。加上这里悠久的人文积淀，以及大量的人文古迹，更令人发出怀古思逸之幽情。

和大多数外国人一样，在葛大卫眼里，成都是个休闲的好去处，来了就不想离开。他把这种韵味称作巴蜀风味，柔润，徐缓，慵懒，又带着一些空灵和内秀，不浮躁，不蛮悍，如小河一般缓缓地流淌在心间。

最让葛大卫惊叹的是，几张坐得发白的旧竹椅，两三悠闲的亲朋好友，懒散地坐在微风徐拂的河岸边或在老街的古树旁，泡上几杯绿茶，就能散淡地，漫无边际地，摆上一下午的龙门阵，他们或是话语轻松悠闲，或是甜润悠扬，直至将一杯茶水喝到清淡无味，还舍不得罢休。

品读儒学思想

除了地道的巴蜀风情，西北部青城山的道教，西南部峨眉山的佛教，都吸引着喜欢哲学的葛大卫。但他最爱的，却是孔子的儒学思想。

"学而不思则罔，思而不学则殆。"儒家思想影响深远，是中国影响最大的流派，成为中国传统文化的主流。来到成都，葛大卫时常捧读到孔子经典名句。读到兴起，他会细心将这些句子摘抄下来，放在书桌显眼的地方，时刻鉴赏，并不忘警诫自己。

哲学能够让人掌握和了解认识生活的基本道理，能够给葛大卫一个全新的视角和思考。他喜欢喜欢孔子的那句"逝者如斯"，他把这句话理解为"活在当下"，并翻译成法语，郑重地写了下来。

他认为，过去的日子，就像清澈的水，固然清晰得历历在目，可是，若想抓住，却是不可能的。过去的已经过去，未来遥遥无期，不可猜测，为何傻傻地去憧憬呢？未来的梦只有靠今天的努力来实现，只有把握住今天，才能抓住未来。要活在当下，珍惜身边的人，珍惜身边的事，领悟身边的物，把握好今天，就已胜过无数个昨天和明天。

是个认真的工作狂

一个认真工作的人，只能称作称职；一个用心工作的人，才能企及优秀。用心不但能够使我们做好本职工作，更能使我们用长远的思考来规划未来；用心不但能使我们积极面对人生的每一次挑战，更能使我们征服人生路途中的每一次困难。一个没有用心工作的人，在人生的舞台上永远只能扮演一个不起眼的角色；只有用心去工作的人，才能完美诠释自己的生命内涵。

葛大卫所在的东风神龙公司成都工厂是神龙集团第五座工厂，总投资 123 亿元，总设计产能为 36 万台 / 年。一期工程占地面积 2484 亩，主要包括冲压、焊装、涂装、总装四大工艺及其分装集成的车间厂房、

183

零部件供应商配套工业园区厂房、试车跑道，以及仓储物流、公用动力站房、食堂等辅助建筑设施。

新工厂定位于 PSA 集团"全球新一代标杆工厂"，作为成都市大力引进的工业重大项目——神龙汽车有限公司成都工厂项目实现了 23 个月建成投产，创造出了令人振奋的"成都速度"。身为该公司成都工厂的质检主任，葛大卫对工作的态度一丝不苟。

经常可见身着黑白色的统一工作服，左臂肩章贴着"安全生产责任人"标签的他，穿梭在工厂的各个车间，如果不是他褐色的头发、高挺的鼻梁和蓝色的眼睛，不知情的人会以为他就是普普通通的一个员工。作为一名资深的汽车行业质检专家，葛大卫的到来对成都汽车产业的提升可谓大有好处，这个全球最现代化的汽车生产车间所输出的产品凝聚的是最专业的技术，经受的是最优质的把关。

令人惊讶的是，葛大卫的办公室布置得特别简单，既没有法式的浪漫情怀，也没有中式的宽敞明亮。一张书桌、一台笔记本电脑，构成了他所有工作装备。在办公室的角落摆放着衣架、工装和休闲服将它挤得满满当当。书桌后面，还矗立着一根裸露的管道，与办公室格格不入。

天哪，这居然是来自法国的质检主任的办公室！也许觉得客人的眼光太过惊讶，葛大卫羞涩一笑，挠挠头："我工作太忙了，没有时间去布置。"转而他又会环视四周，自言自语："也许确实应该布置一下。"可往往是话音刚落，就又埋下头工作或者匆匆拿起文件夹，赶去开会了。

对物质要求低的葛大卫，却对工作异常认真，他常对员工说，一辆车最开始会有许多不起眼的小毛病，可能一个小毛病就需要我们花费数个小时来维修，但这如果在面向市场之前，我们把这些小毛病克服了，就能够带给消费者更好的体验。客户的满意就是我们所追求的，也是我们努力奋斗的原因，我们必须认真且用心地工作。他希望每个人都能够各司其职，在团队工作中发挥自己的力量，达到"1+1>2"的效果。

爱护下属的暖男领导

虽然在工作上一丝不苟，但私下的葛大卫却是关心员工的大哥哥。天气转凉时，他会提醒翻译多添衣服，别感冒了。当看到员工疲倦时，会让他们稍作休息，调整状态。他不喜欢装饰书桌，但却在桌上摆放着前任翻译送他的写有《游子吟》的扇子。

"慈母手中线，游子身上衣。临行密密缝，意恐迟迟归。谁言寸草心，报得三春晖。"认全扇子上的古诗词，对于葛大卫来说是件难事，他最想在离开成都时，找人把它翻译成法语，带回到自己的祖国去。

确实，在成都生活，最大的困难就是语言的障碍，学了几次中文，葛大卫发现拼音的四个音调真的太难了。起初，他也十分苦恼：无法与工作伙伴交流，无法顺利购物，当同事们哈哈大笑时，他只能跟着傻笑。

后来，葛大卫已经喜欢和妻子一起去超市、去市场用肢体语言沟通买菜了，因为对于说成都话的卖菜大爷，相比于他不标准的普通话，肢体语言更简洁明了；工作中，有了法语翻译，他可以与同事更好地沟通交流了，与搭档的配合也能加默契了。

在工作中遇到观点相悖时，在国外生活了许多年，游历了大大小小的国家，能够了解不同国家人们的思想的葛大卫，也看到了每个人思想的独特性，他可以抛下个人认知，求同存异，与同事协同合作，更好地推动了公司的发展。

习惯成都生活

很多人都说，成都是一个来了就不想走的城市。其实，不仅是成都，对很多"老外"来说，四川的美景、美食，休闲的生活都是不小的诱惑，天府之国的魅力已经跨越了国界。

在这里生活久了，葛大卫也从一开始完全不会吃辣椒，吃不惯中国菜，到现在对川菜的热爱并能够吃一点辣椒，他见证着自己的变化。

除了美食，在葛大卫的家里，还有一个区域专门摆放他收藏的茶叶和茶具。他痴迷于中国传统文化——茶艺。

"坐茶馆"是成都人的一种特别嗜好，因此茶馆遍布城乡各个角落。成都茶馆不仅历史悠久，数量众多，而且有它自己独特的风格。无论你走进哪座茶馆，都会领略到一股浓郁的成都味：竹靠椅、小方桌、三件头盖茶具、老虎灶、紫铜壶，还有最有特色的是茶博士，即掺茶跑堂的。

四川的茶倌掺茶技艺高超，还有许多绝活，前些日子，葛大卫就欣赏到了地道的"工夫茶"。只见茶倌摆茶船，放茶碗的动作一气呵成，他们可以把装满开水、有一米长壶嘴的大铜壶玩的风车斗转，他是先把壶嘴靠拢茶碗，然后猛地向上抽抬，一股滚水向直泻而下的水柱冲到茶碗里，再然后他伸手过来小拇指一翻就把你面前的茶碗盖起了，那手法更是叫绝。"苏秦背月""蛟龙探海""飞天仙女""童子拜观音"等花样更是让葛大卫眼花缭乱。

看过四川的工夫茶，葛大卫痴迷上了这种茶艺。他知道，中国的茶是一种文化，品茶是一门学问，清茶一杯，始是浅浅苦涩，而后悠悠一丝清甜从喉中溢出。品茶之道，在于心，在于艺，在于魂，品茶之理，在于境，在于人，在于品。寻得佳时，觅得佳境，品味好茶，一种很微妙的感觉会从心底荡开，只觉气舒神怡，心净神清，浮躁和张扬会一点点地被抽走，恬静和安逸自会一缕缕地流出来。

茶道人生，慢煮茶香，淡看时光。捧一本书，翻到随意的一页。书卷墨香，茶韵悠然，岁月无声。

这里是第二故乡

成都的魅力，不仅在于神奇壮观的自然风光、别具特色的民俗风情和底蕴深厚的历史文化，更在于它海纳百川的包容与开放。对于外国人来说，选择住在哪儿，住多久，其实跟一个城市的包容度息息相关，有包容的城市更显国际化水平和魅力。

对于一些来成都发展的外国人来说，高速发展的都市，可能是吸引他们的原因。但闲适的生活节奏，却让他们扎根。

葛大卫喜欢成都的生活，遇到天气好的闲暇之时，他喜欢带着妻子和两个儿子去散步，踏遍成都街头，寻觅历史的足迹。窄窄的过道，高高的青墙，岁月和风雨磨损了当年的风光。老街里的风，永远不急不缓地吹着。又或是坐在茶馆里听着地道老成都人的"龙门阵"，去社区跳舞，热情洋溢的桑巴是妻子最擅长的。

要么读书，要么旅行，灵魂和身体必须有一个在路上。葛大卫喜欢旅行，去见更广的世面，行走在山水间，更加无拘无束，无论是在郊区还是在城市，他逐渐融入成都，这才是他想要的生活。望向窗外，记录各地沿途的风景，欣赏着各地的美食，有时候在想，成都的山水，怎么都带着秀气和灵性，盆地的地形，大巴秦岭的阻隔，冷风吹不透，烈日照不干，受着天然的庇护，天府如此宜人。

成都是一个充满反差与变化的一个城市，每一年都有不同的变化。人们的生活一年比一年舒坦，心情也越来越惬意。有人曾经告诉葛大卫，成都是中国最适宜生活的地方，这里的生活节奏不会太快，压力不会太大。他再同意不过了，初到成都时，他完全没有想到会和这座城市发生那么多的故事，慢慢地成为一个地道的"成都法国人"。

他喜欢在这里生活，他喜欢这里干净整洁的环境，喜欢这里高科技的设施以及现代化的创业条件。现在，他的生活过得像玫瑰一样绚丽多彩。

葛大卫说，他以后会告诉他的孩子们，他们的爸爸有着两个家乡，一个是法国，一个是中国成都。

Encountering Chengdu by Destiny

Chengdu is a mysterious, poetic city. The crystallizing Jinsha civilization is still lying here, gently relating a story that occurred thousands of years ago; the Wuhou Temple, dedicated to Zhuge Liang, still enshrines the subtle beauty that Zhuge Liang once marveled at; and Du Fu's Thatched Cottage, simple and humble as it is, used to be a comfy shelter for the great poet Du Fu.

Living in France, David, in his young ages, already noticed the little spot on the map. It was a city in west China, which largely aroused his curiosity. Several ancient Chinese poems had paid tribute to its beauty, for example, "Come dawn, we'll see splashes of wet red: the flowers in Chengdu, weighed down with rain", or "Out of God's hand Chengdu was carved, into the canvas thousands of homes adorned.", or "In my window is framed the snow-capped peak of Mount West; Close by my door are moored boats from faraway Wu". That was Chengdu in the eyes of the poets. But what's the city like right now?

This question was not seriously considered by David until 2015, when his boss asked him whether he would like to work in Chengdu and he found himself thinking: "Sichuan has a long history, profound culture, abundant natural resources, and it is also the most developed province in West China. As its capital city, Chengdu comes as a perfect choice, and I just couldn't resist it." So he decided to come. And his wife was also very glad when hearing the news, for she had long heard that Chengdu is the gourmet capital of the world and boasts the core of Chinese cuisine. So the whole family moved to Chengdu, and David's story with the city thus began.

Falling in Love with the "Sichuan Flavor"

Like a lot of foreigners in chengdu, David chose to live in Tongzilin, for the place is inhabited by a large group of foreigners, with special bars and canteens, and is perfect for him to live comfortably and conveniently. It is also in this place that David makes friends from all over the world, while he himself is conquered by the charming Chengduers, who, according to him, are hungry for knowledge, unsophisticated, always smiling and hospitable. In this regard, David would find a famous Chinese poet Lu You sharing his feelings when he wrote that "Never laugh at the look of the liquor, for the peasants have brought out all they can from the good harvest this year to entertain their guests."

The greatest appeal of Chengdu for David is that it has kept up its traditions while pursuing modern development. Boasting a long history, Chengdu is dubbed "the Land of Abundance", "Jiangnan in Sichuan" and "Suzhou-Hangzhou in Sichuan". It is home to Dujiangyan Irrigation System, which is widely accepted as the "ancestor of the world's culture of water conservation", and a famous tourist destination. Its striking culture consists of Sichuan embroidery, brocades, Sichuan opera and tea. Its snacks, unique in taste, varied in kind, are most appetizing. Once coming to Chengdu, you will find yourself bathed in a historical ambiance, and immersed in the unique Sichuan culture.

Moreover, the Chengdu Plain, blessed by the abundant water of the

Minjiang River in the upper reaches of the Yangtze River, has become especially dynamic. Like the small rivers that wind around them, people here live a slow-paced life and enjoy freedom from the hustle and bustle shared by large cities. It is all leisure and ease here. The combination of the profound cultural and historical sites makes it easy to recall the memory of the ancient times.

Like most foreign people, David finds Chengdu the best choice for a leisure life, and a place one could hardly bear leaving after having arrived. He names the taste of Chengdu "Bashu flavor", which is soft, leisurely, lazy, and also ethereal, exquisite from inside, neither fickle nor aggressive, wriggling like a small river in his heart.

What amazes David most is that life could be so easy and yet so unforgettable here. Casually sitting on some old and worn bamboo chairs by the breezy riverside or beside an old street-side tree, with green tea brewed on the table, people could spend a whole afternoon there, chit-chatting in their easeful or resonant tones, and could be reluctant to leave even when their tea has long become flavorless.

A Fan of Confucianism

A die-hard fan of philosophy, apart from the "Bashu flavor", David is also attached to the Taoist Mount Qingcheng to Chengdu's northwest and to the Buddhist Mount Emei to the southwest. But one of his favorites is Confucianism.

The widely influential Confucianism is the largest Chinese philosophical school and has always been the mainstay of traditional Chinese culture.

During his time in Chengdu, David frequently stumbled upon the famous sayings of Confucius, such as "Learning without thought is labor lost, thought without learning is perilous". Sometimes he would even copy his favorite sentences down and place them easily visible on the desk as a reminder or as something to digest over and over in his mind.

Through philosophy, people can learn about and understand the most basic things about life, and also get a brand new perspective for thinking. He perceives the famous Confucius saying "the passage of time is just like the flow of water, which goes on day and night" as "seize the day". He translated it into French and put it down solemnly.

In his eyes, the past is like clear water. Everything seems as clear as they used to be, but they are never likely to be caught in our palms again. Let bygones be bygones and the future extends into a mythical, endless panorama. So why bother dreaming? Dreams can only be realized by hard work. Only by seizing today can we seize the future. When we live in the present, value people and things around us, and make every second meaningful, we are creating a today that eclipses numerous pasts and futures.

A Dedicated Workaholic

Only when one is dedicated to his work can he say that he is doing his duty well, and only through dedication can one be outstanding. Commitment not only makes us more professional, but also enables us to think in the long run; it not only helps us to face challenges, but also weans us off whatever obstacles lying in our way. Without dedication, a man is doomed to be mediocre in his life; while armed with dedication, a man could give full play to the meaning of his life.

The Chengdu plant of Dongfeng Peugeot Citroen Automobile Company Ltd., which David works for, is the 5th plant of the group. With an investment totaling RMB 12.3 billion, it is designed to produce 360,000 automobiles per year. The 1st-stage project covers 2,484 mu (1,656,008 square meters), comprising workshops for the four major steps of automobile manufacturing (stamping, welding, coating and assembly), as well as workshops for sub-assembly or integration, corollary plants of auto parts suppliers, test tracks and auxiliary buildings and facilities such as warehousing logistics, public power stations and dining halls.

Set as an international new-generation landmark plant of the PSA Group, the new plant in Chengdu, also a major project introduced by the municipal government, took only 23 months before being put into use, showcasing the exhilarating "Chengdu speed". As its director of quality inspection, David holds the most rigorous attitude towards his work.

He is frequently sew in his black-and-white uniform, wearing on his left shoulder a badge reading "person responsible for the safety of production", carrying out inspections in the workshops. But for his brown hair, straight nose and blue eyes, he might easily be mistaken for an ordinary employee in the workshops. With abundant experience in automotive quality inspection, David's arrival is surely a good thing for the overall improvement of Chengdu's automobile industry. This PSA automotive plant, also the world's most modern one, is rolling out products that crystallize the best expertise and has stood the most rigorous tests.

David's office is surprisingly simple. It is neither romantic in French style, nor broad and bright in Chinese style. A desk plus a laptop is all his equipment for work. Hangers with his working suits and casual clothing are crammed into the corner. A pipe was exposed from behind his desk, looking a bit strange for the office.

Who will consider such a simple room as the office of the director of quality inspection from France? Responding to my look of surprise, or shock, David gave me a shy smile, scratching his head, and said, "I am just too busy to decorate the room." Then he looked around and muttered to himself: "Maybe I really should decorate it." But as it invariably happens, no sooner had he finished this sentence he hurried away again for work or, carrying a file holder, to a conference.

Casual about material standards of living, David is never a bit casual about his work. He often tells the employees that "at first a vehicle may have many inconspicuous problems, each of which may take hours to deal with. However, if those problems are well solved before the vehicles go to the market, better customer experience will be ensured. To make each customer satisfied is exactly what we pursue and work so hard for. We must be conscientious and dedicated." He is hoping that everyone will do his duty well and play a useful part in his team so that their work could be more efficient and effective.

A Tender Leader in Private

Work has brought out his tough side, but when it comes to daily life, David is very considerate and tender, providing clothing tips for his translator upon cold weather, or giving employees some time off to refresh if they look tired. He doesn't like decorating his desk, but keeps on it a paper fan, a gift from his ex-translator, with a famous Chinese poem Wanderer's Song written on it.

"A thread is in my fond mother's hand moving,

For her son to wear the clothes are leaving.

With her whole heart she's sewing and sewing,

For fear that I'll ever be roving and roving.

Who says the little soul of grass waving,

Could for the warmth repay the sun of spring."

Since it is difficult for him to know every word on the fan, David has wished to have it translated into French and then bring it to his home country France.

Indeed the most challenging thing about living in Chengdu for David is the language. After a few Chinese learning attempts, David is completely baffled by the four tones of Chinese. He remembers being very upset at first. He was unable to communicate with fellow workers, had problems during shopping, and used to pretend to get his colleagues' jokes.

Later, David and his wife began to use gestures when shopping in supermarkets or grocery stores. Compared with his awkwardly pronounced Chinese, they proved clearer and more straightforward. In addition, his work was largely smoothed over with the help of his translator.

Opposing views are never a problem for David, who has years of experience of living in different countries and knows about all kinds of views. He is good at identifying the uniqueness of each thought, deserting his personal prejudices and seeking out something in common, so as to better cooperate with his colleagues and boost the development of the business.

Enjoying Life in Chengdu

Many have said that Chengdu is a city where people who have lived there hardly ever want to leave. Actually, for many foreign people, not only the city Chengdu, but also the scenery, food and leisurely life of Sichuan are all irresistible attractions. The charm of "the Land of Abundance" has transcended national boundaries.

Here already for a long time, David, who came with a chili pepper phobia, suffered from cuisine culture shock, but he has begun to make changes and take to the spicy Sichuan cuisine.

Putting food aside, David has spared a special space in his house for his collection of Chinese teas and tea sets. He has developed a new hobby: the traditional Chinese tea ceremony.

Drinking tea in a tea house is a special pastime for the people of Chengdu, where tea houses have permeated into all corners. Time-honored and numerous, the tea houses boast a unique Chengdu flavor that can be experienced everywhere: bamboo chairs, square tables, three-piece capped tea sets, big stoves to boil water, copper kettles, and the most peculiar "doctors of tea", a nickname for the tea service people.

Local tea houses in Sichuan have the most striking tea service skills, and not long ago David was given a chance to watch one "martial tea performance" closely. The whole process of placing the saucers and tea bowls was super smooth. The large copper kettle filled with boiling water and a one-meter long spout was like a windmill in the performer's hands, who moved the kettle close to the tea bowl, and all of a sudden, before anyone noticed, wrung it back. A rush of boiling water then poured down into the tea bowl, which was then capped with a quick, simple finger flip by the performer. The whole thing was amazing. Afterwards there were more skillful tea performances that dazzled David.

The tea performances thus made David a fan of the Chinese tea ceremony. In his eyes, Chinese tea, beginning with bitterness and ending with a sweet aftertaste, is a kind of culture worth exploring. The taste of it depends on one's sentiments, the craft, one's soul, the whole context, and the very process of drinking. Choose a right moment, find a right place, and sit down for a cup of tea, a very subtle feeling of enjoyment will then fill your heart and refresh your mind, as if all the restlessness and bustle are all relieved and gradually give way to tranquility and ease.

A cup of tea, a book, and the silent passage of time, comprise a most picturesque scene of life.

The Second Home

The appeal of Chengdu not only lies in its spectacular scenery, unique folk culture and profound historical and cultural heritage, but also rests in its extreme openness and inclusiveness. The inclusiveness of a city is an important factor for foreign people to consider when deciding where to live and how long they will stay. An inclusive city will carry a charm of internationalization.

The fast development of Chengdu might initially help to draw in foreigners, but it is the leisurely, slow-paced lifestyle that led them to settle down.

David loves his life in Chengdu, especially when he takes a walk with his wife and two sons on the streets in the fine weather, looking for the traces of history: narrow passages and high celadon walls recalling memory of the past; the breeze on the old streets, caressing as it used to be. Sometimes they relax in a tea house, listening to local Chengduers chit-chat. Sometimes they join in social dancing activities in the community. His wife is very skilled at the passionate samba.

As the saying goes: "You must either read or travel. Either your soul or your body should be on the way." David is a fan of traveling, which rewards him with broader horizons, complete freedom in nature from all anxieties, and a feeling of integration wherever he is. This is his dream life. When he records the scenery along the way and relishes the food, he will find himself always thinking: with a special elegance, nestled in the Sichuan Basin, naturally protected by the Daba Mountain and Qinling Mountain from harsh cold, biting wind and scorching sun, Chengdu is such a nice place.

Chengdu is also a city undergoing constant changes. The quality of life is getting better as the year goes by. David is told that Chengdu is the most livable city in China, for life here is neither too fast nor stressful. And he couldn't agree more. For himself, when he first set foot on this land, he never could have imagined that there would be such a thrilling story waiting to unfold between him and Chengdu, nor could he have expected that he would one day become a "French Chengduer".

He loves living here, with its clean environment, its high-tech facilities and modern conditions geared to entrepreneurship. His life now is as beautiful as a rose.

David said one day he would tell his children that there nere two hometowns for him: one in France, and the other, Chengdu.

吴致远（荷兰）
文化公司创始人

Michiel Roosjen, the Netherlands
Founder of a Culture Company

大慈寺茶园里有个褐发碧眼的文化信使

微微阳光洒落在高高红墙上，斑驳金色光影和零落金色银杏叶相映成趣。这片位于蜀都大道红星路口的红墙很是特别，它像是一道神秘之墙，把成都这座城市悠久历史和繁华当下分隔开来。红墙外，是一栋栋高楼林立，是一串串车水马龙，是一道道时尚风景；红墙内，是一间间低矮庭院，是一阵阵香烟缭绕，是一声声低吟浅唱。在成都的市中心，居然有这样一处特别的地方。

熟悉成都的人或许已经猜出，这便是始建于唐代的成都大慈寺。与繁华、现代的太古里商业区仅仅一墙之隔，大慈寺仍保存着它千百年来的古朴和神韵。因着大慈寺的著名，以至于大慈寺一旁的茶园里人不是很多，四四方方的天井式茶园像是要把所有的闲适都圈在内，坐在一把把竹椅上的人们悠闲自在地品着茶，摆着龙门阵，清脆的茶碗碰撞声与欢乐的成都话组成了一篇生活的乐章。它昭示着，这里是上了年纪的成都本地人的乐土。

常常，在这茶园中会看见有两位身材高大、白皮肤、栗色头发的帅哥，他们在以老年人为主的喝茶人群中，看上去有些格格不入，却似乎对这座茶园很是熟悉，而且面对人们的目光，脸上的神情没有一丝的害羞和拘谨。其中最高大的外国帅哥，就是来自荷兰的吴致远。

最爱大慈寺的盖碗茶

熟练地选好座位，熟练地和小二交谈，又熟练地走到点茶的前台，看着墙上的茶水单子，点上一杯毛峰，看来，吴致远对大慈寺的茶园还真是十分熟悉。

曾经，吴致远还只是个对成都的一切都很陌生的外国游客，吴致远也不叫吴致远，而是叫 Michiel。2011 年，纯粹以旅游观光为目的，吴致远作为游客，第一次来到成都。这个神秘东方的西部都市，让当年只有 23 岁的吴致远大开眼界，他惊讶地发现，遥远的东方古国还有这样一片被称作"天府之国"的宝地，这里有一段段神奇的历史，一座座巍峨的高山，一条条穿城而过的河流，一处处古老的建筑，同时，这里又有一片片现代化的街区，一群群时尚的年轻人……历史与现代、传统与时尚的奇妙碰撞和完美融合，深深吸引了他。

第一次的成都之旅，吴致远和大多数游客一样，去了很多著名的旅游景点，在天府广场、武侯祠、杜甫草堂、宽窄巷子等地都留下了自己的足迹，甚至还听了一次川剧。不过，让吴致远最感兴趣的，竟然是在成都的旅游景点中并不算起眼的大慈寺。

2011 年，大慈寺一带正在进行着轰轰烈烈的城市发展建设，地铁二号线春熙路站正在紧张建设中，还有许多低矮破旧的危房陆续被拆除，取而代之的将是繁华的商业区太古里。吴致远走在这样的街头，望着热闹非凡的建筑工地，有着和其他人不一样的视角。他相信这一带的成都一定会旧貌换新颜，会更加具有现代化大都市的味道，那么处在建筑工地中间的大慈寺会怎样呢？他非常好奇。大慈寺因为它悠久的历史而显得十分陈旧，再加上它地处寸土寸金的商业中心，吴致远不免对大慈寺的未来感到担忧，这一担忧给他的第一次成都之旅留下了悬念。

于是，2012 年，吴致远一到成都，第一时间就怀着忐忑的心情找到他印象深刻的大慈寺，并且惊喜地发现，这个古老的寺院被完好无损地保留了下来，静静地处在忙碌建设的工地中，好似一位遗世独立的智者，静默地等待着他的来到。从那时起，惊喜和感动的吴致远对大慈寺有了更深的感情。不论工作再忙，吴致远每月都必定要抽时间去趟大慈寺，去看看大慈寺是否依然完好，去看看寺院里的环境是否依然安宁，在这片宝贵的闹中取静的净土上找寻心灵的宁静与祥和。再后来，吴致远在每个天气好的周末，都会或是一个人或是约上好友，到大慈寺的茶园里坐下，喝杯清香的盖碗茶。

大慈寺的盖碗茶早已成为吴致远的最爱。在家乡荷兰，人们习惯喝咖啡，而吴致远如今早已习惯喝盖碗茶。对他而言，一碗茶、一把椅子、一本书，不仅是忙碌工作间隙难得的放松方式，更是一种最具成都味儿的生活方式。

与蓉城文艺深入合作

在成都这个文艺气息浓厚的城市，几乎每天都上演着各式各样的文艺演出，一台台扣人心弦的戏剧、一曲曲荡气回肠的交响乐、一场场美不胜收的舞蹈，都给在成都生活的人们增添了许多快乐。这些文艺演出的表演者们，有的来自本土，有的远道而来，他们各具特点，各有千秋，不同的风格才让蓉城这个大舞台更加五彩斑斓。

国外艺术家与中国艺术家的中西合璧，总能制造出别样的美感，那么荷兰著名 DJ 与成都本土小提琴家合作，会碰撞出怎样的火花？这个问题的答案，吴致远可以告诉你。

2014 年秋，吴致远萌生了一个想法，他希望他的故乡荷兰的文化艺术可以被更多的成都人了解和喜爱，而他实现这一目的不想用寻常的宣传方式。在这个崇尚文艺的城市里，人们对新鲜的艺术形式总是有着强烈的兴趣，推出"荷兰 DJ 与中国小提琴手的跨界音乐之夜"一定能受到广泛的关注。于是，在吴致远的提议下，著名荷兰 DJ Mike Ravelli 经过十余个小时的长途跋涉来到成都，与成都的小提琴手会面，并在奎星楼街的名堂创意工作区为蓉城音乐爱好者们献上了一场别开生面的视听盛宴。

此次音乐活动是成都的首次"荷兰日"系列活动的重要组成部分，吴致远创办的荷兰 About Asia 文化传播公司是系列活动的主办方之一。除了音乐活动，吴致远和他的伙伴们还推出了荷兰设计展、微电影之夜等丰富多彩的活动，在蓉城青年群体中取得了很好的反响。

不久之后的 2015 年和 2016 年，吴致远再次参与到"荷兰日·成都"的组织策划中，陆续推出了关于音乐、绘画、时尚、设计等多方面的一系列活动。特别令吴致远难忘和骄傲的是，2015 年，在吴致远的促成下，他在故乡最爱的多米尼克书店与他在成都最爱的大慈寺旁的方所书店达成了合作。

多米尼克书店在世界上有着"天堂书店"的美誉，它其实是一间拥有 800 年历史的古教堂，历史演进中还充当过诸如马厩、搏击场、儿童游乐园、自行车停车场，历史十分悠久，故事十分特别。而 2014 年刚刚在千年古刹大慈寺旁建成的方所成都店，是一个面积约 4000 平方米的"地下藏经阁"式的文化空间，也是中国目前最大的民营书店。

2015 年，多米尼克书店与方所成都店同时被美国《安邸》（Architectural Digest）杂志列入 2015 年世界最美 15 座书店榜单。两家相隔百万公里的书店，一座在"天上"，一座在"地下"；一座 800 岁，一座犹如新生。2015 年 9 月 26 日晚，两座"最美书店"的主人——多米尼克书店店主 Ton Harmes 与方所创始人毛继鸿在方所成都店相会，谈两种不同的"最美"，也谈两家书店如何成为了"最美"，以及怎么继续"美"下去。

吴致远策划的 2015 年"成都荷兰日·创意与城市"活动有了此项文化交流成果，令他十分欣慰。不过他却幽默而谦虚地调侃道，文化交流无非就像他用荷兰的咖啡机磨中国的咖啡豆一样简单。

活力城市充满了机遇

一个不满三十岁的荷兰小伙在成都创业，并一次次促成荷兰与成都的文化艺术合作，着实不是一件容易的事。但吴致远却笑着说，他把自己的成就归功于成都这座美丽的城市。

在处理公司事务的过程中，吴致远越来越发现，原来成都不仅仅有着悠久的历史、秀美的风光，在这个中国西部的城市里，有着一群群充满朝气的年轻人，他们阳光、乐观、勤奋、积极，既会享受生活，又能勇敢地为了梦想打拼。

这里还有着良好的市场环境，吴致远欣喜地看到，时隔一年的成都发生着日新月异的变化，中国政府西部大开发的政策和成都政府对商业的优惠政策让成都的市场经济得以蓬勃发展。这次出差让吴致远意识到，成都是一座充满活力的城市，也有是一座充满机遇的城市。于是，吴致远决定来成都开公司，他相信成都人新潮的思想势必会与他创新型的文化艺术理念不谋而合。

在成都开设荷兰 About Asia 文化传播公司的分公司之后，吴致远决定定居成都。他在这里不仅促进了荷兰与中国文化艺术事业的交流，还促成了他的故乡和"第二故乡"有了更为紧密的联系。2012年，荷兰马斯特里赫特市与成都成为了国际友好城市，在 2015 年的"荷兰日"暨"马斯特里赫特日"活动中，马斯特里赫特市市长安玛丽·潘带领马斯特里赫特市城市文化及重要艺术项目代表来到成都，开启了 Fashionclash 时尚设计展。

Fashionclash 是欧洲顶级时尚艺术节之一，也是马斯特里赫特市首要的年度时尚活动。2017 年 4 月，一个脱胎于 Fashionclash 的时尚文化节即将在成都牛王庙"未来中心"举办，吴致远对此功不可没。

成都，这座既古老又年轻，既安宁又繁荣，既有很深的文化积淀，又有很强的商业意识的城市，随着中国的改革开放和现代化进程，正在发生着深刻的变化。这些变化，吴致远看在眼里喜在心上，他相信在成都蓬勃发展的势头中，自己也会离自己的理想越来越近。

回成都有回家的感觉

从游客到工作者，从工作者到半个"成都人"，如今的吴致远已经打从心底把成都当作了自己的家。作为公司创始人的他时常为了工作出差各地，包括中国其他繁华都市，但吴致远认为，他在其他城市永远只是过客，只有到成都才是"回家"，因为成都才是可以让他彻底放松自己、包容他的一切的温馨港湾。

初来成都时，偶然的一次机会，吴致远欣赏了一场川剧表演，被其美妙动人的唱腔，生动活泼的语言所吸引，此后，他偶尔会和朋友去悦来茶园听正宗的川剧表演，享受铿锵的锣鼓声、婉转的清唱、余音袅袅的帮腔、老茶馆的茶香。吴致远在成都结交了很多四川朋友，也学会了一些四川话，"抵拢倒拐"是他说得最溜的一句。他甚至还学会了唱中文歌，虽然是照着拼音唱，但也是难度不小。他最喜欢的歌曲是赵雷的《成都》：和我到成都的街头走一走，直到所有的灯都熄灭了也不停留……走到玉林路的尽头，坐在小酒馆的门口……

成都独特的韵味让吴致远流连忘返，在他眼里，每一刻的成都都是不一样的。吴致远想要去寻找旧时成都的繁华与秀丽，想要领略这个城市独有的风姿，想去享受那闲适散淡中让人回味无穷的茶文化和麻辣美味，想去感悟那博大精深源远流长的佛文化和道文化的余韵。

成都，一座来了就不想走的城市。好像徐志摩说过："一生至少该有一次，为了某个人而忘了自己，不求有结果，不求同行，不求曾经拥有，甚至不求你爱我。只求在我最美的年华里，遇见你。"吴致远在他最美的年华里，就这样遇见了成都，爱上了成都，扎根在成都。

大慈寺茶园里有个褐发碧眼的文化信使

Tea House of Daci Monastery "Dwells" a Cultural Messenger

The sun casts a gentle golden light upon the high-rising red wall, creating an adorable golden world together with the golden ginkgo leaves here and there—this red wall, located at Hongxing Road intersection on Shudu Avenue, is quite special, for it's like a mysterious screen that secludes the city's ancient history from its bustling life. Outside, there are clusters of tall buildings, busy roads and the ever pervasive fashion; inside, there silently stand low courtyards, with smoke gently wreathing and swirling, and low chanting voices soothing hearts. So what's this special place at the very center of the downtown Chengdu?

People familiar with Chengdu can give a quick answer: it is Daci Monastery in Chengdu, which was built during the Tang Dynasty. Only one wall away from the busy and modern downtown Taikoo Li, Daci Monastery, however, is preserved the way it used to be thousands of years ago. The highly reputed Daci Monastery somehow overshadows the nearby tea garden, which turns out to be much quieter. The square, air-shaft-like yards seem to lock up all of the possible leisure: people sitting on bamboo chairs, sipping tea and chit chatting; clinking tea bowls and the lively Chengdu dialect together producing a piece of music about living. It is, as all signs here show, definitely a paradise for the elderly local Chengduers.

Among the regular guests there are two tall, white and auburn-haired young men, who look sort of out of place amid the aged tea-drinking group. However, they make the tea garden their frequent haunt, rarely disturbed by the surrounding gazes that cast their way. The taller one of the two is Michiel Roosjen, who is from the Netherlands.

Favorite Covered-bowl Tea in Daci Monastery

For him everything is like an effortless routine: picking a seat, having a word with the waiter, coming to the counter, skimming through the menu and ordering his cup of Maofeng tea. Michiel Roosjen couldn't be more familiar with the tea garden.

Michiel Roosjen didn't get to know Chengdu in a day. The city used to be a total stranger to him, and his name back then was Michiel instead of Wu Zhiyuan in Chinese. In 2011, the 23-year-old Michiel came to Chengdu for the first time for a sightseeing tour, ending up awe-struck by this mysterious city in West China. He was amazed to find that in the distant orient there was a "Land of Abundance", a combination of magic stories in history, towering mountains, city-crossing rivers, ancient buildings, and also modern blocks and young fashion fans. The miraculous and harmonious convergence of history and modern life, tradition and fashion, intoxicated him.

Like most tourists, Michiel's first tour in Chengdu was marked by stops at several famous tourist attractions, such as Tianfu Square, Wuhou Temple, Du Fu Thatched Cottage and Kuanzhai Alleys. He even had a chance to watch Sichuan Opera. But his favorite place was the least striking one—Daci Monastery.

Back then in 2011, Daci Monastery was surrounded by thriving urban construction sites, such as the Chunxi Road Station on the Metro Line 2, which was under construction; as a result, many old, low houses were demolished one after another, giving way to the prosperous Taikoo Li of the future. Strolling in the streets and gazing upon the bustling construction sites, Michiel had some different thoughts. The place would surely have a new and modern look, but what would become of the Daci Monastery amid the construction sites? He found himself wondering. The temple looked so old, and given its location at the very center of the expensive downtown area, Michiel became apprehensive about its future and left Chengdu with the question hovering in his mind.

Later in 2012, during his second trip to Chengdu, Michiel, unsure and anxious, went straight to Daci Monastery, which had impressed him so much, and was amazed to find that the temple remained intact, standing erect like a tranquil, fate-spared saint waiting for Michiel's return in his own reserved manner. From that surprising and touching moment onwards, Michiel became more attached to the temple. No matter how full his schedule was, every month he would spare time for a visit there, checking whether it was still intact, or tranquil, and seeking the peace of mind in this precious secluded paradise. As time went on, Michiel began to develop a habit of drinking covered-bowl tea on every fine weekend, either alone or with his friends, in the tea garden neighboring the Daci Monastery.

The covered-bowl tea served at the Daci Monastery has long become Michiel's favorite. Back in his homeland, the Netherlands, people love coffee, but Michiel has become a covered-bowl tea drinker here. For him, a cup of tea, a chair and a book are not only a rare way to relieve stress from work, but also the best of what is a Chengdu-flavored lifestyle.

Launching Cooperative Programs in Culture and Art

Chengdu, as a deeply artistic city, never lacks artistic performances. Its heart-gripping plays, soul-stirring symphonies and visually entertaining dances are adding joyful colors to the life of people here. Those performing artists, either local or from far and wide, are contributing to the big stage of Chengdu in their own way.

When foreign artists meet their Chinese peers, a unique mixed beauty is always anticipated. So what might happen if a famous DJ from the Netherlands is put together with local violinists from Chengdu? That's a question Michiel Roosjen has solved.

During the fall of 2014, Michiel Roosjen had the idea of bringing the culture and art of the Netherlands to Chengdu people through a novel event. Hence the "Cross-border Musical Night of Dutch DJs and Chinese Violinists" was proposed to ignite the interest and thus received wide attention from this city that has always embraced art. At the invitation of Michiel, Mike Ravelli, the most famous Dutch DJ, took a oven the hours to Chengdu, met violinists in Chengdu, and together gave a spectacular performance at Mingtang Creativity Studio of Kuixinglou Street for local music enthusiasts.

The event marked an important opening for the first-time "Dutch Day" series, of which Michiel's Dutch company About Asia was a host. On top of that, Michiel and his partners produced a long list of activities, such as the Dutch Design Exhibition and Micro Film Night, all receiving wide recognition from young people in Chengdu.

Soon in 2015 and 2016, Michiel engaged in a new round of designing

"Dutch Day in Chengdu" and launched a series of activities pertaining to music, painting, fashion and design. One thing that made him really proud was that, through his efforts, in 2015, the Dominique Bookstore, his favorite back in his homeland, struck a deal with Fangsuo Commune, his favorite one here near Daci Monastery.

Dominique Bookstore, the world's well-acclaimed "bookstore in heaven", is actually an ancient church dating back to 800 years ago. Its long history of evolving into a stable, a fighting ring, then a children's amusement park and a bicycle parking lot is vivid and unique. In contrast, Fangsuo Commune, built in 2014 near the ancient Daci Temple, is much like an underground depository that covers around 4,000 square meters. This cultural space is currently the largest privately-operated bookstore in China.

In 2015, the two were both listed in the World's 15 Most Beautiful Bookstores in 2015 by the US magazine Architectural Digest. Millions of kilometers away from each other, the two seem to have little in common: one is "in heaven", while the other is "underground"; one is 800 years old, while the other is newly born. On the night of September 26, 2015, however, the owners of the two "most beautiful bookstores"—Ton Harmes of Dominique Bookstore, and Mao Jihong, founder of Fangsuo Commune—met at Fangsuo Commune in Chengdu. Their talks revolved around their different beauty, the process of becoming "the most beautiful" and how they should carry on.

This meeting proved to be a soothing outcome for Michiel, who had designed the whole series of 2015's "Chengdu Dutch Day: Creativity and Cities" for better cultural communication. But in his humorous and modest way, he joked by saying that "cultural communication is as easy as grinding Chinese coffee beans with Dutch coffee machines."

A City Vibrating with Opportunities

It's not easy for a man under thirty from the Netherlands to start a business in Chengdu, much less to realize so many cooperative programs in culture and art between the Netherlands and Chengdu. But Michiel, with a grin, attributed his success to the city itself.

When dealing with business here, Michiel found that apart from its beautiful scenery and long history, Chengdu, this city of West China, also has a group of energetic youth, who are uplifting, optimistic, hardworking and positive, good at enjoying the journey of life while fearlessly striving for a better future.

To his great joy, the market here was increasingly entrepreneur-friendly, with favorable changes taking place every day. Supportive policy initiatives like the China Western Development and privileged terms for business offered by the local government inject vigor to the economy here. After one business trip to Chengdu, Michiel fully realized the city's vitality and great potential for business. Thus he decided to open an office here, believing his innovative thinking about culture and art would cater to the Chengdu people in their pursuit of novelty and fashion.

After opening a Chengdu office for his cultural communication company About Asia, Michiel decided to move to Chengdu. After that he not only promoted better communication between the Netherlands and China in culture and art, but also helped build closer ties between his home country and his "second home country". In 2012, Maastricht of the Netherlands and Chengdu became sister cities. In 2015, on "Dutch Day" and "Maastricht Day", Mary Pan, the mayor of Maastricht, led a delegation to Chengdu, which was comprised of representatives from Maastricht's urban culture and other major artistic programs, kicking off the Fashionclash fashion design exhibition.

Fashionclash is one of the top fashion and art festivals in Europe. It's also the primary annual fashion event in Maastricht. In April 2017, a fashion festival modeled after Fashionclash was held at the "Future Center" of Niuwangmiao, Chengdu, and the credit must go to Michiel.

Chengdu, ancient but youthful, peaceful but thriving, has a profound culture and a strong sense of business. As China's reforms, opening-up and modernization gather force, the city is going through drastic changes. For Michiel, those changes are good, pleasing signs, for he believes that advancing on the wings of the headway Chengdu is making, he is sure to get closer and closer to his goal.

Chengdu: A Real Home

From being a tourist to working here, to becoming almost a local Chengduer, Michiel has long viewed Chengdu as his home. Though he is seen on frequent business trips across the country, sometimes even in the most prosperous cities of China, he has the impression that only Chengdu is the home he returns to, and anywhere else for him is just a temporary stop. Only in Chengdu can he totally relax and be whoever he wants to be.

When he was still a new-comer here, Michiel once stumbled upon a Sichuan Opera performance. The beautiful singing and the lively words magnetized him. Later, Michiel would sometimes visit Yuelai Tea Garden with his friends to watch the most authentic Sichuan Operas, finding enjoyment in the strong chorus of the drums and gongs, the melodious singing, and the lingering vocal accompaniment in the pervasive fragrance of tea. In Chengdu, Michiel has made a lot of Sichuanese friends and picked up a little Sichuan dialect. He has even learned Chinese songs, which are still difficult for him, even with the help of Pinyin. His favorite Chinese song is "Chengdu" from Zhao Lei, a very sentimental song that depicts the private, subtle emotions of the city.

Chengdu is a uniquely intoxicating city for Michiel, who views every second of Chengdu differently. Every part of the city—its ancient glory, its unrivaled beauty, its leisurely culture of tea and spicy food, and its profound, long-standing heritage of Buddhism and Taoism–appeals to him.

Chengdu is a city one could hardly bear leaving after having lived there. A great Chinese poet Xu Zhimo once depicted love using the following words, "In our life, at least, there must be one time when we should love someone regardless of ourselves, regardless of the prospect, regardless of whether we could join hands, regardless of whether that person could belong to us, and even regardless of whether our love would pay off. At my best age, I have met you, and that by itself is quite enough". So it is with Michiel. In the love story between him and Chengdu, he has met the city at his best age, fallen in love with it and finally settled down there.

HOME IN CHENGDU

Where the Heart Nestles
There the Home Settles

此心安处是吾乡 　下

成都市人民政府外事侨务办公室 编

中国文联出版社
http://www.clapnet.cn

目　录

【乐·享在成都】

CATALOGUE

Enjoying Living in Chengdu

创·梦在成都

冈田正男（日本）
"五月玫瑰花园"经理

Okada Masao, Japan
Manager of Rose de Mai

把爱的玫瑰献给成都

充满浪漫气息的弧形粉红色牌匾，充满设计感的四方形的绿化植物，与植物色调浑然一体的深绿色金属栅栏……在汽车一辆辆呼啸而过的成都温江温郫大道旁，有着这样一处特别的地方。

乍一看，这处地方像是一个不大的公园，高高低低的绿树掩映，深深浅浅的植被交错，星星点点的粉色花朵跃然其间，一条蜿蜒曲折的小径似乎在暗示园内还藏着许多期待被发现的秘密。抬头细看粉红色牌匾，只见上面写着"Rose de Mai"字样，在下方还有一个浅绿色的牌匾，写着"La France 法阁四季庭苑"作为补充，原来，这里是一座法式风格的玫瑰花园。在浅蓝色天空的映衬下，虽然已非玫瑰花盛放的季节，这座花园依然看起来是那么清新和美好，让人不禁想问，它的主人会是一位美丽的少女吗？

与人们的猜测截然不同，它的主人是一位老者，一位来自日本名古屋的 69 岁植物学家，名叫冈田正男。但若你有幸见到这位冈田先生便一定会惊叹，他与这座玫瑰花园的气质浑然一体，简朴的服装、慈祥的笑容，流露出自然的温和与宁静。冈田正男把这座玫瑰花园命名为"五月玫瑰园"，他既是这里的主人又是园丁，这个他亲手培育了 1500 余种玫瑰的花园，这个倾注了他毕生心血的地方，是他献给自己、献给成都的最珍贵礼物。

1994 年　缘分伊始

69 岁的冈田正男，已经和玫瑰花相伴度过了半生时光。早在年轻时，冈田正男就在日本研究玫瑰花的栽种和培育，他在与业内专家们的交流中得知，曾有英国、美国的植物学家在成都研究并实践过玫瑰花的培育，这让他第一次听说到了"成都"这个地方。那时的他对成都还是一无所知，他只知道成都是中国西部的一座城市，似乎有着良好的自然环境。因为日本的土地十分稀缺，冈田正男想在中国培育玫瑰花，然后出口到日本等更多国家，于是便决定，不妨来成都看一看。

1994 年，冈田正男第一次从名古屋来到成都。他细致地考察了成都的土壤状况，考察了成都的花卉种植现状，还考察了邛崃等地。他对成都的土壤环境非常满意，但光照不足的问题让他很是苦恼。当年陪同他考察的成都友人，一位四川大学的老师建议，可以去西昌看看。那里阳光十分充足，但是土壤却并不适合。最终冈田正男决定与友人一起在四川大学进行土壤的研究。

从那时开始，冈田正男就与成都结下了不解之缘。与友人在四川大学的土壤研究工作进展得非常顺利，每当取得新的研究成果，他便会飞回日本，在日本的种植园里进行试验，往返于成都和日本之间成了他的家常便饭。后来，冈田正男还把在四川大学研究出的新的栽培基质出口到了日本。

当然，初来成都的冈田正男从没有想过，自己有一天会定居在成都。在他的记忆中，当年的成都质朴而美丽，就像他儿时的家乡，并不发达，却很亲切。在日益进展的土壤研究工作中，冈田正男发现，自己仿佛已经不能和成都说再见，在成都研究土壤、肥料，并努力把研究成果向世界推广，几乎成了他当时生活的全部。他笑称，自己是不知不觉中"被这块土地留了下来"。

梦想终于照进现实

尽管热衷于土壤研究，但冈田正男最初的心愿始终没有更改，他一直希望能够在成都打造出一座属于他自己的玫瑰花园，把关于土壤和玫瑰花的研究完美地结合在一起。

于是，在四川大学从事研究的同时，冈田正男也在多方打听相关事宜，2005 年，机会忽然向冈田正男招手。他偶然得知，第六届中国花博会将要在成都温江举办，于是在当年 4 月，冈田正男和合作伙伴、成都人徐尧决定报名参加这一国家级的花卉盛会。他来到温江实地考察，发现这里的土壤、气候都较为符合他的需要，当即就看上了这片土地，于是决定就在成都温江打造自己梦想中的玫瑰花园。

万事开头难。虽然冈田正男有着十分丰富的土壤研究知识和玫瑰培育经验，但经营玫瑰花园还是有着不小的难度。第六届中国花博会期间，冈田正男满怀热情地打造出他的第一个玫瑰花园，这放在当年的成都来说可谓是非常超前。精致华丽的花园令他心醉，可是却与周围的农田、苗圃显得格格不入，并没有受到当时人们的关注和认可，不符合当时的市场需求。因此，经营惨淡在所难免，冈田正男两度更换玫瑰园选址，却都以失败告终，令他心痛不已。

然而，不服输的冈田正男还是决定卷土重来，实现自己未竟的心愿。2010 年，冈田正男和伙伴又在温江发现了一片满意的土地，就是"五月玫瑰园"现在的所在地。这里的自然风光深深吸引了他，美丽的田园环境似乎蕴藏着无限的能量。于是，他和伙伴在这 100 多亩的土地上倾注了他们数年来的全部时间、精力和金钱，玫瑰园里的一草一木一花，都是他们心血的体现。

为建成正统的玫瑰花园，冈田正男和伙伴常年到法国引进新的玫瑰品种和培育技术，率先和世界玫瑰领导者、法国玫瑰的代表戴尔巴德在中国独家合作，把这座"五月玫瑰园"打造成了法国戴尔巴德现代庭院玫瑰的展示窗口。2015 年 4 月，从选址成都温江开始，刚好过去了整整十年，冈田正男的"五月玫瑰园"终于正式开园了。这座承载着冈田正男爱与梦想的花园，有着多达 1500 余种玫瑰花，分为原种玫瑰、古典玫瑰和现代玫瑰三大类，每一朵玫瑰都是冈田正男与成都的友谊之花。

因地制宜　交汇融合

"五月玫瑰园"以法式风格为主，在来成都之前，冈田正男就常常与法国的玫瑰培育专家合作，现在玫瑰园里玫瑰花的研究和开发也主要在法国。他致力于把法国的玫瑰花和培育技术引入中国，推广宣传玫瑰文化，此前还从未有过能够展示玫瑰文化的场所。冈田正男的"五月玫瑰园"并不是传统意义上的花园，而是把玫瑰的文化、历史都承载在花园中，再结合精美的园艺，把植物上的、科学上的、美学上的知识有机地结合起来，向公众传递更丰富的内涵。

冈田正男介绍，这座花园是中日法三国特色相融合而成的。法国特色自不必说，园中玫瑰花的品种，园中建筑的风格、绿化的风格、装饰的风格等都流露出浓浓的法式风情。但即便如此，"五月玫瑰园"的中国味道、成都味道并没有丢，因为冈田正男在和伙伴设计这座花园的时候，采取了因地制宜的方法，没有对这片土地的自然风貌进行一丝一毫的破坏，完好地保存了这里独有的地形地貌，与周围的田园风光也能融洽地合而为一，这便是冈田正男对成都最大的敬意。作为一名日本人，"五月玫瑰园"自然也少不了日本的元素。冈田正男独具匠心地亲自在花园进行设计，采用了日式风格的木花架，还专门建设出一个"园中园"，一个日式山水庭院风格的小玫瑰花园。这样匠心独运的设计，让"五月玫瑰园"融入了冈田正男对法国玫瑰的毕生研究，融入了对成都的深情厚谊，也融入了对故乡的深深眷恋。

经过冈田正男的用心经营，"五月玫瑰园"已经在成都牢牢地扎了根。随着成都人生活水平的不断提高，精神文化需求的不断增长，"五月玫瑰园"受到了越来越多人的关注和喜爱，现在日均人流量为 100 人左右。经营状况日渐改善，令冈田正男很是欣慰，但他的追求并不在于收益，而是在于打造他心中的"玫瑰博物馆"。他从未把这座有着 1500余种玫瑰花的花园看作一个纯粹的经营场所，而是看作玫瑰文化的载体，这里的每一枝玫瑰都有明确的品种标牌和介绍，并带出玫瑰背后的历史文化故事，他希望这里能够成为玫瑰文化向世人展现和传递的平台。

凭借着个人的力量进行这项不小的工程，难度可见一斑，但倔强的冈田正男自然不会畏惧，一天天在园中获得的精神上的满足就是他最大的动力。每天到了玫瑰园之后，冈田正男总会先在园子里转一转，观察每一朵花的长势，亲自锄草、浇花。在玫瑰园其他园丁的眼中，冈田正男是一个在工作上追求完美的可爱老人。

一同成长　相伴永远

从 1994 年到 2005 年，从 2005 年到 2015 年，又从 2015 年到现在，冈田正男和成都的故事经历了一个又一个篇章。生活在成都的漫长日子里，他不仅深切感受到了成都人的变化，还看到成都从一个偏远的中国西部城市，发展为一个现代的国际化大都市，成都人的生活品质不断飞跃，人们的物质生活和精神生活都日益丰富。

冈田正男在成都打造玫瑰花园的事业从一开始的无人问津，到现在的广受喜爱，与成都的经济、文化发展有着密不可分的关系。现在，周末郊游、赏花和户外婚礼越发流行，冈田正男高兴地看到，越来越多的成都年轻人和家庭会选择他的"五月玫瑰园"，还有一些文艺工作者会来到园中举办音乐会等活动，这让他对"五月玫瑰园"的未来前景十分看好。

在成都的日子，刚好占据了冈田正男 1/3 的人生，这 1/3 的人生让他感触良多。他见证了成都飞速的发展，见证了城镇化水平的不断提高，这座开放、包容的都市蕴含着无限的潜能，提供着无限的机遇，是他实现理想的最佳所在。因此，冈田正男早已决定，要永远和成都在一起，现在的他早已把成都看作"第二故乡"，每年只回日本探亲一次，虽然没有家人在身边，却有他的挚爱的事业和最好的伙伴，他想要把"五月玫瑰园"打造成成都的文化品牌，打造成"百年玫瑰园"。他最大的愿望，是逐渐把玫瑰园扩散成为玫瑰小镇，让人们在这里收获美的享受，收获精神的满足感，收获心灵的富足。

冈田正男由衷地认为，成都真的是一个很宜居的城市，他感到成都的气候越来越好，环境质量越来越好，美丽的蓝天白云让他心旷神怡。成都不仅是一个宜居的城市，也是一个开放的城市，人们追求心灵的美好，这是"天府之国"自古以来的文明所造就，这样的天时地利人和，让冈田正男不得不爱。

Rose of Love is My Gift for Chengdu

Arched plaques in romantic pink, green plants squared by designs, dark green metal fences that almost merge into the greenery... This is a special place nestling behing the Wenjiang-Pixian Avenue, Wenjiang, Chengdu, with cars whistling by.

At first glance it looks like a park of moderate size, covered with a wavering line of trees and crisscrossing plants that vary in brightness and adorned by pink flowers twinkling like the stars. An indicative path winds and extends, as if there is a mysterious world of secrets in the garden that awaits exploration. The pink plaque overhead reads "Rose de Mai", under which there hangs another light green plaque as a footnote: "La France 法阁四季庭苑 (garden for all four seasons)". So it is a French-style rose garden then! Despite rose season being far away, this garden, against the light blue sky, never loses its freshness and beauty. One might naturally wonder, "perhaps its owner is a beautiful lady"?

That would prove to be a misled assumption though, for in fact the owner is a 69-year-old man named Okada Masao, a botanist from Nagoya, Japan. If you have the chance to meet him, you might be amazed by how his personal manner is integrated with his garden: simple clothing, amiable smiles, all things about him expressing a natural kind of warmth and peace. In this garden which he has named "Rose de Mai", Okada Masao is both the owner and the gardener. He has dedicated all of his life to this garden, which now houses over 1,500 kinds of roses that he has cultivated, which he takes as the most precious gift for both himself and Chengdu.

A Story Since 1994

For 69-year-old Okada Masao, half of his life has been spent together with roses. In his earlier years, he was in Japan studying how to plant and cultivate roses. Communication with related experts revealed to him that some British and US botanists had chosen Chengdu as a place to study and practice rose cultivation. That was the first time when he heard about Chengdu. But then he knew nothing about the city except that it was in West China, and seemed to have perfect natural conditions. Since land resources were scarce in Japan, and Okada Masao thought about cultivating roses in China and then exporting them to Japan, he made a decision to take an inspection tour in Chengdu.

In 1994, Okada Masao made his way from Nagoya to Chengdu. He took a close look at the soil there, the flower cultivation, and also places like Qionglai. He was very pleased with the soil; but the lack of sunshine in Chengdu discouraged him. That same year, he went to try his luck in Xichang upon the advice of a friend from Chengdu who was accompanying him during the inspection tour and was also a teacher at Sichuan University. It turned out that the sunshine was not bad, but the soil was not what he expected. Finally, Okada Masao decided to study soil at Sichuan University together with his friend.

His connection with Chengdu thus began. Their soil study went well. Whenever there was some new achievement, he would fly back to Japan and did experiments in his garden there. He became a most regular guest of the airlines between Chengdu and Japan. Later, Okada Masao exported a new growing medium, an outcome of his study at Sichuan University, to Japan.

But it never occurred to him that he would one day settle down in Chengdu. According to him, Chengdu back then was as simple and beautiful as his childhood hometown. They were both amiable, though not that rich. As his soil study went on, Okada Masao found it impossible to sever his ties with the city, for almost all his time had been occupied by his study on soil and fertilizers in Chengdu, as well as his efforts to expand his achievements to the rest of the world. He joked that he was unconsciously "captured by this place".

Dreams Finally Come True

Though addicted to soil study, Okada Masao never gave up his wish that he had always entertained: to build his own rose garden in Chengdu, where he might perfectly combine his achievements in soil study and rose research.

Accordingly, he never forgot to devote some intelligent efforts to this ambition while studying soil at Sichuan University. In 2005, there was finally an opportunity: he accidentally heard that the 6th China Flower Expo was to be held in Wenjiang, Chengdu, in April of that year. Okada Masao, with his partner Xu Yao who was from Chengdu, decided to sign up for this national floral pageant. During his investigation in Wenjiang, he was instantly won over by the soil and climate there, which perfectly met his requirements, and Wenjiang became his handpicked site for his dream rose garden.

The first step is always the hardest. Though he had a rich academic background in soil study and rose cultivation experiences, running a rose garden still proved to be a great challenge for Okada Masao. The 6th China Flower Expo saw the completion of his first rose garden, which, in the local context, was rather avant-garde. And he was himself intrigued by the delicate and grand garden. However, the garden, which seemed somewhat out of place there among the farmland and nurseries, received little attention and recognition, and proved not in line with the market demand. Sales were consequently poor. Okada Masao was then forced to move his rose garden twice, but to his great dismay, each try ended up in failure.

Okada Masao, who never admitted defeat, took another try for his unfulfilled wish. In 2010, he and his partner found another site in Wenjiang which they took great delight in. It was to dwell the garden "Rose de Mai". The scenery was deeply appealing, and there seemed to be some infinite energies and possibilities hidden behind the natural beauty. Okada Masao and his partner poured all of their time, energy and money into this place that covered an area of over 100 mu (about 66,667m²). Each flower and tree serves as a measurement of their dedication.

To make the rose garden classical, Okada Masao and his partner regularly introduced new kinds of roses and cultivation technologies from France, piloted an exclusive partnership in China with Delbard, a leading rose nursery in the world and the representative of French roses, and made "Rose de Mai" a display window to the modern courtyard roses of Delbard. April 2015 marked the tenth year since the garden was situated in Wenjiang, and Okada Masao's "Rose de Mai" was finally open. This place, loaded with its owner's love and dreams, is covered by over 1,500 kinds of roses that come under three large categories: original roses, classical roses and modern roses. Each of these roses indicates the blossoming friendship between Okada Masao and Chengdu.

Rose de Mai: Adaptation to Local Condition and Tri-national Combination

"Rose de Mai" is mostly in French style, for Okada Masao used to cooperate with rose cultivation experts from France, and the roses in his garden were mostly studied and developed in France. Though always committed to introducing French roses and rose cultivation technologies to China and spreading rose culture, Okada Masao has never found a suitable place to exhibit the culture of roses. Rose de Mai is not a traditional flower garden though. Instead, it embeds the culture and history of roses to the garden's construction and transformation, and organically combines exquisite gardening skills and knowledge of botany, science and arts to provide visitors with something more than it appears to be.

According to Okada Masao's introduction, this garden is imbued with Chinese, Japanese and French elements. French influence is easily felt, since it is pervasive in the rose species, the architecture, the greenery and decoration. It has also kept the Chinese and Chengdu style. During the designing process, Okada Masao and his partner endeavored to keep the landscape intact and make the garden harmoniously fit into the surrounding pastoral scenery, which was the best tribute that Okada Masao paid to Chengdu. Besides, since the owner is from Japan, Japanese elements also naturally found their way here. Okada Masao made ingenious efforts to ornament his garden with Japanese-style wooden flower racks, and more noticeably, a "garden inside the garden", which is a small rose garden with a Japanese-style landscape. Such an ingenious design for "Rose de Mai" represents Okada Masao's life-long study of French roses, his love for Chengdu and also his attachment to his home country.

Okada Masao's hard work has been rewarded, for "Rose de Mai" is now firmly rooted in Chengdu. Higher level of living standard means higher spiritual and cultural demands. "Rose de Mai" is garnering growing attention and popularity, with its daily visitor volume reaching around 100. This improved business performance is encouraging, but Okada Masao never views revenue as and his ultimate goal. Instead, he is always dreaming of building a "rose museum". Thus he never takes this place, home to over 1500 kinds of roses, as a mere money maker. In his eyes, it is more like a carrier of the culture of roses: each rose here has its own brand, profile, and historical and cultural background. It is expected to be a platform where the culture of roses can be displayed to and conveyed to people.

Playing a lone hand in this great undertaking is never easy, but the reserved Okada Masao is fearless. His garden is his biggest source of motivation. Every day, when he arrives at his garden, Okada Masao will first walk around, attentively monitor the growth of each flower, and then do the weeding or watering by himself. In the eyes of other gardeners, Okada Masao is an adorable old man that seeks perfect work.

A Lasting Relationship

From 1994 to 2005, 2005 to 2015, then 2015 up to now, Okada Masao's life in Chengdu has kicked off one chapter after another. It is also over this long course that Okada Masao has witnessed how people of Chengdu has changed, how Chengdu has risen to become a modern international metropolis from a remote city in West China, how people's lives has been improved, and how their material and spiritual life has become enriched.

The development of his "Rose de Mai", which met cold shoulders first and finally rose to wide popularity, is also inseparable from Chengdu's economic and cultural development. More people are taking to weekend traveling, flower watching and outdoor weddings, and Okada Masao is glad to see that more and more young people and families from Chengdu are choosing his "Rose de Mai" as their destination. The garden also attracts people from the art's circle who would like to hold activities like concerts. All that, according to Okada Masao, promises a very good future for "Rose de Mai".

Okada Masao has spent one third of his life in Chengdu, and he has experienced and learned a lot during this period. He has witnessed the rapid growth of the city and its increasing urbanization. This open, inclusive city, which boasts endless potentials and offers infinite opportunities, can be a paradise for his dreams coming true. It is for this reason that Okada Masao has decided long ago that he would never leave the city, which he has long regarded as his "second hometown". He now visits his family in Japan once a year. The lack of family love is well remedied though, for Okada Masao has his beloved career, best partner, and an unrelenting wish to build "Rose de Mai" into a cultural brand of Chengdu, as well as a "century-old rose garden". He even has a bolder idea to enlarge the rose garden until it becomes a rose town, where people may reap beauty, fulfillment and solace.

Okada Masao sincerely believes that Chengdu is a most livable city, especially since its weather and environment is continuously improving, and he is pleased with the beautiful blue sky. Meanwhile, Chengdu is also an open city and people are pursuing an open and beautiful mind, thanks to its long-standing civilization as the "Land of Abundance". Such a perfect combination of nature and culture is irresistible for Okada Masao.

>>> 从云（美国）
成都第一张创业签证获得者

Klimith Philip Walder, USA
The First Foreigner Obtaining the Start-up Visa of Chengdu

用一张蓝图绘制创业之路

云来成都　从语而学

　　与一座城市的邂逅，总是伴随着许多不经意的决定。我们也许是在一座城市结束人生的历程，也许是觅寻许多的城市，最后在最爱的城市来度过我们的一生。选择，总是在不经意的一个念头之下产生，但就是这样一个不经意的念头，或许就改变了我们未来生活的轨迹。当时才九岁的从云定然想不到，爱上了架子鼓并说服父母同意自己打架子鼓的这个选择，会让自己在多年以后因从事乐队鼓手的工作，前往中国，邂逅成都，走上一条汉语教学创业之路。

　　2012 年，从云来到了成都。在此之前的他，先后在北京与重庆有过短暂的停留。体验过北京繁华的都市魅力，品尝了重庆浓郁的山城文化，从云最终选择了成都。古蜀国之都以它高度的包容性、低廉的生活成本、闲适的生活氛围吸引了这位来自费城的年轻小伙。初来成都时，从云的中文水平仅限于最通用的"你好""谢谢""好的"日常用语水平。在面对成都人的方言时，他也只能示之以尴尬又不失礼貌的微笑。此时的从云需要快速地渡过语言难关，让自己更好地融入到这座城市。幸运的是，他很快便找到了学习的方法，正是一本关于如何记住汉字的书，开启了从云最初的中文学习之路。

　　从云感慨地称，这本书，让自己对于中文的学习走了一条貌似曲折，实则基础牢靠、效率高速的道路。大多数的中国人，从牙牙学语之时就是从口语开始接触汉语。我们在口语流利的前提下，开始了字的反复拼写与练习，以此来熟练掌握我们的母语。而成年的外国人并不能照搬此方法，但是选择死记硬背的方法效率又太过低下。所以从云摸索出了立体成像的记忆方法。很快，采用这种学习方法的从云在对中文的掌握上越来越优于其同班的同学们。仅用了两年的时间，从云便取得了汉语等级考试六级的通过证书。如今的从云，早已可以熟练地运用中文来与身边的人交流。跨越了语言障碍后的从云，有了更多的机会去获取许多书本上未记载的知识。当语言不再是我们的阻碍时，我们就有了更多的可能性去激发文化之间的交流碰撞。至于从云是怎样走上了汉语教学这条从业之路的，就不得不提到他的创业伙伴兼朋友英国小伙儿 Luke Neale，中文名叫"宁昊天"。

"蓉漂"落地耕耘梦想

基于一位共同朋友的契机，从云认识了来自英国的宁昊天。志同道合的他们经常聊着关于学习、创业以及梦想的各种话题。或许是在某次吃着火锅热火朝天的讨论中，或许是在一个小酒吧的聚会中，两人对于汉语学习的交流心得孕育出了一个关于教外国人学习中文的"创业宝宝"。

两年前两人都顺利通过了汉语 6 级测试，当时，从云与宁昊天意识到，是时候开启他们的汉语教学创业事业了。

有了这个创业想法后的从云，此刻却面临着又一难题——签证问题。通常外国留学生毕业后想要留在成都工作、创业的话，需要有学士及以上学位外，还需至少两年以上的工作经验。不过幸运的他刚好碰上了最新出台的"产业新政 50 条"规定的新政策，该政策规定，在华高校（含港澳地区的高等院校）毕业的外国留学生，具有在蓉创新创业意愿的，可凭我国高校毕业证书申请 2 至 5 年有效的私人事务类居留许可

（加注"创业"），进行毕业实习及创新创业活动。从云也幸运地成为了第一位拿到四川省"创业签证"的外国人。至此，从云开始同宁昊天安心地将他们辛苦研究的汉语学习方法推向市场并孵化成教育培训机构的产业成果。利用一笔资金，两人开启了他们的汉语教学实验班。基于两个人各自的优势，创造力很高的宁昊天负责面对学生，为他们规划学习内容等；而秩序性很强的从云，则是负责了网络教材的制作与推广，以及部分行政事务。创业的艰辛两人一起体验，创业的磨难两人一起度过。从云与宁昊天这对来自大洋彼岸的年轻人，相识成都，创业成都，不可谓不是一种缘分。

如今，两人的汉语教学事业已经走过了两个年头。这项事业也渐渐走向了更成熟的发展阶段。宁昊天将他们的项目重新命名为汉语蓝图。当问及汉语蓝图这个名字背后的寓意之时，从云表示这样命名是希望学习他们课程的人，能够像拥有一份学习汉语的蓝图指南一样，开启他们的汉语学习之路。汉语的学习有着如蛛网般复杂的体系，两人的这项事业相信可以为更多的汉语学习者带来更优质快捷的学习体验。

从自身的经历提炼出创业的想法，两人也在用心地摸索着最适合他们的方式来让这项事业壮大。目前两人的教学主要采用线上授课的教学方式。依托便捷的网络途径，用直播的方式为他们的学生进行汉语教学指导。渐渐地，从云发现，仅靠两人的时间，已经无法满足越来越多学生的教学需求。所以，两人逐渐萌发了制作教学视频的想法。在考察了大量竞争对手的情况下，两人终于发现了自己的项目在理念上的优势。这一次，他们要将自己的服务转变为产品，用销售视频课程的理念来让项目得到新的飞跃和发展。

从云的教学视频已在 2018 年 1 月推出，相信该教学视频的推出，可以让更多的外国汉语初学者从手机终端以及网页端口等媒介来获取到优质的教学课程，从而得到有效的汉语学习方法。

从最开始的线下小班授课，到现在小规模的线上小组授课与一对一授课模式，再到逐步升级的网络视频课程打造，从云和宁昊天始终坚持着打造精品、精良制作的信念。从云坚信最好的招生方式就是好的口碑。只有通过认真地去制作优质的学习内容，才能让自己的客户们感受到他们的教学诚意，得到良好的教学反馈，从而积累更多的经验以便于提高教材内容质量。在这样的良性循环下，汉语蓝图项目稳步发展，并在 2017 年 9 月遇到了又一次发展的契机。

机会总是在一个偶然的时机悄然来临。一次发朋友圈的时候，从云偶然得知了四川省第一届"天府杯"创业大赛的信息。与搭档宁昊天一说，两人一拍即合，赶紧开始准备参赛的资料，在大赛中从云用生动的例子将汉语蓝图的教学方式做了演示。最终，这两位来自异国他乡的外国友人取得了初赛第二名的好成绩。虽憾失进入决赛的资格，但是通过这样一个平台，让更多的人们认识到了汉语蓝图这个正在成长的项目，或许在未来终会吸引更多的人投入到这个寄托了两人梦想的项目中来。

在获奖之后，从云与他的搭档宁昊天也将汉语蓝图的未来发展工作进一步推展开来。汉语蓝图项目将在成都越来越优渥的创业温床中，孕育出更多无限的可能。在下一步的工作目标中，他们已经联络到了两位美国的程序员对汉语蓝图进行 APP 的打造计划，并计划搬入一个新的办公室，组建一个专业的团队来进行这项工作。

从云化雨　圆梦此地

来到成都的这些年，从云这位费城小伙儿，从最初的乐队鼓手到四川大学的留学生，再到如今的汉语蓝图项目创业者，三重身份的转变也见证了他在成都这座活力四射的城市的成长。一开始的邂逅，一念之间的停留，成都用它千年文化的沉淀与高速发展的经济，让从云与他的伙伴宁昊天在此种下梦想的种子，吸取创业阳光的养分，并慢慢发芽成长。

当提及自己家乡费城的创业环境时，从云感慨到，若是在自己的家乡费城，自己很难有机会参与这类的创业大赛。而成都的政府部门重视对于这类创业活动的支持，对他们这样的外国人也提供良好的创业政策——如创业签证这种政策。加之成都整体的生活成本并不高，减轻了自己许多经济方面的压力，在这样自由的创业环境中，自己与伙伴宁昊天有更多的信心来将项目坚持下去。

在对汉语蓝图项目未来目标的展望中，从云也兴致勃勃地描画出了他与伙伴宁昊天心中的创业蓝图。汉语蓝图未来将从 APP 开发工程开始，通过与中国的相关公司开展合作，来进行 APP 服务的批发售卖。在此期间，从云也计划与四川大学的汉语老师进行合作，拍摄他们的教学视频，丰富汉语蓝图的教学课程。而更为宏大的目标则是，从云与宁昊天寄希望汉语蓝图这个项目来影响英国、美国、澳大利亚等国家对于汉语教学的改革。

谈及成都的未来，这位美国小伙儿眼中闪烁出了充满希望的光芒。侃侃而谈两国的政治经济发展，"中国梦"这个词汇如今让从云体会颇深。中国经济的高速发展，以及自己眼中成都这座城市的万千变化，都让从云赞叹不已。如今的成都人民生活水平提高，科技所带来的生活便捷的改变，都让从云有着切身的体验。

梦想，在成都这片土地上，从来都不是个遥不可及的词汇。这不仅让本地的老百姓们对"中国梦"充满信心，也让从云这位来自远方的青年人才敢于去梦，敢于去闯。从云感叹道，仅仅是微信这样一个小小的社交软件，我们就可以在其中挖掘出无线的商机，创造出属于自己的财富。所以，他寻梦成都，造梦成都，将自己的梦想根植于此。

成都，不再让这位远方的外国小伙伴觉得家在远方，此刻的他心安于此地，筑梦于本土，如一片云从天空中飘来，化作春雨滋润了成都这片创业的土壤。邂逅一座城，寻梦一个家，愿从云及他的小伙伴能够在成都绘制成属于他们的梦想蓝图！

Mapping out an Entrepreneurial Blueprint

Learning Chinese Language in Chengdu

An encounter with a city is always inadvertent. We might live out our lives in them, or we might explore many cities before choosing one to be our home. Such potentially casually-made decisions change our life trajectory. Likewise, nine-year-old Walder never imagined that persuading his parents to support him to learn to play the drums, would many years later enable him to work as a band drummer, and go to Chengdu all the way in China, and then to start a business focusing on Chinese language teaching.

Following a brief stay in Beijing and Chongqing, Walder came to Chengdu in 2012. After experiencing the modernity of Beijing and savoring the local culture of hilly Chongqing, Walder settled in Chengdu. Formerly the ancient State of Shu, Chengdu's inclusiveness, low cost of living and leisurely lifestyle served as a magnet for the young Philadelphian. As a new comer, Walder could only manage the most rudimentary expressions like "nihao (how are you?)", "xiexie (thank you)" and "haode (OK)". In the face of Chengdu dialect, his only reply was to smile politely, embarrassed. Back then, what Walder wanted to do was to adapt to his new life and bridge the language barrier. Luckily, it did not take long for him to hit on an effective learning method: a book on how to memorize Chinese characters helped Walder embark on the road of Chinese learning.

Walder emotionally recalls that this book geared him onto a road of seemingly tortuous yet actually efficient path which eventually laid a solid foundation for him. Native speakers learn the spoken language as children, and can speak fluently prior to learning to read and write, which is then followed by mastery of the mother tongue. Yet such a learning method is impractical for adult foreign language learners. However, rote memorization is too inefficient. Finally, Walder came across a memorizing method featuring stereo imaging, and this method helped Walder overtake his classmates, passing his HSK (Level VI) in only two years. Now Walder can communicate with people in fluent Chinese. With language no longer being a barrier, Walder found more oppotunities to acquire knowledge that was not book bound. And when language no longer poses an obstacle, we are better positioned to engage in meaningful cultural intercourse. The story of his Chinese teaching business start-up story cannot be told without mentioning his partner and friend, an Englishman Luke Neale, who in Chinese is known "Haotian (grand sky)".

Settling down in Chengdu to Start up a Business

Walder met Neale via a common friend. The two like-minded guys often talked about study, start-up and dreams. Their idea of start-up might have been brought up in a discussion while enjoying hot pot, or at a pub. No matter where the idea first took root, the vision of a "start-up" baby was born.

Two years ago, having both passed HSK (Level VI), they realized that the time was ripe to start a Chinese teaching business.

With such an idea in mind, Walder still faced another problem, his visa. Normally, overseas students who wish to work and start a business in Chengdu have to have academic qualifications of bachelor's degree or above, as well as more than two years' working experience. Luckily, the newly released "50 incentive policies to boost industrial development" came to his rescue. The policies stipulates that, for international students graduating from Chinese colleges and universities (including those of Hong Kong and Macao) who want to make innovation or start a business in Chengdu, they can apply for a private affairs residence permit (with note "entrepreneurship") valid for 2 to 5 years with their Chinese university diploma for internship or innovation and entrepreneurship activities. And so, Walder happily became the first foreigner to get the "start-up visa" in Sichuan Province. Since then, Walder and Neale worked to spread their innovative Chinese learning methods to the market, nurturing it for wide-scale application in education and training institutions. With the help of a seed fund, they launched their experimental class. Based on their respective strengths, highly-innovative Neale was responsible for student-oriented services, and designed learning content for them; and systematic Walder took charge of the production and promotion of the network textbook, as well as handling administrative functions. They experienced the ups and downs of entrepreneurship as a team. Destiny preordained that the young Walder and Neale would cross oceans to meet and start a company in Chengdu.

It has now been two years since the founding of their business of Chinese teaching. As business grew, Neale renamed their project "Mandarin Blueprint". When asked the meaning, Walder says that they wish that their students would be able to use this Chinese blueprint to assist them along the road of Chinese learning. Learning Chinese is a spider web-like complex project. But the two guys believe that their courses can help more Chinese language learners gain high-quality and efficient learning experience.

They are dedicated to grow their business in the best way, a pursuit which is based on their own learning experience. At present, they mainly offer on-line courses. The convenience of the internet enables them to provide Chinese teaching guidance via live video streaming. Over time, they found that it was difficult to cater to the needs of an increasing number of students. That was when they had the idea of producing teaching video. After investigating a large number of competitors, they were convinced of the conceptual advantages of their project, and this time, they intended to turn their services into products, and to further elevate their project with the idea of selling video courses.

Walder's teaching videos were rolled out in January 2018, which hopefully would provide more foreign Chinese language learners the access to quality teaching courses and efficient methods to learn Chinese via mobile apps, website and through other media.

As their teaching modes evolve, from the original off-line small-sized class to the present small-sized on-line group teaching and one-on-one instruction, and now upgraded to on-line video courses, Walder and Neale have remained committed to providing quality courses. Walder believes that the best advertising is the praise from their customers. Only well-designed and well-produced learning materials can make customers see their professional inputs, and win their sound feedbacks. In this way, they can gather more experience to further optimize their teaching materials. Driven by such a virtuous circle, Mandarin Blueprint project has been on track. Luckily, they embraced yet another development opportunity in September, 2017.

Good opportunities always arrive at the most unexpected time. One day while browsing WeChat Moments, Walder learned that the first session of "Tianfu Cup" Entrepreneurship Competition of Sichuan Province would be held. After discussion, they prepared materials for the competition, where they would present their teaching method at Mandarin Blueprint with vivid examples. The two foreigners won the second prize in preliminary contest. Though failing to make it to the final, they reached out to a greater number of people, increasing Mandarin Blueprint's visibility. It is possible that more people will want to join them to pursue their dreams in future.

After the competition, Walder and Neale started to channel more energy into the future development of Mandarin Blueprint. Chengdu, an ever more fertile place for start-ups, provides many possibilities for Mandarin Blueprint. They have contacted two American programmers to make an app which will move the project forward. They also plan to move to a new office, and build up a professional team to continue the work.

Realizing Their Dreams in Chengdu

Chengdu has witnessed the young Philadelphian progress from a drummer in a band to an overseas student at Sichuan University, and then to an entrepreneur of Mandarin Blueprint. That transformation is testament to his maturation in such a dynamic city like Chengdu. Chengdu, with its cultural richness and economic boom, persuaded Walder and his friend, who met each other by chance during their original brief stay, to pursue their dream of entrepreneurship and build up a thriving business.

Comparing Chengdu with his hometown, Walder says that it is difficult for him to participate in a similar entrepreneurship competition in Philadelphia. The government of Chengdu highly values such entrepreneurship activities, and offers favorable entrepreneurship policies for foreigners, such as start-up visa. This, coupled with relatively low living cost in Chengdu, has given Walder and Neale more reasons to believe that they can carry the project forward.

When it comes to Mandarin Blueprint's future growth, Walder is animated as he talks about their entrepreneurial plans. The project will seek to develop an app, and work with related Chinese companies for app wholesale services. Meanwhile, Walder also plans to cooperate with Chinese language teachers at Sichuan University, and shoot teaching videos for them, thereby strengthening Mandarin Blueprint teaching provision. For Walder and Neale, their bigger vision is to use Mandarin Blueprint to drive Chinese teaching reform in the UK, the United States, Australia and other countries.

When talking about the future of Chengdu, the American's eyes spark with hope. Mentioning the political and economic development of China and the United States, Walder has a deep understanding of the phrase "Chinese Dream". Both the booming Chinese economy and the ever-changing Chengdu amaze Walder. He himself can feel how living standards have been improved here, and how big a part science and technology have played in that.

A "dream" is not something visible but not out of reach in a magical place like Chengdu. As such, not only are local people more confident about their "Chinese Dream", but young foreigners like Walder are also motivated to pursue their dreams. Walder says that boundless business opportunities are waiting to be tapped, and endless wealth can be created through social networking applications like WeChat. That is why he is determined to pursue and achieve his dream in Chengdu.

It is Chengdu that makes foreign friends feel at home. It is in Chengdu that they gain a sense of belonging, and start a business here. We hope that Walder and his partner make their dream and blueprint a reality in Chengdu.

>> 玛丽亚（俄罗斯）
金融科技创业团队 Scorista 负责人

Maria Veikhman, Russia
Founder of Scorista

成都的好超乎预期

"井络天开，剑岭云横控西夏。地胜异，锦里风流，蚕市繁华，簇簇歌台舞榭。雅俗多游赏，轻裘俊，靓妆艳冶。当春昼，摸石江边，浣花溪畔景如画。"著名宋代词人柳永曾在佳作《一寸金·成都》中这样写道。在他的笔下，成都是那样的繁华和美丽，有数不清的游人，数不清的才俊和美女。是啊，如此好风光的地方，怎会不具有吸引力？

今天的成都，与柳永的词中胜景相比，有过之而无不及。千年之间，物换星移，不变的是成都的魅力和吸引力。行走在成都的街头，不时能看到不一样的面孔，每年都有许许多多的外国人来蓉旅行或是工作。飘逸的金发，湛蓝的明眸，高挑的身材，时髦的装扮……即使看到这样一位女性，也没有人会惊讶，只会认为她是一位时尚的外国美女。不过这位外国美女却并不寻常，她热衷的不是时尚潮流，不是游山玩水，而是自主创业。她，是一位有着时尚外表的女强人。

来自俄罗斯的 Maria Veikhman（玛丽亚）在成都的时间并不长，她现在的工作和生活都主要围绕在天府软件园，她创建的俄罗斯金融科技创业团队 Scorista 入驻在这里。那一片现代化的办公区，那一间小而温馨的办公室，就是她选择的"孵化"自己梦想的地方。而在这段并不长的时间里，玛丽亚却已深深地爱上了成都，并十分庆幸自己当初选择来到成都的决定。

游历多国，追寻梦想

金发碧眼、瘦瘦高高的玛丽亚看起来宛如少女一般，但实际上，她已经在金融科技、风控领域积累了 15 年的经验，也是一位多次创业者。

玛丽亚的家乡距离成都非常遥远，在俄罗斯彼尔姆市（Perm），那是一座工业城市，距离莫斯科都有 1000 多公里。在彼尔姆市长大的玛丽亚在家乡一直读到了大学，主修计算机专业。玛丽亚天资聪颖，从小成绩优异，大学期间，在数学、技术方面表现尤为突出，先后获得在土耳其、美国学习与交流的机会。

毕业后，作为联合创始人，玛丽亚在美国成立了一个在线券商项目 AcclaimDomains，进入信贷风控领域。2010 年，她出售了自己的股份，成功退出。回到俄罗斯之后，她加入了一家提供小微金融服务的公司——Platiza，出任风控总监。

期间她发现，提供小额信贷和无抵押贷款的小微金融公司，服务的人群往往违约率比较高，对风险控制有很高的要求，却并不适用传统银行的金融风控系统。因为，小微金融公司的目标客户往往个人信用低，是银行眼中的"劣质"客户，银行的风控系统并不能完全覆盖这部分人群，但根据统计，这部分人群的数量大约占到了俄罗斯总人口 30%。

抓住这个机会，2014 年 2 月，玛丽亚成立了她现在的公司——Scorista，专注于风控和数学算法领域，通过在数学建模、人工智能领域的优势，为中小微金融服务企业提供风险管理服务。更为重要的是，Scorista 采取按效果收费的模式，足见他们对自己模型的信心。在俄罗斯，中小微金融机构约有 2500 多家，Scorista 用两年时间在这个领域的风控建模细分市场做到第一，甚至比一些国际知名公司在这一领域做得还要好，比如 FICO。此外，Scorista 的发展也获得了俄罗斯产业基金 SKOLKOVO 的支持。

初步获得成功的玛丽亚并不满足，因为她一直有着远大的抱负，她希望自己可以拥有国际性的事业。2015 年，玛丽亚把中国和印度列入了自己的考虑范畴，很快，目光敏锐的她瞄准了中国的经济发展势头，她不禁想到，中国不仅有着广袤的国土、庞大的人口数量，更有着不可限量的发展空间，那何不抢占中国的发展红利，开拓中国市场？

几番考察，情定成都

在考察中国市场之前，玛丽亚对中国的了解其实并不算多，更不用说对成都的了解了。玛丽亚只依稀记得，小时候的课本上曾经有过对成都的介绍，她知道成都是一座中国西部内陆的省会城市，知道成都是中国国宝大熊猫的家乡，其他则都是未知数。

2016 年，玛丽亚正式决定来到中国进行实地考察。根据自己对中国的了解和朋友的推荐，玛丽亚把考察的城市选择为北京、上海和成都。她的行程首先安排在北京和上海，在这两座一线大都市，玛丽亚惊叹于中国的发达和现代，但却总觉得它们并不适合自己。于是，她怀着既期待又忐忑的心情转而来到了成都，期待是因为，她的一位朋友、香港投资人极力推荐成都，而忐忑是因为，她担心偏远的西部城市发展空间狭小。

但在 2016 年 9 月，当玛丽亚第一次踏上成都的土地，她就被这座城市的魔力所深深吸引。从抵达双流机场开始，玛丽亚就真切感觉到了成都的现代化，她看到成都的国际、国内进出港航班数不胜数，看到成都的交通设施十分完善，看到成都的市政建设非常先进，这让她喜不自胜。

虽然是独自一人来到陌生的成都，玛丽亚的考察却很从容。她乘坐公交、地铁，感受成都的城市格局，骑共享单车体会成都的休闲气息，在大街小巷品尝成都的地道美食……美丽的风光、热辣的美食、温暖的氛围，让玛丽亚流连忘返。这趟考察既从容，又不失谨慎，玛丽亚经过反复权衡，终于下定了决心——就将公司选址成都！这是因为玛丽亚了解到，成都虽然是一座中国西部的内陆城市，但发展程度在全国名列前茅，而且作为大省、强省四川的省会城市，成都汇聚了众多宝贵的资源，经济、市场、文化条件都十分优越，成都为创业者提供了众多优厚政策，还有非常丰富的教育资源为成都未来的蓬勃发展做坚强的后盾。而且成都与北京、上海相比较小的城市规模正好符合玛丽亚的需要，可以有效节约中小微企业的经营成本。

玛丽亚相信，这样的一座城市，正是适合她的企业成长的摇篮。

找到伙伴，正式启航

玛丽亚来到成都，带着细致而认真的发展规划。Scorista 的俄罗斯团队在数学建模、统计分析上有很大的优势，且在俄罗斯市场积累了丰富经验，而中国在这一细分市场还有许多空白，风控系统技术研发成本高、数据分析人才相对匮乏。与此同时，在 APP 的开发与应用上，中国市场非常成熟，通过 APP 就可以申请小额信贷，这与俄罗斯在小额信贷申请方面还主要用网页端有很大不同，因此，Scorista 也是来学习的，希望能够把 APP 研发的经验输送回俄罗斯。

尽管有着明确的规划和坚定的决心，但玛丽亚在工作地点的选择上还有些迷茫。玛丽亚首先选择的地点是高新区的一处科技产业园，但很快她就发现，自己的事业与这里并不能融合，因为这里的公司主要是做游戏软件的开发，而自己的公司却是金融科技创业团队。正在玛丽亚发愁的时候，一位朋友告诉她，何不去天府软件园？那里是中国最大的专业软件园区，是中国 10 个软件产业基地之一、国家软件出口创新基地、国家服务外包基地城市示范园区，位于成都高新区南部园区核心地带，已成为成都软件与服务外包产业的核心聚集区。此外，十分重要的是，天府软件园对中小微企业还有着非常诱人的优惠政策，通过竞选和评比脱颖而出的优秀企业可以获得天府软件园免费提供的办公室和员工宿舍，这些正好满足了玛丽亚的需求。

与此同时，玛丽亚通过朋友的介绍，在成都找到了一位好搭档——陈磊，主要为她负责国内市场业务。陈磊曾先后在宜信、恒昌、冠群等公司从事风控工作，在金融风控领域也是一位老兵。这位得力干将的获得，让玛丽亚倍感兴奋，也对未来在成都的发展更有信心。玛丽亚与陈磊一同来到天府软件园找寻机会，并成功享受到了天府软件园的优惠政策，在 D 区拥有了属于自己的领地。

从 2017 年 6 月开始，玛丽亚的 Scorista 正式在天府软件园扎了根。继陈磊之后，玛丽亚又招募了一位优秀的成都软件工程师，与她带来的俄罗斯团队一同打拼，新加盟的工程师也让她十分满意。玛丽亚充满骄傲地说，有了两位成都的得力助手，她在成都的事业做得风生水起，成都不愧是一座人才的宝地、财富的宝地，从公司成立到现在，虽然时间很短，却已经大大超额完成了她的工作目标，这让她又惊又喜。

热爱工作，也爱生活

玛丽亚瘦弱的外表下有一颗顽强拼搏的心。或许是秉承着"战斗民族"的传统，玛丽亚在成都的工作十分勤奋，她不仅管理着天府软件园里新成立的分公司，也依然管理着位于俄罗斯的总公司，这个 CEO 做得很是不易。中国与俄罗斯有着 5 个小时的时差，于是玛丽亚便利用这个时差让自己"分身"。白天主要时间，她忙于处理中国事务，而到了晚些时候，就会开始处理俄罗斯的工作，因此从清晨工作到晚上九点都是常事儿。

但这样高强度的工作并没有让玛丽亚感觉到辛苦，因为她非常喜爱这种充实奋斗的感觉，也非常喜爱工作和生活在成都这座城市。从2016年至今，玛丽亚在成都最大的感受是"很舒适"。每当结束了一周的忙碌工作，她喜欢周五晚上去酒吧小酌一杯的夜生活，也喜欢周六去大慈寺感悟成都的慢生活，小酌、品茶、逛街都是她在成都喜欢做的事。

玛丽亚还是一个"吃货"，她笑称，成都美食是她热爱成都的一个重要原因。她最爱"一个人的火锅"——冒菜，特别是在寒冷的冬日，与三两个伙伴一起吃上一锅热气腾腾、麻辣鲜香的冒菜，仿佛可以驱散一身的疲惫。当丈夫来到成都时，玛丽亚第一时间带着他去吃了最爱的那家冒菜，在谈笑间和丈夫分享自己在成都的欢乐时光。

虽然目前还不会说中文，但玛丽亚喜欢在家里开着电视看中文节目，虽然基本听不懂，但她也能从一点一滴中感受中国味道，感受成都乐趣。在成都的这些日子，已经让玛丽亚深深爱上了成都，因为这是一座让她可以放手拼搏的地方，是一个可以将梦想和生活完美结合的地方，也是一个让她没有距离感的地方。玛丽亚由衷地希望，自己能被成都这座城市真正接纳，自己的事业可以在成都蓬勃发展。她希望未来的时光可以和成都永远在一起，共同发展，共创美好。

Chengdu: A City beyond Expectations

Chengdu was once described by Liu Yong (984-1053), a famous Chinese Ci poet of the Northern Song Dynasty, in a poem like this: "Lying under the heaven as in a well, its Jianling Mountains, being a stronghold against Western Xia Empire, towering into the cloud. Its landscape spectacular, its resources abundant, its silkworm market flourishing, performances of singing and dancing spectacular here and there. People from all walks of life swarming in: young men from rich families smartly dressed, and young girls whose beauty is set off by their clothing. On such a spring day, people are picking stones by the Huanhuaxi River as per prophesy, while the picturesque scenery extends." With such prosperity and beauty, with such smart people, Chengdu is sure to be a destination to attract talent to come.

Today's Chengdu is, if not the same as, much better than Liu Yong's description. Things have changed over a course of thousands of years, but Chengdu's appeal stayed. Taking a casual walk on its streets, one might easily catch sight of some foreign faces. Indeed, Chengdu is attracting a large number of foreign people either traveling or working here each year, such as this lady, with streaming blond hair, bright blue eyes and a slender figure, smartly dressed. At first glance one might easily assume her to be an ordinary beauty from other countries. But her real identity is more than that. Fashion and traveling never prove to be her real love. Entrepreneurship is. And hidden behind her fashionable looks is definitely the heart of an Iron Lady.

Maria Veikhman, who is from Russia, has not been here for a long time. Her major work and life now is in Chengdu Tianfu Software Park, where her credit-scoring startup Scorista has settled. That modern office space and her small, cozy office are the very "incubator" of her aspirations. And though their acquaintance has been brief, Maria has found herself deeply attached to the city, and feels lucky to have made Chengdu her destination for entrepreneurship.

Launching Businesses across Borders

Blonde-haired, blue-eyed, and slender, Maria looks like a maiden, while in fact she is a real veteran entrepreneur with fifteen years' of working experience in financial science and risk control.

Maria's home town is Perm, an industrial city of Russia, which is over 1,000 km away from Moscow, the capital of Russia. Born and bred in Perm, Maria also went to university in the city, and her major was computer science. As a smart girl, she did quite well in her studies. When at the university, her excellent performance in mathematics and technology earned her the chance to study in Turkey and the US as an international student.

After graduation, she co-founded AcclaimDomains in US, an online securities trading program, and entered into the field of credit risk control. In 2010, she sold her shares and successfully pulled out. Later when she returned to Russia, she joined in Platiza, a provider of microfinance services, as its executive of risk control.

Over this course she found that the microfinance companies that provided microcredit and unsecured loans faced a high rate of client defaults.

They demanded better risk control, while the traditional financial risk control systems provided by banks, however, could not serve this purpose. The reason was that, those target clients of the microfinance companies, due to their poor personal credit, always fell into the "inferior" group of bank customers who might not be covered by the banks' risk control system. Yet according to statistics, this is an enormous group that almost accounted for 30% of Russia's total population.

Punctually seizing the chance, Maria founded Scorista in February 2014, which focused on risk control and mathematical algorithms, proving risk control services for small and medium-sized microfinance institutions by drawing on its advantages in mathematical modeling and artificial intelligence. Even more noticeable, Scorista adopted an effect-oriented charging mode, which adequately proved its faith in their models. At that time, there were more than 2,500 medium-sized microfinance institutions in Russia. Scorista took two years to surpass its competitors in market segmentation concerning risk control modeling, even outpacing some well-known international brands, such as FICO. It also obtained support from the Skolkovo Foundation, a Russian organization that fostered startups and venture capital.

However, ambitious and visionary, Maria never drew limits to her success. She hoped to expand her business abroad. In 2015, she began to list China and India as her next destinations. Soon, sharp-eyed as usual, she took a close-up view of China's economic momentum. China, with its broad territory, enormous population, and, in addition, an unimaginable space for business growth, seemed to be a good choice. She could not help but think, "So why not take the initiative to step into the Chinese market and win from it a share of the dividends"?

Finally Choosing Chengdu as the Next Stop

Before her inspection tour, Maria knew little about China, let alone Chengdu. She only vaguely remembered that there was an introduction to Chengdu in her childhood textbooks, which said Chengdu was a capital city in the interior part of West China, and hometown of China's national treasure—pandas. And nothing else.

In 2016, Maria decided to launch an inspection tour in China. She listed Beijing, Shanghai and Chengdu as her candidates after referring to her knowledge about China and friends' recommendations. Beijing and Shanghai, the two first-tier cities, topped her itinerary. She recalled marveling at their level of modern development, yet found out that she did not belong to them. Then, with a longing and worried heart, she came to Chengdu. She was longing, for Chengdu was highly recommended by one of her friends, an investor from Hong Kong. She was worried, for Chengdu seemed to be only a remote western city in China with limited space for growth.

However, in September, 2016, when Maria finally made her way to Chengdu for the first time, she was instantly magnetized by the magical city. The moment she arrived at Chengdu Shuangliu International Airport, she was awe-struck by the high level of modernity there. Seeing international and domestic flights busily leaving or arriving, the perfect transportation facilities and the advanced municipal construction, she felt ecstatic.

Though alone as a foreign traveler, Maria took her travel in Chengdu at a slow-pace. She took buses and the subway to closely watch the city's construction, rode shared-bicycles to fit into the leisurely lifestyle, ate local delicacies as she walked around... The beauty, the spicy food and the warm ambience, made her grudge saying goodbye. After this comfortable and careful inspection, Maria, after repeatedly weighing the risks against the rewards, made the final decision to situate her company in Chengdu. She knew well that Chengdu, though an inland city in West China, was actually leading in its level of development. Plus, as the capital city of Sichuan, a big and strong province, Chengdu was gathering numerous invaluable resources. Its abundant economic, market and cultural resources, preferential policies offered by the authorities, and enormously rich educational resources all made up a solid foundation for its booming development in the future. Its relatively small size compared with Beijing and Shanghai was rightly to Maria's taste, who believed that it would reduce the operating costs of small and medium-sized institutions.

For Maria, such a city was sure to be a perfect cradle for her company.

Starting a Business in Chengdu with Excellent Partners

When she came to Chengdu again, she brought a detailed and serious blueprint. Scorista in Russia was advantageous in mathematical modeling and statistical analysis, and had accumulated great experience concerning the Russian market. In comparison, China had a long way to go in market segmentation, reducing the high cost of developing risk control system and recruiting adequate talent in statistical analysis. But on the other hand, China's app development and applications were quite mature. Micro-credit could even be applied for through apps. That was a completely different picture from that of Russia, where micro-credit application still depended on the Web. To some extent, Scorista saw itself as a student in China, who wished to learn about app development and then bring her experiences back to Russia.

Despite her clear plans and determination, Maria found it hard to find the right site for her company. First she chose a sci-tech industrial park in Chengdu's Hi-Tech Zone, only to find that her career, as a startup of financial science, was out of place, for the companies there mainly specialize in developing game software. The haggard-faced Maria was then suggested by a friend to move to Chengdu Tianfu Software Park, which was China's biggest software park, one of the ten software industry bases in China, Located at the core of the south park of the Chengdu Hi-Tech Zone, it had become the core agglomeration area of the software and service outsourcing industries in Chengdu. Even more important, the park offered very appealing supportive policies for small and medium-sized institutions: outstanding companies who win at competitions and in evaluations are entitled to have free office space and employee dormitories provided by the park. That was exactly what Maria yarned for.

Meanwhile, based on her friends' recommendations, Maria found a good partner—Chen Lei, who was to take charge of the domestic market. Chen formerly worked for CreditEase, Hengcheng Group and Guanqun Chi Cheng in risk control, and was a veteran in financial risk control. Joined by such a capable partner, Maria, largely uplifted, was even more upbeat about Scorista's future. Together with Chen, she went to Tianfu Software Park to try her luck, and finally earned the chance to enjoy the park's preferential policy, which secured her a space of her own in Section D of the park.

June of 2017 finally saw Scorista settle down in Tianfu Software Park. After Chen Lei, Maria recruited an experienced software engineer from

Chengdu, who was to join in the team relocated from Russia. The new engineer's performance satisfied her expectation. Talking of her two capable aides from Chengdu, Maria, extremely proud, said that thanks to them, her career had been going on well here. Chengdu was indeed a place blessed with talents and treasure. Her company, though not founded long, had achieved revenues that far outpaced what she expected. That was amazing news for her.

Loving Work, Enjoying Life

Hidden under Maria's fragile look is the heart of a relentless fighter. It is possibly her blood of a "fighting nation" that makes her extremely diligent. She heads her startup in Tianfu Software Park, and also its headquarters in Russia. Being CEO of the two is not an easy job. For Maria, the five-hour time difference between China and Russia is a blessing, for then she can "split" herself at work: at daytime she mainly deals with the affairs of her Chinese company, while later every day she mainly works for her company in Russia. Thus she might often be seen working from early morning till nine at night.

But high-intensity work never in any way wears Maria out, for she just loves the feeling of fighting for something, as well as her work and life in Chengdu. One thing she knows best is that her life here since 2016 is "very comfortable". Every Friday night, after finishing her work, Maria will find a bar to relax herself in the night life. She also likes to experience the slow-paced life of the Daci Temple on Saturday. Drinking, tea tasting and window shopping are some of her favorites in Chengdu.

As a so-called "foodie", Maria jokes that Chengdu food is the most important reason why she loves Chengdu so much. Her favorite Chengdu food is Maocai (instant spicy steam pot), which has been dubbed as "hotpot for one to have alone". For Maria, eating steaming, spicy and delicious Maocai along with several good friends, especially in chilly winter, is a remedy for all kinds of fatigue. When her husband came to Chengdu, Maria wasted no time in bringing him to her favorite Maocai restaurant. There, accompanied by the good food, punctuated by joyful laughter, she recounted her happy moments in Chengdu.

So far she has not yet learned to speak Chinese, but she loves to stay at home with the TV tuned to Chinese programs. Though barely intelligible to her, those Chinese programs make her feel the real Chinese flavor and fun of the city. Having lived in Chengdu for a while, Maria has deeply fallen in love with it. It is a place where she can fight undisturbedly, perfectly combine her dreams and her life, and feel no alienation. Maria sincerely wishes that she can be fully accepted by the city and that her career can flourish. She is wishing for a better Chengdu to whom she can contribute more and with whom she can stay with forever.

>> 瑞秋（英国）
岩羊手工艺店老板

Rachel Grace Pinniger, UK
Owner of Blue Sheep Handicrafts Store

让爱的杂货铺温暖成都

在成都武侯区高华二街，有一家这样的小店——坐落在居民楼下，却不临街。两间铺面门前用绿植围成一个小院，一把遮阳伞、几张桌子、几把凳子，简单的装饰就让这家店和旁边的礼品店有了明显的区分。步入店里，右侧置物架上满满当当摆放着各种手工皮具和彝族漆器，中间的货架上用小竹编框子装着各种手工刺绣的书签、手工玩偶、木雕等小摆件，左侧墙壁挂着一排大小不等、形态各异的手工包包。沿着左边的小门，便来到店铺另一边，整面墙的格子中摆放着羌绣抱枕、刺绣相框、刺绣杯垫、桌旗等各种小饰品、小物件，三张小桌子可供客人在此喝咖啡、歇息。不同于中国礼品店的整整齐齐，瑞秋的岩羊手工艺店看起来有些许随意，稍显凌乱。

然而，就是这样一家看起来有些随意的店，却多次在各类创意展会上展示着羌族刺绣、彝族漆器、皮具、剪纸等极具中国特色的传统手工艺产品，而让人出乎意料的是，这家店的老板却是一位地道的外国人。

今年72岁的瑞秋来自英国，在成都经营着这家小小的店铺，通过瑞秋，中国传统手工艺人有机会接触到英国、澳大利亚、美国等多地的设计师，经过国际设计师的指导，大大增强产品的实用性和体验感。

现在已经定居成都的瑞秋，早已将成都当成自己的第二个家，她打从心里觉得，自己属于成都，也属于中国，而每一个中国人，也都是她的家人。因此多年来，瑞秋一直用她的爱心和坚持帮助身边的人，在这其中，便有 600 多位贫困的中国手工艺人。

新鲜！热心肠英国老太太转行开杂货铺

出生于在英国的瑞秋，在大学还没毕业的时候，就只身一人去到尼泊尔，当了一名医学生。瑞秋在尼泊尔偏远山区的医院里实习。在那里，她目睹了山区人民看病就医的困难。有的病人为了来趟医院需要跋山涉水，路上来回竟然需要花费两个月的时间。这深深震撼到了瑞秋。她暗下决心：要留在这里，为这个国家培养乡村医生，提高当地的医疗水平。"英国不需要我，那里的事情有人做，我要留在这里，做没人愿意做的事。"就这样，她在尼泊尔、印度、中国等亚洲国家一干就是 45 年。

2008 年，汶川地震发生后，一直都是热心肠的瑞秋，毅然来到四川，参加了当时的灾区救援活动。在救援过程中，瑞秋意外了解到很多灾区手工艺人生存极其困难，大量精美的手工艺品卖不出去。没有了经济来源，这些手工艺人就连生病也不敢去医院。此情此景，令瑞秋百感交集。她当即决定：要帮助这些手工艺人，帮他们把产品卖出去。于是，2014 年 10 月，她拿出了自己所有的积蓄 30 万元，开了这家岩羊手工礼品店，以此来帮助困难的手工艺人。

瑞秋店里销售的每一件工艺品，都出自贫困山区少数民族或者残障人士之手。这里既有来自苗族的传统手工钱包，也有来自彝族的木质餐具，还有来自藏族的手工毛毡饰品，也有来自特殊困难家庭的小装饰品……每件手工艺品，瑞秋都分好了类，并通过小卡片介绍产品背后的故事。

虽然有些手工艺品并不是那么精美华贵，但制作它们的人或许是病重孩子的父亲，或许是大山里供子女读书的母亲，或许是身有残疾、行动不便的年轻人。一针一线、一点一滴都融入了他们对生活的渴求和追求。

暖心！往来顾客国际友人统统来帮忙

每天上午十点，瑞秋会准时打开店铺的卷帘门。这个点儿一般很少有客人，瑞秋会趁着空当，仔细规整和摆放店里的商品，做好一天的准备工作。日常店里不忙的时候，瑞秋则选择去成都周边的手工艺人家里主动收购产品，这样既能看看手工艺人的生产生活环境，又能给他们提出一些改良的建议。"看到手工艺人的很多产品，因为款式落后并不好销售，我就会建议他们改变一下样式。"在瑞秋的店铺中，有一部分客人都是外国人，因此，瑞秋通常会建议手工艺人用中国的原材料、中国的技艺制作一些外国人生活用品。

心韵绣坊是一家由失聪及残障人士组成的个体经营机构。2000年，在来自英国的英恩梅女士的带领下，很多生活在昆明的失聪及残障人士聚集到了一起，开始学习一些简单的拼接布块和刺绣技艺。经过几年打磨，心韵绣坊的产品已经能上市销售。瑞秋关注手工行业后，很快了解到心韵绣坊的存在。"他们的产品不是最精美的，但却是很用心的。"在瑞秋的思维中，买一个东西，一定要具有实用性，才会购买。于是，瑞秋建议心韵绣坊的工人们，制作丝绸餐垫套装、相框等人们日常生活中需要的东西。具有中国刺绣元素的圣诞袜，告别了原有的红白单一颜色，大胆采用翡翠绿色、玛瑙红色等中国古典服装特有颜色，没想到这批圣诞袜在瑞秋店里一上市，就深受众多顾客喜欢，被一抢而空。

瑞秋店里很多羊毛制品都是来自青海的安多手工制品。瑞秋和他们对接后，岩羊也成了安多手工制品主要销售商。立体卡通的微波炉手套，款式简单大气，材质却是中国传统的羊毛制品，也成了瑞秋店里的爆款之一。简单的羊毛抱枕却融入了羌绣、彝族刺绣等多种元素，极具中国民族感的创意，不仅深受外国人的喜欢，很多中国人也十分钟爱。

家住附近的插花师张小姐就是瑞秋店里的老顾客。"从他们开业我就一直在这里买东西，不少东西很实用，而且也被瑞秋的行为感动。她真的很不容易。"一来二往，张小姐和瑞秋成为了朋友，只要一有时间就会来店里帮忙布置商品。"受她启发，做点自己力所能及的事情。"帮着布置完店铺后，张小姐还一口气买下来了8个手工玩偶。

瑞秋的善举不仅感动了身边的人，也让远在大洋彼岸的朋友纷纷行动起来，来到成都支持她。今年6月，荷兰夫妇Martin和Debra，不顾路途遥远，从荷兰飞到成都兑现当初对瑞秋的承诺，帮助她重新装修了一遍店铺。远在澳大利亚、英国的朋友们不仅积极帮忙联系设计师设计产品，还热心帮瑞秋拓展销路。一些在蓉国际友人也纷纷出谋献策，帮瑞秋联系各种活动，拓展小店的知名度。刚刚参加完创意设计周，瑞秋又连续接到多个组织的圣诞活动邀请。"可以认识更多的人，能把产品推广出去。"瑞秋很乐意参加这类活动。如今，经过多方的努力，瑞秋和她的小店，也渐渐走上了正轨。

感动！残障家庭获益

戴安是瑞秋店里的职员，也是瑞秋的主要翻译。早在大学时期，戴安就经常到瑞秋的店里来做志愿者。大学毕业后，戴安顺利在一家外资银行谋求了一份体面的工作。当她回到店里探望瑞秋的时候，正遇到瑞秋最艰难的时期，看着瑞秋一个人在店里忙里忙外，戴安的心久久不能平静。"一个英国老太太尚且如此，我又怎么能无动于衷呢？我想跟她一起来完成这件有意义的事儿。"戴安毫不犹豫选择了辞职，成了瑞秋的全职店员。

"以前店里生意并不好，经常很长时间都没收入。"戴安说，为了节省开支，瑞秋经常吃着即将过期的食品，但省吃俭用的她却坚持全款收购手工艺品，对待手工艺人从不讨价还价。有的手工艺品因为制作难度大或者残障人士自身条件受限，根本达不到销售的标准。"我经常劝她，那些做工不是特别精美的产品，我们其实可以拒绝的。"但瑞秋总是很坚持。她总说："我们挣钱的方式可以有很多，但他们确实很难。"在戴安看来，瑞秋更希望能通过这种方式鼓励手工艺人，让他们对生活充满信心。

今年 6 月，二更视频"更成都"栏目将瑞秋和她的爱心杂货铺，拍成小视频对外发布，瞬间便获得 10 万＋的阅读量，也是"更成都"上线以来，在微信平台最快获得 10 万＋的推送。人们感动于这个英国老太太的善举。越来越多的人慕名而来，选购自己钟爱的小物件。

"我就是看了网上的视频，专门倒了 3 趟公交车过来的。"24 岁的张悦。一直以来都非常喜欢这种民族风情的小摆件，她精心为自己挑选了一根苗族的银项链和几个刺绣外壳包装的笔记本。短短几个小时里，店里来了好几拨和张悦一样慕名前来的客人。"买的东西正好也是我家里需要的，如果能在买东西的时候顺便帮助一个困难人士，我还是很愿意这样做的。"客人们的反馈，让瑞秋越来越感到欣慰。"不要仅仅因为公益来买东西，而是要买自己需要的。"

如今，随着瑞秋和岩羊的名气越来越大，店里的生意越来越好。现在小店一周的销售量相当于以前两三个月的总销售量。今年下半年，瑞秋还盘下了旁边的店铺，把岩羊在原来的基础上扩大了一倍。

店铺更大了，客人更多了，瑞秋也更忙了。或是理货，或是帮客人准备咖啡，对待每一位进店的客人，瑞秋总是微笑着欢迎。即便还是听不懂中文，但在瑞秋眼中，只要进店消费的顾客，都是怀揣着帮助他人的善心而来。客人每购买一件工艺品就能为一个困难家庭或者一位残障人士贡献了一份力量。

对于未来，瑞秋并没太多的计划。"未来也许会去其他城市，也许会留在成都，甚至也有可能会回到英国。"在这位 72 岁的英国老太太看来，她依旧很"年轻"，自己还能做很多事情。而目前，她只想帮助更多的困难人士。

在瑞秋看来，如果成都是她的家，那么这些她帮助的人也就是她的家人。成都给了她温暖和爱，她便也用爱来回馈成都，心怀爱意，不忘善心，便是瑞秋一直以来，最坚持的事情。

A Loving Shop Warms Chengdu

A small store tucked away from the street sits on the first floor of a residential building on 2nd Gaohua Street, Wuhou District, Chengdu. The space before its two front rooms, enclosed by plants and shrubs, forms a small courtyard. Although only adorned with a parasol along with several tables and stools, this simple gift store stands out ameng others nearby. Inside, the shelves on the right are stacked with a variety of handmade leather goods and Yi lacquer ware; the shelves in the middle are filled with small bamboo cases containing ornaments like hand-embroidered bookmarks, handmade dolls, and wood carvings; and a row of handmade bags of all shapes and sizes hang on the left wall. The small door on the left leads to the other side of the store. There are also various small ornaments and objects such as Qiang embroidered cushions, photo frames, coasters, and table flags. The three small tables are provided for guests to drink coffee and relax. Unlike a neat Chinese gift shop, Rachel's Blue Sheep Handicrafts Store is more casual and a little chaotic.

This casual-looking store exhibits traditional Chinese handicraft products with Chinese characteristics such as Qiang embroidery, Yi lacquer ware, leatherware, and paper cuttings at various creative exhibitions. Surprisingly, its owner isn't a local Chinese but a foreigner.

Rachel, a 72-year-old British lady runs this small store in Chengdu. She acts as a bridge between Chinese artisans of traditional handicrafts and designers from countries and regions including the UK, Australia, and the United States. The guidance provided by international designers has greatly enhanced the products' usefulness and improved consumer experience.

Since taking up permanent residence in the city, Rachel has long considered Chengdu as her second hometown. She feels that she has an extremely deep connection with Chengdu, China and Chinese people. As such, over the years, Rachel has been helping the people around her with love and persistence, and her kind ness has assisted more than 600 impoverished Chinese artisans of traditional handcrafts.

Elderly UK Lady Switches from Medicine to Selling Ethnic Handicrafts

Rachel was born in the UK. She traveled alone to Nepal when studying medicine at university. She gained experience working in a remote hospital in a mountainous region of Nepal. There, she witnessed how difficult it was for the local people to access treatment. Some patients had to make a treacherous two-month trip to and from the hospital, which shocked Rachel deeply. She resolved to stay in Nepal and improve the local medical standards by training the rural doctors. "The UK has more than enough people to meet its needs. I will stay and do what no one wants to do". says Racbel. This determination motivated her to work in Asian countries such as Nepal, India and China for 45 years.

Kind Rachel came to Sichuan and participated in the disaster rescue efforts in the wake of the 2008 Wenchuan Earthquake. During this period, Rachael learned that many craftsmen there were engaged in a struggle for survival and that a lot of exquisite handicrafts lacked market access. The lack of a source of income made a hospital trip intolerable for sick craftsmen. It is this sad fact that caused a whole range of different emotions to well up within her. Following this, she immediately decided to help these craftsmen sell their products. In October 2014, she invested RMB 300,000 in the Blue Sheep Handicrafts Store to help those poor craftspeople.

Each piece of handiwork sold in Rachel's store has either been made by a minority craftsman living in an impoverished mountain area or by a handicapped person. Traditional Miao hand-made purses, wooden Yi tableware, handmade Tibetan felt ornaments, trinkets from families with special difficulties—Rachel classifies them under different categories, and on the small cards there are stories of each product.

Some handicrafts are neither exquisite nor luxurious, but the maker might be the father of a seriously ill child, a mother in the mountains who provides for her children at school, or a young person with disability and mobility problem. Every piece of thread they sew into the cloth reflects their aspirations of life.

Heartwarming! Customers and Foreign Friends Passing by Offer Help

Rachel opens her rolling shutter at 10:00 am every day. Normally, few buyers come at this time, and Rachel will prepare for the day while she is free by carefully arranging and displaying the items in the store. When the store does not have many visitors, Rachel goes to areas near Chengdu to purchase products from the craftsmen's homes. In this way, she can not only see the environment in which craftsmen work and live, but also give them helpful advices. "Many handcrafts do not sell well because their designs are too old fashioned. I give them some small suggestions about how they might go about redesigning them." As some of her customers are foreigners she usually recommends that craftsmen make practical articles suitable for daily use by foreigners using Chinese raw materials and techniques.

The Xinyun Embroidery Workshop is a self-employed organization employing deaf and disabled people. In 2000, Ms. Enmehmei from the United Kingdom gathered together many deaf and disabled people living in Kunming and taught them simple stitching and embroidery skills. Years of hard work resulted in the Xinyun Embroidery Workshop's products doing better in the market. Rachel soon learned about the Xinyun Embroidery Workshop after she switched to handcrafts. "Their products are not the most beautiful, but they are carefully made." In Rachel's view, practical products have customers. Rachel suggested that the Xinyun Embroidery Workshop make silk placemats, photo frames and other practical articles. Colorful Christmas socks featuring Chinese embroidery bid farewell to the former monotonous red or white color. Colors such as jade green and agate red, traditionally unique to ancient Chinese clothing were used instead. In Rachel's store, these Christmas socks proved very popular with the customers, and they are sold out very quickly.

Many of the wool products in Rachel's store are handmade Ando products from Qinghai. Rachel works together with them, and Blue Sheep becomes a major retailer of Ando handcraft products. 3D-cartoon microwave oven gloves are simply designed, but they are made of wool, the traditional Chinese material. The gloves also proved very popular at Rachel's store.

Various elements such as Qiang and Yi embroidery have been incorporated into simple wool cushions. Such creative Chinese features are welcomed by foreigners and Chinese alike.

Flower arranger Miss Zhang, who lives nearby, is a regular visitor to Rachel's store. "I have been buying things here since she opened shop. Many things are very practical. What's more, I'm touched by what Rachel has done. It has not been easy for her." Miss Zhang and Rachel became friends after they met several times. Usually, when she has time, she would come over to help arrange the items. "I have been inspired by her. I'm doing something that is within my power to help." Upon offering help, Miss Zhang bought eight handmade dolls at once.

Rachel's kind actions have touched not only those around her, but also friends on the other side of the ocean who have been sufficiently moved to travel to Chengdu to help her. In last June, the Dutch couple Martin and Debra flew across continents, from the Netherlands to Chengdu, to honor commitment they made to Rachel—the redecoration of her store. Friends in Australia and the UK have also given substantial help. They contacted designers and increased her sales. Some international friends in Chengdu gave advice and contacted the organizers of various events, and successfully raising awareness of the store. Shortly after Creative Design Week, Rachel received invitations to several Christmas events. "You can promote your products when you meet more people." Rachel is very happy to participate in such activities. Such teamwork has pushed Rachel's store onto the right track.

Moving! An Effort that Benefits Families with Disabled Members

Diane is Rachel's employee and translator. When she was still in college, Diane often volunteered in Rachel's shop. Following graduation, she got a decent job at a foreign bank. When she returned to the shop to see Rachel, Rachel was in her most difficult time of life. For a long period of time, Diane found it difficult to keep calm while Rachel bustled around the store. "How can I remain indifferent when an old lady from the UK can do so many wonderful things? I do want to help her in this meaningful endeavor." Without hesitation, Diane resigned from her post and became a full-time assistant at Rachel's store.

"Business used to be bad, and there were often long periods of time when no money came in at all." Diane says that in order to save money, Rachel often took food passing its sell by date. She was thrifty but always paid in full for the handicrafts she purchased. She never bargained with craftsmen. Some of the handicrafts were not up to market standards either because they were difficult to make or because they stretched the abilities of disabled craftsmen. "I told her time and again that we could actually refuse to accept flawed products." But Rachel thought otherwise. "She always said that we had many ways of making money, but the craftsmen didn't." In Diane's view, Rachel hoped this could encourage craftspeople and provide them more confidence in their lives.

In June, Rachel and her caring shop were featured in "Better Chengdu" on Ergeng Media Platform. The video clip was quickly viewed by more than 100,000 times. This repost hit its target number of views faster than any other since the launch of "Better Chengdu" on the WeChat platform. People were moved by this old English lady's charity, and more and more people came to buy their favorite trinkets.

"I watched the video on the Internet and then came. My trip took three bus transfers." 24-year-old Zhang Yue has always liked such small ethnic ornaments. She selected a Miao silver necklace and some notebooks with an embroidered covering for herself. In just a few hours, the store was visited by several groups of people who, like Zhang Yue, came out of admiration. "What I buy is what my family really needs. I'm happy to help someone in difficulty when I just buy something." Customer feedback delighted Rachel. "Do not compel yourself to buy anything because that will help people in need. Buy what you yourself need."

Rachel and Blue Sheep are enjoying growing popularity, and business is on the rise. Current weekly sales volume now equals previous total sales volume over a period of two or three months. In the second half of last year, Rachel bought the shop next door, doubling the size of Blue Sheep.

The larger the store is, the greater the number of customers is. Rachel is now busier, tallying or preparing coffee for guests and welcoming visitors always with a smile. She doesn't understand Chinese, but for Rachel, those peple that come into the store have desire to help others. Each handicraft purchase contributes to a family in difficulty or to a disabled person.

Rachel does not have many plans for the future. "I may go to another city, or stay in Chengdu, or even return to the United Kingdom." According to the 72-year-old British lady, she is "young" enough to do many things. At present, she only wants to help more people in difficulty.

"If Chengdu is my home, then the people I'm helping are my family", Rachel says. Chengdu has once given her warmth and love, and she has repaid it with kindness. Love and kindness are what have motivated her from the very beginning.

教・学在成都

>> 麦轲瑞（美国）

四川大学匹兹堡学院校长

Michael Reed, USA

Associate Dean of Sichuan University-Pittsburgh Institute (SCUPI)

爱一所校，恋一座城

走过深深浅浅的银杏林，穿过一阵阵青春烂漫的笑声、歌声，便又是一个银杏的世界。四川大学江安校区东门附近的银杏生长在水岸边的广场上，水天一色，银杏树金色的倒影中泛着浅浅的涟漪，好一派诗情画意的景象，实在赏心悦目，令人流连忘返。在银杏树林的掩映下，有一排不算高的教学楼，来来往往于几栋教学楼间的，大多是青春的中国面孔，但在文科楼四区却有一些年长的外国人，他们是四川大学匹兹堡学院的教授们。其中一位灰白色鬓发、身量富态的外国绅士从中国学生中走来，面带灿烂的笑容，他就是这个学院的副院长、教授——来自美国的 Michael Reed，中文名叫"麦轲瑞"。

一见锦城误终身

"拂窗新柳色，最忆锦江头。"南宋著名诗人陆游在诗篇《春晓》中如是说。陆游的蜀中生涯并不长，却对成都这片热土爱得深沉，甚至曾萌生"终焉于斯"的念头，虽然最终并未能得偿所愿，但却留下了许许多多关于成都的不朽诗篇。

其实，不论在任何年代，都有数不清的像陆游一样的人，他们来自他乡甚至异国，对成都从陌生到了解，又从了解到爱上，这座城市的魅力千百年来都不曾变过。

曾经有人告诉麦轲瑞，成都是一座独具特色的中国西部城市，它流传着一个"让人来了就不想离开"的传说。2013 年，麦轲瑞怀着无限的好奇来到中国旅行，其中成都毫无疑问地列入了他的必去目的地。几经辗转，麦轲瑞第一次踏上了成都的土地，虽然与成都的第一次亲密接触只有短短的一周时间，但成都却给他留下了十分难忘的记忆。行走在成都的街头小巷，他感受到了和美国、中国其他城市迥然不同的气质，成都的街道和建筑流露出历史与现代碰撞的独特韵味，成都的自然风光呈现出西部内陆的独有风情，成都人的热情洋溢给他留下了许多欢乐的回忆。麦轲瑞不仅游历了成都的各个景点，还领略了乐山大佛之壮美，峨眉胜景之神秘，如此种种，让他不由得对成都萌生情愫，回到家乡后依然对成都津津乐道。

2015 年 8 月底，命运的安排让麦轲瑞得以与成都再续前缘。2014年，在四川大学与美国匹兹堡大学的共同努力下，四川大学匹兹堡学院正式成立，一年之后，麦轲瑞在美国匹兹堡大学获悉，四川大学匹兹堡学院有扩充师资力量的计划，与妻子商量之后，当即便决定来到成都任教。时光飞逝，麦轲瑞已经在成都生活两年有余，深入的生活让他获得了与当年旅游成都不同的感受，他不仅喜爱成都的美景，更喜爱成都的文化。而且在与中国学生的交流中，他逐渐学会了一些中文，现在的他不仅有"麦轲瑞"这个中文名字，还可以骄傲地用中文说："我喜欢成都，这里是我的家了。"

致力发扬创新型教育

从家乡美国来到遥远的成都工作，麦轲瑞并没有不适应的感觉，这是因为他所任教和管理的四川大学匹兹堡学院与一般的中国高校学院不同，教学模式与西方国家无异。经教育部批准成立的中美高校合作办学机构在全国只有 5 所，而四川大学匹兹堡学院则是西部地区的第一家。这个学院采用全英语授课方式，鼓励创新性学习、开放式讨论、独立性思维，提升学生的领导力、团队合作和创新思维能力。学院设立了美国匹兹堡大学的三个最强学科——工业工程、机械设计制造与自动化、材料科学与工程学，学生所修学分可以得到美国匹兹堡大学的承认，达到双方学校要求的学生可以同时获得四川大学和美国匹兹堡大学的本科学士学位。

这样一个独特的学院，让麦轲瑞身在成都也能如鱼得水。麦轲瑞对四川大学匹兹堡学院的教学环境赞不绝口，现代化的教学设施、丰富的教学资源、灵活的管理机制、勤奋的中国学生，给了麦轲瑞施展抱负的极佳空间。作为一名教授，麦轲瑞也经常会亲自给学生们授课，充实的工作让他收获了许多快乐。

经过教学实践，麦轲瑞真切地感受到了中国大学生和美国大学生之间的区别，在他看来，由于从小受教育方式的不同，中美大学生各有优势和不足，中国大学生不仅十分刻苦，而且从不抱怨遇到的困难，有热情、有雄心、有志向，勤奋聪明好学的中国大学生们总能又快又好地解答老师提出的问题，让他非常欣慰。而美国大学生有着很强的创造性，善于人与人之间的交流和自我表达，擅长团队协作，而且阅读较为广泛。

于是，麦轲瑞就在这样的感悟中给自己设定了工作目标，那就是让中国大学生取长补短，把美国大学生的优点结合到中国大学生身上，培养出综合优势更加显著的优秀人才。他在教学中不断培养学生创新型思维模式，鼓励学生们在探索答案的过程中加深思考，并努力培养学生们的团队合作精神。麦轲瑞认为，中国是一个有着五千年悠久历史的文明古国，成都也是一座历史文化底蕴深厚的城市，这样的国家、这样的城市必然是人才辈出。拥有众多优秀高等学府作为支撑，成都的人才丰富程度和优秀程度完全不亚于北京、上海等一线城市，再加上 2017 年《成都实施人才优先发展战略行动计划》（"成都人才新政 12 条"）的发布，成都的人才吸引力进一步提高，将会会聚更多青年才俊。麦轲瑞希望通过自己的努力，培养出更多现代化的高精尖人才，为成都、为中国的发展尽一份力。

中国情缘命中注定

辛勤的工作离不开家人的支持，麦轲瑞在成都并不孤独，因为他的妻子也从美国来到了成都，与他一同居住在倪家桥附近。有爱，有家，有事业，这样的生活让麦轲瑞感到既幸福又满足。与其他美国教授相比，麦轲瑞在成都生活得更加适应，这不仅因为他有妻子的陪伴，更是因为他的妻子是一位中国人，一位出生于上海的知识女性，而他自然就是一个纯正的"中国女婿"。

麦轲瑞与妻子吉玮有着一段浪漫的爱情故事。2006年，妻子吉玮赴美留学的时候在网上发帖，想要找一名美国人与她成为学习伙伴，教她学习正宗的美式英语。机缘巧合，麦轲瑞看到了这个帖子，此时的他正想要找一位网友学习西班牙语，看到帖子上并没有写明发布者的语种，他便给发布者回信，进行询问和交流。尽管并不是自己想要寻找的西班牙语网友，但这位好学、可爱的中国女孩却深深打动了他的心，在逐渐深入的交流中，他确定这位来自遥远东方国度的女孩就是自己一直寻觅的另一半。

也许正是这样的跨国恋情让麦轲瑞发现了自己命中注定的中国情缘。麦轲瑞坦言，如果不是有一位中国妻子，或许他并不会想要来到中国。在和妻子的生活中，他领略到了许多中国文化的独特魅力，感受到了中国人的善良、热情和勤劳。当麦轲瑞决定来到成都发展时，妻子欣然支持了他的想法，并选择伴他左右，同他一起开启了在成都的小日子。

妻子吉玮现任 Barbri 公司亚太地区的法务经理，同样与教育相关，夫妇二人在事业上相互扶持，一起感受着成都的发展速度与城市活力。而在生活上，二人更是相互陪伴，走过市井与历史交融的宽窄巷子，逛过文人骚客留下无数足迹的杜甫草堂，赏过神奇华丽的川剧变脸，看过憨态可掬的国宝熊猫，吃过麻辣鲜香的火锅串串……这样安逸的日子让麦轲瑞不禁感叹，原来成都的生活才能叫作"享受生活"！

公园里的品茶常客

麦轲瑞和妻子都非常喜欢生活在成都，但他笑称，还是他对成都的喜爱更胜一筹。拿出手机，打开地图，麦轲瑞熟练地指出成都的一个个公园，能够如数家珍一般，分别说出各个公园的具体位置和特色，尤其是各个公园的茶馆所在。原来，麦轲瑞是一位品茶爱好者，成都最流行的茶馆文化正合他的口味。

提到品茶，麦轲瑞的表情瞬间变得更加放松，脸上流露出灿烂的笑容。在母亲的影响下，麦轲瑞从小就对茶有着特殊的感情，长大之后更是和一般的美国人不同，不爱喝咖啡，而是爱品茶。麦轲瑞曾经以为自己的爱好很奇特，而来到成都后他发现，原来这里的人们对茶的热爱比他更甚，而且成都的茶还有和美国不一样的喝法，人们可以在热闹的坝坝头喝，可以边打麻将边喝，可以晒着太阳喝，可以赏着流觞曲水喝，老少咸宜，动静皆宜。成都公园里的茶馆或茶摊是麦轲瑞最钟爱的品茶场所，工作之余，麦轲瑞最喜欢做的事就是和妻子或朋友在公园里品茶。除了他最爱的浣花溪公园、百花潭公园，望江楼公园和文化公园里也常常出现他的身影，麦轲瑞一边说着，一边不由得为他爱的公园竖起了大拇指。他开心地说，自己非常喜欢成都的公园，因为公园里不仅有着极佳的生态环境，而且有着非常温馨、欢乐的氛围，这让他倍感放松和惬意。

如今的麦轲瑞已经切身领悟到"来了成都就不想离开"这种感受。诚如他自己所说，成都已经是他的家，虽然生活的时间不久，但在他心中却已然算得上是"第二故乡"。

家在成都，爱在成都，梦也在成都。麦轲瑞深深爱上了成都山清水秀的自然环境，爱上了成都蓬勃昂扬的发展势头，爱上了成都闲适温馨的人文环境，爱上了成都爽朗热情的百姓性格。从美国来到成都，麦轲瑞从不曾后悔当年的决定，并对成都这个"新家"越发地充满热爱、充满信心。成都这座城市正在经历着日新月异的变化，麦轲瑞很庆幸自己身在其中，他相信，未来的日子里他将会见证成都更加美好的前景，这个具有魔力的城市，将会是他实现理想的地方，他与成都的缘分，必将收获一个最美丽的结局。

Love a School, Love its City

Beyond a ginkgo forest, golden here and still more golden there, a youthful peal of laughter brought us to another world of ginkgo that lies beside the east gate of the Jiang'an Campus of Sichuan University. The ginkgo trees here guard a square along a river that almost melts into the sky at the horizon. The rippling water and the golden ginkgo reflections make up a most pleasant picture exuding endless poetic beauty that tends to stay one's feet. Back dropped by the ginkgo trees are a row of classroom buildings of moderate height. Among those buildings, youthful Chinese faces come to and fro. However, the 4th section of the Arts Building also gathers some older foreigners, who are rightly the professors of SCUPI. Among them is a portly gentleman with greyish white and curly hair coming to us from a crowd of Chinese students, smiling all the way. He is Michael Reed, an American, and also a professor and the associate dean of SCUPI.

A Good First Impression that was to Last

Lu You, a famous Chinese poet from the Southern Song Dynasty (1127–1279) once wrote in his poem "Dawn of Spring" how he felt about Chengdu: "The window frames a beautiful picture of green willows, and how I miss life along the Jinjiang River". His stay in Sichuan was not long, but his love for it was deep and sincere. He even thought about "spending the rest of his life here". Though this thought never became action, he still contrived a large number of poems about Chengdu, which would prove immortal.

The truth is that, whatever the age, Chengdu has always been drawing numerous people like Lu You, who come from alien places or countries, to become acquainted and fall in love with the city. For thousands of years, Chengdu always magically wins their love.

Michael Reed once heard that Chengdu was a special city in West China, so appealing that "once one comes, he or she can hardly bear to leave it". In 2013, Michael, loaded with curiosity, kicked off a journey to China, during which Chengdu was listed as an unquestionable must-go destination. When he finally set foot in Chengdu, despite a only seven-day schedule, he harvested a memory that would last forever. Walking on the streets of Chengdu, he dug out something different from what he would find in either the US or any other Chinese cities. The roads and buildings displayed a unique combination of archaic and modern elements; the natural beauty was typical of the west inland; and the joyful and vigorous Chengdu people carved many happy moments for him. Michael toured around Chengdu, and also managed to visit the magnificent Leshan Giant Buddha as well as the mysterious Mount Emei. These experiences left him intoxicated, and even after returning to the US, he still couldn't help recommending Chengdu to others.

At the end of August in 2015, as if predestined, another chance lay before Michael that would tie him with Chengdu. In 2014, jointly arranged by Sichuan University and the University of Pittsburgh in the US, SCUPI was established. One year later, SCUPI planned to increase its faculty size, and Michael, on hearing the news from the University of Pittsburgh, instantly made a decision to be a teacher in Chengdu after obtaining his wife's support.

Time flies, and Michael has lived in Chengdu for more than two years. As his exploration goes deeper, his feelings towards Chengdu are now largely enriched, which differs greatly with his impression of Chengdu as a foreign traveler: it is not so much the beauty as the culture that he really loves. And good for him, he has picked up some Chinese from his Chinese students. Now he has a Chinese name, and he can speak in Chinese, loud and proud, "I love Chengdu. It is my home".

Committed to Innovative Education

Traveling a long way from the US to Chengdu, Michael has never encountered culture shock. The reason is that SCUPI, where he works as a teacher and a manager, is completely different from its Chinese counterparts, and precisely follows Western countries in its teaching methods. So far, only five institutes in China jointly founded by Chinese and American universities have been approved by the Ministry of Education of the People's Republic of China, and among the five, SCUPI is the first one in west China. With classes delivered in English, it encourages innovative study, open discussions and independent thinking, and it is committed to enhancing students' leadership skills, spirit of team work and innovative thinking ability. The three most prominent disciplines of the University of Pittsburgh—industrial engineering, mechanical design, manufacturing and automation, and material science and engineering—are introduced into SCUPI, and SCUPI student credits are also entitled to be recognized by the University of Pittsburgh. SCUPI students who meet the requirements of both sides can get a Bachelor's degree from both Sichuan University and the University of Pittsburgh.

This unique institute is definitely a blessing for Michael by making his life in Chengdu like a duck taking to water. He pours praise on SCUPU's environment, modern teaching facilities, broad teaching resources, flexible management and hard-working students. He has finally found an outlet for his aspirations. As a professor, Michael also gives regular lessons to his students, which makes him fulfilled and joyful.

Practice as a teacher allows him to identify the real differences between Chinese students and American students. According to him, on account of different educational methods used as they grow up, Chinese students and American students have distinct strengths and weaknesses. Chinese students are hard-working, and they rarely complain about hardships. Warm, ambitious and aspirational, these smart Chinese students always long for knowledge and are quick to answer his questions in a precise way, which he feels is quite encouraging. American students, on the other hand, are highly creative, sociable and expressive. They are good at team work and always read extensively.

Bearing such an insight, Michael has made his work plan, namely encouraging Chinese students to draw on the strengths of American students while trying to cultivate better comprehensive talents. Thus in his teaching, he continuously encourages his students to build innovative thinking models, to deepen their thinking while looking for an answer, and to strengthen their team spirit. Michael believes that, since China has an ancient civilization that spans five thousand years, and since Chengdu possesses profound historical and cultural deposits, it is atural that talents should abound here. Backed by a large number of universities and colleges, Chengdu is not in any way inferior to first-tier cities like Beijing and Shanghai in the range and level of its talent.

With the release of the Chengdu Action Plan to Implement Talent Priority Development Strategy (or the 12 New Policies Concerning Chengdu Talent) in 2017, Chengdu is set to attract and gather more talent. For Michael Reed, his wish is always to make dedicated efforts to cultivate more modern, top talented individuals for Chengdu and China.

A Godsend Chinese Wife

Without his family's support there would be no Michael's full dedication to his work. He never feels lonely in Chengdu, for his wife has also come to Chengdu from the US, and they together live near Nijiaqiao. Having love, a family and a career, Michael can't feel happier and more contented with his life. Compared with other American professors, he fits in much better, for he has his wife together with him, and more importantly, she is Chinese, a female intellectual born in Shanghai. That makes Michael a real "Chinese son-in-law".

The couple's love story is like a romantic novel. Back in 2006, Ji Wei, who was to become Michael's wife, was a foreign student in the US. She posted online that she was looking for a language partner from the US who could teach her native American English. Michael, who was also looking for a language partner to learn Spanish, happened to see her posting, but it revealed nothing about its author's mother language. Michael thus replied, inquiring and messaging to and fro. It turned out that she was not at all the Spanish language partner he expected to find, but he found himself deeply attracted to this diligent and adorable Chinese girl. As their communication deepened, he was convinced that this girl from the faraway East was the one he had always been seeking for.

It might be this cross-border love, as if arranged by fate, that tied Michael with China. Michael confesses that, without his Chinese wife, he might have never come to China. With his Chinese wife around him, he feels the special appeal of Chinese culture, as well as the kindness, warmness and diligence of Chinese people. When Michael decided to move to Chengdu, his wife was totally supportive and joined him in building their future in Chengdu.

Ji Wei is now the legal Manager of Barbri Asia Pacific, a company also related to education. On careers, the couple supports each other, feeling the strong beat of Chengdu's development; in life, they intimately accompany each other, leaving their footprints together in the Wide and Narrow Alleys that combine secular life and history, and Du Fu's Thatched Cottage that has been a popular destination for poets and writers, marveling at the face-changing performances of Sichuan Opera, chuckling at the adorable pandas, marveling at the spicy, tasty hotpot and food strings... With such comfortable moments always around the corner, Michael cannot help but exclaim, "You may never find a better place quite like Chengdu to enjoy life!"

A Regular Tea Sipper in the Parks

Michael and his wife both love living in Chengdu, but he jokes that his love for Chengdu is superior. Taking out his cell phone and opening the GPS app, Michael turns into an expert on the parks of Chengdu, locating them effortlessly, while pointing out their addresses and characteristics, especially where their tea houses are. The reason, actually, is that Michael is a fan of tea tasting, and the tea houses of Chengdu are definitely to his liking.

On mentioning tea tasting, Michael's face relaxes into a bright smile. Influenced by his mother, he has been born with a special attachment to tea since a very young age. When he grew up, unlike ordinary Americans who only love coffee, Michael preferred tea. He used to see his taste as very peculiar, but when he came to Chengdu, he found that the people here were even more addicted to tea. Tea tasting here seems completely different from that in the US. People can sip tea at noisy squares, or beside mahjong tables, during a sun bath, or when relishing the beauty of nature. Tea tasting here is suitable for the young and the old alike. It can be either dynamic or static. The tea houses and tea booths in the parks of Chengdu are Michael's favorite places for tea tasting. And his No. 1 hobby after work is to sip tea in the parks with his wife or friends. Apart from his favorite Huan Huaxi Park and Baihuatan Park, Michael is also a regular visitor to Wangjianglou Park and Wenhua Park. He gives all thumbs-up while talking about these parks, gladly admitting that he is a fan of parks of Chengdu. Their ecological excellence and warm and joyful ambience always soothes him with relaxation and coziness.

Now Michael indeed feels that "Chengdu is a place that one never wants to leave once he or she comes"; just as he says, Chengdu has become his home. Despite his not-so-long stay here, Chengdu for him is a kind of "second hometown".

Chengdu is a place where Michael is blessed with a family, love and chances to pursue his dreams. He is deeply attached to its beautiful landscape, its booming development, its leisurely and soothing culture, and its cheerful, vigorous people. He never regrets his decision to move to Chengdu from the

US, but finds that, as days go by, he is more passionate and confident about his "new hometown". Michael feels lucky to have the chance to live in a city that is going through changes every day. He believes that he will see a better Chengdu in the future, and this magical city is to witness his dreams coming true. There is sure to be a happy ending to his story with Chengdu.

>> 何健铭（马来西亚）
高尔夫球金牌教练

Ho Kien Min, Malaysia
A Golf Gold Medalist's Coach

我与高尔夫"川军"共成长

　　每当遇到阳光明媚的日子，人们总喜欢走到户外，沐浴在灿烂的阳光下，拥抱在自然的怀抱中，品味生命的美丽。对于热爱生活的成都人来说，这样的休闲方式更是必不可少，每逢好天气，成都的公园里总是熙熙攘攘，河边的茶铺里总是欢声笑语，运动场上也总是有许多青春的身影在挥洒着汗水。

　　热爱生活的人，常常会热爱运动。随着时代的发展，随着生活方式的变化，人们的运动方式越来越多种多样，其中，打高尔夫球已成为不少成都人青睐的运动休闲方式。在麓山大道旁的麓山高尔夫学院，蓝天白云映衬下的绿色草坪甚是美丽。在宽阔的高尔夫球场上，昂扬的活力扑面而来，在挥杆的人群中，有一个身影很是特别，他时而展现出十分潇洒的动作，时而走到他人身边，细致认真地进行协助。他标准的动作、高超的技法和耐心的指导无不说明着，他不是一名普通的高尔夫爱好者，而是一名优秀的高尔夫教练。

　　这位高挑帅气的教练头戴棒球帽，身穿轻便的运动装，乍一看似乎是一位英俊的少年，而事实上他是一位有着30余年教学经验、多次荣获全国"十佳高尔夫教练"的马来西亚籍资深教练，他的名字"何健铭"早已被成都的高尔夫球爱好者所熟悉。

误入蓉城深处

　　来成都之前，何健铭从没有想过自己会和成都结下不解之缘。他没有想到，1998 年才第一次了解到的这座城市，竟然会成为不是故乡胜似故乡的地方。

1997 年，何健铭受马来西亚的朋友之邀，在南昌的高尔夫球场做了为期三个月的培训和指导工作，在工作中偶然结识了一位湖南老总，从他的口中，何健铭第一次听到成都这个名字。1999 年，何健铭接到了一通来自那位湖南老总的电话。那位老总告诉他，自己来到了成都的牧马山，那里的高尔夫球场正在寻觅一位优秀的外籍教练，条件十分优厚。在老总的力邀下，何健铭爽快地接受了这份工作。

于是，2000 年 2 月，何健铭第一次来到成都。他记得，当年的成都还是一座较小的城市，但牧马山的四川国际高尔夫俱乐部却不错，让他在惊喜中首次在成都开始了交流和教学工作。但当年高尔夫还并不流行，打球、学球的人非常少。一年之后，何健铭在学生的介绍下转到东莞，那边的工作十分得心应手，但何健铭却总是忘不了成都，总是挂念在成都结识的学生和朋友，所以短暂离开成都的时间里，何健铭还是常常飞回成都，也在找机会重新回来。

成都不会辜负爱它的人。2004 年，机会再次向何健铭招手，当年在牧马山的同事告诉他，自己在麓山国际乡村俱乐部任职总监，该俱乐部有意打造高尔夫学院，邀请他和自己一同发展。何健铭欣然答应，回到成都后发现，这里的情形已经发生了很大的改变，高尔夫爱好者增加了很多，当年曾教过的学生成了现在的行家，有些还做了教练，而他作为"师父的师父"，感到非常亲切和自豪，这让他坚定了自己重新留在成都的决心。

兜兜转转，终于还是被成都留了下来。何健铭说，他总能在成都感受到一种热情，也能感受到一种尊重，让他既能体会到家一样的温暖，又能展望到事业发展的前景。这样的成都，何健铭再也不愿离开。

引领四川高尔夫成长

来到成都工作，何健铭感到很幸运也很开心，幸运的是，由于来到成都时间较早，他成为了成都高尔夫行业的先驱者；开心的是，十余年的辛勤工作受到了成都、四川乃至全国高尔夫行业的认可，更为重要的是，他在这些年间培养出了超过 8000 名学员，其中有的学员甚至成为了位列中国前 20 名的高尔夫职业选手，也培养出了很多优秀的青少年学员，这让他非常有成就感，也非常庆幸自己来到成都发展的决定。

有一位学员让何健铭印象十分深刻，也让他倍感骄傲。这是一位出生于 1999 年的成都女孩，名叫何沐妮。何健铭清楚地记得，2006 年的时候，年仅 7 岁的何沐妮在父母的带领下第一次走进他的球场，这个清秀文静的小女孩非常乖巧懂事，每当布置学习任务，总是勤奋地完成。何健铭回忆道，有很多次，何沐妮早上带着面包来到球场，辛苦练习一上午，中午吃完面包又继续练习，让身为教练的他既心疼又赞许。

同时，何沐妮还非常善于思考，总会在学习中大胆提问，不放过一个难点。这样一个天资聪颖又勤奋自律的女孩，很快便在何健铭的培养下脱颖而出。何健铭骄傲地说，2009 年，何沐妮在全美著名的 USKG 世界青少年冠军杯赛斩获女子 10 岁组亚军，一战成名。2015 年 7 月，通过资格赛入围大满贯美国女子公开赛的何沐妮成功晋级，12 月，她在美国青少年巡回赛（AJGA）-POLO 精英赛中一举夺魁，赢得个人首个 AJGA 邀请赛冠军，在 2016 年 2 月的安妮卡邀请赛 (ANNIKA Invitational) 中，何沐妮收获并列第五位。

虽然现在何沐妮已经以高尔夫特长生的身份成为美国南加利福尼亚大学的大学生，很少回到成都，但她和启蒙老师何健铭一直保持着紧密的联系，时常通过微信向何健铭请教，逢年过节的问候也是从未间断。

何健铭非常欣慰，成都的优秀学员远不止何沐妮一个。熟悉高尔夫球的人或许听说过杨光明和严斌这两个名字，他们都曾在四川的权威高尔夫锦标赛上夺得冠军，这两位优秀的职业球员都是何健铭的学生，并且是由业余爱好者被逐渐培养为职业选手，何健铭对此功不可没。

众望所归，2009 年和 2011 年，何健铭两度被评为"中国十佳高尔夫教练"，随后还受聘成为高尔夫四川省队的主教练，带领四川高尔夫军团一路过关斩将杀入第十二届全运会的决赛，远远超乎人们的预期，让四川高尔夫取得了有史以来的最好成绩——全国第六名。这次比赛让四川高尔夫军团收获了巨大的信心，也让何健铭看到了四川高尔夫的成长，看到了自己多年心血的成果。

扎根成都，奉献力量

2017 年，第十三届全运会在天津举办，由于工作忙碌，何健铭没有继续担任高尔夫四川省队的主教练，由他推荐的朋友带领出战。虽然意外的伤病使省队此次取得的名次不太理想，但队员们优良的职业素养和精神风貌依然为四川高尔夫树立了良好的形象。

从 2000 年至今，何健铭真切地感受到，四川成都的高尔夫行业进步了太多太多。从当年的鲜为人知，到现在超过一万名球友，而且每年都会涌现出优秀的职业选手。同时，高尔夫球被列入奥运会项目，使得人们对这项运动的重视程度不断提高。

何健铭说，他当年在东莞结识的中国职业女子高尔夫运动员冯珊珊给了他很大的影响。现年 28 岁的冯珊珊是中国历史上第一块奥运高尔夫球奖牌获得者，2017 年 11 月 11 日，她又在 2017LPGA 蓝湾大师赛决赛中夺冠，登顶女子高尔夫世界第一。年轻有为的冯珊珊给了中国高尔夫行业很大的鼓舞和震撼，也让何健铭更加坚信，在成都从事高尔夫人才培养是一个非常具有前景的行业。何健铭记得，当年刚到成都时，高尔夫球场上人数最多不过 20 人，而现在成都经常打高尔夫球的人数多达 3000 余人，常常要提前预约才能打球。并且，成都的现状与很多其他城市不同，高尔夫爱好者多为本地人。随着成都经济水平的发展，随着人们生活品质的提高，越来越多的成都人乐意尝试新的运动，愿意走进高尔夫球场，享受高尔夫这项运动的乐趣。

在这样的大环境下，何健铭将在成都继续从事高尔夫人才的培养工作。1996 年从打亚洲巡回赛的职业球员转型为教练，何健铭的工作重心就主要放在青少年教学方面，因为根据他的个人经验和对高尔夫行业的了解，只有不断涌现出优秀的青少年球员，这个地区的高尔夫水平才能持续提高，因为优质的后备力量是发展的必要条件。同时，只有通过青少年球员的成长，随着新一代球员认识的改变，才能让高尔夫这项运动被人们重新认识和更好地接受。现在，何健铭每年要新接触 500 余名青少年高尔夫学员，其中既有成都中小学校组织上公开课的学生，也有受父母的影响来学习的孩子。

何健铭说，每 80 名来上课的青少年中大约会有 4 至 8 名有潜力，而这 4 至 8 名学员中只要有 2 人能坚持下来，认真走上高尔夫道路，就能让他倍感满足。和朝气蓬勃的青少年学员们在一起，何健铭感到非常开心。更让他开心的是，学员们不仅对他十分尊重，更是十分认可，这是他坚持下去的最大动力。

心之所系，一往情深

时光如白驹过隙，转眼间，何健铭迎来了他在成都的第 18 个年头。这些年里，何健铭明确了自己的职业规划，找到了自己的人生方向，实现了事业的新高度。成都也在这些年里与他一同发展着，何健铭切身感受到，成都几乎发生了翻天覆地的变化，曾经的小城已然变成了一个国际化的大都市。

何健铭看到，成都的环境变得越来越好，荣获了"首批创建生态文明典范城市"称号，生态文明建设走在全国的前列，人与自然和谐发展，美丽的公园和青山绿水是他闲暇时间的最爱；成都的美食越来越丰富多彩，除了传统意义上的川菜，还融入了全国乃至全球的众多菜系，更加无愧于"美食之都"的称谓，美食的诱惑令他对成都更加难以割舍；成都的城市建设不断发展，城市规划日益扩大，随着"建设全面体现新发展理念的城市"概念的提出，未来的成都还将发生巨大的变化，让他非常期待。

在成都生活了 17 年，何健铭已将成都视为自己的"第二故乡"。2017 年，何健铭完成了一件大事，了却了自己的一桩心愿——成了成都自贸区首个"中国绿卡"申请人。多年前，何健铭就有了申请"中国绿卡"的想法，但门槛太高、手续复杂，2017 年，成都市公安局出台"成都出入境改革创新十五条"，降低了"中国绿卡"的门槛，拓宽了申请途径，何健铭便立刻申请。未来，何健铭想在成都买房，想把马来西亚的家人邀请来成都同住，他希望家人们也能与他一同分享成都的美好。

Grow up with "Sichuan Golf Legion"

Whenever the weather is good, people enjoy going outdoors to bask in the sunshine, embrace nature and appreciate the beauty of life. For those people of Chengdu who have a love of life, these activities are a must. Chengdu's parks forever bustle with visitors and the riverside teahouses brim with laughter, and the young are always to be found sweating on the sports ground. All of these seem to be a "ceremony" held by the city to celebrate the advent of good weather.

People who love life often love sports. As society evolves, lifestyles evolve in tandem, and people nowadays are engaging in more diverse sports. Golf has become the preferred sport and entertainment for many of those in Chengdu. The green lawn against the backdrop of blue sky and clouds is simply gorgeous at Lushan Golf Academy on Lushan Avenue, and the energy of high-spirited players is overpowering on the vast golf course there. One of the people there looks somewhat different as he swings his golf club. Every now and then, he makes a cool move or approaches others to give them detailed assistance. His standard moves, superb techniques and patient help all hint that he is not an ordinary golfer at all, but in fact an excellent golf coach.

The tall, handsome coach wears a baseball cap and lightweight sportswear and at first glance seems to be a handsome teenager. Actually, he is a Malaysian golf coach with more than 30 years of teaching experience and the winner of the title "Top Ten Golf Coaches in China". His name, "Ho Kien Min" has long been known to golf lovers in Chengdu.

Lost in the Depths of Chengdu

Before coming to Chengdu, Ho Kien Min never once thought that one day he might have a close relationship with the city. He never expected the city he first learned about in 1998 would eventually become a second hometown.

In 1997, Ho Kien Min engaged in three months of training and mentoring on a golf course in Nanchang at the invitation of a Malaysian friend. He ran into a Hunan executive while he was there. It was this executive who first told Ho Kien Min about Chengdu. In 1999, Ho Kien Min received several calls from him where the executive told him that he had come to Mumashan, Chengdu, where a golf course offered preferential treatment to any good foreign coach who would like to work there. At his invitation, Ho Kien Min readily accepted the job.

Ho Kien Min first came to Chengduin February 2000. He remembers that Chengdu was still a small city then, but the Sichuan International Golf Club at Mumashan was pretty good. Pleasantly surprised, he started exchanges and teaching in Chengdu. However, golf was not popular at the time, and very few people were playing or learning it. One year later, one trainee introduced Ho Kien Min to Dongguan. He was comfortable working there, but Chengdu was always on his mind: he missed the students and friends he met in Chengdu. During the brief period when Ho Kien Min was away, he often visited the city, looking for an opportunity to return.

Chengdu never turns its back on those who love it. In 2004, opportunity knocked the door again. A former colleague in Mumashan told Ho Kien Min that he was the director of the Lushan International Country Golf Club. The club was building a golf academy, and so his former colleague asked him to join it. Ho Kien Min eagerly agreed to return to Chengdu. Upon arrival, he discovered that the scene had evolved. There were more golf enthusiasts, and some of his former students had become experts, some were even coaches. As the "master of masters", he took pride in this familial relationship. This time, he resolved to stay.

His trip to Dongguan ultimately ended in Chengdu. Ho Kien Min says that he can always feel the passion of Chengdu as well as its respect. Chengdu gives him the warmth of a family and affords him amazing development prospects. Ho Kien Min will not leave such a good place again.

Leadership Role in the Growth of Golf in Sichuan

Ho Kien Min is happy and considers himself lucky to work in Chengdu. He considers himself lucky because his early arrival made him a golf pioneer in this city; he is happy because Chengdu, Sichuan and the whole country recognize his dedication over a decade to golf. More importantly, he has trained up more than 8,000 players over the years. Some have become the top 20 golf professionals in China and some have become outstanding golf players. Such success gives him a sense of accomplishment, and he is very grateful at having made the right decision.

Ho Kien Min is very proud of one impressive student. It is He Muni, a local girl who was born in 1999. Ho Kien Min recalls that in 2006, 7-year-old He Muni walked onto his golf course with her parents. This small, quiet girl was very clever and sensible. She would always diligently perform whatever activity assigned to her by her coach. According to Ho Kien Min, He Muni often came to the golf course in the morning with some bread. She practiced hard and after eating the bread at noon, she went on practicing in the afternoon. This made Ho Kien Min, her coach, both tenderly care and proud of her.

Also a strong thinker, He Muni asked bold questions while training, refusing to leave any problems unsolved; and as a result of Ho Kien Min's training, this talented, hard-working and self-disciplined girl rapidly grew in her abilities. Ho Kien Min proudly tells us that He Muni came second in the women's 10-year-old group at the prestigious USKG World Youth Championships in 2009. And in July 2015, she was qualified at the qualifying tournament for the Grand Slam Women's Open and was promoted. In December, she won the AJGA-POLO Classic, winning her first AJGA Invitational Championship. In the February 2016 ANNIKA Invitational, He Muni achieved a ranking of fifth place.

Although He Muni now studies at the University of Southern California as a gifted golf student and seldom returns to Chengdu, she maintains close contact with this inspirational teacher, frequently consulting him on WeChat and sending him greetings during festivals and holidays.

Ho Kien Min was delighted to discover that in addition to He Muni, there were also many other outstanding golf students in Chengdu. People familiar with golf may have heard of Yang Guangming and Yan Bin, both of whom have won titles at Sichuan's prestigious golf championships. These two amateur-turned outstanding professional players are former students of

Ho Kien Min. His contributions to their professionalism cannot be overstated.

To popular acclaim, Ho Kien Min was named as "China's Top Ten Golf Coaches" in both 2009 and 2011. He became the head coach of the Sichuan Golf Team and led the Sichuan golf corps into the 12th National Games after a series of competitions. The finals far exceeded everyone's expectations—the Sichuan Golf Team put in its best showing ever, coming sixth in the national sports event, the result of which gave Sichuan's golfers immense confidence, and Ho Kien Min was able to witness the growth of golf in Sichuan and the fruits of his years' hard work.

Settling Down in Chengdu to Make Even Greater Contributions

The 13th National Games was held in Tianjin in 2017. Having other commitments, Ho Kien Min did not continue serving as the head coach of the Sichuan Golf Team, and he recommended a friend to coach the team in his stead. Although accidental injuries affected the team's ranking, its professionalism and dedication exhibited the worthy characteristics of Sichuan Golf.

Deep down, Ho Kien Min feels that golf in Sichuan and Chengdu has made rapid progress since 2000. Golf evolved from a little-known sport to one with more than 10,000 players. Excellent professional players emerge every year, whilst the inclusion of golf into the Olympic Games has raised awareness of the sport.

Ho Kien Min says that Feng Shanshan, a Chinese professional female golf player whom he met in Dongguan, exerted a great influence on him.

28-year-old Feng Shanshan is the first Olympic golf medalist in Chinese history. On November 11, 2017, she won the 2017 LPGA Blue Bay Masters Finals and topped the world in women's golf. The youthful, promising Feng Shanshan is an outstanding star who has greatly encouraged both golf of China as well as Ho Kien Min. He believes the golf training in Chengdu is a promising career. Ho Kien Min recalls that when he first arrived in Chengdu, there were at most 20 players on the golf course. Today, more than 3,000 golf players regularly play golf in Chengdu, and people often have to make reservations. And modern Chengdu is different from many other cities— the golf lovers are mostly locals. Economic development and higher living standards in Chengdu have made it possible for more people to try new sports. They want to go to the golf course and enjoy the sport in all its glory.

In such a favorable environment, Ho Kien Min will continue training golf players in Chengdu. Since 1996, when he switched from a professional player playing the Asian Tour to coaching, Ho Kien Min has focused on youth training. From his personal experience and understanding of golf, he knew that a continuous flow of outstanding young players is key to higher standards in the sport because high quality players are necessary for the sport's further development. In addition, the growth in the number of young players combined with the changing attitudes of the new generation is a prerequisite to foster a better understanding and wider acceptance of the sport. Ho Kien Min teaches more than 500 young golf students every year, including students in open classes organized by primary and secondary schools in Chengdu, and children who are encouraged to attend by their parents.

Ho Kien Min points out that about four to eight out of every 80 youngsters who attend his classes have potential, and that he would be more than satisfied if just two of them dedicate themselves and their future to the sport. He enjoys spending time with these young enthusiastic protégés. What makes him even happier, and the greatest motivation behind his continued efforts, is that they both respect and value his input.

A Life-long and Unfaltering Devotion

Time flies, and in the blink of an eye, Ho Kien Min has already been in Chengdu for 18 years. Over the years, Ho Kien Min has defined his career plan, found his life path, and performed outstandingly. Chengdu has made great strides as she has worked out so many miracles day in and day out over the years. Deep down Ho Kien Min feels that Chengdu has undergone earth-shaking changes. The small town he first met has metamorphosed into an international metropolis.

Ho Kien Min has witnessed the improvement of Chengdu's environment. Its progress in melding the ecology with civilization has won the city the title "First Batch of Demonstration Cities to Create Ecological Civilization". Here, man and nature coexist. The numerous surrounding beautiful parks and verdant mountains and rivers are his favorite destinations in the free time. Chengdu's cuisine is unique for its diversity: apart from the gene of traditional Sichuan food, by absorbing the essence of other cuisines from across the nation and from all over the world, Chengdu is transforming itself into a genuine "culinary capital". It is the allure of this food that really explains why he finds it so hard to leave. Urban development constantly expands the city's boundaries. The slogan "building a city that fully reflects the new development concepts" is set to dramatically remake Chengdu, and

Ho Kien Min is looking forward to these changes.

Having lived in Chengdu for 17 years, Ho Kien Min sees Chengdu as his "second hometown". And in 2017, he fulfilled his wish by becoming the first applicant for the "China Green Card" in Chengdu Free Trade Zone. Many years prior, Ho Kien Min had been contemplating about obtaining a "China Green Card". At that time he was not successful because the threshold was too high and the procedure too complicated. In 2017, Ho Kien Min applied immediately after Chengdu Municipal Public Security Bureau released the "Fifteen Rules for Entry-Exit Reform and Innovation", which lowered the threshold of "China Green Card" and increased channels for application. Ho Kien Min wants to buy a house in Chengdu in the future, and move his family in Malaysia to Chengdu, because he wants his entire family to share the beauty of this city, Chengdu.

>> 张龙（尼日利亚）

蒲江县实验中学外教

Kwesi Michael Samuel, Nigeria

A Foreign Teacher at Pujiang Experimental High School

黑皮肤的"老成都"一家人

从前的世界很大很神秘，许多人或许一生都从未离开过自己的半亩方塘，而时移世易，今时不同往昔，交通、科技的飞速发展给人们的生活带来了巨大的变化，地点与地点之间的距离、人与人之间的距离都大大缩短，城市之间乃至国家之间都形成了更加紧密的联系，地球从一个神秘的浩瀚星球变成了"地球村"，因而人们在生活中时常有着"潇洒走一回"的率性。

从前的成都，由于"蜀道难，难于上青天"的阻碍，是处于西南内陆的闭塞之地，而今天的成都，早已成为一座开放、便利、时尚的国际化大都市。走在成都的街头，你常常能看到不一样的面孔，他们来自五湖四海，因成都无限的魅力不约而同地选择了这里。

在位于天府广场的成都市出入境接待中心，不同肤色的面孔更加多见。这里的外国人或是在成都旅行，或是在成都工作，与成都百姓一同分享着这里的美好。在这些外国人中，有一对黑皮肤的夫妇非常显眼，不仅是因为他们出双入对十分恩爱，更是因为他们可以用中文熟练地和工作人员交流。这对夫妻 Michael 和 Rita 来自遥远的尼日利亚，他们都是地地道道的"外来客"，但十余年的成都生活已然深深地改变了他们，让他们有了中文名字"张龙"和"张百合"，让他们成了"成都通"，还让他们从一个小家庭变成了幸福快乐的五口之家。

初到成都　一见如故

大千世界，茫茫人海，缘分本就是一种说不清道不明的东西。

早在张龙还身在尼日利亚时，便偶然在和朋友们的聊天中听到了成都这座城市。朋友告诉他，成都是神秘东方古国中国的一座西部城市，那里不仅有着浓浓的中国味儿，还有许多非常独特的地方，那里有新奇炫酷的川剧变脸，有麻辣鲜香的四川火锅，有憨态可掬的大熊猫，还有数不清的名胜古迹……这席话瞬间勾起了张龙对成都的好奇心，于是在一年之后，2004年，张龙来到成都旅行，在杜甫草堂、武侯祠、金沙博物馆等著名景点都留下了自己的足迹，还把火锅吃了个过瘾，连变脸秀都看了一场。短短几天的旅行充实而快乐，让张龙对成都十分恋恋不舍。虽然张龙此前曾游览过中国的许多其他城市，但成都却带给他从未有过的感觉，那种感觉似乎是亲切，似乎是温馨，他明白了，原来这就叫作"一见如故"。

这奇妙的感觉让张龙萌生出大胆的决定——我要住在成都！短暂的旅行让他真心爱上了成都，他爱上了这里丰富多彩的文化，爱上了这里妙不可言的美食，爱上了这里山清水秀的自然环境，也爱上了这里热情友好的人们。张龙不禁感叹，成都实在是一个宜居的城市，他希望可以和家人一起生活在这里，共享成都之美。于是，这座让人"来了就不想离开"的城市，就这样留下了张龙，成了他在异国他乡跋涉途中停留下的第二故乡。为了感谢初到成都时帮助自己的张姓好友，他索性将自己的中文名字选定为张姓，再加上他非常喜爱的中国龙，取了"张龙"这个名字。

在成都游览的时候，张龙非常青睐蒲江的生态环境，于是就把家安在了那里。定居成都蒲江之后，张龙先是在学校教书，后又做起了进出口贸易，把成都以及中国各地的特色商品销往世界各地，生意做得风生水起，日子过得渐入佳境。

第二年，张龙便把妻子 Rita 也接到了成都，入乡随俗，妻子把自己最喜欢的花和张姓结合，取了中文名字"张百合"，夫妇二人在成都正式开启了幸福的家庭生活。

对于不常旅行的张百合来说，成都更是一个新鲜的地方，这里是她在中国的第一个目的地，也是一见钟情之所在。当丈夫张龙初次来到成都旅行后，给她描述了许多关于成都的美丽画面，早已让她心驰神往，于是十分支持丈夫留在成都的决定，并毅然追随丈夫而来，把一岁多的大儿子托付给了家中父母照顾。张百合对成都的喜爱与丈夫不相上下，她由衷地感叹，丈夫真是做了一个英明的决定！

五口之家　幸福生活

张百合来到成都之后，放弃了原先的教师工作，专心做张龙的得力助手。她一边协助张龙的生意，一边悉心料理着小家。两年后，他们的小家又有了两个可爱的新成员—— 一对龙凤胎呱呱坠地。新生命的降临让张龙、张百合夫妇喜悦不已，这两个小宝宝是他们爱的结晶，是他们在成都生活的新的动力，更是他们与成都缘分的进一步加深，因为小宝宝虽然是纯正的尼日利亚血统，却是出生于成都的"成都人"。张龙为小宝宝也取了中文名字，男孩叫张文，女孩叫张明。随后，由家乡的爷爷奶奶照顾的大儿子也来到了成都，和爸爸妈妈、弟弟妹妹团聚在一起，并有了中文名字"张德"。

从一到二，从二到五，张龙决定留在成都时只有自己一个人，而短短的三年之后，他就在成都有了一个幸福的五口之家。有了家人的陪伴，张龙和张百合在成都的生活更加适应，他们时常一起在成都的大街小巷寻觅美食，时常一起在阳光下的河岸边喝茶休闲，也时常一起在公园里嬉戏野餐。张龙说，孩子们最喜欢的地方是石象湖公园，在春暖花开的日子里，他总会带着妻子和孩子们到公园里赏花、玩耍，那里花草繁茂，空气清新，环境优雅，是成都绿色健康生态环境的最佳体现。尼日利亚人的口味与成都人相似，也是热衷麻辣风味，这让张龙一家在成都如鱼得水。他们不仅酷爱成都火锅和串串，还热衷于品尝和研究川菜，特别是张龙，已经学会了几道川菜拿手菜。每当有朋友到家中做客，张龙总喜欢亲自选购食材，为朋友们做上一桌丰盛美味的川菜，酸菜鱼、麻婆豆腐、回锅肉、宫保鸡丁都是他的拿手菜，每当看到朋友们吃得赞不绝口，他的心中满是骄傲和喜悦。张龙对川菜赞叹不已，他赞叹四川人的无穷智慧和创造力，赞叹普普通通的食材居然能用四川特有的方法变成无与伦比的美味，与家乡尼日利亚的美食既有相似之处，又截然不同，相似之处在于麻辣的口味，而不同之处则在于烹饪方式，显然张龙已经更偏爱川菜的做法了。

还有一个让张龙惊叹自己与成都的缘分之处，那就是川剧变脸。初次来成都旅行时，张龙在朋友的陪同下，在宽窄巷子里第一次欣赏到这一神奇的艺术形式，让他颇受震撼，念念不忘。与家人定居成都后，他又带着妻子和孩子们再次欣赏，并惊讶地发现，川剧变脸竟然与尼日利亚的民族特色艺术"换面"有着异曲同工之妙，让他很是激动。

成功之都　共同发展

如今，张龙夫妇在成都的生活温馨而安定，大儿子在蒲江读中学，小儿子和小女儿在蒲江读小学，三个孩子都非常喜欢生活在成都，学会了一口流利的蒲江话，还在学校和社区结交了许多亲密的伙伴，特别是每逢龙凤胎兄妹的生日，总会有很多小伙伴来到家中一同庆生，其乐融融，热闹非凡，而且若非看到兄妹俩的外表，实在难以相信他们是尼日利亚人。

有了幸福的家庭和贤惠的妻子作为坚实后盾，张龙得以更加专注于自己生意。在成都的日子里，张龙早已熟悉了成都的方方面面，特别是作为商人，他充分熟悉和了解了成都的市场经济状况。张龙非常了解成都的物产特色，也非常了解世界的流行风向，他所销售的蜀绣、成都特色小吃、大熊猫玩偶等商品在国外市场上广受欢迎。张龙在这些年来切身感觉到，成都在不断扩大对外开放，成为西部对外交往中心，世界上越来越多的人知道成都、来到成都。成都正在经历着飞速的发展，成都的经济水平正在不断地提升。在他初次来到成都时，虽然感觉成都很美很宜居，但是现代化水平还不高；而今天，他认为成都的经济水平已经迈上了新的台阶，如果要选择一个中国城市作为全球新经济成长和崛起的样本，成都再合适不过。

乐不思归　爱城如家

十余年的成都生活，让张龙一家对这座城市有了很深厚的感情，他们与这"第二故乡"的亲密程度，已经超过了尼日利亚的故土，每年的大多数时间都在成都度过，只回老家探亲一两次。最有趣的是，出生在尼日利亚的大儿子竟然认为英语比中文更难，从小学会的语言似乎已经被忘在了老家。

远离故土十余年，张龙一家的选择令老家的一些亲友不解，但张龙和张百合却不以为然。他们认为，亲友之所以不解，是因为不曾了解过这座遥远的东方城市，而当他们来到成都，在夫妇二人的陪伴下游览成都的人文与自然风貌之后，便转而支持他们的决定。张百合说，故乡有些人也来到了中国定居，选择在北京、上海等地，并邀请他们前去同住，但他们从未动摇过留在成都的决心。在她的心中，唯有成都才是真正的宜居城市，不仅有着优越的生态环境，而且有着深厚的文化底蕴，交通、医疗、教育等方方面面的水平都在迅速地提高，让她和家人都受益匪浅。

让张龙一家离不开的，还有成都的人。张龙深深地觉得，成都人非常亲切和友善，给予过他很多热心的帮助，让他一直感怀在心。张百合亦是认为如此，不管走到成都的何处，亲切的成都人总会给她家的感觉。孩子们如今也不愿离开成都，每当从尼日利亚探亲回来，总是比回老家更兴奋，因为成都的小伙伴们还等着他们一起玩耍。张龙和他的家人真心爱着这座城市，在他们口中，已经把"成都是我家"说成了一种习惯。未来的日子里，这个幸福的非洲五口之家，将会在成都的温暖怀抱中，收获更多的欢声笑语。

A Family of Dark-Skinned "Chengdu Locals"

The world used to seem vast and mysterious. Many people never left their hometown. Times have now changed and the world today is different from the world in the past. Rapid developments in transportation and technology have dramatically changed people's lives. The distance from one place to another and the distance between different people are shorter than ever before. Cities and countries are bound together. The earth has developed from a mysterious, vast planet into a "global village". These changes have made it possible for people to make the snap decision to go on an "extraordinary journey".

In the past, "Shu road was as taxing as ascending heaven". Chengdu sat in the southwest hinterland, blocked on all sides from the outside world. Today, it has already become an open, convenient and stylish international metropolis. You can often notice the faces of different nationalities from all corners of the world when strolling down the streets. The infinite charm of this city has drawn them together.

There are even more people of different skin colors at the Chengdu Exit and Entry Reception Center in Tianfu Square. The foreigners here intend to either travel or work in Chengdu. They share the beauty of the city with the locals. A dark-skinned couple stands out among these foreigners in that not only they are very affectionate towards each other but also they communicate proficiently with the staff in Chinese. This couple, Michael and Rita, come from the remote country of Nigeria. They are genuine "guests", but over a decade's living in Chengdu has transformed them profoundly, giving them the names "Zhang Long" and "Zhang Baihe". Their interaction with this city enables them to nearly "know everything about Chengdu", during which their family, a small intimate unit consisting of only husband and wife before, has turned into a large happy family with three children.

"Chengdu, Like an Old Friend, When We First Met"

This world is thronged with people, and the way it ties people together is not easy to explain.

When Zhang Long was still in Nigeria, he first heard of Chengdu when talking with friends. A friend told him that Chengdu was a city in the west of the mysterious, ancient China. It is a typical Chinese city with many unique features, where one can watch "Face Changing", an intriguing technique of Sichuan Opera, taste the spicy Sichuan Hotpot, see charmingly naive giant pandas, and visit countless places of historic interest... These words aroused Zhang Long's curiosity about the city. One year later, in 2014, Zhang Long traveled to Chengdu for the first time, leaving his footprints in famous historic and cultural sites such as Du Fu's Thatched Cottage, Wuhou Temple, and Jinsha Site Museum. He also ate a lot of hotpot and watched the "Face Changing" show. This short vacation gave Zhang Long a sense of fulfillment and happiness. He ended up being reluctant to leave. Zhang Long had visited many other cities in China before, but he sensed something different about Chengdu. It was bursting with cordiality, warmth and sweetness. He came to realize that on their very first encounter, Chengdu and he had already become intimate friends.

This wonderful feeling led Zhang Long to make a bold decision— he would move to and live in Chengdu! During this short trip, he fell in deep love with the city. Its vibrant culture, fantastic food, beautiful natural environment, and hospitable people led him to marvel at Chengdu, saying that it is a truly livable city. He hoped to live here and admire its beauty with his family. Zhang Long then decided to stay in this city that "you do not want to leave once you come". Chengdu thus became his second hometown on his travels in foreign lands. To thank the friend with the surname of Zhang who helped him when he first arrived in Chengdu, he gave his Chinese surname as Zhang, and his first name as Long for he is fond of Chinese dragons (pronounced "long" in Chinese).

While touring Chengdu, Zhang Long was attracted by the natural environment of Pujiang. He decided to set down roots there. Zhang Long worked there first as a teacher. Later, he became engaged in import and export trade, selling the specialties of Chengdu and other parts of China to the rest of the world. Success in business gave him the trappings of a comfortable life.

The next year, Zhang Long arranged his wife Rita to come to Chengdu. Rita adapted to Chinese customs by combining her favorite flower with her husband's Chinese surname of Zhang, and her chinese name became as "Zhang Baihe (meaning 'Lily')". Following her arrival, the couple began their life as a family in Chengdu.

For Zhang Baihe, who did not travel much, Chengdu was a new place. It was her first destination in China, and it was her love at first sight. Her husband Zhang Long told her how beautiful Chengdu was after his first trip to this city. She was so fascinated that she supported her husband's decision, leaving her eldest child, her one-year-old boy to the care of her parents at home, and came to Chengdu to live with her husband. Now Zhang Baihe loves Chengdu as much as her husband does. She claimes that her husband has made a wise decision!

The Happy Life of the Family of Five

After Zhang Baihe came to Chengdu, she gave up her former job as a teacher and dedicated herself to helping her husband. She helped run his business whilst taking care of the small family. Two years later, they welcomed a delightful pair of twins into their lives. Their advent brought the family endless joy. The two children, who embodied the mutual love of their parents, became a new driving force behind the family's life in Chengdu. Their birth further strengthened their parents' relationship with Chengdu, and their pure Nigerian blood running through their veins did not contradict the fact that they were "Chengdu locals". Zhang Long also gave the two little kids Chinese names: the boy was named Zhang Wen; the girl Zhang Ming. Later, their eldest son, who had been under the care of his grandparents back in the Nigerian hometown, came to Chengdu. He joined his mom, dad, and younger brother and sister, and received the Chinese name "Zhang De".

The size of the family grew from one to two, and then from two to five. When Zhang Long decided to stay, he was the first of his Chengdu family. And, in just three years, he had a happy family of five in Chengdu. And surrounded by their family, Zhang Long and Zhang Baihe enjoy life in Chengdu more. They would often walk down the high streets and back lanes in search of delicacies, drink tea together on riverbanks in the sunshine, or play and have a picnic in the park. Zhang Long says the children's favorite place is Shixianghu Park. On spring days, he takes his wife and children to the park for flower-admiring and game-playing. The luxuriant flowers and plants, fresh air, and the elegant environment there epitomize Chengdu's green and healthy environment.

Zhang Long and his family feel just like a fish in the water of Chengdu, for both Nigerians and the people of Chengdu like hot and spicy food. They love Chengdu hotpot and barbecue and are keen to try out and learn about Sichuan cuisine. Zhang Long, in particular, has mastered the knack of cooking some Sichuan dishes. Whenever guests come, he would buy the ingredients himself and cook a delicious Sichuanese meal to entertain them. He is particularly good at boiled fish with pickled cabbage and chili, Mapo Tofu, twice boiled pork, and Kungpao chicken. He would watch with pride and joy when his friends give him the thumbs-up during the meal. Zhang Long marvels at Sichuan cuisine, the infinite wisdom and creativity of the Sichuan people, and how ordinary ingredients can be turned into unparalleled delicacies using methods unique to Sichuan. They are similar to yet different from the cuisine of his hometown. The similarity is the spicy taste, and the difference lies in the cooking method. Apparently, Zhang Long prefers Sichuan cuisine.

Another factor that has contributed to the intimate relationship between Zhang Long and Chengdu is the "Face Changing" of Sichuan Opera. Zhang Long experienced this magical art form in the company of friends in Kuanzhai Alley on his first visit to Chengdu. He was absolutely amazed by it and mesmerized by the visual performance it provided. After settling down in Chengdu with his family, he watched it again with his wife and kids and was surprised to find that "Face Changing" in Sichuan Opera was strikingly similar to "Switching Faces", a Nigerian ethnic art.

Thriving Together with Chengdu

Today, Zhang Long and his wife live a sweet and stable life in Chengdu. Their eldest son attends high school and their younger son and daughter attend primary school in Pujiang. The three kids enjoy their life in Chengdu. They are fluent in the Pujiang dialect and have made many friends at school and in the community. The birthday of the twin brother and sister is a special occasion, when many little friends would come over to celebrate. It is a time when joy overflows. And it can be hard to believe they really are Nigerian.

With a happy family and a wife supporting him, Zhang Long can devote more time and effort to his business. Zhang Long's life in Chengdu has informed him about all aspects of the city. As a businessman, he is well acquainted with the status of Chengdu's market and economy. Zhang Long is well aware of the uniqueness of Chengdu's products; he is also aware of what the world currently needs. The Shu embroidery products, characteristic Chengdu snacks, and giant panda dolls that he sells and promotes on overseas markets are popular. Over the past several years, Zhang Long feels that Chengdu is expanding more widely to the outside world and becoming the center for foreign exchanges in West China. More and more people in the world are learning about and coming to Chengdu. The city is experiencing a rapid development, and its economy is improving. When he first came, he found it a beautiful and livable city but not modern enough. Today, he finds Chengdu has raised its economy to a new height. In his view, Chengdu is the best example of a Chinese city rising in global economic development.

Reluctant to Leave the City He Calls Home

Zhang Long and his family have forged an intimate relationship with Chengdu during their decade-long stay here. They now feel closer to their "second hometown" than to their native hometown in Nigeria. They spend most of the year in Chengdu, going home only once or twice to see relatives. Most interestingly, the eldest son, born in Nigeria, thinks English is harder than Chinese. He seems to have totally forgotten the language he has acquired at a younger age.

Zhang Long and his family have been away from their native land for more than ten years. Some of their friends and relatives back home find this difficult to understand, but Zhang Long and Zhang Baihe think otherwise. According to them, their relatives and friends do not understand it simply because they know so little about this distant oriental city. However, after some of them have visited Chengdu and the couple has taken them to see its culture, history and landscape, their former disapproval has been replaced by approval. Zhang Baihe says some people in her hometown also have left Nigeria and settled down in other Chinese cities like Beijing and Shanghai. They have asked them to live together with them, but they never waver in their determination. She believes that Chengdu is the only city with a great standard of living, which not only boasts a superior environment, but also an ancient culture. She and her family also benefit a lot from the rapid development in transportation, healthcare, and education of the city.

Another factor that makes Zhang Long and his family reluctant to leave is the local people. Zhang Long is impressed by their kindness and friendliness. All of whom have been extremely enthusiastic to help, for which he is extremely grateful. Zhang Baihe agrees with her husband, saying kind Chengdu locals always give her a sense of family wherever she goes. Similarly, the kids are reluctant to leave. Each time when they return from their trips back to Nigeria to see the family, they are more excited than they are in Nigeria because they have so many friends in Chengdu who are waiting for them. Zhang Long and his family love the city. They often say, "Chengdu is my home". In the days to come, there will be much more laughter in this happy African family of five in the comfort of Chengdu's warm embraces.

>> 洪毅全（新加坡）
世界著名青年指挥家

Darrell Ang, Singapore
World Renowned Young Conductor

引领乐声壮阔

在高新科技公司齐聚的天府新区，有一处汇聚高雅音乐艺术的场所，那便是四川交响乐团。沿着天府二街的干道向西直行，便能寻得此处。四川交响乐团一直以来都是一个充斥着艺术气息的地方，与周围的科技氛围相比，恍若与世隔绝的桃花源地。推开它的大门，便能见到简约的沙发与卡座，像一个咖啡厅。办公区外其他的装潢、摆设也在告诉来到此地的人：这里是艺术家的世界。琴师乐手偶有经过，无论是坐在沙发上认真地交流音乐，或者是聊起闲天，都有一种与众不同的气氛。后台排练时时传来的管弦之声，恢宏而悠扬。

成都既是古都，也是一座现代化的城市，除去"宜居"这个广为人知的特性，成都最大的优点便是它的文化包容性。所谓"兼容并蓄"，并非每个城市都能做到。对于优秀的文化，不论古今中外，成都城以及成都人，都能欣然接纳。也正是在这里，艺术能得到长久丰盈的滋养。也有很多他乡之人，被成都的魅力深深吸引，徙居于此，为自己和成都建立一番事业。

洪毅全来自新加坡，是四川交响乐团现任的艺术总监，也是享誉世界的交响乐青年指挥家。2016 年，他来到成都，随后的一个月便加入了四川交响乐团。一次合作引来三年之约，洪毅全的加入，给整个成都的交响乐带来了新的天地。

邀得才俊为栋梁

洪毅全 4 岁的时候便开始学习钢琴和小提琴，也正是在那时候他天赋异禀的音乐才华开始得以彰显。天性追崇艺术的人，对艺术的理解远胜常人，而洪毅全对艺术的好奇和痴迷，也促使他义无反顾地投身于音乐的世界。从学习乐器到学习作曲，再到研习指挥；从维也纳音乐学院到圣彼得堡音乐学院，再到耶鲁大学，洪毅全并非出身豪门，仅仅怀着对音乐的无比热爱与执着，艰难前行至今，成为享誉全球的音乐指挥家。

洪毅全能流利地用汉语、英语、德语、法语、意大利语、俄语六种语言进行交流，曾留学于不同国家，对各国的音乐文化都涉猎颇深。在他的艺术生涯里，他曾指挥过世界各地知名交响乐队的演出，也拿下了许许多多的国际指挥大奖；他载誉归国，曾是新加坡交响乐团最年轻的副指挥，还曾任新加坡国立青年管弦乐团艺术总监，2011 年率团出席了英国著名的 Aberdeen 国际青年音乐节，紧接着参与了 2012 年在柏林 Konzerthaus 举办的青年欧典音乐会。如此蜚声世界的青年才俊，自然有许许多多的国际知名乐团向他抛来橄榄枝，而他选择了成都，于 2016 年正式出任四川交响乐团的艺术总监。

2016 年，他第一次来到成都，为四川交响乐团的一场音乐会担任指挥。四川交响乐团求贤若渴，为了这一次音乐会，也是费尽心思地邀请到他合作。也正是那一场结缘，让他在随后的一个月里拥有了四川交响乐团艺术总监的身份。当他踏上成都土地的那一刻起，这里的文化与气氛便与他的音乐世界产生了强烈的共鸣。诚如他所言，成都对他有一种天然的吸引力，这里似乎预示着将成为他音乐生涯的再度腾飞之地。他喜欢这个城市充盈的温柔情怀，成都是一个可以沉静学习的地方，也是一个升华艺术的唯美之地。同样地，经过那一次合作，他感受到了与乐团成员合作的默契和四川交响乐团的巨大潜力。所以，面对全球各大知名交响团纷至沓来的邀请，他毫不犹豫地选择了尚在成长期的四川交响乐团。

"我想去肩负更重的责任，迎接更大的挑战，我要把四川交响乐团打造成中国一流的交响乐团，而我也深深喜欢成都这个城市。"他平和的语气里，不经意地流露出他的壮志雄心。诚如他所言，四川的交响乐起步晚，跟欧洲国家比起来更是有相隔百年的历史差距，很多地方还不够完善。他选择这里，是一种责任与挑战，而四川交响乐团的求贤之心与为之付出的努力，也令他深为感动。成都正值大力建设音乐之都的时期，这里有未来交响乐的无限潜力，如果发展顺利，成都还有望成为全中国乃至世界的音乐圣地。推波助澜，也正是洪毅全的壮志雄心。

倾力，与蓉城共扶摇

成都的冬日不似北方严寒，温柔的阳光透过浅浅的云层，却也弥散着微微的清凉，尽管如此，比起四季如春的新加坡，成都还是显得有些冷。但是这份寒冷，并没有动摇洪毅全对成都的热爱，他在这里感受着四季的分明，路两旁的行道树早已被金黄色染透，偶有银杏褪却裙摆，裸露着枝杈任风徐徐轻抚。他的心也在这样的环境中沉淀了下来。洪毅全望了望玻璃窗外，来不及更深地思索，便转身投向了忙碌的工作中。

一头鬈发，些许胡楂，打着英伦结的灰色围巾，洪毅全的精神面貌冷静而从容，像一个年轻而绅士的"大叔"，也自然地流露出一个音乐艺术家的风骨。从外人的角度看，他那张脸时刻都保持着严肃与冷静。他是一个"乐痴"，一个不苟言笑、认真严谨的指挥家。他的世界里，除了音乐便再容不下其他了。洪毅全现在的住所离四川交响乐团咫尺之地，就近而居也是为了方便工作。

许多外籍朋友来到成都之后，可能都尽情地体验了成都的当地风情，逛遍了具有成都风味的大街小巷，尝遍了各色美食。对于成都，他们也许能绘声绘色地给别人讲述各种各样的所见所闻。"你对成都的印象是什么样的？"若是如此问洪毅全，他并不像其他人一样能答出来许多。虽然来成都有一年的光景，但他待在成都的时候并不固定，仍然需要往来奔波于世界各地，不断地演出、学习、交流。而他去过的成都的地方，更是屈指可数——天府广场、宽窄巷子，除此之外也就是四川交响乐团的所在地了。而他体验过的成都地方文化，除了熊猫与川菜，也不能聊出再多了。洪毅全选择成都的原因正如他所说："我是来这里工作的，而不是旅游的。"不论身在何处，工作，是洪毅全每日的必修课。音乐事业，是他的全部，而成都最吸引他的，正是四川音乐文化焕发出的生机与契机。成都良好的就业创业氛围与工作环境，给了他源源不断的激情与动力。

他自来就没有闲情逸致去培养其他爱好，也无心娱乐游玩。成都闲逸而慵懒的生活节奏，他应该不会去尝试了。"忙碌于工作，醉心于音乐"足以形容洪毅全在成都的全部生活。他的故事写满了世界各地，但在成都却被每一天充实而紧张的工作而代替，生活中的小惊喜早已被乐团的事务淹没，一些趣事也就此淡漠。他可能随时拖着一个登机箱来上班，与乐团的成员们进行排练或者开完会之后，他又得奔赴其他国家继续工作。时间对他来说弥足珍贵，他对时间的使用甚至已经精确到了分钟。身边的助理为他安排好行程演出、交流、学习——他在不断为自己和四川交响乐团注入新的生命力，如同一个往来汲水的战士，滋养着一个蓬勃发展的交响乐团队。

江河聚，碧海波澜起

虽然没有那么多时间去采风，但耳濡目染之下以及通过与乐团成员们的交流，洪毅全对成都文化的认知和理解也在与日俱增。曾留学多地的他，把各国优秀的交响乐理念和文化分享给乐团的同时，也不断尝试在音乐中融入成都的本土文化，创造属于成都独特魅力的交响乐。

2017 年末，洪毅全率领乐团的其他两位青年驻团指挥一同完成了四川交响乐团跨年音乐会的排练和演出，并执棒了著名旅德青年钢琴家贾然演出的莫扎特第 23 钢琴协奏曲。这场音乐会的下半场，四川交响乐团演绎了与民乐相结合的两首曲目：《冬之梅》和《巴蜀风情》，地方色彩相当浓厚。身为艺术总监，洪毅全率领四川交响乐团，通过这场演出向成都人民展现出了乐团无限的艺术创造力。

轰轰烈烈的故事向来引人入胜，也更容易赢得读者的垂青，但洪毅全在成都的故事并无波澜。他以另一种方式在书写他的每一寸光阴，那便是厚积薄发。成都闲适、亲和、慢节奏的地域文化与生活方式，一点一滴地加深着他对音乐艺术的进一步理解，使他的艺术造诣有了更高层次的提高。一天天，一步步，他与乐团都在改变。

洪毅全在四川交响乐团出任艺术总监的时期为三年。四川交响乐团期望他能利用三年的时间，形成乐团的艺术风格，建立演奏员的职业乐手意识，但他却已为乐团做好了 5 年、10 年的规划。"因为乐团需要时间来沉淀和成长"，洪毅全如是说。初到乐团，他便开始与每个成员进行交流、磨合，对乐团的制度进行整顿。在他的改革下，每次排练结束，乐手们的谱架上都空空如也，说明大家开始带谱子回家练习了。也从其他许多细节里可以看出，成员们现在对乐队和音乐投入了更多的努力与激情，这令所有人都感到振奋。不仅如此，洪毅全不断招贤纳士，为四川交响乐团吸引各国音乐人才，为成都的音乐未来筑下坚实根基。

指挥家手中的指挥棒大约是一场音乐会上最小的"乐器"，但却担着最大的责任；它无声可作，却引导着恢宏的协奏曲。从乐声响起到结束，唯有乐团指挥是无从休憩的，不容有半点差池。当一个青年指挥家在舞台上浑然忘我地指挥着乐团，每一个节奏都恰如其分地表达着曲子的情感，那是洪毅全与四川交响乐团的飒爽英姿。在音乐的世界里，他们都是肆意驰骋的骏马。精彩的演出换来雷动的掌声，惊叹之余，观众都能知晓：在成都，有四川交响乐团和一名来自异国他乡的艺术总监，与乐团所有成员一起，写意着四川交响乐的美好未来。

　　未来，洪毅全会因为对乐团或成都的眷恋而继续留下，抑或是去往他地迎接另一个挑战，这些都是未知数。常人难以去忖度一个艺术家的思想，也无法理解他的执着，但洪毅全在任的每一天里，他都将乐团的事务放在第一位。在他的努力之下，四川交响乐团的改变与成长有目共睹，而乐团成员们对这个严肃而率真的艺术总监皆是交口称赞。四川交响乐团前进千里而积的跬步，都隐在他挥舞着指挥棒的身影里。

Directing Magnificent Music

In the Tianfu New Area, home to a large number of high-tech companies, there is a refined place for art—the Sichuan Symphony Orchestra. Walking along Tianfu Second Street and heading west, you may find the place. A place with an artistic atmosphere, Sichuan Symphony Orchestra is like a reclusive haven amid those high-tech companies. Walking inside, you may find a simple yet refined sofa and partitions that make the place look just like a coffee shop. The decorations and furnishings in areas other than the offices constantly remind visitors that this is a place exclusively for artists. Occasionally, there come some music players. They may sit on the sofas and exchange ideas about music or just chat freely, creating a special atmosphere around them. The wind and stringed instruments rehearsal backstage frequently sends magnificent yet melodious sounds.

Chengdu, a modern city that evolved from an ancient capital, except being described as "livable", is also known for its cultural inclusiveness. Not every city is capable of being "inclusive". Chengdu and its people are ready to embrace every type of advanced culture, regardless of its origin in time or place. Here, art can be richly nourished. Attracted by the charm of Chengdu, people from other places have moved here to build a better future for both Chengdu and themselves.

Darrell Ang, a world famous young symphony conductor, comes from Singapore and now serves as the art director of Sichuan Symphony Orchestra.

he came to Chengdu and joined Sichuan Symphony Orchestra one month later. The three-year contract was the result of the cooperation between Darrell Ang and the orchestra. The arrival of Darrell Ang brought something new to the symphony of Chengdu.

Man of Superb Talent

Darrell Ang started learning the piano and violin at the age of four when he demonstrated his musical talent. As a born artist, when compared with ordinary people, he usually excelled in the understanding of art. Due to curiosity about and a passion for art, Darrell Ang finally devoted himself to the study of music: from practicing musical instruments to studying composition and conducting skills; from Vienna Conservatory of Music to St. Petersburg Conservatory of Music and Yale University. Darrell Ang was not born in a rich and powerful family. With a genuine passion for music, he overcame various difficulties and challenges along the way and finally became a world famous conductor.

Darrell Ang can speak Chinese, English, German, French, Italian and Russian. Having studied music in various countries, he had acquired a wealth of knowledge about the musical culture of those countries. He had directed the performance of famous symphony orchestras around the world and had received numerous international prizes for conductors. Back to Singapore with honors, he once served as the youngest assistant conductor for the Singapore Symphony Orchestra and the art director for the Singapore National Youth Orchestra. In 2011, he led the orchestra to attend the famous Aberdeen international youth music festival held in the UK. In 2012, he attended the youth European Classics Concert held in Konzerthaus, Berlin. With world fame and musical talent, Darrell Ang was always a favorite of internationally renowned orchestras which were eager to invite him on board. However, he finally chose Chengdu and became the art director of the Sichuan Symphony Orchestra in 2016.

In 2016, Darrell Ang came to Chengdu for the first time and conducted a concert for the Sichuan Symphony Orchestra. Eager for talent, the Sichuan Symphony Orchestra had tried every means to invite Darrell Ang to conduct for the concert. The cooperation finally led to his appointment as the art director for the Sichuan Symphony Orchestra one month later. When Darrell Ang stepped on the soil of Chengdu for the first time, his musical pursuit found an echo from the city which boasted of rich flavors of culture. As he says, Chengdu is an appealing place which seemed to promise a more successful career for him as a musician. He was attracted by the tenderness of the city which was an ideal place for quiet study and artistic pursuit. Additionally, through the cooperation, he was deeply impressed by the team spirit of the members of the orchestra as well as the great potential of the Sichuan Symphony Orchestra. As a result, he finally decided to work for the still growing orchestra in face of invitations from various world renowned orchestras.

"I want to shoulder more responsibilities and take on new challenges. I want to build the Sichuan Symphony Orchestra into the leading orchestra in China, and I love Chengdu." His gentle tone does not hide his ambition. As Darrell Ang says, the Sichuan Symphony Orchestra was created almost one hundred years after those in European countries and therefore it is still weak in many areas. Due to the desire to take responsibilities and address challenges, he finally made the decision to work for the orchestra. He was also impressed by the orchestra's eagerness to seek talent and the efforts it made to that end. As Chengdu is striving to build the city into a "capital of music", a bright future for the development of its symphony is promised here. It is also expected that Chengdu may become the music shrine of China and the world. Therefore, Darrell Ang is determined to make contributions to this ambitious undertaking.

Working Hard and Growing up Together with Chengdu

Chengdu is not as cold as the north in the winter. When the gentle sunlight penetrates the low clouds, it still feels a little chilly. Compared with Singapore which enjoys warm weather all the year round, Chengdu is cold in winter. However, this does not dampen Darrell Ang's love for Chengdu. He enjoys the four distinct seasons of the city. The leaves on the trees on both sides of the road have turned yellow. Ginkgo leaves have fallen, leaving the bare branches resting in the breeze. He feels settled down as well. Looking outside the window, Darrell Ang, having no time for more meditation, returns to work again due to his busy schedule.

Curly hair, a face not cleanly shaven and a gray scarf with an England-style knot—the young and genteel "uncle" Darrell Ang looks cool and confident. As a musician with an artistic disposition, he always looks calm and serious. He is a devotee of music and a very serious conductor who always pursues perfection. His life is dominated by his work. To reduce his commuting time, he chooses a domicile that is just a stone's throw away from the Sichuan Symphony Orchestra.

After arriving in Chengdu, some foreigners make full use of the opportunity to learn about the local customs, visit Chengdu-style streets and alleys and have a taste of the delicious food. They can vividly describe their experiences and adventures in Chengdu when someone asks them, "What is your impression of Chengdu?" For Darrell Ang, however, this might be a very difficult question to answer, and most of the time he is unable to offer a vivid description of his life in Chengdu. During the one year period after he chose to live in Chengdu, he had to travel around the world for performances, study and exchanges, not always staying in the city. Outside of the site of the Sichuan Symphony Orchestra, the only places he has visited are Tianfu Square and the Wide and Narrow Alleys. And the only two things he can tell you about Chengdu are the pandas and Sichuan cuisine. As Darrell Ang says, "I come to Chengdu to work instead of travel". Wherever he is, work is an integral part of Darrell Ang's daily activities. Music means everything to him. The vitality and opportunities promised by the musical undertakings of Sichuan is what appeals to him most about Chengdu. The favorable conditions offered by Chengdu for start-ups and those who are willing to work here continuously give him inspiration and motivation.

He does not have the leisure to pursue other interests or engage in entertainment. And it is impossible for him to adopt the slow and leisurely lifestyle of the Chengdu people, as he is preoccupied with "work and music" every day. His story is known to people around the world, but he just concentrates on his work and his busy schedule everyday while staying in Chengdu. The pleasant surprises and anecdotes of everyday life have been totally ignored due to his preoccupation with the work of the orchestra.

He may take his boarding suitcase to the orchestra for rehearsal or meetings. Afterward, he has to rush to another country for work. Time is precious to him and he has to make full use of each minute. His assistant arranges everything from performance tours to exchanges and study for him. Like a solider drawing water from different sources, he has continued to inject new vitality into his own career as well as the development of the flourishing Sichuan Symphony Orchestra.

Rivers Flow to the Sea and Waves Surge

Although he does not have time to collect local songs, Darrell Ang's knowledge and understanding of the culture of Chengdu has increased steadily thanks to the daily influence of and the communication with members of the orchestra. Having studied in different countries, Darrell Ang has made continuous efforts to introduce orchestra members to first-rate symphony ideas and the culture of other countries. At the same time, he has been seeking ways to incorporate the local culture of Chengdu into music in order to compose Chengdu-style symphonies.

At the end of 2017, Darrell Ang, along with two young conductors of the orchestra, rehearsed and performed for the year-end concert of the Sichuan Symphony Orchestra. He also conducted the Mozart Piano Concerto No. 23 performed by Jia Ran, a young pianist living in Germany. During the second half of the concert, the Sichuan Symphony Orchestra performed two pieces of music which borrowed elements from folk music: "Plum Blossom in Winter" and "Charm of Bashu". The performance exuded rich local flavors. Through the concert, Darrell Ang, as the art director, and his team from the Sichuan

Symphony Orchestra, demonstrated for the people of Chengdu the limitless artistic creativity of the orchestra.

Fascinating stories appeal to people and entice readers more easily. Darrell Ang's story is not a fluctuating one, He has spent his time in Chengdu in a different way, i.e., by being well-grounded in his artistic pursuits in order to present artistic works with ease someday. The leisure, friendliness and slow pace of life featuring the local culture and lifestyle of Chengdu has helped him to gain more understanding of music day by day and thereby increase his artistic attainments. Actually, he is growing up together with the orchestra.

As agreed between Darrell Ang and the Sichuan Symphony Orchestra, Darrell will serve as the art director for the orchestra for three years. During this three-year period, he is expected to help create a unique artistic style for the orchestra and help all performers develop a sense of professionalism. However, Darrell Ang has already made a five-year or even 10-year plan for the orchestra. "It takes time for an orchestra to grow", says Darrell Ang. After working for the orchestra, he made efforts to interact with each member of the orchestra and improve the rules for the orchestra. With his efforts for reform, the score rack is usually left empty after rehearsal because the performers take music books home for more practice. When observing carefully, you may find that members of orchestra have become more devoted to the music and the group, which is an exciting change. Darrell Ang has also helped the Sichuan Symphony Orchestra to attract people with musical talent from across the world with a view towards laying a solid foundation for music development in Chengdu in the future.

Albeit the smallest "instrument" in a concert, the baton used by a conductor shoulders the greatest responsibilities. Sending no sound, it guides the magnificent performance of the concert. From the start to the end of the concert, only the conductor must stay focused every moment for fear of making any mistakes. When the young conductor directs the performance attentively and each rhythm appropriately expresses the intended emotion, you may be impressed by the enterprising spirit of Darrell Ang and the Sichuan Symphony Orchestra. In the world of music, they both are galloping horses. His marvelous performances have won thunderous applause. While admiring the performance, all of the audiences know that there is a foreign art director in the Sichuan Symphony Orchestra who, along with the other members of the orchestra, is writing a new chapter for Sichuan symphony development.

No one knows whether Darrell Ang, out of his affection, will stay in Chengdu to continue to work for the orchestra or not, or whether he will leave for another place to meet new challenges. It tends to be difficult for ordinary people to know exactly the mind of an artist or understand his perseverance. Whatever is the result, for Darrell Ang, work is the first thing on his agenda as long as he still works for the orchestra. Thanks to his hard work, no one can deny the changes and growth experienced by Sichuan Symphony Orchestra. This serious yet sincere art director is praised unanimously by all the other members of the orchestra. The small steps taken by the Sichuan Symphony Orchestra are the results of Darrell Ang's striving efforts. The baton waving in the air just promises a brighter future for the Sichuan Symphony Orchestra.

乐·享在成都

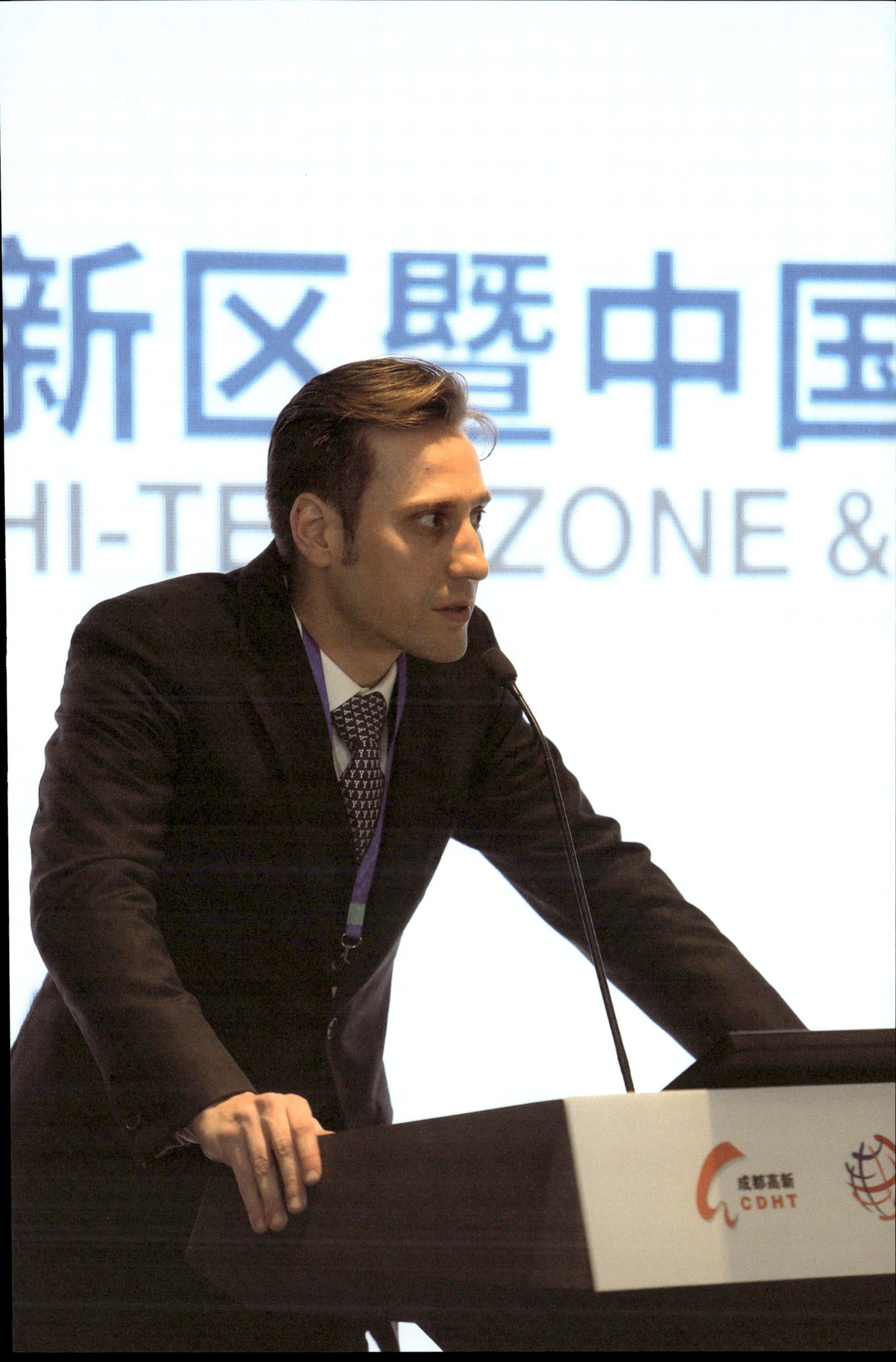
新区暨中
ZONE
成都高新
CDHT

>> 柯文（美国）

成都高新自贸试验区管理局外籍雇员

Alexander J. Cohen , USA

A Foreign Employee of Administration of Pilot Free Trade Zone of
Chengdu Hi-Tech Industrial Development Zone

自贸区来了个 "洋雇员"

这一天的成都，天空中飘着微微细雨，时间尚早，天色却有些阴沉。但即便是在这样的天色下，这里的人们依然活力不减，不仅迈着轻快的步伐，而且在行走间谈笑风生，一张张带着笑容的面孔青春洋溢，仿佛为阴冷的冬季平添了几分暖意。

这样的一处环境，并非是繁华的商业街区，也非热闹的城市公园，而是高楼林立的成都高新区。在这座历史悠久的城市里，高新区有着不一样的特点，它虽然没有老城的历史沉淀，但却有着强烈的现代感、浓郁的时尚气息，方方面面透露出它的年轻和朝气。高新区的特点还不止于此，它不仅是成都现代感的突出代表，更是成都发展前景的最佳展现，它汇集着成都许许多多的现代高科技产业，也会集着成都许许多多的高精尖人才，这里正奋力谱写着成都更加美好的未来。

在高新区的年轻人群中，多数为黑头发黄皮肤的中国人，但也会不时地出现几个别样的面孔，他们来自全球各地，却不约而同地被成都的蓬勃发展所吸引，在这里实现自己的人生价值。2017 年 6 月，成都高新自贸区抛出高薪招贤纳士，招聘职位从自贸办副主任到各个处室、项目负责人，在网络上引起高度关注，要知道，政府公开招聘外籍员工，可谓是一次巨大的突破与改革。而实际上，高新区早在四月份就已经启动对外招聘，意在全球挖掘优秀的国际人才。

来自美国康涅狄格州、毕业于耶鲁大学的美国高才生 Alexander J. Cohen，在机缘巧合的情况下参加面试成功被录取，有了一个新的身份——成都高新自贸试验区管理局办公室国际项目负责人。这个工作，不仅可以让柯文有充分的空间发挥自己的价值，还能够实现其职业发展的定位，并在自贸区的大家庭中找到家的归属感。

一口流利中文，与华缘分从小开始

曾有人说，中文是世界上最难的语言，对于想学中文的外国人来说，它就仿佛是一座难以攀登的高峰。然而柯文的中文水平却很高，他在工作中、生活中都能用中文和人们轻松沟通，"哥们儿""宅""要得"这样的俚语也都不在话下。

柯文的中文水平可并非是一朝一夕练就的。早在柯文读初中八年级的时候，他的中文启蒙就正式开始了。他的学校开了一门"中国历史"的课程，授课老师是一位从宁波交换而来的中国老师，课程让他对上下五千年的中华文明有了初步认识。在老师潜移默化的影响下，年少的柯文对中国逐渐萌生了强烈的兴趣，也跟老师学会了一些简单的中文词汇。

之后从九年级到大学期间，柯文都一直在学习中文，考入耶鲁大学后，柯文又选修了中文课程，继续把对中文的爱好与未来的人生发展规划相结合。在大学里，他的中文水平取得了突飞猛进的进步，对中国的了解也越来越丰富。

不过柯文与中国的缘分还不止于此。由于柯文的父母都喜欢中国也有中国朋友，从很小的时候，父母就会每周带他去一次中国餐厅用餐。此外，柯文与一些中国小伙伴交了朋友，从他们身上，他了解到更多中国人的性格特点和民族习惯，使他对中国更加具有认同感和亲切感。

一眼相中成都，在这里有家的感觉

尽管从小就对中国有了一定的了解，也能熟练地听说中文，但成都对于柯文而言，依然是一个陌生而神秘的地方。在踏足成都之前，柯文对成都几乎不曾有过了解，他只知道这是一座中国西部的城市，只知道这里有他和家人都非常喜爱的川菜，而其他的信息都是一片空白。

然而命运却把柯文带到了这里。2010 年 9 月，原本在上海从事红酒经销的他，受公司的派遣来到成都，独自一人在人生地不熟的成都开设一家分公司，柯文对成都进行了方方面面的考察，特别是成都的市场经济现状和发展潜力。他在考察中发现，成都蕴藏着非常巨大的发展机遇，它是一座正能量满满的城市，它未来的发展前景势必不可限量。他还了解到成都人的生活习惯和消费习惯，发现成都人对生活十分热爱，并且善于享受生活，乐观面对生活，与这座城市和谐相融。

于是，从 2010 年 10 月开始，柯文就正式开启了在成都的工作和生活。柯文把自己在成都的家安在了桐梓林，对成都满满地又有了更深的感悟。与上海相比，柯文感觉成都的生活节奏相对慢一些，更休闲舒适，成都人也非常热情好客，在成都很快就结交了许多中国和外国的朋友，这让柯文非常开心，哪怕身在遥远的异国他乡，只要有好朋友们陪伴，就不再孤单。柯文感叹道，成都人既能认真工作，又会享受生活，这样的人生态度让他很欣赏。

柯文喜欢劳逸结合，哪怕工作再忙，也会抽出时间来放松自己，打篮球、打网球都是他的兴趣爱好，每年还要参加成都篮球国际联赛。静下来的时候，柯文还喜欢读书，阅读让他能够与自己的内心对话。柯文说，美国有一种说法叫作"work-life balance"，就是找到工作和生活的平衡点，他感觉在成都实现了这个平衡点。

与蓉城同发展，感叹变化日新月异

　　2017 年 6 月，柯文在机缘巧合下参加了成都高新自贸区高薪招贤纳士的面试，大学所学的是经济学专业，又有着很好的中文水平，这个工作似乎正是为他量身打造。果然，柯文的才华得到了成都高新自贸试验区管理局的肯定，获得了新的工作，开始了新的职业生涯。

　　新的工作让柯文得心应手。前几年柯文一直从事教育相关的工作，虽然也较为符合他的兴趣，但与他所学的专业仍有差距，他有时会遗憾自己的专业水平无法很好地施展。而在成都高新自贸试验区管理局，他的工作和所学专业非常贴近，给了他极佳的施展才华的空间，令他感到非常幸运。同时，柯文也很庆幸，作为一名"老外"，能在成都获得好的工作机会，这是成都这座包容性的城市赐予他的红利。在新的工作环境中，柯文和领导、同事们都相处得十分融洽，工作得非常愉快。目前，柯文正在推进全球顶级科技园区合伙人计划（TSPPP），柯文由衷地希望，成都能够吸引到更多的国际人才，并为之不断努力。继柯文之后，成都高新自贸试验区管理局又招聘到一位法国高才生，很快便与柯文成了好朋友。

　　从 2010 年到现在，柯文最黄金的青春岁月都在成都度过。回想这些年来成都的发展变化，柯文身在其中，感触良多。他犹记得，2010 年刚到成都时，成都的地铁刚刚开始建设，二环路高架桥也还没有修建，而现在，二环路高架桥上每天都飞驰着很多车辆，成都的地铁也已经开通了 6 条线路，而且城市的格局变得越来越大，开始逐步向着三环外延伸，还在修建第二座国际大机场，日新月异的发展让成都已然成为了一座现代化、国际化的大都市。柯文坦言，根据他自己对中国、对成都的了解和感受，成都在中国已经可以称得上是准一线城市。而在这段时间里，柯文自身也发生了不小的变化，柯文相信，未来的自己还会与成都一同发展和进步。

四川妻子相伴，离不开的"第二个家"

柯文说，刚到成都的时候曾有人对他说，成都是一座来了就不想离开的城市，那时的他并未当真，可是现如今却应验了这句话。这不仅仅是因为柯文在成都有了满意的工作，还因为柯文和一位四川女孩恋爱结婚了。

2010 年 9 月，在柯文到成都的第二天，就遇到了他现在的妻子Grace。柯文清楚地记得，这个女孩外表端庄秀丽，待人接物落落大方，他对她一见钟情，于是，果断地展开了追求，并成功赢得了她的芳心。约会几次后，柯文就觉得有一天他肯定会娶这个女孩，终于在 2015 年，柯文与 Grace 在成都领证正式结为夫妻，使他在成都的生活更有归属感。

说起妻子，柯文的脸上不禁流露出幸福的笑容。有了妻子的陪伴，他在成都的生活更加安定，每年也会回美国看望陪伴父母两三次。柯文笑着说，现在他有两个家，父母在的地方是一个家，自己和妻子在的地方是第二个家。

成为一名"洋女婿"之后，柯文在成都的生活更加丰富有趣。柯文记得当自己第一次跟着还是女友的妻子回到雅安过春节的时候，准岳父岳母对他十分热情，完全没有因为他的外国人身份而介怀，让他悬着的心落了地。他第一次体会到了正宗的四川春节，浓浓的年味让他很是欢喜。年夜饭上，准岳母做了非常丰盛的饭菜，一桌菜里，最合他口味的是一道烂肉粉条，他边吃边对准岳母赞不绝口，没想到这几句夸奖引得准岳母接连好几天都特意为他做了这道菜，直到现在，每次柯文跟着妻子回娘家，岳母还是会特意为他准备这道菜，让他既感动又尴尬。柯文心里明白，这就是四川人的热情好客，因此他总是会带着暖暖的感动吃得很开心。

在成都、在四川有了亲人和很多好朋友之后，柯文坦言，恐怕这辈子都不会真的"离开"成都。哪怕今后自己和妻子因为工作的需要要去其他地方，但由于对成都深厚的感情，和对亲人、朋友们的深深的牵挂，他也会经常回来这里。柯文笑着说，也许很快他会和妻子生一个混血的"成都宝宝"，那将会是他成都情缘的最美丽结晶。

A Foreign Employee in Pilot Free Trade Zone

It's a rainy day in Chengdu and the sky is overcast. But instead of being upset by the weather, people here are energetic and in high spirits. Their vitality warms the dark cold winter.

This is neither a busy business district nor a bustling city park. It is Chengdu Hi-Tech Industrial Development Zone. Chengdu Hi-Tech Industrial Development Zone is a new district in this ancient city, featuring a modern and fashionable environment, reflecting its youth and vitality. Far more than that, Chengdu Hi-Tech Industrial Development Zone is also a hallmark of the city's development embedded with a great amount of modern hi-tech industries as well as an array of high-quality and sophisticated talent. It is striving to create a brighter tomorrow for the city.

The local raven haired, yellow skinned Chinese account for the majority of the young workforce in the Hi-Tech Zone. These foreigners, although coming from different countries, are attracted by Chengdu's prosperity and come for the high quality of life on offer. In June, 2017, "Pilot Free Trade Zone" of Chengdu Hi-Tech Industrial Development Zone posted recruitment for well-remunerated posts such as Deputy Director of Office of Administration of Pilot Free Trade Zone of Chengdu Hi-Tech Industrial Development Zone, as well as leaders of departments and projects among others. The recruitment aroused wide online discussion about the breakthrough signified by the government's willingness to advertise for overseas employees. In fact, the Hi-Tech Zone launched its own global recruitment since April, aiming at attracting outstanding international talent to work in Chengdu.

Alexander J. Cohen, coming from Connecticut State of America and graduating from Yale University, got a new title of Officer of International Projects at the Office of Administration of the "Pilot Free Trade Zone", Chengdu Hi-Tech Industrial Development Zone after performing well during the interview. The job allows Cohen to dig deeply into his potential and find a direction for his career development. Furthermore, he feels completely at home at the "Pilot Free Trade Zone".

Fluent Chinese Comes from Ties with China as a Child

People say that Chinese is the most difficult language in the world. Chinese is to foreign learners what Mount Everest is to mountain climbers. However, the language is not a problem for Cohen. He can communicate with his colleagues and friends in Chinese fluently, even with some pieces of slang like Gemer (Chinese for "bro"), Zhai (a state of staying at home) and Yaodei ("OK" in Chengdu dialect).

However, Rome was not built in a day. Cohen began learning Chinese in Grade Eight. Back then, his school launched a course named "Chinese History", which was taught by an exchange teacher from Ningbo, China. It was the beginning of his interest in China's 5,000-year-old culture. Young Cohen was attracted to this mysterious eastern country and picked up some simple Chinese words from his teacher.

In fact, from Grade Nine to university, Cohen never gave up learning

Chinese. At university he selected Chinese as an optional course. He endeavored to integrate Chinese into his career development goals. Efforts brought reward, and Cohen made impressive progress in Chinese in Yale and got a better understanding of China.

Cohen's ties with China are not only mirrored by his fluent Chinese. He also loves Chinese food. His parents, who were also fans of China, would take him to Chinese restaurants once a week to meet their Chinese friends when he was young. With the help of his own Chinese friends, Cohen's sense of recognition and intimacy with the country also improved, and he increasingly understood the distinctive characters and habits of Chinese people.

Fall in Love with Chengdu at First Sight

Although Cohen's understanding of China began at a young age and he had a sound language ability, he had no idea what Chengdu looked like before he came. The city's location in West China and the origin of Sichuanese cuisine were the limits of his knowledge.

Eventually he arrived in Chengdu. Engaged in red wine distribution in Shanghai, he was assigned to Chengdu to launch a new branch in September 2010. Since then, Cohen had conducted a detailed investigation on Chengdu, its current economic environment and development potential. What he had found was that Chengdu was prosperous with great growth opportunities. He believed that a promising future beaconed for the city. He also found out about the lives and consumption habits of the local people, discovering that they were enthusiastic and optimistic towards life. They knew how to relax. He concluded that the people and the city were in harmony with each other.

Therefore, Cohen started his work in Chengdu in October, 2010. Living in Tongzilin, he began to get a better understanding of the city. Compared to Shanghai, he found Chengdu more relaxing and more livable. The pace of life was much slower. Hospitable locals and foreign friends here helped alleviate his loneliness and homesickness. He said he admired the ability of the locals to balance hard work with a carefree lifestyle.

Apart from work, Cohen also tries to devote time to his hobbies. He likes playing basketball and tennis as well as reading. He says sports help relax him and reading helped him think and reflect. He even plays in the Chengdu International Basketball League every year. Cohen tried to explain this by talking about the work—life balance, a theory popular in America. He thinks that he has found it in Chengdu.

Growing with Ever Changing Chengdu

In June, 2017, Cohen applied for an interview run by "Pilot Free Trade Zone" of Chengdu Hi-Tech Industrial Development Zone almost by chance. As he majored in Economics in Yale University and was fluent in Chinese, he was expected to be qualified for the role. And as it turned out, he won the post.

Cohen has adapted well to his new job. Having worked in education industry for the past couple of years and also interested in this sector, he felt some regret that there were few chances for him to utilize the knowledge that he had learned in school. However, the Administration of "Pilot Free Trade Zone" of Chengdu Hi-Tech Industrial Development

Zone gives him an opportunity to stretch himself. Cohen feels lucky to get such a promising job in Chengdu as a foreigner. He attributes this to the city's inclusiveness. The Administration not only provides him a space to give full reign to his potential, but also comprise a group of friendly leaders and colleagues. Cohen is now developing a global Top Science Park Partnership Program (TSPPP). He says he will dedicate himself to working on this program, so as to attract more international talent to Chengdu. Another French intellectual employed by the Administration became a good friend of Cohen.

Since 2010, Cohen has devoted the best years of his youth to Chengdu. Witnessing Chengdu's growth over the years, he feels excited. He recalls that when he first arrived in Chengdu in 2010, the metro system was just getting off the ground and Second Ring Overpass had yet to be constructed. But now, the former has 6 open lines and the latter carries many cars every day. Additionally, Chengdu is ever expanding, now comprising more than three ring roads and is currently constructing a second international airport. Fast-changing development has turned Chengdu into a modern and international metropolis. His understanding of China and Chengdu leads him to believe that Chengdu is a first-tier city in the making. Growing in tandem with the city, Cohen has also matured. He believes that there will be more growth in the future in his time at Chengdu.

A Sichuan Wife and the Second Family

When Cohen first arrived in Chengdu in 2010, he was warned that it was a very difficult city to leave, and although he had initially laughed at the idea, this was how things turned out. His willingness to stay finally comes from both his satisfying job and his local Sichuanese wife.

Cohen met Grace the very next day after arriving in September, 2010. He fell immediately in love with her. She was beautiful, demure and well-mannered. He asked Grace to be his girlfriend and she accepted. After several dates, Cohen was convinced that this girl would one day be his wife. And in 2015, they married in Chengdu.

Speaking of Grace, Cohen cannot help showing his happiness. After marriage, his life in Chengdu is more stable, though he still flies back to America to see his family several times a year. Cohen says he has two families, one in America with his parents and the other in Chengdu with his wife.

Life became more exciting following his marriage. To his great relief, when Grace took him to Ya'an, a city in Sichuan, for Spring Festival, her parents took a shine to him and did not mind that their daughter's boyfriend was a foreigner. This was Cohen's first experience of a real Sichuanese Spring Festival. He says he liked the atmosphere. Grace's mother prepared a tasty New Year's Eve Dinner, his favorite dish was vermicelli noodles with spicy minced pork. Unexpectedly, his praise encouraged her mother to make it for him again over the next few days. Even now, whenever they return to Ya'an, his mother-in-law goes out of her way to prepare this dish for him, which embarrasses him while he is also moved each time. He understands the care and love behind it, so each time he gladly tucks in.

With so many relatives and friends living in Chengdu and other places in Sichuan, Cohen admits that he would never leave the city. Even if work requirements mean that either he or his wife need to move, their affection of the city as well as their friends and relatives living here would pull them back. Cohen says that maybe he and his wife are going to have a Chengdu baby in the near future, which would be the best gift that Chengdu could give him.

>> 伯尼（毛里求斯）
"丛林"咖啡店老板

Hans Bernard Pierre Noel, Mauritius
Owner of the Jungle Coffee Shop

一段跨国恋：艰辛中的浪漫

"沃野自兹始，浮云喜乍晴"，应了这"世界水利文化鼻祖"的滋润灌溉和千年历史文化的滋养，青葱的树木，湿润的空气，都江堰这座小城散发着它独有的悠然自得而又不失厚重的气息。在这样的城市氛围里，"丛林"的诞生似乎也是顺理成章的事情。

"丛林"是一家咖啡店，这家咖啡店和他的名字一样特别，店主人独具匠心地将音乐、鲜花、比萨等多种主题融进了咖啡店里，店面虽小，却也精致而丰富，因而也吸引了不少客人的光顾。至于为什么要将店名取名为"丛林"，店主人伯尼说，他很喜欢 the Jungle 这个词，因为它包罗万象，可以容纳下你喜欢的一切。而"丛林"里的一切，便是店主人伯尼和露露这对跨国夫妻共同爱好的结晶。

每天上午十点左右，伯尼和露露会一起来到店里，开始一天的准备工作。露露负责修剪花草，伯尼负责摆放桌椅。整个咖啡小店弥漫着独特的味道，鲜花的香气伴随着现磨咖啡的醇香；轻快而富有律动的爵士乐按摩顾客的耳朵；伯尼夫妻俩不经意间的眼神交流，总流动着掩藏不住的爱意。

缘，妙不可言

缘分是一种妙不可言的东西，能让生活在地球两端的两个人相遇相知并相守。相遇之前，他们循着各自的轨迹按部就班地生活着。伯尼出生于毛里求斯，成长在澳大利亚，然后就职于墨尔本当地的汇丰银行，

153

拿着非常可观的薪酬；露露出生并成长于四川都江堰的一个农村，是个典型的四川姑娘，是成都某高校的一名英语专业的大学生。

2007年年底，伯尼第一次来到成都，因为共同的好友，伯尼在一次聚会上认识了露露。第一眼见到露露，伯尼就被深深吸引，但落花有意，流水无情，当时的露露对伯尼并没有其他想法。伯尼离开成都之后，虽然他们经常用Email联系，但露露始终无法放下内心的包袱。

二人看似无望的感情在一年后出现了转机，2008年，伯尼告诉露露，要来成都看她。露露并没有把他的话放在心上，毕竟他们只见过一次。但没想到的是，在露露生日那天，伯尼真的出现在她面前，这样的惊喜渐渐使露露内心的坚冰开始融化。再想到当时的成都刚刚经历过汶川大地震，而伯尼不顾危险地来找露露，这样的真情最终使露露敞开心扉，尝试着接受伯尼的爱，半年之后，他们终于走到了一起。

不平凡的开始注定要经受更多的磨炼，正如大家所能想到的，二人的跨国恋要经受时间和距离的双重考验。短暂的相处后，伯尼不得不回到墨尔本工作，露露却要留在成都继续她的学业。在"用你的晚安陪我吃早餐"的日子，他们的感情靠E-mail延续着。露露承认，在这期间，她动摇过，也想过放弃，但每次伯尼都用耐心和温暖，给露露坚定继续的信念。

经过两年辛苦的异地恋，怀着对爱人深切的思念，2010年，露露去了墨尔本，也就是在墨尔本待的三个月，彻底改变了露露的人生。初到墨尔本，人生地不熟的露露面临着多方面的压力，找工作经常忙得不可开交，第一次离家那么远，难免心情低落。有一次露露发了很大的脾气，伯尼并没有开口，他只是很冷静地抱着她，给她温暖。在墨尔本这短暂的三个月生活转瞬即逝，由于露露的签证只有三个月的时间，期满她必须回国，离开之前，露露做了一个惊人的决定，她决定嫁给伯尼！终于，他们两人就在墨尔本登记结婚，历时三年的感情终于修成正果。

154

2011 年，毕业后的露露去了墨尔本，给这段长达四年的异地恋画上句号。在墨尔本的四年时间里，露露每天上完班，"好丈夫"伯尼都会在家做好夜宵，烧好热水，然后接露露回家。他们的生活看似平淡，却又无比幸福。

听从内心，走好漫漫创业路

上天似乎想给这对幸福的夫妻更多的考验，2015 年，露露妈妈的身体突然出现问题，露露不得不放弃墨尔本惬意的生活回国陪伴家人。要和露露一起来到都江堰生活，就意味着伯尼要放弃墨尔本高薪的工作，远离亲人和朋友。当他把"定居都江堰"的想法告诉家人时，却意外地得到了家人的支持。伯尼的哥哥鼓励他说：听从自己的内心，和自己心爱的人一起选择自己想要的生活，去中国也会收获不一样的人生经历。于是，2015 年年底，伯尼和露露回到都江堰，开启了他们的创业之路。

对于两个从来没有创业经验的人来说，走出第一步无疑是个艰难的决定，还好伯尼是一个天生的乐天派，他相信"车到山前必有路"，任何苦难都会被他们的热情打倒。他们准备从事一份自己真正喜欢的职业，这就考虑到两人的兴趣爱好，他们都喜欢咖啡，露露又喜欢鲜花，那么开一个鲜花咖啡店再好不过。于是，"丛林"就这样诞生了。

突然从一个高级金领转换成自由职业者，完全不一样的人生体验，伯尼坦言自己并没有太多不适应，因为现在做的工作才是自己真正热爱和想追求的，而且还可以每天和爱的人一起生活在这样一座美丽的城市，享受生活才是最重要的事情。创业初期，处在探索阶段的小店只经营咖啡和鲜花。每天清晨会有师傅给小店送花，露露满心欢喜地修剪、装饰着这些鲜花，伯尼则开始调制咖啡，伴随着爵士的律动，这种简单舒适的生活使他们远离了城市的喧嚣和复杂的人际关系。

开店初期，"丛林"位于并不繁华的都江堰，客流量小是二人遇到的最大的难题。如何吸引更多的人认识他们的店呢？经过一番思考后，伯尼突然想到了"比萨"，他想：如果把咖啡、鲜花和比萨融合到一起，会不会吸引更多的人来消费呢？对于比萨，伯尼有特殊的记忆和感情。他小时候生活在毛里求斯，他的外婆特别喜欢做比萨，而他也特别喜欢看外婆做比萨，从和面到烘焙，这些过程让他感到非常有趣。

带着这样的思考，在都江堰待了四个月后，伯尼抱着试一试的态度，回到了墨尔本学习做比萨。现在大多数的西餐厅为了追求利益最大化，都采用机器加工制作比萨；为了追求更鲜美的口感，伯尼决定学习最原始的比萨制作工艺：纯手工制作。他所学做的这款比萨工序繁复，光做好面坯就要48个小时。曾经的银行金领，挽起袖子，系上围裙，就这样开始做起了一名制作比萨的大厨。

在墨尔本学习了将近一年，伯尼才学会手工比萨的制作方法，如果不是真的热爱这门手艺，想必也没有人能像伯尼一样，付出这么多的时间和金钱，还要忍受远离爱人的痛苦。伯尼离开的这段时间里，店里的工作都是露露一个人在打理，这段时间里，露露没有一点埋怨，因为她知道短暂的辛苦是为了日后的幸福。

2017年2月，比萨正式加入到了"丛林"这个大家庭，成为继咖啡、鲜花之后的新元素。由于比萨都是纯手工制作，伯尼和露露每天很早就要开始做准备。比萨所需的面粉、芝士直接从国外进口，蔬菜和肉类也是精选当地最好的，做好一个比萨大概需要15分钟，整个制作的过程都在吧台，顾客可以看得清清楚楚。

现在，"丛林"的生意越来越好，比萨经常供不应求，伯尼一个人有点忙不过来，未来他想多请几个师傅一起来做比萨，他对这些人最基本的要求是：必须真正热爱这份职业，享受这份工作。对于未来"丛林"的发展和设想，伯尼坦言想把它做成一张有特色的名片，有机会还会多开几家分店，把"纯手工制作"这种理念分享给更多的朋友，为人们提供一个可以真正放松、休闲的场所，并且每个店都会融入不同的元素，但都是源于手工。

静待花开

来到都江堰后，伯尼认识了很多新朋友，有了自己的圈子，每周五下午，他都会和露露在小店门口举办一场烧烤 party，邀请朋友们参加，大家一起分享美食，享受生活；咖啡店晚上收工后，伯尼经常会做好一个比萨带到朋友家，大家边看电影，边吃比萨；闲暇时刻，露露会带伯尼到周围景区走一走，学习中国文化，了解中国礼仪。

现在，伯尼已经完全融入了都江堰的生活，他爱上了这里的干锅，爱上了大熊猫，爱上了这里的一切。谈起当初的选择和现在的变化，伯尼表示自己一点也不后悔来到都江堰，每天和爱的人在一起，和鲜花、咖啡、美食相伴，他很享受现在的生活。最近他还应邀参与了一本书籍英文版的校对工作，这本书由都江堰本地作家编著，收集了许多都江堰的历史文化故事。他说，能为自己妻子的家乡做一些事情，让更多的人了解到都江堰的文化，向世界介绍都江堰这座城市，这是他的荣幸。

中国有句话叫"七年之痒"，转眼间，伯尼和露露已经认识十一年了，在生活中，他们相互理解、扶持，才能走过这漫长的十一年。露露说，从伯尼身上，她学到最多的东西就是包容。我们每个人都有自己的生活，所以，不要随意评价他人，过好自己的生活就好。

露露和伯尼打算举办一场婚礼，对于这场爱的婚礼，他们有很多想法和期待，伯尼打算在都江堰办一场中式婚礼，邀请亲朋好友来见证他们的幸福时刻。从他们彼此互望时的深情眼神中，你可以体会到什么是真正的幸福。

也许就像他们说的那样，如果没有遇到彼此，露露也许还在成都做一个翻译，或是老师；而伯尼可能会一直在汇丰银行做他的金领。但缘分就是个神奇的东西，可以让两个陌生人变成恋人，变成对方生命中最重要的人，相守彼此。都江堰这座城市并没有让这位远方的外国小伙伴觉得家在远方，此刻的伯尼，心安于此地，筑梦于本土。邂逅一座城，寻梦一个家，祝福这段在都江堰落地生根的跨国爱情早日开花结果，愿伯尼和露露在都江堰一直幸福下去！

Transnational Love Story: Romance with Trials

Dujiangyan, "a vast fecund land where clouds give way to sunshine" have nurtured the "forefather of world water conservation culture". With a history of more than 2,000 years, with lush trees and a humid climate, Dujiangyan is a place of both leisure and refinement. In such a place, the birth of the "Jungle" seems to be preordained.

Both the coffee shop and its name are unique. The owner has created a variety of themes for the shop: music, flowers and pizza. Small but intricately designed to a delicate taste, the coffee shop has enticed customers ever since its opening. Regarding its name, the shop owner, Bernard, claims that the Jungle was his favorite word because it had connotations of inclusiveness, and the embrace of all that we loved. Everything in the shop is the fruit of interests shared by the shop owner and his Chinese wife Lulu.

Bernard and Lulu arrive at the coffee shop around 10 am each morning to prepare for the coming day. Lulu attends to the plants while Bernard arranges the tables and chairs. A romantic atmosphere permeates the entire shop: with the pleasing aroma of flowers mingling with the scent of freshly ground coffee; whilst the lively and rhythmic jazz music is an aural feast. Under the seemingly accidental eye contact between the couple flows their deep love.

Unfathomable Predestined Love

The unfathomable, unknowable predestined love can lead two people born at the opposite ends of the world to meeting and falling in love with each other. Before meeting, Bernard and Lulu had followed the social conventions of their respective cultures: Bernard was born in Mauritius and grew up in Australia. He then worked for HSBC in Melbourne, earning a handsome salary. Lulu was born and grew up in the countryside of Dujiangyan, Sichuan. As a typical Sichuan girl, she then went to a university in Chengdu to study English.

At the end of 2007, Bernard went to Chengdu for the first time and met Lulu at a common friend's party. Bernard fell in love at the first sight, but his love was unrequited. After Bernard left Chengdu, the two young people maintained email contact, but Lulu never opened up her heart.

Their seemingly hopeless relationship started to turn around a year later. In 2008, Bernard told Lulu that he would go to Chengdu to see her. As they had only met once, Lulu didn't take his promise seriously. But on her birthday, Bernard surprised Lulu by visiting, an action that made her heart melt. For the Wenchuan earthquake had just struck Chengdu, yet he had still come, in spite of such danger. She gave way to his love and they became lovers six months later.

An unusual beginning usually signals further trials ahead. As expected, their intimate romance was tested by distance and time, when after a short stay in China Bernard returned to work in Melbourne whilst Lulu continued her study in Chengdu. Reverting to disparate lifestyles, their romance endured via email, a time during which Lulu admitted she occasionally wanted to give up, but Bernard's patience and love proved to be a constant source of strength.

After missing Bernard intensely for two years, Lulu visited Melbourne in 2010. The three-month stay in Melbourne changed the course of her life. Living in a new place far away from home for the first time, Lulu felt under immense pressure. Her ultimately futile job search resulted in her developing depression. One day, Lulu lost her temper, yet Bernard said nothing and remained calm. He gave Lulu such a big hug that Lulu was reaffirmed of his abiding love for her. Her visa was only valid for three months, and so she prepared to leave Australia. Prior to the visa expiration date, Lulu made a surprising decision: She would marry Bernard! Finally, after three long years they married in Melbourne.

In 2011, Lulu visited Melbourne following graduation and the four-year transnational love finally bore fruit. During Lulu's four-year stay in Melbourne, Bernard proved to be an attentive husband who picked her up after work and prepared midnight snack and hot water drinks—a common yet happy life.

Listening to Inner Voice and Starting a New Business

However, more trouble lay in store. when Lulu's mother's health problems compelled her to relinquish her married life in Melbourne to return to China to care for her. For Bernard, living in Dujiangyan with Lulu meant giving up his high-paying job and living far away from his own family and friends. When he told his family about his plan to "settle in Dujiangyan", however, they gave their support, his brother told him to "just listen to your inner voice and live the life you want with your beloved wife. There may be exciting experiences ahead in China". And so, at the end of 2015, Bernard and Lulu made their way to Dujiangyan and started their own business.

For new entrepreneurs, taking the first step is always the most onerous. Fortunately, Bernard is an optimist who believes that "things will eventually sort themselves out". Such optimism and passion is enough to overcome any difficulties. In order to engage in something they really love, they decided to open a combined flower & coffee shop, for both of them like drinking coffee and Lulu loves flowers. And so, the Jungle came into being.

The switch from high-powered city professional to small town entrepreneur didn't pose any difficulty to Bernard because this new job was his dream vocation. Besides this, there was the joy of living in such a beautiful town with his beloved wife, something which he ranked extremely high. When the shop first opened, they only sold coffee and flowers. Every morning, after the worker sent flowers to the shop, Lulu would happily trim them while Bernard began brewing coffee. Surrounded by jazz music, this simple yet care-free life was a world away from the hustle and bustle of city life and troubling interpersonal relationships.

Since Dujiangyan is only a small town, in the beginning the Jungle struggled to attract customers. The challenge of how to attract more visitors was a frequent headache. After much consideration, Bernard hit upon the idea of pizza: why not combine coffee, flowers and pizza? That might attract more customers. Bernard had a special love for pizza. When in Mauritius as a child, his maternal grandmother often made pizza and he loved watching the whole process, from kneading dough to baking—it had been such an enjoyable experience.

To try out this new idea, Bernard returned to Melbourne after just a four month stay in Dujiangyan and started to learn how to make pizza. To maximize profits, pizzas are produced by machine in most western restaurants. However to make a better tasting product, Bernard, decided to learn the oldest way of making hand-made pizza. This traditional method involves a rather complicated procedure, the dough taking 48 hours to produce. This former high flying city professional rolled up his sleeves and put on an apron, finally becoming a pizza chef.

After one year's study in Melbourne, Bernard finally grasped the techniques of this traditional craft. Without a genuine passion for the craft, Bernard would have been unable to survive such a taxing period: not just spending money and time but also separated from his wife. Lulu managed the coffee shop alone during his absence, however she did not complain for she understood this temporary trial would lead to future happiness.

In February 2017, pizza joined the family of coffee and flowers at the Jungle. Preparation meant that, Bernard and Lulu had to start very early every day. The flour and cheese were imported while vegetable and meat were sourced from the local market. Pizza usually took 15 minutes to make, and it was made at bar counter allowing customers to watch the whole process.

Nowadays the Jungle is flourishing and the demand for pizza often exceeds supply. Struggling to run the business alone, Bernard is considering hiring more people to help. The basic job requirements are: to have a genuine passion for this profession and love the job. Regarding his vision for the future growth, Bernard said he wanted to build the Jungle into a unique brand name and if possible to open several outlets. He wants to share the idea of "traditional hand-made pizzas" with more people and provide a place to relax.

Each outlet may have different characteristics and elements, but hand-made is a must.

Awaiting Bloom of Flowers

Bernard has made a lot of new friends in Dujiangyan. Each Friday afternoon, he and Lulu will invite them to a barbecue party held in front of their shop. After a day's work, Bernard of ten makes a pizza and takes it to a friend's house. Then all the friends watch a movie together while eating pizza. During their spare time, Lulu will take Bernard to scenic spots to teach him about Chinese culture and Chinese etiquette.

Bernard has already adapted to life in Dujiangyan. He loves everything about it including the spicy dish, dry pot and of course, Sichuan's famous pandas. Bernard has no regrets towards moving to Dujiangyan. He enjoys life with his beloved wife, and surrounded by flowers, coffee and delicious food every day. Recently, he has been entrusted with the proofreading for an English language book written by a local writer. The book contains a lot of stories pertaining to the area's history and culture. Bernard is honored to contribute to his wife's hometown and introduce it to more people around the world.

Eleven years have passed since Bernard and Lulu first met each other. With an eleven-year mutual support and understanding, the seven-year itch passed without a hitch. Lulu says that she has learned a lot from Bernard, especially how to be an inclusive person. Each has the right to pursue his or her own lifestyle. As such, it's unwise to comment on how others live. Just be yourself.

Lulu and Bernard want to hold a wedding ceremony someday. They have come up with several ideas about the wedding. Bernard wants to have a Chinese-style wedding and invite his friends and family along. From the love in their eyes when they look at each other, you may know the meaning of true happiness.

They say that if they had never met, Lulu might be working as a translator or teacher in Chengdu while Bernard would still be a high flier at HSBC. Predestined love works its magic, binding two strangers together and refocusing their attentions on each other. Bernard, a foreigner from a distant land, doesn't feel that he lives in a strange place because he's already physically and emotionally adapted to life in Dujiangyan. To find such a city to pursue your dream and to establish a new life is precious. We hope that the love between Bernard and Lulu will blossom further, in the town where their story began, and that their life will be filled with love and happiness!

刘杰森（美国）

成都环球医生

Jason A. Logan, USA

Doctor of Global Doctor Chengdu Clinic

用药医治疾病，用爱温暖心灵

在科华北路的力宝大厦，有这样一处地方，走到二楼，穿过大厅和一条长长的走廊，便能看见它，推开它的大门，便能感受到温暖的暖气向自己袭来，暖气仿佛能够透过皮肤钻进人的心里，让人产生一种回到家里的错觉。紧接着，映入眼帘的是简洁的装修风格、完整的医疗设备、让人倍感亲切的医生，这温馨的氛围，让每一个来到这里的病人，都能在诊疗之前，感到无比踏实。

这里，就是环球医生成都国际医疗中心。在这个地方，人们可以看到许多从国外来到成都的医生，而刘杰森医生就是其中之一。作为一名全科医生，刘杰森一直致力于心血管疾病的预防，胆固醇疾病、儿科的诊疗和研究，他每天都会在环球医生接见他的病人，而他的病人亦总是无比信任他，彼此之间，不像医生和病人关系，反而更像朋友。

病人的信任让刘杰森感受到生活的意义和价值，忙碌的工作也让他倍感充实，如今一家人都已定居成都，从生活到工作，一切看起来都是那么的幸福美满，然而回想当年，青年时期的他一定不会想到，自己有一天会离开美国，来到成都，拥有今天的生活。那时的他，只有一个小小的梦想——长大后要做一名帮助别人摆脱痛苦的医生。

探寻广阔天地，结缘天府之国

为什么要来成都呢？

很多人都这样问刘杰森，要知道，这不是一次出差，亦不是一次旅行，它是真正地将自己扎根在另一个遥远的彼岸，远渡重洋，要跨越的不只是海岸和公路，还有年轻而稚嫩的心灵。

刘杰森本人也有过踌躇，有过怀疑，但是从来没有后悔过，用他的话来说，也许从选择到安居，一切都是一种冥冥之中早已注定的缘分。

缘分的种子生根于童年时满怀梦想的心灵，在孩童时期，刘杰森就已经将医生这一职业当作自己毕生努力的事业，虽然从小就坚定地想要成为医生，但他那时从来没有想过有一天会来到成都。怀着对梦想的虔诚信念，及至 2002 年，刘杰森终于获得美国田纳西大学的医学博士学位，人生浩瀚，如山脉层峦叠嶂，人总要不断翻越，去看更广阔的天地。因此彼时的刘杰森，心里其实已经燃起了一个火种——要去一个新的环境，去学、去看自己没有见识过的东西，并用自己所学去帮助那里的人摆脱疾病的困扰。

打那之后，这个火种便在刘杰森的心里燃烧着，它象征着一种希望——时刻提醒着刘杰森，自己的人生将有无限的可能。这种希望使得刘杰森兴奋、期待，进而推动着他更加热爱自己的事业，终于，在 2004 年，刘杰森和自己的妻子订下了计划——去中国，让自己内心的火种在那块充满魅力的土地上，燃烧得更有意义。

在中国的第一个脚印，刘杰森和妻子落在了澳门。在朋友的带领下，刘杰森见识了澳门的美丽，但却并没有对澳门产生一见如故的感觉，他知道，他想要停留的地方并不是这里。随后刘杰森又去了广东并和妻子在农村生活了一段时间，令刘杰森感到很庆幸的是，那里的人们并没有因国家和文化的差异而排斥他们，相反，人们非常热情，生怕怠慢了这两个国外的朋友，而刘杰森亦竭尽所能，乐此不疲地用自己的专业帮助这些热情好客的朋友。

虽然没有留在澳门，也没有留在广东，但这一段经历使得刘杰森对中国和中国人产生了一种非常难得的亲切感。他喜欢中国城市里的现代文明，亦喜欢农村里自然淳朴的田园风光，最重要的是，中国人对他的友好，让他在中国找到了归属感，这更加坚定了他要留在中国的决心。

决心是有了，但是中国那么大，留在哪里仍旧是个问题。刘杰森走过的诸如澳门、广东，虽然也好，但待在这些地方，刘杰森仍然感觉自己只是一个游客，他要寻找一个能让他产生家的感觉的地方，他不知道这个地方在哪里，但他知道这个地方一定存在，而且就在中国。

很快，一位朋友告诉刘杰森——在中国的西部地区，有一座城市叫成都，那里不仅适合居住，而且近几年，全科医生的发展空间很大，会有很多机会。

就这样，刘杰森得知了"成都"这个地方，为了给自己的事业找到更好的基石，在 2007 年的时候，刘杰森和自己的妻子来到了成都。初来成都，刘杰森就像寻常的游客一样，爱到一些著名的景点，如武侯祠、宽窄巷子、春熙路等地留下自己的足迹，工作时间，刘杰森便常来华西医院交流学习。经过一段时间的了解，刘杰森发现成都果然如朋友所说，是一个非常适合居住的地方，但与此同时，他也会想，还会不会有比成都更好的地方呢？如果因为眼前的风景而错过了自己心底的那个"家"，那多可惜啊！

因此，那时的他产生了两种想法——留在成都或是继续去寻找更加合适的地方。这两个想法不停地在刘杰森的脑海里交战，使得刘杰森纠结不已，就在这时，一件意想不到的事情发生了——2008 年 5 月 12 日，汶川大地震。

2008 年的地震，不仅震垮了无数人的家，更震碎了无数人的心，看着电视新闻上面那无数张纯真而悲痛的面孔，刘杰森和他的妻子心碎不已，没有过多地犹豫，他们毅然决然地以医务志愿者的身份来到了灾区，帮忙救助那些受伤的人。在那里，他们用纱布包扎人们血流不止的伤口，亦用乐观的精神和不离不弃的陪伴包扎了人们血流不止的心灵。

用药医治疾病，用爱温暖心灵

在举国悲痛的时候，刘杰森虽然不是中国人，但却深刻地感受到，自己是四川、是中国的一分子，也正是因为这段做志愿者的经历，让他对四川这块土地产生了深深的依恋，最终决定和妻子一起留在四川的省会——天府之国成都。

初遇重重困难，感受人情温暖

冬天虽然已经到来，但是成都这座城市，并没有被严寒笼罩。在人民公园，人们有说有笑地喝着大碗茶；在春熙路，商场与店铺里顾客熙熙攘攘；在宽窄巷子和武侯祠，游客们左手拿着小吃，右手拿着相机，他们没有因寒冷而心情郁闷，反而在寒冷的衬托下，更能体会到温暖的存在。

这就是成都，一座无论何种季节，都能让人感觉到温暖的城市。这份温暖，感染着每一个扎根在成都的异乡人。朝着大街小巷放眼望去，我们常常能够看见不同肤色的外国朋友，他们状态轻松自然，也用笑容温暖着来来往往的成都人。

相互温暖，并且用温暖的态度相互感染，这就是生活在成都的外国朋友和成都人之间，最真诚的默契。作为成都的一分子，刘杰森早已养成了这样的默契，然而刚来成都的时候，一切都并不容易。

异国生活，语言不通给刘杰森带来了许多不便。比如有一次他去超市买牛奶，结果因表达错误买成了酸奶，回去之后发现是酸的，还以为牛奶是坏的。诸如此类的事情还有很多，一开始也闹了不少笑话，每每提到当时那些糗事，刘杰森都忍不住笑，但是他打从心里觉得，他要感谢这些不便，因为正是通过它们，刘杰森才结识了那么多友善帮助他的成都朋友，他们有的帮他办宽带，有的带他学着买东西，生活中大大小小的事情，只要刘杰森一家人有困难，这群朋友总能第一时间赶到，久而久之，刘杰森渐渐习惯了成都的生活，语言的障碍也被慢慢克服。

除了生活上的不便，工作上也有许多难题，在华西交流学习的时候，中西方不同的诊疗模式让刘杰森感到有些不适应，虽然这样，但他依然没有打退堂鼓。作为一个全科医生，刘杰森不仅关注病人的身体病症，更关注病人的心理健康，他会像个朋友一样，定期探访病人，不仅帮他们摆脱疾病的困扰，还为他们做心理建设，避免他们因疾病而产生消极的情绪。

就在这个时候，环球医生向他抛出了橄榄枝。一直以来，成都都是一个与国际紧密接轨的城市，随着经济和文化的发展，越来越多的外国朋友来到成都定居，而他们中的大部分人，往往对本地的医疗系统一无所知，从而面临着一个看病难的问题，正因如此，才会有环球医生这样的诊疗机构。在这里，病人都以外国朋友为主，在他们需要帮助的时候，环球医生会为他们提供紧急治疗，并通过绿色通道，协助他们转诊到当地医院。

彼此契合的诊疗模式和诊疗习惯使得刘杰森选择留在环球医生工作，最重要的是，这里的病人需要他，留在环球医生可以帮助到更多的人，这也是他从医的初衷。

习惯成都生活，收获爱与善良

除了在工作上帮助无数的病人，在生活中，遇到需要帮助的人，刘杰森和他的家人也会不遗余力地帮助他们。2011 年，刘杰森的妻子在街上遇到一个患有地中海贫血症、在街上乞讨的孩子，孩子布满心酸的脸颊和无邪的眼眸深深地触动了她，她想要帮助这个孩子，于是从包里掏出一百块钱，递给了对方。

回到家里，刘杰森的妻子对刘杰森说了这件事，两人内心久久不能平静。一百块钱在乞讨的钱里算数额很大的了，但是却不能真正地帮助到这个孩子，经过一番商讨之后，第二天，刘杰森带着儿子来到那个孩子乞讨的地方，邀请他和他的家人到家里吃饭。

在聊天的过程中，刘杰森一家人了解到这是一个不幸的家庭——两个儿子都患有地中海贫血症，为了给孩子治病，孩子的父母从农村搬到城市，但是来到城里，只会做农活的他们却不知该如何赚钱。

为了帮助他们，刘杰森介绍了一个会做手工牛皮制品的美国朋友给这家人认识，并教会他们靠手工艺品赚钱。不仅如此，刘杰森还召集朋友，为他们募捐，帮他们减轻一些经济上的压力，而这样的帮助一直持续到现在。

两个完全陌生的家庭，能够在一个城市里相遇，这是一种难得的缘分，更令刘杰森感到欣慰的是，自己的家人和朋友，也都愿意跟着自己去帮助对方。当看着自己的孩子们跟这个生病的孩子成为朋友，一起玩耍的时候，他深深地感觉到，善良是可以相互传染的，自己在帮助别人的同时，也是在为身边的人做一个很好的榜样，让他们学会付出，学会包容。

成都就像一个大家庭，无论你是什么种族，是贫是富，是美是丑，在这里，只要你愿意敞开心扉，就能收获无数爱与善的回馈。

想起刚来中国的时候，刘杰森总想着找到那个能让自己"一见如故"的家，而如今他才知道，"家"的含义并非只是一个居住地，它应该是一个连接陌生心灵的桥梁，只有当自己完全融入到一个地方的时候，这个地方才能算作自己的"家"。

那时不能确定，但是现在，刘杰森已经可以很肯定地说，成都就是自己的家。他的三个孩子在成都上学，四川话说得比他还好；他的妻子喜欢川菜，成都的饮食文化已经深深地根植于她的心中；而对于他本人来说，在成都可以实现自己的事业理想，更重要的是，这是一个让他深深眷念的地方，每当走在成都的街头，看着熟悉的高楼大厦，他的内心便会感到温暖和安稳。

因此，刘杰森一家人并不打算回美国。2018 年，他和妻子获得了中国的永久居留权，成都市市长亲自为他们颁发中国"绿卡"。他希望与成都的缘分能够一直延续下去，他希望他的孩子，以及孩子的孩子，能够永远记得，他们除了远在美国的故乡，还有第二个家——一个属于他们、温暖他们、爱着他们的家。

用药医治疾病，用爱温暖心灵

Curing Diseases with Medicine and Warming Hearts with Love

Jason A. Logan's place of work is at LIPPO Tower on Kehua North Road. On the 2nd floor, you arrive at it after walking through the hall and a long corridor. Upon opening the door, a wave of heat warms both body and heart, a kind of coziness that only home can offer. Within the clinic, it is cleanly decorated, and a full range of medical equipment is on display. Visitors are warmed by smiling greetings from amicable doctors. The warm ambience would make every patient feel secure even before stepping into the doctor's office.

This is the Global Doctor Chengdu Clinic. You can find many foreign doctors who have settled down in Chengdu, including Jason A. Logan. As a general practitioner, Jason A. Logan has constantly been committed to the prevention of cardiovascular diseases, the diagnosis and treatment and research of cholesterol diseases and pediatric diseases. Here in Global Doctor, he meets his patients every day, who hold him in high regard. The harmonious relationship between them is more like that of friends.

It is such trust that inspires Jason A. Logan to find the meaning and values of life. Despite a hectic schedule, he finds his work rather fulfilling. Now his family has settled down in Chengdu, making both life and work seem perfectly carefree and happy. Yet back in his youth, he never imagined that one day he would ever leave America and live such a life here in Chengdu. Back then, the only dream he cherished was to become a doctor and cure the sick.

Falling in Love with Chengdu while Exploring the World

Choosing Chengdu, why?

The same question has been raised by many people. Rather than a business trip or a journey, working in Chengdu means traveling across the oceans and taking roots in another country, traversing both geographically and mentally.

Jason A. Logan has had his share of doubt, yet never a trace of regret. In his words, everything, from choosing Chengdu to settling down here, seems to have been predestined.

All of that can be traced back to his childhood dream, namely, devoting his heart and soul to medical services. Whilst becoming a doctor was a long-cherished dream, living in Chengdu had always been beyond his wildest imagination. Driven by his firm belief, Jason A. Logan finally got the Doctor of Medicine in University of Tennessee of the United States. Life itself is like row after row of mountains, emboldening us to search far and wide, and high and low for newer, broader horizons. Back then, Jason A. Logan's heart was ignited by another dream. He wanted to go to a new place, to learn, to explore, and to cure the sick.

This new dream burnt like a flame in his heart. It represented hope, a reminder that, for him, the future holds infinite possibilities. Such a hope made Jason A. Logan excited, expectant, energetic, which translated into greater passion for his career. In 2004, Jason A. Logan and his wife finalized their plan to go to China. He wanted to see his dream flourish in that charming land and live a more fulfilling life.

They first set foot in China in Macao. A beautiful city impressed him after his friends accompanied him to explore Macao. Yet he did not feel at home there and felt that it was not a place he could stay. Then he went to Guangdong, living there for a while with his wife. Luckily for him, national and cultural differences never posed any obstacle to him. On the contrary, he found the people warm-hearted and they tried their best to make them feel at home. In return, he did everything he could, returning their hospitality with medical expertise.

Neither Macao nor Guangdong managed to make James settle down. Yet his experiences made him feel closer to both China and its people. He loved the modernity of urban China and the idyllic scenery of its rural areas. Furthermore, the fantastic friendliness of the Chinese people made him feel at home, making him ever more determined to stay.

Then, out of all the places in a country as large as China, where should he choose to live? In the places where he had been to, such as Macao and Guangdong, Jason felt more of a tourist. What he was looking for was a place that evoked in him a feeling of home. Though he did not know where it could be, he knew that such a place surely existed. and could only be found in China.

Soon, a friend informed him of a city in West China called Chengdu, which was not only a good place to live, but also offered growing and enormous opportunities for general practitioners.

Now knowing the existence of the city, he came with his wife in 2007 in search of a strong foundation for the development of his medical career. As a new comer and like other tourists, he frequented the famous scenic spots, like the Wuhou Temple, Broad and Narrow Alley and Chunxi Road. In the course of his job, he often visited West China Hospital for exchange and learning.

Over time, Jason found that Chengdu was just as liveable as his friend described. Yet he still wondered whether there might possibly be another place even better than Chengdu. Would it be such a pity to lose out the "home" in his heart because of the attractions of his immediate surroundings?

He fought with the two opposing ideas — staying in Chengdu or questing for somewhere better. Just as he wrestled with these two conflicting ideas, a tragedy struck out of the blue. On May 12 of 2008, the Wenchuan Earthquake reverberated around the world.

The earthquake ruined the homes of thousands of people and tore the hearts of the afflicted. The countless pure, sad expressions on TV deeply moved Jason and his wife. Without much hesitation, they went to the disaster area as medical volunteers, and came to the rescue of the wounded. There, they bandaged the bleeding wounds of injured with gauze, and comforted them in their misery with optimism and companionship. Whilst the whole nation was heartbroken with grief, Jason A. Logan, though not Chinese, felt that he was a part of Sichuan, a part of China. It was this experience as a volunteer that made him feel attached to Sichuan, and finally persuaded him and his wife to stay in Chengdu, a city regarded as "the Land of Abundance".

Feeling Warmth in the Midst of Difficulties

Even during winter, Chengdu is not cold. People chat and drink Big Bowl Tea in the People's Park; on Chunxi Road, shopping malls and shops throng with customers; on Broad and Narrow Alley and in the Temple of Marquis, tourists enjoy local snacks and take pictures. The cold weather never makes them feel gloomy, but they find more reasons to feel happy against the backdrop of winter.

This is Chengdu. A city warms the soul no matter what the season is. Each time, Chengdu can warm a stranger who is settling down here. Walking along the streets and alleys of the city, you can easily spot foreign friends of all colors. They look at ease and smile and greet the locals passing by.

A tacit understanding has grown between foreigners living in Chengdu and the local people. They interact with warmth and care. As a resident of Chengdu, Jason is long accustomed to such tacit understanding, for it sharply contrasts with what has happened when he first arrived, a time when he was struggling with many difficulties.

Language barriers resulted in many problems for Jason. On one occasion he went to a supermarket to buy some milk, but when he returned home he found what he had actually bought was yoghurt, initially mistaking it for spoiled milk. That was just one of many embarrassing accidents, which cause much amusement when mentioned. However, he was grateful for such mishaps, because they gave him the opportunity to meet many kind Chengdu locals. Some helped him install broadband, and some taught him how to shop. Whenever he and his family encountered any difficulty in their life, whether big or small, they could rely on these friends to immediately come to the rescue. As time passed, Jason has become accustomed to life here, gradually overcoming the language barrier.

Besides such inconveniences, he also encountered difficulties at work. During his time of study at West China Hospital, the Chinese mode of diagnosis and treatment confused him. Yet the idea of giving up never once crossed his mind. As a general practitioner, Jason showed concern for both the physical and mental health of his patients. He would pay regular visits to patients, just like a friend. He also offered them psychological counseling to help them avoid sadness and depression.

At that time, Global Doctor gave him an opportunity. As Chengdu's economy and culture was flourishing, the city's long history of international exposure attracted more and more foreign friends to come and settle. Yet most of them had little understanding of the local medical system, and therefore had difficulty making use of such services. It was against such a backdrop that Global Doctor was founded. At Global Doctor, the majority of the patients were foreigners. Whenever they were in need, the doctors there would offer them emergency treatment and transfer them to local hospitals via their "Green Channel".

The more familiar diagnosis and treatment methods attracted Jason to stay at Global Doctor. More importantly, the patients there needed him, and by working there he could help more people, which was exactly his original dream.

Getting Used to the Life in Chengdu and Reaping Love and Kindness

Apart from helping patients in his work, he also reached out to people in need in his daily life. In 2011, his wife encountered a child beggar with thalassemia on the street. The child's painstaking expression deeply moved her, and she felt compelled to give him RMB 100 yuan.

She told her husband about the beggar upon returning home, a fact which disturbed the couple for a long time. Though 100 yuan was a large number for a beggar, it was not sufficient to make any fundamental changes to the child's circumstances. After some discussion, on the second day, Jason A. Logan took his son to the beggar's location, inviting him and his family to have a meal at his home.

During conversation, they found that the child came from a very unfortunate family, with their two sons suffering from thalassemia. The parents moved to the city from countryside in order to treat the children. Yet they had no means to make a living.

To provide assistance, Jason introduced them to an American friend adept at making hand-made leather products. This friend taught them how to earn money through handicraft. Furthermore, Jason sought friends to raise money for the family and help ameliorate the financial challenges they faced to some extent. This help has been continuing.

That two different families, who would otherwise be strangers, should meet each other in such a city was destiny. Jason was gratified that his families and friends were willing to assist this poor family. Seeing that his children and the ill child became friends and played together, Jason was aware that kindness was contagious. When you are helping others, you are also serving as a role model for those around you, encouraging them to learn to give and to be tolerant.

Chengdu is like a big family, where different people, regardless of their race, wealth or appearance, can always reap endless love and kindness as long as they open their hearts.

Recalling those initial feelings he had upon his first arriving in Chengdu when he was always searching for a so-called home, Jason has realized that "home" is not only a place of residence, but also a bridge connecting disparate hearts together. Only when you fully integrate in to a place, can it be called that you have found a "home".

Though in the past he was unsure whether he would stay on, he now can answer with certainty that Chengdu is his home. All his three children are studying in Chengdu, and they speak Sichuan dialect better than he does. His wife loves Sichuan cuisine, and Chengdu's culinary culture has taken root in her heart. For him, he can realize his career goals in this city. More importantly, it is a place he loves deeply in his heart. Whenever he walks on the streets of Chengdu and watches the familiar towering buildings, he feels a sense of warmth and a sense of security.

And so, the family does not intend to return to America, in the year of 2018, they successfully got the "Green Card" of China, and the mayor of Chengdu Mr. Lou Qiang issued the Card to him. He hopes that his love for Chengdu can be sustained, and that his children and grandchildren will always remember that, besides their home in America, they also have one more home that belongs to them, nourishes them and loves them.

>> 丹尼尔·德弗朗西斯（意大利）
成都音乐界知名人士

Daniele Defranchis, Italy

A Famous Foreign Musician in Chengdu

圆梦锦城

从蜀汉时期的锦城，历经1700年的嬗变，成都如今已然成为中国最具幸福感的城市之一，它发展快速，其悠闲、乐观、宁静、繁华又洒脱的独有特质和极具包容性的城市风貌吸引着一批又一批国内外游客的到来，而丹尼尔·德弗朗西斯就是其中之一。

2014年，丹尼尔从米兰来到成都，开始了他的新生活。来成都之前，他已经是意大利专业音乐家和教师。他毕业于米兰国际音乐学院，专业为古典吉他音乐和19世纪吉他音乐，同时还获得了管理学硕士学位。

他致力于古典音乐和现代音乐领域的工作与表演，曾受邀到中国多地与当地音乐家和艺术家同台演出，使他能与中国音乐环境和教育系统直接接触。

两座城市，两种不同的文化，同时交汇在一个人的身上，并在年轻的心灵里，碰撞出了绚烂的火花。

梦·初次遇见锦城

丹尼尔是个酷爱旅行的人，他在全世界许多国家都留下了足迹。在此之前，他来过中国两次，先后经过北京、上海、广州、重庆和成都等地，并在旅行的途中，结识了许许多多来自五湖四海的朋友。

2013年暑假期间，丹尼尔再次来到成都。上次来的时候，为了体验生活，他曾从事过一份短期工作，回到米兰后，成都的一个朋友介绍了一份长期 offer 给丹尼尔，这份工作既可以让他更深刻地了解中国文化，又能发展自己的事业。

其实，那个时候的丹尼尔就已经在心中埋下了梦想的种子——他一直坚信音乐是没有国界的，他希望自己的音乐可以被成都人接受、喜欢，甚至带给他们温暖和力量。

这对他来说是一次挑战，但却意义非凡。于是正处在快速发展，又有着深厚文化底蕴和浓郁音乐氛围的成都深深地吸引了丹尼尔。正是因为这样的不解之缘，丹尼尔和成都完美邂逅。

梦·自由的生活在这里

在成都定居后，丹尼尔感受到了成都和米兰的各种不同。文化的差异、饮食的不同，深深地困扰着丹尼尔，但他非常乐观，不断学习汉语，适应中国美食，他要靠自己去独立地生活。他一直坚定着一个信念，如果都不能与自己和谐相处，谈何与人相处。

经过他持之以恒的学习，如今，丹尼尔已经完全融入了成都生活，也有了自己在成都的朋友圈。

在成都，他喜欢青羊宫和望江公园，一有空闲，就去走走看看。望江公园有很多竹子，早上有很多人打太极、练武术。很快，丹尼尔爱上了太极，因为在练习音乐的过程中，需要长时间的低头和弯腰，这让丹尼尔的身体承受了很大的压力，而练习太极又恰好能放松身体；另一方面，每天面对城市的紧张与纷繁之后，练习太极也可以让人心境得到放松，以此来平衡心态、释放压力。

来到成都，就不得不提及成都的茶文化。丹尼尔很小的时候就喜欢喝茶，他对茶的热爱，和他的父亲有很大的关系。上世纪 70 年代，丹尼尔的父亲常到中国出差，经常有朋友送他很多茶，这培养了丹尼尔对茶的兴趣。丹尼尔认为，茶馆就是成都的一张名片，很多国外的朋友因为慕名茶馆文化而不远千里来到成都，他也会经常送茶叶给自己的外国朋友，把他们邀请到家里来喝茶、聊天。

除了太极和茶，丹尼尔还非常喜欢旅行，他喜欢学习新的东西，他认为旅行就是学习新东西的一个过程，并且会一年出去一次或两次。他在旅行之前不会做太多的攻略，因为他认为旅行本身就是一个自由体验生活的过程，做太多的攻略反而会束缚了自己。他去过很多国家，比如西班牙、瑞典、比利时、奥地利、英国、爱尔兰、葡萄牙、希腊、越南、日本、老挝、土耳其、摩洛哥，等等。与我们大多数人不同的是，丹尼尔喜欢一个人去旅行，他认为旅行不仅能了解不同的人和文化，也能反思自我。在旅行的时候，最重要的是认识自我，要学会和人打交道，学会把旅途中的经历和体验带入自己的音乐创作中。在选择旅游目的地时，他不喜欢游景点，他认为大多数的景点已经被商业化的气息笼罩，并不能真实反映当地的特色和文化；在旅行的过程中，他喜欢接触当地的人，尽可能与当地人沟通交流，亲身体验当地人的生活。

丹尼尔爱中国功夫、爱茶、爱旅行，他永远都在尝试新的东西，而这些新的东西，为丹尼尔的音乐注入了不同的新鲜元素，这些都由于在成都，他有很多机会去体验他的兴趣爱好，也正是在成都这样的一种环境里，丹尼尔的音乐初心始终没有变得浮躁。每当他走在成都的街头，悠闲自由的风吹过他的脸颊，他都能够感受到一种难得的宁静与惬意，这份感觉，常常能给他的音乐创作带来新的灵感。

成都这座"懒城"，正如它优哉游哉的调性一样，比起惊涛骇浪，它更擅长水到渠成。丹尼尔迷恋这里的高山流水、痴狂于这里的山肤水豢。被称为川西第一道观的青羊宫、五大仙山之一的青城山、拥有2000多年历史的峨眉山……现代化并没有阻拦这座城市本该有的历史遗风，这个城市保留了自己最厚重的味道。

梦·落地生根的人生

众所周知，成都在中国算是出了名的"慢城市"，茶馆遍地，到处是喝茶聊天、搓麻将的人。随处可见人们坐在竹篾编的躺椅上，时不时端起一杯茶，抿一口，便仰靠椅背，椅子随之前后摆动起来；或者四人坐一桌，打牌的人抓起一张张牌，噼噼啪啪地甩了出去。对这种悠闲的"慢节奏"，丹尼尔却没有太多共鸣，他说他只在纪录片中看到过。这主要是因为他每天的工作太忙了，忙得甚至作息混乱。

丹尼尔在成都教意大利语，因为每天面对的都是一群中国学生，这就需要他每天不断地阅读中文书籍，他必须把一些中国的思维方式带入到意大利语的教学中，这样才能让学生更好地理解，同时也提高了自己的中文水平。

除了教意大利语，丹尼尔也会担任吉他老师。他教的学生水平参差不齐，有些才刚开始学，有些已经很专业了。在他看来，他与学生们的关系不是"授课与被授课"的师生关系，而是"相互分享音乐、共同进步"的朋友关系。对于未来的吉他教学，他虽然没有太多的规划，但他明确地表示，自己不会成立吉他培训中心，因为他不想成为一个商业化的人；而且成都有很多家吉他培训机构，他并不想跟他们去竞争；他喜欢让自己的教学变得更加自由，他可以和学生们聊聊音乐、喝喝茶，交流中国文化。

在日常的工作和生活之余，丹尼尔并没有忘记自己的梦想，他一直致力于创作优秀的音乐，并将自己的音乐和音乐理念传递给更多的人，很幸运的是，近几年来，成都市正在大力支持音乐产业的发展，打造"音乐之都"，越来越好的音乐氛围给丹尼尔提供了优质的创作和演出环境。

丹尼尔平时的演出机会很多。在成都的这几年，他在大大小小的场合演出了一百多场，加上还要兼顾意大利语和吉他的课程，这些工作经常交叉在一起，非常不容易。没有人能随随便便得到演出的机会，这就需要丹尼尔自己不断地和别人谈合作。丹尼尔不喜欢在酒吧和餐馆演出，因为在这些场所演出经常会有歌曲的限制，而且在这些地方，音乐家只是作为背景，没人认真欣赏。丹尼尔想要演唱自己的音乐，所以他一般会在有认真的听众的地方表演，这些听众感兴趣于高品质音乐并愿意欣赏，如剧院、音乐节、音乐酒吧等。

赵雷的那首《成都》中描写了这样一个非典型性古都。"成都，带不走的，只有你。和我在成都的街头走一走，直到所有的灯都熄灭了也不停留。"灯火喧嚣和寂静怅惘的结合，阳春白雪和下里巴人的碰撞，这座最天然的创作环境无疑对丹尼尔的吸引力极大。来自天南地北的一群年轻人因为音乐这个梦想集合到了一起，分享、交流……而丹尼尔如今正在做的，就是将自己对成都的感受，将自小的童年记忆融合到一起。东西方文化交汇的那一刻，也是丹尼尔最感动的那一刻。

对于未来在中国的音乐计划和工作规划，丹尼尔还没有明确的方向，他说他会继续专心地进行音乐创作和教学，把更多的知识、经验传递出去。他不想变成明星，因为如果变成明星，很多事情会变得身不由己，甚至没有时间去做纯粹的音乐。他只是希望自己能有一些"小"的名气，有一点粉丝，可以跟更多的艺术家合作，交一些在音乐上更有造诣的朋友，大家一起把全部的热情投入到音乐中。

虽然在外人看来，丹尼尔似乎没有太大的抱负和追求，但实际上他是一个特别务实，对本职工作极其认真负责的人。在充满诱惑力的当下社会环境中，他还可以纯粹地去做音乐，安心地做自己喜欢的事情，不受外界影响，把兴趣当作工作，把工作当作享受，这就十分难得了。

在丹尼尔心中，成都就像第二个家，在这里，丹尼尔不再感到孤独，他不知道未来会怎么样，但是可以肯定的是，他的故事将一直在成都延续。

圆梦锦城，成都和丹尼尔必定会擦出更亮的火花！

Dreams Come True in Chengdu

After 1,700 years' growth, Chengdu has developed into one of the happiest cities in China. Its fast development, unique combination of leisure, optimism, tranquility, prosperity and inclusiveness have attracted tourists from all over the world, one of whom is Daniele Defranchis.

Daniele left Milan to start his new life in Chengdu in 2014. He was a professional musician and teacher in Italy prior to relocating. Daniele graduated from International Academy of Music, majoring in Classical Music of Guitar and Music of Guitar in Nineteenth Century. He also has a Master's Degree in Management.

He has devoted his life to classical and modern music. His experience of performing with local musicians and artists in cities all across China, has given Daniele a direct understanding on China's musical environment and its education system.

Daniele has tasted two different cities and cultures, the essence of which inspired and enlightened him to see marvelous and creative sparks.

Dream · The First Meeting with Chengdu

Daniele is obsessed with traveling. Apart from China, he has visited many other countries. During his two visits, he went to cities like Beijing,

Shanghai, Guangzhou, Chongqing and Chengdu, making friends with people from all over the world.

During his 2013 summer vacation, he visited Chengdu again to get a long-term job offer introduced by a friend in Chengdu. This job gave him the opportunity to acquire a better understanding of Chinese culture and to further his career. This job was not his first in the city. On his first trip to Chengdu he found a short-time post, which expanded his life experience.

And that was the beginning of Daniele's dream to give people of Chengdu the opportunity to enjoy his music, or even to get warmth and be empowered by it, for he always believed that music can straddle cultural divides.

Therefore, although challenging, this long-term job was important. Chengdu's fast development, profound cultural heritage and its musical environment appealed to him. It was such alluring qualities that made Daniele settle down in Chengdu.

Dream · A Comfortable Life in Chengdu

After settling in Chengdu, Daniele became aware of the differences in many different areas of life between it and Milan. He found the differences in cuisine and culture that are especially hard to adapt to. He threw himself into learning Chinese language and devoted himself to appreciating the local cuisine. He firmly believed that one must find harmony within oneself prior to getting along with others.

The diligence paid off, for now Daniele is accustomed to life in Chengdu and has made many friends here.

Two of his favorite places to spend time are Qingyang Palace and Wangjiang Park. People love to play Tai Chi and Chinese martial arts in the Bamboo Woods in Wangjiang Park. Soon after he came, Daniele fell in love with Tai Chi, for it was an exercise that could relax a body tired from music practice, and alleviate the stress and worries that came after work.

Another hallmark of Chengdu is its tea culture. Daniele's love of tea comes from his father. In the 1970s, Daniele's father often visited China on business and was gifted with tea by his friends. Tea culture can be seen everywhere, an industry which Daniele regards as being a symbol of the city, and one which is very enticing to foreigners. He also takes tea as a gift for his foreign friends and invites them home to drink tea.

Daniele enjoys learning new things, and apart from Tai Chi and tea culture, travel, his other hobby, is something which helps facilitate this process. He usually travels once or twice a year. He prefers to travel without a guidebook, for he feels that guidebooks restrict opportunities to have fresh and exciting life experiences. He has been to many countries, including Spain, Sweden, Belgium, Austria, England, Ireland, Portugal, Greece, Vietnam, Japan, Laos, Turkey and Morocco. Daniele prefers to travel alone because he feels that this makes it easier to gain an understanding of other peoples and cultures, and it also facilitates self-reflection. He states that the most important thing to be learnt from travel is self-understanding, social skills and how to infuse his music composition with these experiences. Daniele is critical of tourist honey pots, feeling that the majority are over-commercialized and not representative of local features and culture. Instead, he enjoys communicating with local people and experiencing local life.

Daniele's love of Tai Chi, tea and travel are a reflection of his tireless pursuit of novelty, which in return infuses fresh elements into his music. All of these are the fruit of his time in Chengdu, a period which has given him chance after chance to develop his hobbies. This inclusive city also allows him to stick with his original dream. Calmness and comfort are his source of inspiration, things which leisurely Chengdu easily provides.

Chengdu is a slow paced city, suitable for people pursuing dreams with great patience and consistent efforts. Daniele is mesmerized by the beautiful scenery and enticing food here. Modernization has not destroyed Chengdu's ancient charm, the home of such heritage as the Qingyang Palace, known as the best Taoist Temple in West Sichuan; Qingcheng Mountain, one of the five most beautiful mountains in China, as well as the more than two-millennia-old monastery at Emei Mountain.

Dream · Settle in Chengdu

Chengdu is famous for its slow pace of life, with teahouses spreading all over the city and people drinking tea, chatting with each other and playing mahjong. These are common scenes here. Someone would lie in bamboo recliners and slowly sip tea while a group of four people play mahjong nearby. However, Daniele says he only sees such things in documentaries because he is too busy to experience the "laid-back" life.

Daniele teaches Italian in Chengdu. Given that his students are Chinese, he has to read piles of Chinese books to adjust his teaching method to their learning habits and to facilitate their Italian language acquisition. This work has a welcome side effect of improving his Chinese level.

Daniele is also a guitar teacher with students covering different levels from freshmen to specialists. He says that their relationships extend beyond the classroom and they become friends who can share music and help each other grow. Although he has a clear career plan around future guitar teaching, he states that he would not open a training center. This is because he prefers being a teacher to a business man; he does not want to compete with existing local training organizations; and also he enjoys a free style of teaching, which gives him the opportunity to chat with his students about music and Chinese culture.

Even when he is busy with teaching, Daniele never forgets the original force driving him to Chengdu. He has devoted himself to music composition as well as the promotion of musical concepts in spare time. Fortunately, Chengdu has provided substantial support for the music industry over the past few years to develop itself into a City of Music, giving him a fantastic opportunity to realize his dream.

Daniele is frequently invited to perform, and during his time in Chengdu, he has performed over a hundred times. It is difficult to balance his performance schedule with teaching Italian and guitar. Lacking an agent, Daniele has to seek out opportunities by himself. He says he doesn't like playing in pubs or restaurants where musicians are not respected and have little power on song selection. He prefers to sing his own songs and play in places where audiences appreciate high-quality music, including theaters, music festivals and bars.

Chengdu, a song written by Zhao Lei, depicts the private, subtle emotions of the city. Chengdu perfectly fuses the hustle and bustle of the city with seclusion and gloom, as well as that of elegant art with folk art, which allows Daniele to immerse himself in music composition. Chengdu attracts many young people to pursue their musical ambitions and compare notes on their works and opinions. Daniele writes songs which reflect his feelings about Chengdu combined with memories from childhood. He feels the greatest thrill when the interplay between eastern and western cultures causes creative sparks to fly.

He is still unsure about his future musical and professional career in China. But he will continue to focus on music composition and teaching, thereby passing on his knowledge and experience. Daniele says he has no desire to become famous because it would change his life too much, giving him much less opportunity to focus purely on music. He just wants to gain some local recognition, a few fans, and more opportunities to collaborate with other artists, and get to know some musically talented friends, so they can all concentrate on making great music.

Although one could criticize Daniele for lacking ambition, he is in fact a practical man who is responsible for his work and devotes to his music. It is admirable that he resists external influences, focuses on his dream and enjoys what he is doing.

Daniele does not feel lonely here anymore, regarding Chengdu as his second home, and a place where he will write the next chapters of his life story.

It is quite possible that there will be more creative sparks ignited from the interaction between Chengdu and Daniele in the future!